THE DAUGHTER GAME

Kate Long is the author of *The Bad Mother's Handbook*,
a top-ten bestseller. She lives with her family
in Shropshire.

Also by Kate Long

THE BAD MOTHER'S HANDBOOK

SWALLOWING GRANDMA

QUEEN MUM

KATE LONG

THE DAUGHTER GAME

PICADOR

First published 2008 by Picador

First published in paperback 2008 by Picador

This edition first published 2010 by Picador
an imprint of Pan Macmillan, a division of Macmillan Publishers Limited
Pan Macmillan, 20 New Wharf Road, London N1 9RR
Basingstoke and Oxford
Associated companies throughout the world
www.panmacmillan.com

ISBN 978-0-330-47978-3

The publishers are grateful to Carol Ann Duffy for permission to
reproduce 'Anne Hathaway' from The World's Wife (Picador, 2000)
and to Allison McVety for permission to reproduce 'Offspring'
from Miming Happiness (Smith/Doorstop, 2010).

1 3 5 7 9 8 6 4 2

A CIP catalogue record for this book is available from
the British Library.

Typeset by Intype Libra Ltd
Printed in the UK by CPI Mackays, Chatham ME5 8TD

Visit **www.picador.com** to read more about all our books
and to buy them. You will also find features, author interviews and
news of any author events, and you can sign up for e-newsletters
so that you're always first to hear about our new releases.

For Ben and Toby

Many thanks, for their feedback and support,
to Peter Straus and Ursula Doyle.

Thank you also to Rachel Black and Louise Scull
for their excellent book *Beyond Childlessness*.
(More information at www.beyondchildlessness.com.)

Thanks to Phil Hughes of H.T. Hughes (Caerwys) Ltd
for providing background information on the running
of a timber yard; and to Edward Mitchell for his
advice on professional procedure in schools.

And thank you to my ex-colleagues and students
who were always inspiring, even though none of them
is to be found in these pages.

Offspring

Someday, all the children I didn't think to bear
will come to find me. In their twin-sets
of egg and sperm they will bombard me
with questions I haven't learned to answer.

Why didn't you let me have a dog, or puberty?
they'll ask. The girls will demonstrate
the flounce they never got to wear
and the boys will brood like storms.

Hundreds of them, each a calendar-cross
apart, queuing up to say: *you are hopeless,*
mother, we cannot talk to you. And fathers

will get away scot-free, dodge the flak,
bugger off down to the garden shed,
propagating with tools they'll not pass on.

From 'Miming Happiness'
by Allison McVety

Chapter One

Jackson was melting. Anna played the flame-thrower up and down his body and watched him shrink like a wax model, his head disappearing into his neck and his outline sweating away in fat tears. Next she applied the flame, now a Bunsen burner, to his middle and grew a hole in his stomach. His top half fell off.

And she was home.

Putting down her bags of folders and the roll of sugar paper she'd carried up the drive, she opened the front door, then scooped everything up again to dump in the hall. Come back to it after dinner.

'Hello?'

No reply, but the answerphone was showing two messages. She pressed play and listened as she pulled her cardigan off. The house was stifling. Had the heating been on all day?

The moment when you left, said Jamie's voice, *was the second between two heartbeats. Beeeeep.*

I am the rose beneath the hammer – I am a rose, the rose, I am a rose beneath your hammer—

She left it playing and went into the kitchen to put the kettle on, sloshing water about needlessly, trying not to think about the day.

Jackson had flicked the *No Admittance* light on and come out from behind the desk – she'd known she was in trouble then. She closed the door herself and he'd leaned against the desk as though overwhelmed by the mighty burden of headship.

'Anna,' he said. 'I know you must be very busy today, setting the rooms up, and unpacking your books—'

She allowed herself a very slight nod.

'Yes. Well, I won't keep you long. So. Year Ten. A difficult year, tricky age, I mean. And one or two colourful characters this time round.'

She waited.

'And you do a marvellous job with them.'

He let his eyes flick to the window, to the horizon, so as to demonstrate sage consideration.

Prick, Anna was thinking. Sad fat prick.

'Because I wouldn't want you to think we didn't appreciate you. I know you're one of the most dedicated members of my staff. But I'm sure you can understand, after last term, why I'd want to have a little chat with you. Before we get too busy.'

Still she'd said nothing. Why should she give him any help?

'After last term . . .' Jackson said again, as if the phrase encompassed everything he needed to express.

'I thought that had been dealt with.'

'And it has, it has.' A sort of smile. 'Absolutely. But you and I know that pastoral tutors – all teachers, really – tread a fine line. I do myself. There's a lot goes on in the privacy of a Head's office. Sometimes I have very delicate situations to deal with, very delicate. And it's hard not to become overinvolved, the very process of learning can create a certain intimacy—'

'I never made him come to my house.'

Jackson held up his hand. 'This isn't about Adam Gardiner. As you said, that's over and done with. It is, isn't it?'

It bloody well is, Anna thought. She managed another nod. If she opened her mouth now, God knows what might come out.

'This is more a general chat, just to remind you of what we might call the professional parameters. Because it's easy to get drawn in, especially if you have a caring nature. Some of these children can be, what, manipulative. Teenagers are much more sophisticated these days than we were at that age.'

Anna fixed deliberately on the wall clock next to his head. He turned to see what she was looking at.

'Sorry,' she said, not sorry at all, 'I have a departmental meeting at twelve.'

Jackson detached himself from the desk and came forward. For one awful moment she'd thought he was going to touch her.

'We've decided to give you a break from being a form tutor this year,' he said. 'Less work for you. Three nice easy terms, no pastoral reports or meetings to attend. You can concentrate entirely on your lessons. There.'

He walked past her and opened the door wide.

I did nothing wrong, she'd wanted to say. But Les was outside, holding a sheaf of papers and looking harassed. So she'd just walked out. That was – she checked her watch, 4.30 now – nearly five hours ago. Did other people get this memory loop thing? She opened the freezer, saw the damn pork steaks she'd intended for tea still in there. Jackson's face smiled on.

She brewed two coffees and climbed the stairs, stopping at the airing cupboard to switch the heating off. Even from the first landing she could hear Jamie's Bix Beiderbecke. That meant he'd finished working for the day, if he had ever started.

He was at the desk, anyway.

'Hello,' he said, as if it was a huge surprise to see her.

'Coffee.' Anna held the cup out to him and he rose to take it.

'Top girl.'

There were three empty mugs on the windowsill.

'Good day? Get much done?' She leaned in the doorway and scanned the room for evidence of industry. On the computer side, two noticeboards, a hand-drawn chart, two calendars, her NUT wall planner; also shelves of box files and two tables covered with wire trays. On the wall opposite the window, a set of plastic drawers for stationery, and a floor-to-ceiling bookcase. Next to the door, a bed-settee covered in loose books. More than her life was worth to shift any of them. His systems. She'd read in one of the Sunday supplements about a Paperless Office: imagine.

'Bits and pieces. Research.' Jamie lifted one corner of a computer printout.

She'd tried to work in here herself when they first moved in but he said her presence interfered with his creativity. Anna's office area should have been the spare bedroom, but there wasn't much space and the table was taken up with the dolls' house. She did her marking in the lounge.

'I don't know how you can work in this temperature. It's boiling up here.'

'Is it?'

'Top floor's always the warmest room in the house. Heat rises.'

'You should've been a physics teacher.' He turned to the keyboard and typed something in. 'Sorry. While I remember. Oh, you haven't wiped the answerphone tape, have you?'

'As if.'

'I had this fantastic idea while I was out—'

She waited while he typed some more. Bent over the desk he looked such an academic, with his longish grey-blond hair and his open-necked shirt. Still attractive at fifty. He clicked on save and closed the screen down.

'That's nailed him. So, sorry, good day at school? Get everything done you wanted?'

Anna sighed. 'Jackson was a git. As usual.'

'Uneasy lies the head that wears a throne. Specifically gittish, or just generally?'

'I've been sacked from being a form tutor. He tried to sell it as a sabbatical, but basically I've been demoted.'

Jamie arched his eyebrows in sympathy.
, though.'

was his line. But I like having a form, it's nice.
I've got to take Nathan sodding Woods into my
GCSE set.'

Nathan Woods. Your nemesis, Mel used to say. Anna
hadn't taught the boy for a year, but even so, on nights
she couldn't sleep her mind sometimes played a Nathan
slideshow: the wide-legged stance; the folded arms; the
way he leant against the display boards, crushing paper;
his grin. Once Anna had come across Nathan and Les in
a corridor when the rest of the school was in assembly.
Les, normally so cool, had been twitching with fury but
Nathan had just looked bored. He was taller than Les; a
lot taller than Anna. Jackson avoided him.

'Nathan the Bastard? I thought you'd shifted him
onto someone else.'

'That's what Mel promised last term. She said
Andrew could have him, it was his turn. But Mel's
not there any more, and this new head of department,
Chrissy—'

'The one with the rigid hair?'

'Yeah. She's decided to give Andrew all the A-level
Language, so his timetable's full.' Nathan taking someone's shoe and throwing it over the wall into the road;
that had been in his very first week. Just a joke, Miss. 'It's
not spectacular disobedience, he never does anything
we can chuck him out for. It's low-level disruption, arrogance, continual abrasiveness. And I suspect he's much
worse out of lessons. God only knows what it's like to
be a pupil in his year.'

'Poor Anna,' said Jamie.

'I can handle him, I'm not *worried*. But he will be a damn nuisance.'

'You'll show him.'

'I wish Mel was still around.'

Mel. Gone all the way to Liverpool.

'Give her a ring tonight. She's probably had just as tough a day. Tougher. It's all new for her, remember, not just a couple of fresh faces in the department and a bunch of Year Sevens who'll wet themselves if you go boo. Anyway, you like it, really, all the argy-bargy, the pressure. You were like a lost soul over the holidays. Be honest, you couldn't wait to get back to school, could you?'

'You forgot to take the chops out again,' said Anna.

I am a bad wife, she wrote. *A good teacher but a bad wife. That is why, despite the brain-numbing meetings, the recycled assemblies, and Jackson, I would rather be here in school and not at home with Jamie.*

She paused to enjoy the quiet of the classroom for a few seconds. A few feet away, Nathan had his hand up. Already his shirt collar was pulled apart, his bead choker on show. Which was against the rules but not worth the confrontation; not now, with the others so immersed in writing. Anna shook her head at him and put her finger to her lips. To her relief, he only dropped his arm with a sigh.

Jamie thinks I am jealous of him, which is ironic. I am bloody angry with him, but not jealous.

Nathan was tapping his teeth with his biro, click-click,

click-click. She opened her mouth to say something, but at the same moment he took the pen away from his face and began scribbling earnestly. Through the wall she could hear a jolly French song, children's voices dragging behind it.

'I want you to write a letter,' she'd told them. 'To yourselves. As you'll be in ten months' time, at the end of the year. Its contents will be completely private, only you will ever read them. You'll need to move your desks apart, like an exam – no, when I've finished speaking – because I don't want you looking at anyone else's work but your own. And at the end of the twenty minutes you're going to put what you've written into an envelope and seal it up. I'll then take your letters away and lock them in a cupboard till next July.'

'You're not going to mark them?' Lin from the front row.

'I'm not going to see them at all. What you write will be entirely up to you. Entirely private.'

Glances round the room, smirks.

'Entirely honest.'

'She's going to take them in the staffroom and read them out.' That was Nathan.

'No one will see what you write, you have my promise. And I shall do one too, one of my own. I always do.'

Hands had gone up.

'How many words do you want? – Mrs Lloyd, can I say about my athletics training? – Is it OK if I use—'

She waved them quiet. 'I'll put some questions on the board to start you off. Which you choose to answer is up to you.' She wrote quickly across the whiteboard:

Who are the most important people in your life right now? Which material possessions do you most care about? What are your goals for the months ahead? What is your biggest secret? If you could change one aspect of your life, what would it be? What scares you? Are you looking forward to this year?

'Why are we doing it, Mrs Lloyd?' This was from Lin, so she knew it was a genuine question and not cheek. 'What's the point in writing to yourself?'

'Because you can sometimes learn a lot from looking back, see how much progress you've made. A lot can happen in a year, you know.'

Lin nodded thoughtfully.

The class settled.

Anna wrote: *I want not to be having an affair any more. I want to be a different person. In ten months' time I want to have turned my life right round.* Then she took the Tippex and blotted it out, just in case. She felt a bit sick.

Across the room, Nathan smiled to himself. She could see even from here he was drawing a huge cannabis leaf.

At the end of the day, with the corridors quiet again, she sat in the staffroom going through the envelopes. You could tell a lot just from the outsides. Lin Keane had formally addressed hers, c/o the school, postcode and all. Sally Marsden had drawn a heart-shaped seal with *4 U* in the middle. Anna shuffled through to find Nathan's. *This envelope is <u>BOOBY-TRAPPED</u> if you try to open it you will get your fingers BLOWN OFF!!!*, he'd scrawled across the flap. She could make a good guess at the kind of things he'd written about.

She put the sheaf of envelopes into a cardboard wallet, labelled it, and slid it to the back of her locker. Somewhere under the folders of work was her own letter from last year, which she had not opened because she knew the kind of wishes and promises she'd made, and what had happened to them.

Outside the work annexe in the coffee area she could hear snippets of conversation: *Did you get down to St Remo in the end? – Yes, Cathy did very well in her exams – I can't believe Frankie's started nursery already!*

It was like a club, a society that she'd never learned to infiltrate. It wasn't that she disliked her colleagues, just that a lot of the time she couldn't think of what to say back to all the mumsy twitter. She knew some of the women thought she was cold.

Yes, a little girl, eight pounds four. She's sending a photo in for the board.

Anna went out of the staffroom when people brought babies in.

Chrissy poked her head round the door. 'Everything OK?'

I should be the one asking that, thought Anna. 'Fine. And you?'

'Getting there!' Chrissy smiled and rolled her eyes. How did she make her hair go like that? Anna wondered what it would feel like to touch that crispy fringe, feel its mesh give under her fingers.

'And Nathan? Did he give you any trouble?'

'Not a peep.'

Chrissy gave a pleased tut that meant, There, I told you so.

But it's only lesson one, Anna wanted to say. They're all subdued at the start.

'So, first day over with. I hope you're not going to sit and mark all evening, Anna. Not on the first day back.'

No indeed, thought Anna. I'm off to meet my lover shortly.

'Jamie's busy this evening at his writing group. He has to be out early so it doesn't matter if I get back late.'

'Well, don't overdo it,' said Chrissy. 'I won't be staying tonight.' She gave a twisted wink, and disappeared.

'Has he sold any scripts yet?' asked Les, coming through the door with a box of files. 'When's he going to be on TV, that's what I want to know. ITV Drama Premiere, written by Jamie Lloyd. Then we can all boast that we know him.'

'He's trying something experimental,' said Anna, decorating the pages of *Walkabout* with mini-Post-its. 'He says television needs more than cops 'n' docs.'

'Get him to write a good comedy. There's nothing decent on, even after the watershed.'

'No.' She did a quick calculation on the bottom of an Oxford pad. Three weeks, plus homeworks, would get this book read and discussed. She paused and looked up. Les was staring at her.

'You all right, Anna?'

He seemed to have gone greyer over the summer, and more lined. She'd found out last term that he was only a year older than she was.

'Fine. Why?'

'You look really pale.'

'Do I? I'm fine.' She shrugged. 'Tired. You know.'

'God, if you feel like that now, at this stage, you'll be on your knees by Christmas.' He shook his head, mock-stern, and pushed the files onto a shelf above her head. 'Take it easy, girl.'

'I will.'

She'd told Jamie that she'd be staying late to get all the boards backed and rejig the stock cupboard. Sugar paper lay in inviting sheets across the far tables; in her pigeonhole were envelopes full of Scholastic invoices that had to be gone through, and ticked, and filed. Anna pushed her cuff aside to check her watch. Given the choice between meeting Russ and stamping new books, *Get Set for English* would have won hands down.

When Anna had decided to have an affair with Russ seven months back, she'd first arranged the rental of a caravan on a park outside Chester, then set up a direct debit to pay for it from an account Jamie didn't even know she had. If any communication ever came from the Halifax, Anna would drop it casually in the bin and call it junk mail, fishing it out later and clipping it into the back of a ring binder where she kept her Key Stage 3 worksheets. She'd had an extra copy of the key cut, bought new bedding, and spent some time cleaning the interior of the caravan and going round the windows with sealant. Only when she'd finished did she approach Russ.

One of the worst things about the place was the awful decor. She longed to smarten it up, but you don't personalize a place like that because you don't want to leave clues about. When Anna lay pinned to the bed by

Russ, she'd turn her head and let her eyes rest on a bobbly copper ashtray and a crappy shell owl. She always meant to move them, always forgot afterwards. 'Someone must have left these,' Russ had observed brightly when he first saw them, as though there were any other kind of explanation. She'd put her own curtains up, though; thick brown velvet ones from a second-hand shop. Impossible to see through. She'd have liked to hang a good watercolour above the bed.

It was ten minutes' drive from school, twenty from Russ's timber yard. Tonight Anna was first there, which gave her time to put the kettle on and go round quickly with a duster. Then she sat with the curtains drawn and ate a biscuit, and tried to read *The Times* that she'd filched from the staffroom.

At last she heard the car engine, silence, door slam, footsteps on gravel. An impatient scrabble at the door. Russ thought she was going to have sex with him tonight.

She called, 'Hi!' and he turned the handle like a thief, peering in. For God's sake, she wanted to say.

A smile of relief spread across his wide face. 'Oh, 'sgood to see you again. Jesus. We've got this new bloody undermanager, wanting to go through some orders for tomorrow, as if he's not paid to sort it out on his own.'

She let him embrace her but he must have sensed her stiffness because he faltered and took his arms away.

'All right? Hey?'

'Not really.'

'Oh, hell.' His alarm was instant and electric. 'What's

happened? Has someone said something? Does Jamie – Ruth—?'

'No. Calm down.'

He stepped back and she moved across to sit on the sofa.

'What, then? What?'

She'd decided before he came to make it quick. Straight to the point. What else was there to do?

'I think we should finish it.'

'Finish?'

'We need to end our affair.' Russ always needed things spelt out.

'Oh. God. No. No, Anna, no.'

She swivelled away from him and studied the interlocking squares pattern of the cushions. Russ was never a handsome man, but at his best he'd had a boyish charm which had been quite attractive. He'd inherited his mother's flushed and cherubic features while Jamie looked like his father, manly, classical. Russ suffered in hot weather, Jamie stayed cool.

'Don't make it difficult, Russ.'

To her dismay he lunged and dropped to his knees before her, grabbing her hands. From this position she could see how thin the hairs on his crown were. He'd be bald in five years.

'Anna, love, you can't just decide to stop like that. This is about both of us. Let's at least talk it through. What's the matter, what's changed? Is it something I've done? Is it Jamie?' His eyes bulged. He had not been expecting this.

'Nothing's the matter. It's time for – we need to

wind things up, we're not going anywhere and I'm not happy.' She nearly added 'with the deceit', but that would have been too provoking. She'd been all right with half a year's worth of deception, he'd say, justifiably. God, what a mess.

'*I* was happy. I don't get what's going on. You never said anything. What can I do?'

Get up, she wanted to say. 'Nothing.'

'You've decided?'

'Yes.'

He knelt back, sulking. After a moment he said, 'Don't you love me?'

She didn't answer.

'I know you never said, but I thought . . . I love *you*.'

'Sorry.'

'Shit.'

Russ shifted awkwardly then got to his feet, looked down at her. 'I still don't understand. Jamie's said something, hasn't he?'

'No. It's me. I'm not comfortable doing this any more.'

'But—' He waved his arm around the caravan. 'All this—?'

Stick a bomb under it as far as I'm concerned, thought Anna. 'The lease ends on March 1st. I'll hand back the keys then.'

'We could have another six months. Please. I know I can talk you round. You need these meetings. You said Jamie's so cold. What about that first time, and after you'd come back from Wales? You *cried*.'

She shook her head.

'What about me, Anna? What am I going to do?'

'Go home. Love Ruth.'

'I can't. Not that way, you know what she's like.'

Then go home to your kids and be damn grateful, she thought.

Suddenly he sank down next to her, embracing her hard, kissing her and pushing her back against the cushions. '*Please*.'

For a split second she wondered whether to go with it, just to shut him up. Then she felt nauseous and turned her head away from his wet mouth. His erection jutted into the top of her leg.

'It won't do. No. Stop, Russ. There's no point any more.'

At last he was angry, which was easier. 'No point? No fucking *point?*' He jerked his body upright, glared at her, and swept her newspaper off the table onto the floor. Nice one, Russ. That was about as violent as he could manage. And yet, when he stood up and grabbed his coat, she flinched, wondering whether he was going to take two strides across the room and hit her. Instead he wrenched the door open, slammed it behind him.

That was that over with, then.

Chapter Two

Jamie came in at half nine, which was early for a writers' group night.

'Didn't anyone want to go for a drink this evening?'

He threw his coat over the newel post, lazily. 'Nope. They were all busy.'

'What, even Clodagh?'

'Clodagh's on holiday.'

'Ah.'

It was safe to tease about Clodagh because she was the wrong side of sixty-five. Clodagh's crush on Jamie was something to joke about. Anna wasn't so sure about the rest of them, though.

'They're all females in your writing group, are they?' Russ had asked last time he was round; just that hint of bitterness in his voice.

'Yeah, I suppose they are.' *But, hey, what can you do?* Jamie's smile said.

'Nice for you.'

'Anna's not jealous, are you, love?'

'God, no. Too busy to be jealous. Too tired.'

But it was a fact: Jamie ran a weekly writing group

in an upstairs room at the Red Lion where he was the only man.

Now Anna started to gather her spelling lists together in year order. 'Successful evening, then? Did the Muse call?'

Jamie poured himself a Jack Daniel's and reached for the remote before he answered.

'The problem with writing is that it can't be done to order. Half of them – more than half – turned up saying they hadn't done anything this week – dog's died, mother's in hospital, unexpected visitors, you know the sort of thing. It's like when the kids don't hand in their homework. 'Cept you can't put my lot in detention.'

'Some of them would like that. Most of them fancy you.'

'So? Half the sixth form fancy you. It's when you start fancying them back you've got problems.'

Anna's cheeks prickled.

Into her mind flashed a school trip, seven years ago, where the man giving out the lecture tickets had scanned the group and said, 'Isn't your teacher here with you today?' Anna had been thirty-five then. Russ had marvelled many times about how young she looked. 'It's because you're so petite,' he'd said. 'You're like a girl. It's only the way you walk makes you look older, and the way you dress.' It was true she'd had to watch her body language, especially in the early days. When she moved along the corridor she did it briskly. In class she sat up straight and serious.

'You didn't get through very much, then?'

Jamie eyed his bourbon, held it up and looked at the

fire through it. She could tell he was thinking up lines of poetry. Any minute now he'd snatch for the phone pad. But no, he sighed instead and put the glass back on its mat.

'The problem is, I'm in no position to criticize. My Muse hasn't been terrifically busy either, of late.'

Tell me something I don't know, thought Anna. She secured the papers with a bulldog clip and laid them in a box file. As she closed the lid, clicked it into place, she thought how he used to wade through marking too, sit through staff meetings, grumble at every new syllabus. But where Anna was meticulous, Jamie had skimmed, writing undrafted reports on the last evening with the TV on, framing his lessons as he walked along the corridor to the classroom. No one had ever complained, either. His easy manner was half his charm.

'Did you ever fancy any of your pupils, then?'

He looked up in surprise. 'Those snotty little kids? Good God, no. Not likely! Bizarre question, Anna.'

'Just wondered. With you saying. Evelyn Waugh reckoned that's the only reason men go into teaching, to ogle young girls. Youth is beautiful, isn't it?'

He made no response except to turn on the TV. Anna dragged her tapestry bag from under the chair and loaded up the files she needed for next day. So much churning round inside her. Her head felt swimmy with fatigue.

'Hey, you OK?' Jamie put the remote down and turned in his chair. 'You've gone white.'

What would he say if she told him? I've been having an affair with your brother but it's over now because I think he's got me pregnant. She said, 'Nathan Wood's going to be trouble, you know.'

Jamie sat back again. 'Oh, that little shit. Don't go worrying about him. Any bother, chuck him out, send him to Les or your distinguished leader. Honestly, Anna, it's not your job to sort his behaviour out. Your role is to deliver the curriculum, and if Nathan Smartarse isn't fit to take it in, shift him onto the pastoral care team. That's what they get their extra scale-point for. Sod him. I never had any truck with kids like that.'

'What, you never had any kids muck about in your class, ever?'

'Not what I said. Listen: it doesn't matter what your teaching style is, some kids are always going to behave like dickheads because that's the way their brains are wired. The trick is not to let it get to you. I never did.'

That she could believe. She'd gone in once, long before they were married, to watch him teach. Terms at Montcliff were shorter than at the comp, so she'd been on holiday a whole week by then. She'd called in at the staffroom one break to pick up some videos he was lending her, and he'd said, 'Don't go just yet, come and see my Year Nines.' She'd sat at the back like an inspector, and been struck immediately by the difference in his style from her own. He'd perched on the edge of the desk (Anna always sat behind) with his shirt sleeves rolled up and an open body posture. The children weren't always putting their hands up before calling out. Jamie used his arms a lot, dropped slang into his speech. When he saw a child who wasn't listening he didn't simply say, as Anna would have, 'Stephen, can you pay attention, please.' He asked a question he knew the boy wouldn't be able to answer because he'd missed the information, waited for the audience laugh, then pretended to use a radio for contact: 'Calling planet Brooker. What's the atmosphere like where you are, Ste?' The other children liked it. She'd wondered at the time whether she was doing it all wrong.

'I'll bear your advice in mind,' she said.

She could not get comfortable in bed. When she lay on her front, it felt as though her internal organs were falling against the mattress and squashing together and causing damage. She turned on her back and they lurched again; she kept imagining liver on a butcher's scales. Across the ceiling slanted a faint bar of light from the gap in the curtains and she watched it for a while, her hands on her stomach. Finally she got up, filled a glass with water, and went to sit in the spare room with the dolls' house.

She'd come across the green and white tin-fronted Triang in an antique shop, and it had been a serious restoration project. It wasn't a toy. Jamie said the house was creepy by moonlight. 'Like the M. R. James story. You might peep through those latticed windows one night and see a horrible crime committed in miniature.' Except there was no one inside to be murdered. Anna didn't agree with adding dolls; they destroyed the realism. You were supposed to look in at each room and feel as though the occupants had just left. She peered now into these silent, ordered rooms.

What would Russ be doing at this moment? Could

he sleep tonight? In his messy, overcrowded semi that Anna always longed to clear and redesign properly, taking up those God-awful carpets and sanding the boards; repainting the sills and finishing the papering in the hall; sweeping all the crap into a skip. That shell owl would have been right at home in Ruth and Russ's house. Of course, kids made a lot of mess. If she had a baby, she'd keep its toys in an antique wooden trunk that could stay on show all the time. But she mustn't think about the baby, it was important not to think about the baby yet. See what happened when you let your mind go sliding? She fought to bring up Russ's living room again – there were French windows at one end but the curtain rail was coming away from the wall and Russ had never got round to fixing it. Ruth was too wet to pick up a drill. So the curtain sagged on one side, the material pooled on the floor, and every so often someone would tread on it or catch their foot and yank it a bit more. 'One day it'll fall right out on someone's head,' Ruth would say, looking meaningfully at Russ. And there was no proper room for a dining table, at least not one that would seat more than four, so often as not they ate off their laps among Tom's Duplo and Bethany's Bratz and Tasha's magazines and all the other assorted junk they insisted on piling up. Ruth collected pot pigs, for Christ's sake. 'Sometimes I just can't stand it any longer,' Russ told Anna when they were at the caravan one time. 'I have to get out. Do you understand?' Absolutely, Anna said. Sometimes Ruth left the ironing board up for days.

Anna unhooked the front of the dolls' house and

pulled the metal wall open. One of the tiny willow-pattern plates had fallen off the dresser and needed righting. She set it back in place and neatened an antimacassar while she was in.

If Russ's house was hers she'd paint the whole place cream and ban all ornaments. She'd pave the scraggy front garden and invest in some decent prints for the hallway, take out the gas fire and scour the reclamation yards for a good Deco surround – but too late, the image was sliding away again to be replaced by a hospital room and a doctor's voice: *What I'm saying is, there's no actual foetus.*

She picked up the metal Speedway cooker and pushed its feet into the skin on the back of her hand until she was back in Russ's world. Ruth pregnant; no. Ruth as she was last week, complaining about her weight, slapping her hip as though she could beat some fat off. 'I need to be Ruth-less!' she'd quipped, very pleased with the line. 'No more HobNobs for Mummy. Tom, if you see Mummy with the biscuit tin you've to shout, "Stop!", OK?' Tom watching *Scooby Doo*, not showing the slightest bit of interest, not even turning round. If Tom ever tried to stop Ruth eating she'd probably whack him. No, that wasn't fair; Ruth wouldn't hit her children. Just whinge them into submission. 'How do you keep so slim?' she'd said to Anna, her gaze moving up and down Anna's body. 'You're so lucky.' The temptation to go, Well, I don't sit around stuffing my face half the day.

She replaced the cooker, then pushed at the little porcelain sink with the tip of her finger to line it up with the skirting board. Good. The house front swung back round and she clicked it into place. If she put her eye to the bedroom window she could see the tiny nightdress case sitting on the repainted Lloyd Loom chair.

Imagine Ruth naked. Imagine Ruth and Russ naked. No, she didn't want to think about them together like that. And anyway, he said they never did any more. The trouble with Ruth was she'd stopped behaving like a wife, apparently.

What was it going to be like when she met Russ again?

They were looking at 'Anne Hathaway' by Carol Ann Duffy. Everyone except Nathan had their anthologies open; he was colouring the Os on the front of his to make them look like cartoon eyes. Anna went over and, without fuss, without looking at him, flipped his booklet to the right page.

'I'm going to read the poem through with you and then I'll put a question on the board. I want you to write the answer in note form, for discussion. You can work on your own or with a partner. OK?'

Their silence she took for assent. Anna cleared her throat and read:

> *'The bed we loved in was a spinning world*
> *of forests, castles, torchlight, clifftops, seas*
> *where we would dive for pearls. My lover's words*
> *were shooting stars which fell to earth as kisses*
> *on these lips; my body now a softer rhyme*
> *to his, now echo, assonance; his touch*

> *a verb dancing in the centre of a noun.*
> *Some nights, I dreamed he'd written me, the bed*
> *a page beneath his writer's hands. Romance*
> *and drama played by touch, by scent, by taste.*
> *In the other bed, the best, our guests dozed on,*
> *dribbling their prose. My living laughing love –*
> *I hold him in the casket of my widow's head*
> *as he held me upon that next best bed.'*

The beauty of the words couldn't touch her today; she was a thousand miles from this classroom, and unbelievably tired, as though someone had tied stones to her limbs and neck. Something flickered at the edge of her memory: she thought she might have dreamed about Nathan. In front of her, the students waited blankly.

'So. To begin with.' She took up the marker and stood by the whiteboard. 'What do we learn about Anne's relationship with William?'

Sweet Jesus, it came back to her now, this dream that she'd been *kissing* him, and *enjoying* it. No explanation, no context, except that they'd been on the top of a high building somewhere and she'd been late for a class. No Jamie in the dream, either. She imagined asking Mel, Do you ever have erotic dreams about people you detest? and Mel laughing and saying something like, Yeah, all the time, don't worry about it. She could recall now Nathan's sleepy hooded eyes and his faint moustache as he'd held her face and loomed in. You thanked God at times like this the pupils couldn't see into your brain.

She sat for a minute watching the class, alert for signs of disengagement. There, Felix's hand was up, he needed help already, probably hadn't been listening when she gave out the instructions and where were his coloured lenses that he was supposed to wear? But before she could make a move there was a knock at the door, and when it opened, it was Les.

'Mrs Lloyd? Sorry to interrupt your lesson. We've got a young lady here who's starting late.'

Anna was out of her seat and moving forwards when the girl stepped in.

'Kali Norman.' Les's gaze was shifting around as though there was something he should not look at. 'She's going to be in Mr Maye's tutor group. And the headmaster said your set for English . . .?'

'Thank you, Mr Weston.'

Everyone was staring at this tall girl who stood with her shoulders back and her copper hair spread out over her shirt. *I know you from somewhere*, thought Anna. Or had she seen that face in a painting? Something struck a chord.

She became aware that they were waiting.

'Kali, would you like to come and sit at the front with Lin so you can share her anthology? I'll sort you out with one of your own for next lesson. Do you have something to write with?'

The girl reached into her shoulder bag, held up a tobacco tin and rattled it. Extraordinary, but under her white school blouse she was wearing a red bra. Not a standard blouse either, because it was too fitted. It gave her a different shape from the other girls: narrower, more slender. Where the two fabrics touched you could see the actual details of the lace. First day at a new school; surely her mother would have said something as she walked out of the house?

Anna motioned to the empty chair and Kali sat. From where she was now, Anna could see the line of natural brown hair colour at her parting, before the henna kicked in. Then Kali raised her eyes and Anna unaccountably found herself blushing. At the next desk, Lin tugged at her WWJD wristband and drew her elbows in, even though there was plenty of room.

'Felix, is it quick?'

'Oh, yeah. What's assonance again?'

'Repeated vowel sounds. If you're not sure of the line, though, leave it. We'll be going over the whole poem in ten minutes.'

Felix nodded and Anna went to stand by Kali. 'If you just read the poem for now and listen to what we say in discussion, I can give you a homework for copying up the notes.'

''Kay.'

'Is it Carly as in the singer, or Kali as in the goddess?'

A smile. 'The goddess.'

'Ah. By the way, we don't—' Anna felt her collar digging in as she leant over. '—allow nail varnish in school. If you could make sure you remove it tonight.' She spoke lightly to show it wasn't a telling-off. Kali reached for her tin. 'Excellent.'

Kali's plum nails squeezed under the lid. There was a metallic pop and the tin came open to reveal ink cartridges, a set of studs and a kohl pencil. Behind Anna, Nathan sniggered over some private joke.

'So, you're sorted?'

'Yeah. Thanks.'

'And I'll have a chat with you after.'

Nathan made a choking noise and something clattered to the floor.

'Do you *want* me to move you?' said Anna, over her shoulder.

'You said we could work with a partner.'

'Yes, work being the operative word. What is the matter? Are you stuck?'

'This poem, it's filthy.'

The boy next to Nathan, Martin Fallow, had his head in his hands and was shaking with laughter.

'Go on, Martin,' he said.

'I'm not saying it.'

'What?' Anna turned and straightened up.

''Sabout muff-diving, isn't it?'

Nathan had lowered his face and slurred the words but they were quite audible. Martin picked up his anthology and held it, like a child would, in front of him. She could see by his shoulders he was still laughing.

'It's this line here, about diving for pearls. 'Cause they're in bed and they're at it, yeah, and then it says he goes pearl-diving. That's what it means, isn't it?'

God, thought Anna, this for another two years.

'The wonderful thing about poetry,' she said, looking round for a moment to take in all the class, 'is that it's open to individual interpretation. So *if* you can justify yourself in appropriate language, if you can support your point of view in a clear and sensible way, by reference to the text, then an examiner would accept your argument. But you would have to express it properly. Maturely.'

'So if I use posh words I can put that it's about—' Nathan stuck his tongue out as far as it would go and wiggled it.

A huge geyser of loathing welled up inside her. She had to fight to keep her hands by her sides and her voice calm. 'I'm going to have to send you out if you don't modify your behaviour.'

Some of the girls on the front row were whispering, not sure what had been said.

'And that means a letter home via the headmaster to explain why you were excluded from a lesson. I take it you'd rather not go down that route?'

'No, Mrs Lloyd.'

'Well, then.'

'Sorry, Mrs Lloyd.'

'I'll see you afterwards.'

'Yes, Mrs Lloyd.' Insolence radiated off him.

Quarter of an hour to get through till the bell went. She walked back to the desk and sat down behind it. Then she pretended to study the poem while she took some deep breaths. After a minute she took the board rubber, wiped the question away and began to take their ideas: Anne loved William a lot, yes – she misses her husband now he's dead – he made their relationship seem magical, good. Nathan sat dumb and Anna acted as though he wasn't in the room. When she glanced at Kali, the girl was watching her with, she thought, something like admiration. But it was hard to tell.

*

'The thing was, he was technically right so I didn't feel I could send him out.'

'Hmm?' Jamie nodded, though his eyes were on the TV listings. 'You don't want to put up with any nonsense, Anna. Crush him early. I'd have told him to fuck off, little tosser.'

'No, you wouldn't. And he's not so little.'

Jamie leaned across the sofa as if reaching for a kiss. Instead he picked her red pen from the spine of her open mark book so he could circle his favourite programmes. Research, this was. 'So go on, what did you do, in the end?'

'The usual. Talked about needing to approach lessons more seriously now he was a GCSE student, reminded him of the discipline procedure, explained what would happen if he did it again. Blah, blah, and he's rolling his eyes and sighing – I swear if he'd looked at his watch I'd have lost it. Then I tried the upbeat ending, you know. You've got potential, I know you're able, sort of thing.'

'Oh, yeah. We talk some shite, don't we? Is he bright?'

'Not bright. Clever-clever. He thinks he's terrifically streetwise.'

'I expect he is.'

'Yes.' Those awful hooded eyes. 'God knows what the new girl thought.'

She wrenched her mind off Nathan and tried to focus on a lesson plan, but her thoughts slid to Kali's velvet shoulder bag, the wavy tinted hair all different shades, that red bra. Those silver bracelets would have to come off because, hell, they couldn't allow any individualism in the school.

Anna had left Jamie drawing his critical rings and was on her way to make coffee when she heard the letter box snap. Who was posting stuff at this time? But when she pulled the door curtain back there was nothing on the carpet. She glanced back to check the living room: no movement there, only a theme tune floating out and then the excited muffle of a voice-over. In another second she'd clicked the latch open and was looking out into the night, across the green. And there he was, Russ, standing under the lamp post opposite. Fuck. He waved his hand as though he'd been greeting her in the high street. He had no coat on. It looked as if he'd stepped out of his house on a whim.

He came swiftly across the road towards her and it was all she could do not to shut the door in his face.

'Don't, Anna,' he said as he got near. 'Wait.'

She hung onto the Yale lock as he pushed a piece of paper at her. She took it out of fright more than anything. 'Go,' she hissed. 'Please.'

To her relief he turned and walked back down the street, towards the main road, away.

Trembling, she slid the paper up the sleeve of her jumper like an exam cheat, pushed the door gently to, and sprinted upstairs to the bathroom where she could lock herself in. Then she ran to the window to peer out again, but dropped the blind in panic a second later to yank the light off. From darkness she scanned the road below. Nothing. Gone. She sat down on the toilet seat and closed her eyes. There was a faint cramping below her stomach.

After a while Anna made herself get up and switch the light back on. Then she turned the taps on full because she wanted nothing so badly as to lie in a warm bath.

The letter. She drew it out, blood thumping in her ears, and began to unfold it.

'Anna?'

Jamie was knocking at the door, fucking hell. 'Yeah?'

'You having a bath?'

No, I'm climbing Mount Everest. 'Yes. Why?'

'Nothing. I made the coffee.' A martyred pause. 'Shall I leave yours outside, then?'

'OK.' . . . *kind of beacon in my life* . . . she read with horror . . . *feel I haven't been given a chance to put things* . . .

She stripped off her clothes and laid them across the heated towel rail, then climbed into the water. You weren't supposed to have the bath too hot when you were pregnant.

Dear Anna,

Please read this all the way through. I know I should try to give it you at work but I can't wait till tomorrow. You can text me. I'll be up all night. I'm sorry for panicing in the caravan. (Even in her stressed state Anna winced at the spelling error.) *It was a shock. I said I loved you and I know that's not what you want to hear, but now I've had a chance to think it over I don't think I do. That was a mistake. So if you're feeling frightened off because I'm getting involved then don't.*

But please please Anna, can't we carry on as we were?
You've been a kind of beacon in my life and I don't want
it to stop. All I want to do is talk things through with
you because I feel I haven't been given a chance to put
things right and I'll do <u>whatever it takes</u>. Please will you
see me just one more time to get things straightened
out? I think we owe it to each other to finish it right.

I don't owe you anything, she thought. Not yet,
anyway.

She guessed he'd intended to post his note through
the letter box, then realized how mad an idea that was
and drawn it back. She hadn't thought of Russ as having
a reckless side. That certainly had not been in the plan.

If it did all come out, what then? She could imagine
too well Ruth's collapsed face, the stares of the children.
Ruth would call her something like a cold hard bitch
because she secretly thought that anyway. She'd cry a lot
and comfort-eat and go round to her parents' begging
sympathy; she spent half her life round there anyway.
Anna would be at a stroke the most evil woman in history. Russ would run between them, or run away.

Jamie's reaction she didn't dare consider.

She mashed Russ's note in the bathwater and fed it
down the plughole in tiny scraps. She had no intention
of acknowledging it. If she replied, the whole situation
would drag on and on. But she couldn't help checking
the street again before she went downstairs.

'You didn't drink your coffee.' Jamie saw her carrying the full cup to the kitchen. 'What's up?'

'Nothing. Why should something be up?'

He raised one eyebrow. 'Because you look a bit strange this evening. Spacey. You coming down with something?'

'I might have a cold coming on,' she said.

Chapter Three

On Monday the Head called a four o'clock briefing, which was a surprise as well as a damn nuisance. Jackson avoided staff meetings where he could. Groups made him nervous. He coped better with private interviews; operating to maximum effectiveness in a face-to-face environment, he'd probably call it. On rare occasions he'd take a lunchtime stroll across the playing fields, attempting to engage some of the pupils in banter, flinching from stray footballs. Anna suspected the boys kicked the ball at him deliberately.

She watched his ugly face working now as he waited for his staff to get their coffees and take their seats. One day she might stand up and shout, 'What are you doing in this job?'

Jackson took the dais and stood waiting. The chat continued. He held his chin up in an authoritative pose, but there was still no noticeable lull. Then Les, stationed next to him but a step below, tapped his spoon on the side of his mug and the meeting began.

'Quick student update,' announced Jackson. 'I have some pastoral information that needs to be cascaded, and I wanted us all to have the opportunity to feed back on any problems or concerns we might have at this early point in term.'

Anna looked down at the coffee table, tried to read the *TES* headline upside down.

'So firstly, Amy Carter's mother is out of hospital and is being looked after at home. But it's palliative care. She's not expected to live more than a couple of months. So, be understanding about homework deadlines, not having the right books, sort of thing. Any concerns, see Amy's form tutor, Mrs Yates. Yes, it's very very sad. Very sad.' He paused to show how sad he was. Above him the corner of a laminated Health and Safety poster pinged away from its Blu-tack. 'Mr Weston?'

'Right, yes.' Les consulted his notes. 'We have a new pupil this term in upper school, Kali Norman, Year Ten, under Mr Maye. Pleasant girl but we do have a bit of a blank where Kali's history is concerned, don't we, Headmaster?' Jackson nodded. 'She's been living a nomadic life. Came to us from a comprehensive in Manchester but because she was only there half a term they haven't got any records for her. They never received anything from her previous school—'

'Her mother says she was off with glandular fever for several months,' Jackson broke in. 'And before that they'd been in Ireland. So she's out of year, in fact. We've agreed she can repeat Year Ten even though technically she should be in the class above. But I've spoken to the mum and she seems keen, and I think Kali's able enough. Anyway, our Mrs Hislop is pursuing the girl's school records for me and I'll let you know when we catch up with them. Or they catch up with us. Ha ha.'

'However,' Les went on, 'what we do need to keep in mind is that Kali's had a slightly unsettled background and we need to be sensitive to that. There was an allegation of abuse – not sexual, physical – against one of her mother's ex-partners three years ago. By her own admission, mum's had a lot of boyfriends – father's not on the scene at all – and she feels that Kali can sometimes act in an attention-seeking way. She doesn't want us to label her daughter from day one, but she does want us to be aware.'

Jackson raised his voice and scanned the room. 'So that means re-reading the chapter in the staff handbook on appropriate conduct to pupils, and, particularly if you're a male member of staff, taking the usual sensible precautions. Not closing the door if you happen to be in a room on your own with her, that kind of thing. Nothing—' He held up his hand in a calming gesture. 'Nothing to get worked up about. It's simply being professional. Modern times, I'm afraid. That's all.'

There was muttering and shifting round the staffroom. The telephone by the door rang twice, then stopped. Anna looked at her pile of unmarked books, then at the clock. Jackson made no sign of getting down off the dais.

'So we're pretty much up to speed there,' he said loudly. The staff fell silent again. 'And Mr Maye or Mr Weston or myself will keep you informed of latest developments. Now, before we finish, any concerns about other pupils? Form tutors?'

Andrew Maye raised an index finger. 'I'm not happy about Nathan Woods.'

'Who is?' That was Les. Some polite laughter. 'Sorry; in what sense?'

'I'd say he's come back with even more of an attitude this term. He's, I don't know, simmering. You see it in registration. He walks in first thing and he's *looking* for trouble.'

'Has he done anything specific?'

Anna turned to where Chrissy was sitting. You made me have him, she wanted to say, and he's already tried to disrupt one of my lessons with smut. A real head of department would have taken a pupil like that herself. But Chrissy was doodling in her planner and didn't see Anna's face.

'. . . animosity between him and Justin Coates,' Andrew was saying, 'and he winds Martin Fallow up. Also, I think what Nathan gets up to outside the classroom is worse than anything we get to see.'

'So we'll all keep our eyes open while we're on duty,' – Jackson again – 'and report anything of note. Communication is the key.'

'I never have any problem with Woods.' Tom Maxfield, this; middle-aged idealist, friend to all misfits, twat. 'I reckon it's because we share a passion for guitars. If you talk to him, I mean really talk to him rather than telling him off, you get so much more back.'

Fuck off, Anna thought. And cut your hair, too.

'Thank you for the words of wisdom, Tom,' said Les.

Jackson waved his hands as the murmuring began again. 'Well, I'm going to say That's all folks, and if you have any further comments or, yes, I know you're anxious to get home but, if you have any difficulties, do try and go through the form tutors and use the pastoral care system, see if you can sort things out at ground level . . .'

Don't come bothering me, was what he meant. As soon as he stepped down, Anna scooped her books to her chest and took them through to the work area. If Chrissy came over to chat now—

But it was Andrew who pulled up a chair on the opposite side of the table and got his mark lists out, set his coffee down, unwrapped his Tracker bar. 'Wanker,' he said companionably. Anna glanced up and gave a quick smile. 'Bloody waste of space. Come the glorious day.'

Les stepped into the doorway. 'Just be aware that the wanker is still only round the corner,' he mouthed.

'I don't care,' said Andrew, but he shut up.

'How's Kali getting on in your English set?' Les came over and perched on the edge of the desk next to Anna. 'How've you found her?'

Anna thought of the bracelets and the tobacco tin and the knowing looks.

'Difficult to tell so far. Orally she's excellent, very incisive. She's got a piece to hand in tomorrow, so we'll see what the written work's like.'

'But behaviour in class is OK?'

'All right at the moment. At least her bra's white this week.'

Andrew raised his head. 'You can still see her tattoo, though.'

'She's got a tattoo? I never noticed. Where?'

'Upper arm. A bird, about the size of a ten p.'

'I thought you weren't allowed tattoos under the age of eighteen. Is it real?'

'Who knows. I'm certainly not getting close enough to find out. She strikes me as one of those girls who know they're good-looking, and I don't trust that type.'

'Very wise,' said Les, grinning. 'Remember the two-foot rule.'

'She's not our usual clientele, is she?' Anna put her pen down for a moment to consider. 'She gives off "I'm different" vibes, and it's not just the way she looks. Or the fact that she's older.'

'Sixteen going on twenty-five,' said Andrew. 'And that's going to mess our GCSE stats up for next year, isn't it? Has it occurred to Jackson?'

'What's her mother do?'

'Flits about attaching herself to the nearest wealthy man, I think. It's the fiancé who's paying Kali's fees; he runs a big garage or something. It's a cycle, though, isn't it: crap parenting, dodgy kids who become crap parents who have dodgy kids.'

'Not necessarily,' Anna began hotly.

'Anyway. I'm not going to be left on my own in a room with her, I know that much. I've enough on my hands trying not to take a swipe at bloody Nathan.'

'Neither of them worth ruining a brilliant career over,' said Les, getting to his feet again. 'Our litigious society. Let me know if you have any problems, though.'

Anna opened her mouth to speak, then shut it. Nathan could have another chance.

*

She thought for a moment Russ's car was parked in the bay opposite the school entrance, and her stomach lurched. But when she looked again, it wasn't the right registration. Still, she was shaken. The trouble was, she didn't really know Russ at all.

PM was on the radio, wall-to-wall gloom, so she switched to *drive time* and tried to listen to the songs rather than letting her thoughts run.

> *It's a damn damn shame*
> *You're leaving me, you're leaving.*

The way home – if she didn't go via the caravan site – was a straight, fast A-road through fields. In the winter the clouds would be spectacularly red, like driving into hell.

She didn't dislike the time alone in the car.

> *'Cause I don't think*
> *That I can live without you.*

Except it was difficult sometimes not to use the space to brood.

> *I guess you've opened up my heart*
> *And I'm gonna bleed forever*

Before she knew it, her mother's voice came in over the music: *What the hell do you think you're doing?* Anna was back on the boat, leaning over the water and watching a dark fringe of fish eat her sandwich. *Do you think we've got money to burn?* Money to drown, Anna had replied dreamily, and Miriam had slapped her legs. That would have been just after they moved up to Nantwich

– she'd have been ten. Most of the time Miriam had kept the boat moored in one place; so much for the big adventure. They'd spent a freezing winter tied up outside a pub where the owners had a boxer dog that barked incessantly. (Russ and Ruth had a mongrel dog, which meant there were hairs everywhere, and it smelt. She'd once seen baby Tom sucking on its rubber bone.) Anna remembered her mother wearing a suede coat and knee boots, her hair long and straight down her back. The *Weasel*, their boat had been called.

Thinking about it now, they'd have been following some man, or escaping from one. (The problem was, people changed when they were thwarted. You saw this whole new side. She was going to remind Russ, if they ever spoke about it again, how he'd agreed the rules, how he'd been perfectly happy to play it her way. She'd said quite clearly from the outset that either one of them could stop whenever it suited them. He hadn't raised any objection.)

The boyfriend-before, Beard-Man, had lived in a caravan, so perhaps that was where Miriam's boat idea had come from. That had been down in Exmouth, where they'd stayed for four years. Anna had the chance to settle at school and there was the sea and good shops selling toys. Her best teacher had been Mr Woollard, who did speed drawing with them. He'd put a potted plant on the table and say, Sixty seconds, go! And you had to sketch the outline in really fast, no good getting bogged down in detail, though there was always someone who only managed a single leaf or half a stalk before he told the class to stop. She wouldn't have minded having him as a dad, except he was taken already and on the old side for Miriam. The day after her mother said they were leaving Exmouth, Anna had stood on the beach during a fog so thick she couldn't see the water. It was like the end of the world. (What if Russ did tell Jamie?)

She came out of it to Led Zeppelin's 'Black Dog' and Chris Evans wondering where he'd put his old air guitar – was it still under the bed or had it gone up in the loft with all his O-level notes. The landscape of middle age was a strange one.

Because she didn't dare think about the baby she imagined a conversation with Kali. She could tell her she understood. *I know what it's like to keep moving around the country after your mother. It's difficult when you do stop because you don't want to put down roots in case you're off again, I've always found it hard to make friends. And I absolutely cried my eyes out when we had to leave Devon. My mum must have had gypsy blood in her. She looked like a gypsy. Do you know, we used to live on a boat near Nantwich!* 'That's why you're so square,' Jamie teased her sometimes. 'It's your rebellion against your hippy roots.'

And just like that, with 'Black Dog' still pounding the dashboard speakers, she was back at the hospital waiting to go in for her D and C; Jamie reading *Maxim* and looking grim and bored. A booklet on the bedside locker with a logo of two cupped hands holding a foetus.

If there did turn out to be a baby, it would be worth whatever happened.

The house was very quiet when she got in: no upstairs music, no TV or radio. Either Jamie wasn't home or he was working super-hard. She went through to the lounge and started at the sight of the bouquet on the table. Russ has sent me some flowers, she thought, with a message that Jamie's read, and he's left me.

She ran straight up to the office, because if Jamie had gone he would have taken his computer. But his room was still the usual mess, no evidence of any crisis. And there he was, she could see him through the window, in the back garden talking to a neighbour over the fence. She waved but neither of them saw her. When she tapped on the glass he looked up quickly. There was a sheet of paper in his hand.

'Good news,' she heard him call as she went back down the stairs.

'You've sold a script!'

'No—' He was leaning against the newel post, holding the paper in front of him like a speech.

'You've finished a script?'

'*No*. For God's sake, Anna. I've won a prize.'

'A prize?'

'For poetry. Look.'

Anna took the letter. 'TellTale Writers' Group . . . your poem "Six Ways to Dissect the Human Heart" has won second prize in our annual competition . . . to be included in our anthology . . .' She made to hand it back. 'Very good.'

'See, though. They're giving me seventy-five pounds for it. Seventy-five quid and it's only eighteen lines long, so that's over four pounds a line! Not bad for an hour's work, eh?'

He took the letter back and scanned it again. 'I sent the thing off on a whim. Seventy-five pounds.'

'Yes, terrific.'

It was important that she didn't let her irritation show. They weren't short of money, but it all came from Anna, Anna's job.

'For an hour's work.'

'Yes, fantastic.'

'I brought you flowers.'

'Oh!' She'd forgotten them for a moment. 'Thanks, that's nice.' And a relief, she could have added. 'So you're going with poetry now?'

He shook his head. 'It was one of those days when I had writer's block, couldn't get a thing out. I just switched off the computer and went for a walk. When I came back, I'd written a poem. Amazing the way the Muse operates, isn't it?'

She didn't reply.

'I still want to write for TV. That's my, what, my vocation. It's just finding an original angle . . .'

'Did you remember to get some more tea bags in?'

'Fuck,' said Jamie. Then he went quiet for a while.

Eventually, over the pizza that he only pushed around his plate, he said, 'Fucking tea bags. You always have to spoil it, don't you? Why can't you ever simply be glad?'

And that was the evening ruined.

Later she rang Mel but only got the answering machine. Anna wouldn't have known what to say anyway. That was the problem when you kept so many secrets from your best friend.

Now she lay in the dark, Jamie's sulky form beside her, and considered Russ.

The first time she approached him, how had he reacted? No, further back than that: what had he been like the first time she ever saw him? She'd been going out with Jamie for almost a year before he introduced them. Anna would have been thirty, Russ too. He had more hair then and his round face suited his youth. Ruth thought she had done well for herself, you could see. But even then there was a trapped look about Russ, hooked up with this swelling woman and the evenings and nights full of crying, toys and clutter so that work was actually an escape, even though that was a barrow load of stress too. He'd looked Anna up and down with such obvious envy it was embarrassing. 'Trust my brother to pick a stunner,' he'd said, though only she noticed the bitterness in his voice because Jamie laughed and Ruth was sniffing Tasha's bottom and going, I think she's done a nappy, so she missed any nuances of tone. 'What do you think of my little bro, then?' Jamie had asked when Russ and Ruth had gone home. 'I practically brought him up, you know. Not like me, is he?'

She'd invited Russ to have an affair with her eleven years later; ten years of being unremarkably polite family members, doing emergency baby sitting and delivering Easter eggs, sponsoring charity swims, coaching Tasha with her reading for a while. Then one day she'd phoned and made an appointment to see Russ at the timber yard – she wanted to speak to him away from home, didn't want to be reminded of the children, because Tasha and Bethany were so sweet in those days and Tom was pretty new, only a toddler. She'd closed his office door and he'd said, all smiles and then slightly worried, 'What's this about?' And she'd just moved round behind the desk and kissed him, and there was so much longing in that kiss that it left him weak and he had to sit down, panting. Then she'd given him a slip of paper with the address of the caravan and a time on it, and walked out.

So by the time he came to her, he was desperate with lust and fear and barely listening. He'd sunk against her groaning and afterwards kept saying Thank you, thank you, though if he'd realized how unattractive gratitude is in a lover he'd have stopped at once. She remembered him baring his teeth and explaining how he'd taken a sponge bag into work with him so he could freshen up. But the sex had been better than she'd expected because of his absolute passion; it was impossible not to be carried away by it. Perhaps it was a power thing, too.

It was on about the fourth meeting that he asked, Why? She'd been ready for this question. 'Because the sex in my marriage has become meaningless,' she'd said. Which was true. 'Oh, it's the same in mine, too,' Russ had replied, and she'd thought, Not in the same way, it isn't.

The idea had been to make sure of a baby, then get out. An affair with a stranger would have been too complicated to arrange, too risky. When could she have found the time to trawl a bar or a club? Never mind what kind of man you might pick up in those places, with what history or intentions. The same issues surrounded clinics – who knew the crazy, mangled genes you might receive? Horrible strangers masturbating into pots; the idea made her feel ill. But Russ was family. He was solid and dull and dependable and bored. He'd had enough of babies, would never stake any kind of claim over a pregnancy, had too much to lose all round by not keeping quiet. He was hers for the taking.

And if it was a crazy plan, it was no madder than stealing a child from a pram and that happened all the time. She just could not bear any longer to stand passively by and feel herself withering up on the inside and Jamie not caring.

A few weeks in, Russ went through a phase of standing in front of the mirror and asking what on earth she saw in him, which was off-putting. Eventually she had to ask him to stop doing it.

Then came his guilty phase. 'Do you ever feel guilty?' he asked one time after the sex had not been so brilliant.

'Do you?' she'd said, to avoid answering.

'Of course. It's not me, this.' Well, who else is it rocking the caravan of a Tuesday evening, she wanted to say. 'I'm not a bad person.'

'No.'

'The problem is' – he'd turned to her confidentially – 'marriage isn't what you expect, is it? You're led to believe certain things, then it all shifts round and – it's like, on Sundays we trail off to Homebase and there are all these miserable-looking blokes there, you can see from their faces they're thinking, How did I get here?

Because you start off in a relationship having a stack of sex and mucking about, and she keeps herself nice, wears make-up, diets, what have you. Then as soon as you've signed on the dotted line that's it, you're just a household asset. I sometimes feel like climbing up on one of their patio tables and shouting a warning to all the young lads, *Get out now*. I never have any time to myself, even when I come home she wants me to help with the kids or go round to her parents' or some neighbours' do. And even though I work all the hours God sends there's never enough money, bloody car's clapped out and dropping to bits but I can't get a new one because we need to repair the bay window before it falls off. And I could cope with all this if I got the sex, but there's no sex, there really isn't. Even when we do get it together I don't fancy her. You've no idea what having three kids does to a woman's body.'

Anna had seen the Tena Lady pads in Ruth's airing cupboard. Serves you right for marrying a mother-figure, she could have said.

He'd raised himself up on one elbow and looked down at her naked length. 'Your body's so intact.'

Strange word to use, she thought.

Towards the end he started talking about Jamie. Why had she married him? How were things? ('I mean, obviously not *great*, I know, or you wouldn't be here.') It was funny, wasn't it, the way their dad's will had worked out? But he wasn't jealous, because when the will had been made, Dad had no idea that property would be worth so much and shares so little; he'd meant them to have the same, he'd meant it fairly. That was what mattered. Though God knows it would have come in handy. But Jamie was older than him; if anyone deserved to take early retirement, it was knackered old Jamie and good luck to him. Did Anna mind supporting him financially? Sometimes he'd thought it didn't seem very manly, very gallant. But he was sure Anna wouldn't have agreed to something she wasn't happy with.

She never said anything much; at last he got the message. She'd known he felt those things anyway.

Russ was angry but he was weak. He'd never do anything to rock the boat now, surely? The strange thing was, in her school work she was such a planner, so organized and forward-thinking. Proactive, Jackson once called her 'like the margarine'. But life didn't run itself along those kind of lines. All she had thought about, when the affair had begun, was getting herself pregnant. Everything after that had been in the shadows.

Chapter Four

Three years ago the sixth-form media-studies group filmed a promotional video for the school, and for the first time ever Anna had seen herself as the students saw her. Small – smaller than a lot of the Year Eleven girls with their long swinging hair and stack soles – and dark and neat in a navy outfit with white cuffs and collar. Jackson had held a special screening of the pre-edited version in the staffroom and attempted a jokey commentary. But his quips were drowned out by yelps and laughter as one by one the teachers spotted themselves. Oh my God, it's me. Look at that haircut. My voice!

Then it was Anna's turn and there she was, delivering notes on *To Kill a Mockingbird* to a quiet class. Nothing spectacular, just getting on with the job. Cut to Liz Yates's Geography and Liz stalking round the room, perching flirtily on the edge of the table, swinging her legs. A great one for treats, Liz. Always bringing in sweets or some junk, couldn't run a lesson without add-ons. 'They see through that stuff, though,' Mel had told her later, when Anna found her section had been edited out and Liz's retained. 'Kids aren't stupid. You can't win them over with a Creme Egg. They might not be able to articulate it but they do appreciate good plain teaching in a calm environment. That's why you get all those cards at the end of term. That's why they come to you with confidences.'

Not that that was always a good thing. That was how the business with Adam Gardiner started.

She'd decided to beat Nathan Woods with sheer, bright, unremitting professionalism. Draw him into the lessons, offer lots of praise, challenge him intellectually. That way he'd have less chance to be distracted; if he was involved, he'd enjoy himself more. Anna wasn't going to let him sit at the back and draw ranks of phalluses.

Today, though, he wasn't here.

'I asked you, for homework,' she was saying, 'to think about what the two women in these poems got out of their relationships with their husbands. And to make some notes so that we can put together an essay plan today in which we think about Comparison and Contrast.'

Some pupils were looking up, some were bent over their desks doodling; some were staring past her through the window at the distant hills. Martin Fallow was playing with his calculator. She'd moved him away from his mates next to one of the serious girls and he was sulking about it. Kali had come late and was seated by the door, a faraway expression on her face.

'So, who'd like to start?' said Anna. 'Let's concentrate on the Duffy first because that's revision.'

She wrote some prompt words on the board, then turned back.

'Lin?'

'Erm, the relationship made her feel special, better than, you know, the guests – in the other bed – they had ordinary dull marriages. But he kind of transported her to another level when they had sex—'

Some tittering.

'Go on.'

'And he was like a part of her – no, I mean she was part of him, he was in control of the relationship, but that's probably 'cause of the times? Women were below men, sort of thing?'

'Was it "the times", or was that just the way he made her feel?' Anna tilted her head, smiling. 'Good start, anyway. Let's get some of that down . . . OK . . . Sally?'

The momentum of the lesson had started. She glanced down at her planner; what did she need to get through in the next forty minutes? More hands were going up. She could set a timed essay for Thursday and afterwards show them the *Poets Talking* video, that always went down well. Put them into discussion groups for the exercises at the end—

Then the door banged open and it was Nathan, very flushed, no tie. Everyone turned to see because he'd brought in with him an abrasive field; the room was charged at once. Something had happened to him that morning and he was sparking with it.

'Whoops,' he said. 'Bit late.'

'Put your tie on and sit down,' said Anna. 'There.' She pointed to the front but he'd already slumped next to Martin at the end of the middle row. Martin looked at her from under his fringe, waiting.

Well, he could wait. She'd freeze Nathan out and carry on with her notes, then tear a strip off him at the end, during break. She could tell from the mood Nathan was in that a confrontation now, with an audience, was what he wanted. He had pulled his rolled-up tie from his blazer pocket and draped it round his neck, but made no effort to knot it.

'So Duffy portrays Anne as being incomplete without William, is that correct? Sally, what were you going to add?'

But Sally was spooked and had lost the thread. 'She, um, misses—'

Nathan had unzipped his sports bag and was stirring the contents round and sighing. Anna knew he had no textbook. 'Share,' she mouthed.

Martin shoved his book across, grinning. Nathan made to grab it and they scuffled briefly.

'—Erm, she misses the intimacy—'

Never wrestle with a pig, Mel always said. You both get dirty and the pig likes it.

Anna took two steps towards the boys and said in a low voice, 'If you don't settle down you will both be out of the lesson.'

She ignored Martin's mock-amazement and moved back to the board.

'Good.' Sally was put out of her misery. 'Intimacy. Now, what about the casket image; why has Duffy chosen a casket as a place for Anne to hold her memories? What's special about a casket?'

No hands up now, damn it. And then another knock on the door and it was Les.

'Mrs Lloyd, may I have a quick word?'

She could have kicked the desk in frustration, but she went straight over. Let them have half a minute to twitter, then she'd start over again.

Les drew her round the other side of the door. 'Just to fill you in,' he said, 'there's a legitimate reason for Nathan's lateness. I don't know if you've said anything to him?'

'I was going to leave it till the end.'

'Right, well, if you send him back to me as soon as the bell goes, that's probably simplest. We have some unfinished business.'

Anna glanced back into the classroom. Everyone was still in their chairs though Martin was tipping his back, his arms spread wide like a clever circus performer.

'Anything I should know about?'

'Jackson's put a notice up about it in the staffroom. Nathan's been running an illegal lottery, extorting money from other pupils and fixing the draw so his mates win and split the proceeds. He's been using the school photocopier to print off tickets: that's how we found out. He left the master on the glass. Saves on computer ink, see?' Les pulled a sneering face that was meant to look like Nathan. 'So we've had him in the Head's office till now trying to find out how much cash has gone through the system and which kids have lost out. He won't give, though, so we thought we'd pack him off to lessons, get him out of the way while we did some digging and phoned his parents. Sorry. Is he all right?'

'Unstable. Could go off at any minute.'

'As normal, then.' Les sighed and looked at his watch. 'Seriously, any trouble, boot him out. I'll only be across the way, in the office.'

Anna nodded and went back in.

'So,' she announced. 'So—' The hum subsided. Kali still looked vacant; was she ill? Anna clasped her hands and stood very still while she waited for complete silence.

Nathan's hand went up.

'Yes?'

'I know the answer.'

'To?'

'You said why a casket, yeah?'

'Oh, that's right. Why not any old box; why not a—?'

'It's because it's like a treasure chest, so her memories are like her jewellery, like these, you know, precious things.'

Everyone was listening, anticipating.

''Cause William would've given her stuff, jewellery, wouldn't he?'

'Oh, yes, I'm sure he would. Good.' Probably Nathan was trying to ingratiate himself with her, hoping she'd put in a good word for him with Jackson. 'And you do keep jewels in caskets, in fact the casket image comes into several—'

'I know something he gave her.'

'Do you?'

'I do, yeah.'

'And what's that?'

'It says it in the poem.'

'What?'

'A pearl necklace. You know.' He gave a snort of mirth. 'Her husband gave her a *pearl necklace* while they were in bed together.'

His gaze locked on hers. Grins of disbelief round the room, a gasp from someone, eyes swivelling between her and Nathan while they tried to work out whether Mrs Lloyd had got the joke.

Anna swallowed once and said, 'Leave your books on the table and go and stand outside.' Even as she spoke she was thinking, I could have pretended not to understand, I could have glossed over it and avoided a row.

Nathan didn't move.

'Now, please.'

He rose as slowly as he could, jerking his chair back so it hit Neil Frank's desk behind him. Neil jumped and even Kali looked up.

On his feet at last, Nathan glanced round the room, then slouched towards the door. Get out, get out, Anna screamed in her head. But as he drew near he made a sudden swipe at Kali, grabbing at her hair.

'Oh! Shi—' Her hands flew up to protect her face. He hadn't touched her, though. Nathan half-turned and raised his fist to show them the earpiece; lifted his arm and the iPod was dangling above Kali's desk-line. When he was sure they'd all seen, he dropped it back into her lap.

'You wanna have a go at her,' he said to Anna, and walked out.

Almost immediately she heard Les's voice booming and when, after a few seconds' stunned delay, she went to see, Nathan was being escorted down the corridor in the direction of Jackson's office.

'Mr Weston?' she called after them.

Les paused by the fire door. 'I'll catch up with you, Mrs Lloyd. Fill in a problem slip for me at break, will you? Let me know the details.'

As she passed Kali's desk again she held out her hand automatically. Kali placed the iPod in Anna's open palm and started to speak.

'Later,' Anna told her.

She went to the desk and sat down, feeling shaky. There was perfect quiet.

'The casket,' she said after a moment. 'It's an image to suggest precious contents. Write that down if you haven't already got it. It means her memories are precious.' She swallowed again. 'Yes, Neil?'

'Shall I close the door, Mrs Lloyd?'

'That would be helpful,' she said.

Anna was driving home in the fading light, Kali's music in her ears.

> *What's in the dark? A friend or foe*
> *The monster that you only know*
> *The glimmer of your lover's eyes*
> *The spectre of your childhood's cries*

'He thinks no one can touch him,' Andrew Maye had said when the notice went up about Nathan's suspension. 'He won't believe someone's taken action at last. It'll certainly make my registrations easier for three days, anyway. Good bloody riddance; shame he's coming back. What did his parents say, Les?'

'What they always do: It wasn't him, it must have been someone else. But this time there was too much evidence against him.' Les rinsed his mug out over the sink. 'And they mentioned taking the school to court and how legal fees would be no problem for them. You've heard it all before. Mr Woods' method of defence is attack. That and waving his chequebook around. The man's arrogance personified. He does his son no favours.'

'I hate the way he sits with his legs wide apart at Parents' Evening,' said Anna. 'It's really off-putting.'

'Primitive male crotch-display. He'll be baring his bottom next.'

They laughed; Anna had felt marginally better.

> *What's in the water? Crystal light*
> *A siren swimming out of sight*
> *The shipwreck of a lonely year*
> *The silent shark that scents your fear*

For the first time this term she'd left school before 4.15, throwing her bag of marking in the passenger seat and slamming the door on the day. The bag had fallen over and the exercise books had all slid out, along with Kali's confiscated iPod. Anna wasn't sure what had made her clip it on and listen.

Kali came knocking at the staffroom that lunchtime, just as Anna got her sandwich out. Chrissy had gone to answer.

'Is Mrs Lloyd in?'

Chrissy saying, 'You do know you aren't supposed to knock between 1 and 1.30. Is it urgent?'

Anna had got up anyway.

The girl had been standing in the corridor subdued, feet together, head down, but she brightened when she saw Anna.

'Mrs Lloyd.'

'Kali.'

'I've come to apologize for my behaviour in the lesson.'

'Ah.'

'I realize it was very rude of me to be listening to my music while you were teaching.'

Close up you could make out faint freckles under the girl's clear skin. Undamaged, glowing youth. Had she really spoilt herself with a tattoo?

'I see,' said Anna. 'Do you understand how important it is for you to follow the notes we're making now? That you need these notes to be able to answer in the GCSE exam? It's no good coming to me in eighteen months' time in a state because there are gaps, it'll be too late by then.'

'I understand. I won't do it again.'

'No.'

'Thanks, Mrs Lloyd. And – yeah, thanks. It's difficult when you're new.'

She felt herself begin to soften. 'I can appreciate that.'

''Cause there are all these new rules to follow, everything's different.'

'I'm sure.'

'And sometimes I get it wrong. I'm sorry.'

'Let's forget about today, start again.'

'I wanted to ask—'

'Yes?' Anna leaned forwards. 'What is it?'

'I was wondering when I can have my iPod back?'

So, not an apology at all. 'End of the week,' she snapped. 'Provided you behave yourself in lessons.'

'I will, I will,' she heard Kali say as the door swung shut between them.

> *What's in your mind now? Petrol bands*
> *Bars of sunlight across your hands*
> *Splitting colours' fragment glare*
> *The dazzle fades, there's no one there . . .*

'What are you doing?'

Jamie was standing in the doorway watching Anna as she bent over his computer. She glanced up, unconcerned. 'Trying to work out how to download some music.'

He scowled as he came over. 'For God's sake, don't mix those files up. There's all my work there.'

'I haven't touched your files. I'm not even using that folder, look.' She pointed to the screen. 'Territorial or what?'

'It's my *work*, Anna.'

It was only because they'd been showing an ITV Drama Premiere that she'd managed to get near the machine. She stepped back and counted ten while he brought up his documents and went through them, click, click, click.

'Haven't you got them all backed up, then?'

Jamie ignored this, choosing instead to close the program and open up Anna's music file. He read down the list. '"Cut the Wire"? "Brood"? Not your usual thing.'

'One of the students recommended it to me.' She saw again the iPod dangling in Nathan's fist. 'It's quite good. Interesting lyrics. Sort of a raw sound.'

Jamie snorted. 'Make a change from your perpetual Bach.'

'Make a change from all your jazz, too. You should give it a go. I've got a whole new soundtrack to my life.'

He pushed the mouse away. 'I'll pass on that.'

'We can't always carry on the same,' she said. 'The same things all the time. Don't you ever want to try something different?'

'Not if it means listening to – ' he squinted at the screen ' – "Don't Know Don't Care".'

One day, she thought, I'm going to make a bonfire of this computer. That'll take the smug look off your face.

Russ's truck was in the school drive. It *was* Russ's truck. Anna drove past with wide eyes, heart pounding. Here at school! What was he playing at?

The second she was parked – and she made herself go down to the bottom of the slope to her usual spot, maintain normality – she scrambled out of the car, waded across the gravel and ran up the main steps to the big wooden doors, keeping her breaths even. Nothing to be gained by having a fit.

Better to find him and tackle him than have him burst in on her, she was thinking as she pulled on the handle; maybe he could be fobbed off, and then, oh, God, in her face, something buffeting her hair and skittering off past her, wetness on her cheek. A kid's thrown something at me, was her first reaction. Then she saw, at the bottom of the entrance hall stairs, Stu the caretaker with his overalls on and a fishing net in his hand. Chrissy was behind him.

'Are you all right, Anna?' Stu came forwards with his hand outstretched. 'Did it get your eye?'

'It's gone, anyway,' said Chrissy from the back somewhere.

'What was it?'

'A little robin got himself stuck inside. When you opened the door he took his chance. We've been nearly half an hour trying to catch him. It's, ah, your blouse is marked.'

'Hell.'

Chrissy produced a tissue from her handbag. 'Not what you need first thing in the morning, is it?'

You have no idea, Anna thought.

'That's good luck, though, when a bird does it on your head.' Stu winked amiably. 'You'll have good luck all the day now.'

'I thought robins were bad luck?'

'I s'pose it evens out, then.'

'Right.'

'Actually,' Chrissy said, 'I was looking for you. Can I have a quick word?'

Oh, Jesus wept, Anna almost shouted. Will you lot just leave me to find my ex-lover before he wrecks my life?

'I'm in ever such a rush; how about break-time?'

'Has to be now. I wanted to catch you before you see the Head.'

Anna scanned the balcony above, then turned to check the view through the window, but there was no sign of Russ. 'All right.'

She let Chrissy lead her across the parquet into the library and close the door behind them. If only she was anywhere but here, and all the time Kali's music played on in her head.

> *What's in your lover's fearful touch*
> *The kiss of one who loves too much*

'What it is,' said Chrissy, and there was a strained kindness in her voice that made Anna want to panic. 'Mr Woods has complained to the Head that the content of your lesson . . . was, inappropriate.' She held up her hand. 'OK, OK now. Don't get upset, we can easily dismiss the claim. I know it's only an attempt at revenge on his part because Nathan's backed himself into a corner. The father's as silly as the son. But we do need to respond, so what I need from you is a quick outline of what you've been doing with Year Ten.'

Lose Yourself in a Book said a banner over the front desk. *Feel the Power of Words*, cartoon poster of a little man standing on top of a giant dictionary.

'You know what I've been doing,' said Anna. 'The GCSE course we're all following, all of us. Poems prescribed by the exam board.'

'OK. Fine. Which poems specifically?'

'I can show you.'

Anna pulled the blue file out of her bag and began to flick through. There was a knock and Jackson peered round the door. 'Aha,' he said as if he'd somehow caught them out. 'Just the ladies I wanted to see.'

'Anna was showing me the poem Nathan's alleging is indecent.'

Jackson nodded and came forward to see.

'It's on the syllabus. It's about Shakespeare.'

'Well, then.' He rubbed his hands together and peered at the text. 'Shakespeare. Good-good.' He won't understand it, thought Anna, watching his eyes scan back and forth. 'Yes, I see,' he said unconvincingly.

'The point is, it's on the syllabus. Each text is chosen by the examinations body and we have to teach it so Nathan can pass his GCSE. Mr Woods can't allege anything improper.'

'Excellent,' said Jackson. 'And this reference to, erm, a pearl . . . ?'

'A magical moment in their relationship,' said Anna quickly.

'Oh. Good.'

'Do you want me to talk to Mr Woods?' said Chrissy.

'If you would.' Jackson's gratitude was palpable. 'Excellent.'

Anna started to put the folder back but Jackson stopped her. 'If I could have another minute—' Chrissy, who had been making a move for the door, halted. 'No, you're fine, Mrs Knight. It's just Mrs Lloyd I want.'

When the door clunked shut he said, 'Will you take some advice?' He didn't wait for a reply but shifted his body weight from one foot to the other so that he was in her personal space. 'Anna, I think you need to go carefully. If you read the staff handbook, allusion to anything of an adult nature is inappropriate.'

'But if it's part of the syllabus, if it's in the poem.'

Jackson, oh horror, laid his hand on hers. His skin felt cold and dead. 'Yes, but you don't always have to *spell it out*. Eh? Remember, these are children you're dealing with. Children. You must never forget that, Anna. You must never project your own adult experiences and understanding onto them.'

Did she ever do that?

As soon as Jackson released her – another second and she'd have had to slap him, and damn the career – she ran straight to the office. Out past the piano and display boards, across the polished wood, and up the staircase. God knows what mischief Russ had been making while she was stuck in the library being lectured.

Mrs Hislop looked up from her typing as Anna came in. 'Are you all right?'

'Yes. Why?'

'You're very pink today.'

Anna touched her own cheeks. 'Oh, you know. Rushing about.' Through the leaded window she could see the roof of the timber lorry. There didn't seem to be anyone in the cab. '. . . I was after the key to the stationery cupboard.'

'Here you are.' Mrs Hislop pulled open a drawer in her desk. 'You have been looking peaky recently. I worry about you.'

'Anaemia,' said Anna off the top of her head. 'I'm supposed to take supplements.' Then casually, as if she'd just spotted it, 'Hey, that's my brother-in-law's lorry outside! How weird. You haven't seen him about, have you? Has he been up here, I mean?'

Mrs Hislop shook her head. 'I wouldn't know him. There was a very young lad came up here to deliver an invoice earlier, I'd say only just out of school.'

'God, no, Russ is my age.'

'It's been busy all term with deliveries for the lab extension. The noise has been unbelievable. There were cement mixers, diggers, all sorts here in the summer when it started.'

Anna moved near the glass so she could look right down onto the drive. A boy in Timbershop overalls appeared from round the side of the building and stood waiting by the cab for a few seconds. Then, at a distant shout, he wrenched open the passenger door and climbed in.

'Is it your brother-in-law?'

Next came Stu, still with his net, and some bloke wearing a hard hat and safety boots, the site foreman perhaps. Finally an oldish man whom she recognized from the lumber yard, though she didn't know his name. They were all talking and pointing at something she couldn't see. The man in the hat patted his own leg with a clipboard.

At last the old guy hauled himself into the truck and started up the engine. Definitely no Russ, then. Thank Christ. She watched as the lorry rolled away through the main gates, and went hot at a sudden memory of Russ putting his hand up her skirt once at a school fete. In these grounds, round the back of the leylandii that screened the wild area. God, she'd torn a strip off him for that. Never, never touch me if we're outside the caravan, she'd snarled at him.

'No, not my brother-in-law.' She became aware of the key in her hand and of Mrs Hislop staring at her. 'Right, then. I'll go and get some paper,' she said. 'Back in a mo.'

Anna set off towards the stockroom. She felt physically lightened and full of energy. It hadn't been Russ and everything was going to be all right, and anyway, if he was going to make some dramatic gesture he'd have made it by now, wouldn't he? She didn't notice Kali sitting in the reception area until the girl stood up and spoke.

'Mrs Lloyd?'

'Oh! Kali Norman, what are you doing in here? It's not 8.50 yet. You shouldn't be inside for another fifteen minutes.' But she couldn't make her tone harsh, she felt too buoyant.

'I needed to speak to you.'

'You want your iPod back.'

Kali's body language was shy and young. 'No. Not that. I needed to give you something.'

'Oh?'

'I don't mean give, I mean lend. Something for you to look at. It's a bit private, though.'

Anna waited. She observed the rise-and-fall moulding of Kali's upper lip, her white skin, the line of kohl inside the wet rim of her eyelids.

'It's some poems.' She lowered her lashes modestly. 'I write poetry when I'm, when I feel a lot about something and I can't stop thinking about it. I have this special book I put it in. I thought you might like to have a read.'

'Isn't it too personal to share with a teacher?'

'Well, it is personal, but not – dodgy. It's not about things I've *done*, it's more, you know, thoughts and emotions. I thought you could maybe tell me whether any of the poems were any good and how I could improve.' When Anna didn't reply, she said, 'I thought you'd want to see them; it's English.'

It wasn't unusual to have a student share extra-curricular writing like this. Anna knew the form. 'Of course, thank you. I'd be delighted. Have you been writing long?'

'About a year.'

The book was a hardback with lined pages inside. Anna flicked through and saw poem-shaped jottings, blocks of longer text, and doodles of thin, sad girls. On the cover was a postcard of Millais' *Ophelia*. The drowning woman's face shone out against the green background, her expression thoughtful rather than distressed.

'She looks like you,' said Anna.

'Yeah, I know. That's why I stuck it on. You look like that actress, don't know her name. She's really old.'

'Thanks!'

'No, she's from the old films, I mean. Do you know who I'm talking about? She's got her hair the same shape as yours.'

But Anna was looking from Kali to the painting. 'Elizabeth Siddal, that was the name of the artist's model. Now she was a fascinating character. I'll tell you about her one day.'

'Hey, did you know they had a bird in here this morning?' Kali nodded to where there was a streak of white across the banister and another up the sash window. 'It died, I think.'

'No, it didn't. I let it out.'

'Honestly? That's cool. You set it free, wow.' Kali glanced over to the entrance as though she might catch the moment of release re-enacted. 'So keep the poems as long as you like. Let me know what you think of them.'

'I will, thank you.'

'No problem.'

She ought to have told Kali to remove her bangles and wipe her eye make-up off, Anna thought as the girl swung away down the corridor. But it hadn't been the right time. It didn't matter.

She would phone Mel tonight, be positive and chatty. Nathan was away, Chrissy was sorting his father out. Russ was not stalking the building. Just at that moment, she felt invulnerable.

Chapter Five

Jamie wanted sex that evening. More irritating still, he wanted it while she was finishing off her marking. The good mood at the start of the day had evaporated by home-time and when Anna got in she could feel temper pricking at her insides; the last thing she needed was intimacy. But Jamie hadn't been able to read that, or had decided to ignore it.

He came up behind her as she knelt on the floor in front of the fire.

'Mmm, you feel nice,' he said. He ran his hands up and down her back while she struggled to get debriefing notes down for the A-level essay she'd just marked. 'I love the firelight. So D. H. Lawrence.'

It would have been churlish to point out that they only had Living Flame gas. The coals glowed uniformly inside a rectangle of steel and black granite; the fireplace had come brand new with the house. Anna clamped her arms to her sides as his fingers tried to move round to her breasts. She knew she should relax and let him touch her but she couldn't bring herself do it.

'Mmm,' he said again.

Define your terms at the start, she scribbled hopelessly.

His hands dipped lower and under her buttocks, stroking and probing. *Make that your opening paragraph.*

When he got no response, he shuffled forward on his knees so he was pressing right against her back. She found herself pinned between husband and grate. 'Oh, Anna,' he said, and made a more determined move for her chest. That was it, there was no pretending it wasn't happening now. Best go with it.

Jamie leant sideways so he could shove the Teacher's Planner out of the way across the carpet. Then he straightened and felt for the zip at the neck of her jacket, but she moved his fingers away and drew it down herself. She could hear him thinking, *home and dry*. At last he backed off her and she was able to turn round and take the pressure off her kneecaps.

A memory dropped into her mind of Russ, shortly after they'd started their affair, standing in the caravan shirtless and holding a cassette player. She'd been lying on the bed waiting for him and wondering what the delay was, when he laid the cassette player on the table, pressed Play and the tail end of 'Another One Bites the Dust' blared out. He remained perfectly still. There was a hissy pause, a muffled clunk, then the boom-boom-clap of 'We Will Rock You'. He put his shoulders back like a fighter and advanced. 'What, what are you doing?' she said, laughing and at the same time realizing she shouldn't. He'd scowled at her and jabbed the machine off. 'Is this what you play when you have sex with Ruth?' she'd asked. 'No,' he said. That was probably right; she couldn't imagine Ruth having any truck with

Queen in the bedroom. But there was a lie in there somewhere. Perhaps he'd lost his virginity to the track.

Jamie locked his mouth against hers and, fused, they lowered themselves so she was lying on her back. He pulled her bra up so the wire raked her nipples painfully. 'Oh, Anna, God,' he said.

She'd only had two lovers before Jamie; Hitch, her first, and Phil, who'd almost been her fiancé while they were at university. It was difficult to remember them now, their quirks and preferences. Hitch had been pretty awful. She'd been in love with Phil.

Now Jamie was lifting himself up on one elbow, holding himself away to tug at her waistband. Her skirt and knickers slid down over her hips and when they reached her knees she kicked to get them off. The seams of his Wranglers were rough against her skin and his belt buckle caught her an icy kiss on her stomach. I've made a doctor's appointment today, she could have said. Can we leave off sex till my second trimester?

She watched as he reached behind his head and drew his T-shirt quickly off. There was no fat on him, his muscle tone was still as good as it had been when they met. No doubt about it, she was married to an attractive man. Plus, in technical terms, Jamie was good at sex, dextrous and confident where his brother was hasty and awkward. It was just that she felt no connection any more, with Jamie or with her own body.

He stood up and unfastened his jeans.

Russ once told her that he loved her *tightness*. She remembered this now as Jamie's burning cock butted between her legs and immediately she tried to stop her thoughts, but too late because they were running on to what had come later which was that Ruth's birth canal was shot to pieces and there was hardly any sensation for either of them, and then Anna and Russ had had an enormous row because Anna had pointed out Ruth might as well have been in bed with them, so conscious were they of her presence. Russ had cried, but that meant nothing because he cried easily. Anna, who had been about to remark that she thought he didn't have sex with Ruth any more, had held her tongue because a major part of having an affair is knowing when to keep silent.

Jamie began to thrust. After half a minute she shifted her hips so the angle became more awkward for him, a small rebellion. He never broke his rhythm.

By pretending to stroke Jamie's hair she could bring her watch into view. 10.15. That wasn't too bad, she could still get half an hour's work in before they went to bed. The problem with this essay was that most of the group had misunderstood the term Romantic. 'It has a special literary sense,' she would tell them. 'It comes out of a whole reactionary artistic movement, nothing to do with treating your partner to a red rose and a box of Milk Tray.' She would do them a special crib sheet with the main points on it and they could stick it into the front of their files for reference.

Without warning Jamie spasmed against her, his face a grimace. That hadn't taken long.

'Oh, God, sorry,' he said, blinking.

'OK.'

'It's been a while.'

'Yes.' It had been over a month since the last time.

'Can I . . .?'

'No, I'm fine.'

He rolled off her, heaved himself up, and padded naked to the cloakroom. She lay with her eyes closed for a minute, wishing she'd finished her notes. But on the plus side, that was sex out of the way for at least another fortnight, one more To Do ticked off her list and she was feeling quite pleased about it when Jamie wandered back in and said, 'I forgot to say, Russ has invited us over for Sunday lunch. So make sure you put wine down on the shopping list this week.'

The night before they went to Russ's, Anna had a teaching dream. She was taking Year Ten (in the assembly hall for some reason) and they were about to sit an exam. She was scanning the room for Kali but the girl wasn't there. Nathan, who was wearing his own clothes and not uniform, stood up and said, 'I don't need to do this exam because I'm going to be a pilot.' Then she understood that she was Kali, and that was why there was an empty seat at the back. It was Kali who was taking the lesson, so where was Anna?

Bethany was stringing beads by the aquarium and Anna had knelt to help her.

'That's a lovely necklace you've made.'

'Yeah,' said Bethany. 'It's for Tom.'

Tom rocked in the armchair and grinned. God, he's effeminate, thought Anna. Even at four. She peered into the tank while she waited for Bethany to decide on a fastener. 'Is that fish dead?'

Her eyes tracked a loach as it skimmed the gravel stiffly, rose up the side and floated across the surface, driven by the current from the filter.

'Yes, I think it is,' said Ruth, and carried on laying the table.

The fish began to sink down the other side.

'Shouldn't you take it out?'

Ruth licked her finger and rubbed at one of the place mats. 'There's a net by the pellets. Kids, you'll have to have the lap trays on the sofa again.'

Tom slid off the chair and came to see the dead fish. Bethany took the opportunity to drape the necklace over his head. 'If you put that velvet cushion on your head you'll look like an Eastern prince,' she said. 'The king of Persia, is that in the East? Hang on, we'll go get my dressing gown.'

Russ and Jamie were over in the bay and Anna could tell by the way he was standing that Russ was holding forth about something. As she went past with the dripping net she caught the word 'taxes' and saw Jamie look away, bored.

'Ready,' said Ruth. 'Can everyone come to the table now, please?' There was a snappish edge to her tone that spoke of tantrums if her gravy went cold.

'So what shall I do with this fish? Do you want me to flush it down the toilet?'

'No, stick it on the windowsill so the kids can bury it later.'

'Three hundred thousand we turned over last year,' said Russ sourly. 'But I saw damn all of it.'

Ruth's voice in the hall. 'Beth! Tash! Tom! Come down!'

Russ had so wanted a son, and oh, God, here he came again, blue velvet hat, purple chenille robe and glittery beads across his chest. No one said anything, though Russ made a slight noise in his throat, snatching the cushion off the boy's head as he glided past.

'That was my crown.'

'Sit,' said Ruth.

When Anna had contemplated meeting up with Russ again in front of everyone, she'd felt ill with fear. But now she was here and nothing had happened she was beginning to fade out, as usual. Another track of Kali's had implanted itself and she had to force herself not to mouth some of the words as they played through her head.

> *You'll never understand the pattern of my mind*
> *You're a different nature a different kind*

'Which wouldn't be so bad,' Russ went on, 'if you saw anything for it. But there's no police on the streets—'

> *No one can follow where I go*
> *It's not a place I could ever show*
> *To you to you*

'Tom! Your beads are going in your coleslaw. Take them off, for God's sake. Beth, help him.'

'Looks like you've got a little fashion designer on

your hands there.' That was Jamie, unwisely. Russ shot him a murderous look.

'He'll grow out of it,' said Ruth, pushing tureens about the table.

'I remember Russ wearing one of Mum's dresses.'

'I did not! It was a coat and you were wearing one too. God, you've got a selective memory.'

> *If one day I could if one day I could*
> *Let you through*
> *What would you do*

'But look at him now, father of three.' Jamie was smiling.

'How's school?'

Anna jerked out of her reverie. 'Sorry?'

'I was asking,' said Ruth, 'how school was going. Tash, I can see you hiding your carrots under the fat, stop it.'

She said, 'Good. Yes, same as usual.'

'We thought you were looking tired,' said Russ. 'Stressed.'

'And what happened with that naughty boy? Is he behaving himself?'

'He got suspended, but now his parents have taken him on a two-week skiing holiday to spite the Head. They didn't agree with his punishment.'

'That's not right. You have to support the school,' said Ruth through a mouth full of potato. 'What did he do to get suspended?'

'I don't know.' She couldn't be bothered to go into it.

'We've got a new girl in the same class, though, who's very pleasant.'

> *Heart like a wound*
> *Can you heal me*

Ruth nodded as though there was something to agree with. 'Perhaps she'll be a good influence.'

'Perhaps.'

> *Heal me heal me*
> *Steal my pain away*

Anna saw Tom, who was squashed in the middle of the sofa, spit out a stringy piece of meat into his palm and then dangle it between his thumb and index finger. His sisters made gagging sounds and shifted away. The tartan throw at their backs slid down to show a rip in the sofa fabric.

She turned and caught Jamie's eye.

'That your Kali you're talking about?'

'Mmm.'

'Anna's new pet,' Jamie explained. 'Comes from a deprived background.'

'No one at your place is deprived,' said Russ at once. 'Bunch of rich kids.'

'Emotionally deprived. And she's not my pet.'

'She lent you her private diary.'

'It was her poems, actually. She lent them to me because I'm her English teacher.'

'That's nice,' said Ruth. 'Do finish the cauli, there's plenty more. I always make too much.'

'Anna's having a second teenagehood. She's moved

on from dolls' houses now and she's downloading this girl's iPod collection. What was it, "Brood"?'

Ruth gave a ghastly wink. 'Oh, I like to listen to Tasha's stuff. Some of those boy bands are lovely. I pop a disc in and have a bit of a bop while I do the ironing.'

What am I doing here, thought Anna. Across the table, Russ used his fork to stir a fragment of beef round his plate and load it with gravy. Ruth fiddled with her waistband next to him. Jamie sat with his fingers interlocked like a TV presenter on a late-night arts show. She became fixed on Russ carrying the meat to his mouth, a drop of gravy sliding down the neck of the fork onto his fingers. Those fingers had been inside her.

'Sorry to say it again,' Russ spoke as soon as he had swallowed, 'but you do look really grim, sis-in-law. You coming down with something? You've aged about five years since I last saw you.'

'Russ! What a thing to say,' said Ruth, though Anna could tell she was secretly pleased. 'You look lovely, take no notice. And you'll soon pick up your colour again in the holidays. Do you take supplements?'

'Folates . . .'

'I've heard flax is good for the menopause.'

'Good God,' said Jamie, 'she's not that old. Give the lady a break.'

'Well,' said Russ, 'you could do with something.'

So this is how it's going to be, thought Anna. I'm going to run the gauntlet of Russ's spite for the rest of my life. Which would be crap in itself, but sooner or later Jamie was going to notice and wonder why. She began to rehearse a story in her head. *He was cross with me because I tackled him for sniping about money while you were in the garden.* That was plausible.

'It is easy to let yourself get run down.' Ruth leant an elbow on the table and cupped her chin in her hand. 'Those three wear me out.'

Anna glanced across at the sofa, where Beth was now sitting astride the arm and Tom was lying full length, using the rolled-up dressing gown as a pillow and kicking at Natasha's lap. Any minute a plate was going to go over.

'Still, we wouldn't be without them, would we, Russ?'

It was far too warm in the room and Anna thought she could smell the fish drying on the windowsill.

'Pudding,' said Ruth, as if it was a challenge.

'I need to . . .' Anna scraped her chair back, got up and went out into the hall. She felt heavy and not right.

Something made her go upstairs to the proper bathroom rather than use the toilet-in-a-cupboard off the kitchen. She could feel wetness between her legs as she climbed the steps. She knew then. But it was still a shock to see all that blood pooled there when she lowered herself onto the seat and drew her knickers down. She stared, and in one sense wasn't surprised: what else had she truly expected? But even so the sight made her weak and trembly, as though she were looking down at an amputated limb, and to lose it here, in this dirty bathroom— She made herself pull the knickers right off and placed them in the empty sink. Twisting her skirt round, she could see that it was OK, thick black crepe with a lining; if it had caught, it wasn't going to show through.

She slid the garment off, turned it inside out and laid it on the floor. Then she took a fist full of Kandoo and began to wipe herself down.

It was exactly like last time. There were clots of blood down the toilet, on the white tissue in her hand, and there was the dragging sensation over her pubic bone that she'd not consciously registered while she was downstairs. What she wanted most at this moment was lie down on the floor, clear aside the plastic toys and the measuring jug and the ripple-edged magazines, and curl up there with her fingers over her eyes.

Instead she took dry paper and blotted between her legs, her thighs, then the back of her skirt lining, then her knickers, pressing hard to absorb as much as she could. Last time she'd been frantic to find something that could have been a baby and the doctor said there isn't always one and she didn't know whether that made it better or worse.

Thinking that way nearly started her crying so she began to clean round the bathroom, the sides of the sink and the toilet seat, flushing and checking and flushing again. To mask the sick-iron smell of blood she found a bottle of bleachy spray and doused everything she thought she'd touched. The chemicals stung her eyes and the back of her nose. Any minute now someone was going to come up and ask what was wrong.

Finally she stood still, gazing at the enamel sheen. Through the streaky mirror she saw how mad she looked, her eyes pink and strands of hair across her face. But there was no time: she went to the airing cupboard and shifted old bottles of shampoo and descaler and an inflatable turtle and a length of plastic home-brew tubing until she found Ruth's cache of giant sanitary towels, Christ, how many did the woman get through? Then she dressed herself. There didn't seem to be as much blood now. Maybe it was over.

She thought she might find Jamie outside the door, or someone, but the landing was empty. There was laughter coming from the dining room.

Anna went down the stairs, opened the front door, and walked away.

Chapter Six

Anna was thirty-three when she married, thirty-four when she heard from an acquaintance that her mother was dead, and thirty-five when she stopped taking the pill. It had been a unilateral decision to get pregnant, though at that stage Jamie hadn't specifically declared No Babies. He hadn't said anything other than that he 'liked things the way they were'. 'But life doesn't stay the same,' Anna had argued. He'd turned it into a joke, bending his back and pretending to use a stick. 'I'm too old to cope with change. Too feeble.' He'd been forty-two.

Once she asked him outright: Do you want children? 'Do *you*?' he'd replied, with such conviction that suddenly she wasn't sure. Because she did love him. 'Aren't I enough?' he said. Then at thirty-seven, after two years of trying and with Ruth's belly swelling visibly, she'd taken herself to the doctor and asked for a course of Clomid. She got pregnant and stayed that way for three months. Ruth went on to have Tom.

Some lines that people say lodge in your head forever. Once, while she was still pregnant that first time, she was sitting quietly in the staff workroom when she happened to overhear two women from the French department discussing their divorces. 'There are some moments in a marriage you never forgive,' one of them said. Anna had replayed the line when she stumbled out of the hospital scanning room and recognized relief on Jamie's face; and when three months afterwards he left her to wrap Tom's present of a newborn sleepsuit; and when, a year later and the doctors having drawn a blank on her, he refused to go for tests.

Sometimes she watched him with his nieces and nephew. They were never encouraging scenes. True, none of the children was especially engaging, hampered as they all were by Ruth's genetic inheritance. But Jamie clearly found them irritating, made no allowances. 'God, no, coal isn't made in factories,' he'd exclaimed at Tasha when she was only seven. What a fool! his expression said. 'They know nothing, do they?' he'd complained later in the car. 'And why are they always such a mess?' When toddlers ate, he said, he had to look away because it put him off his own food. Sometimes Tom or Beth tried to climb on him, but he peeled them away politely. As far as she could remember, she'd never seen him hold any of them as babies.

When his father passed away after a series of strokes, Anna thought that might alter Jamie, lay some demons, make him aware of his own mortality. But that turned out to be the kind of twist that only happens on TV. He stayed the same; perhaps slightly more cynical.

'What if you come to regret your decision and it's too late?' she asked him more than once. 'You'll have missed your chance.'

'I won't change,' he always said. 'It's the way I am. Stop trying to make me feel as though I've done something wrong, because I haven't. I'm happy, you're the one who wants to upset things. You're enough for me.'

'You act like it's some selfish whim. I'm not doing it to be awkward, Jamie. It's a *drive*.'

There was no way to explain it that he could understand.

He said, 'Children are boring. No one admits it, but it's a fact. Russ thinks they're boring; you can see it all over his face. He'd send them back if he could. If Russ could start his life again tomorrow, he'd take an entirely different route.'

She asked him how he could possibly know what having children would be like.

'Because I'm a teacher, Anna. I deal with kids every day. And I tell you, I get more than my fill during the day of repeating instructions and squashing idiotic behaviour.'

His other argument was that he'd done his stint, he'd had his fill of childcare by the time he was eighteen. And of course you couldn't argue with that: what a marvellous boy to bring up his own brother after their mother had died, and sacrifice his youth etc. (although Russ had a slightly different take on events).

'So what about me?' she asked Jamie. No answer. There's no compromise to be had with babies. What he did at least do was keep the secret. People assumed she didn't want children, and that had been easier for her than being pitied.

So she'd waited for him to come round; let him use

his father's inheritance to give up teaching, pursue his writing, move house, buy a new car. Then, when all the rows had been had and it became clear he wasn't going to budge, she went back for another course of Clomid and started seeing Russ. All her life she'd understood that if you worked hard and applied yourself, you would succeed, and yet here she was failing the most basic test of womanhood. Something had to be done urgently to put things some way back under her control, and serve Jamie right, *serve him damn well right* for having denied her access to the obvious and legitimate path. But now the baby was gone, if there ever had been one; the affair had been a waste of time after all.

World's End, they called the hill overlooking Llangollen. Where else was there to go two weeks after a miscarriage on a desperate Sunday afternoon when your husband wasn't speaking to you? Anna was a cautious driver but she'd got here on adrenalin, throwing the car around the bends, crunching gears to get up the gradient. Wind buffeted the car. Somewhere along the ridge she parked, but keeping the key in the ignition and the radio on loud.

The grass was grey-green and scattered with stones. It looked unfriendly soil. To her right was a slate scree slope, to her left a bank of orange bracken. Bands of shadow and light moved across the valley below so that details were spotlit briefly: a white cottage, a cluster of trees.

She tried opening the car door and that was like battling with an invisible lunatic on the other side, someone pushing against her then wrenching away. The chassis rocked as she fought to save the hinges and she swore and yelled into the wind. When she did get out and manage to slam the door, her hair whipped across her eyes and her sweater plastered itself against her chest. She was chilled through at once.

'Your urine sample shows a weak positive. Do you still feel pregnant?' the doctor at the EP unit had said. She said she didn't. But then she never had. She'd never truly believed in this baby. 'Is it my fault?' she asked. 'Is it something I've done?' 'We can't tell why most miscarriages happen,' he said, and turned the lights off. Only the screen glowed in the dark, lighting up his grave face. 'What we would expect at this point of gestation is a pretty visible foetus, about ten centimetres long. But you can see—'

Her eyes stung now as she looked over the spread of Llangollen. 'Cast yourself off,' didn't the devil say to Jesus. 'Throw yourself from this high tower. The angels will catch you.' She could so easily have climbed back into the Mondeo, jammed down the accelerator and revved into the void. 'That scintillation at the bottom of the screen is bleeding,' she heard the doctor say again.

The pressure of the wind against her eyeballs blurred the scene around her and the air boomed in her ears. She imagined herself as a film; climbing over that stone wall, running across the shivering grass to lie down somewhere in the middle of the field on her back with her arms spread out like a crucifixion and the camera would zoom away in an aerial shot so she became tinier and tinier until the screen faded to black. Her tears blew to the sides of her face along the top of her cheekbones, drying almost instantly, to spite her.

By the time she got back in the car she was almost too cold to make her fingers work the heater switch. And, God, who was that mess of a woman in the driving mirror? Her nose was running and her hair tangled like a crazy wig. It would not do. She dropped open the glove compartment with her left hand and simultaneously fired up the engine with her right, only to shriek as the car lurched forward because she'd left it in gear. For three terrifying seconds she thought she was going to plunge over the side after all. The car stopped with a jerk and a pile of exercise books fell off the passenger seat into the footwell. 'Well fucking, fucking hell,' said Anna. Her planner was down there, too, with all the loose sheets she kept in the back spilled out. Her relief at not having thrown herself off a mountain, even the sadness before, disappeared under a wave of irritation; she'd spent an hour sorting those books by grade. Plus half the kids hadn't stuck in their acrostics even though she'd told them to, so those were all mixed up too, fuck it.

She leant across and began to gather pages together. Then she spotted, half under the mat, the cover of Kali's poetry collection. She'd been meaning to give it back, but first she'd had to have two days off for the bleeding to calm down and after that Kali had been absent for a week, no one knew why.

Anna thought the poems were good.

'There's a surprise,' Jamie had said.

'I don't mean they're flawless. She makes the usual errors. But for a sixteen-year-old they're tremendously aware. It's not the usual splurge of romance-and-self-loathing.'

'That age, what's left to write about?'

She hadn't bothered to explain; no point when Jamie was in that sneery mood. There are lines, she could have said, that feel as though they were written about me. As she pulled now at the book's spine, one of them came to her:

> *We bleed in secret you and I*

Where was it, that poem? She drew the book up towards her and flicked through the pages once more. Titles stood out afresh. The miscarriage cast a tint through which she viewed everything differently. *Red Secret*, *Emptied*, *The First Pains*. Of course these poems weren't about losing a baby, but some of them were about loss. Here was one now, not the one she'd been after, but still, so true –

> *When you were part of me I was whole*
> *a drop of perfume oil*
> *but when you left*
> *my shape broke*
> *I scattered out across the water in a film*
> *one molecule thick*

That was how she felt, stretched to nothing. How could she explain to Jamie that extent of hopelessness and lack of identity? Yet Kali had put it into words. Then there was this:

> *We bleed in secret you and I*
> *A secret blood that mingles grief*

And bonds us while our faces lie
You play the fool and I the thief

The effect had been ruined slightly by the tiny list in the margin: *belief relief thief leaf reef chief beef*. Then there was a couplet on its own at the bottom of the page:

Under my heart lies an empty place
Where once was love is only space

Kali, deep and pre-Raphaelite, always apart somehow from the others, watching her across the room. It was as though the girl had got inside her head.

Evening by the time she got home. Jamie was, as ever, in front of the computer. She could see the light through the top-floor curtains as she pulled into the drive. Smeary plates in the sink showed he had eaten. She took herself upstairs to face him.

'I didn't know where you were or when you were coming back,' he said without looking up. 'If you were coming back.'

'Don't be so melodramatic. I had my mobile. You only had to call.'

'You seem to have got into this habit of just taking off.' He tapped crossly at the keyboard.

'Hardly a habit. And anyway, why should you always know where I am? You'll be wanting me tagged next.'

Jamie swivelled in his office chair. 'I'd like to see your face if I disappeared for half a day without warning. What is going on with you, Anna? Is this going to be a pattern of behaviour from now on, because I could do with knowing. I need to warn other people; you know, hosts—'

It took all her strength not to back out of the room.

He rose and came towards her, arms open. 'Please, Anna, tell me what's going on. Is it the same as when we were at Russ's? A claustrophobia thing, a panic attack? Are you ill? Anna, are you having a breakdown?' He reached her and placed his hands on her shoulders, an ambiguous gesture. Could have been restraint, could have been love. 'Don't shut me out,' he said.

Behind his back the screensaver switched itself on, a quill scribbling lines of black ink against an aqua background.

'Anna?'

'I think I am ill.' This was what she'd told him before. She never mentioned a baby. 'I might be suffering from depression.'

He looked at her doubtfully. 'Dad got depressed after Mum died. But he couldn't get out of bed and he cried all the time. He didn't run off in the middle of Sunday lunch.'

'Do you want me to explain or not?'

'OK.'

He stepped back a pace.

'I can't—'

'Look, do you want to sit down? I'll get you a drink, you need one. Yeah? Only you seem like you're poised for flight again and I can't cope with that again. Sit, Anna, and sort yourself out. I'll open some wine.'

She peeled off her jacket and kicked away her shoes,

settled herself among the piles of books on the sofa. She could see Jamie's 'Work in Progress' file from here; it didn't seem to have grown any bigger for a long time. She thought he spent a lot of time surfing the net.

At last he came back with a bottle and two glasses. 'I needed something myself,' he said, pouring almost to the brim. 'Go on, then. Get it down you, and talk to me.'

'It's hard to explain.'

Jamie moved in next to her, pushing books onto the floor without ceremony. He leant back against the sofa arm and waited, a detached teacher-expression on his face. Nobody leaves this room till the culprit owns up. Only his thumb moving up and down, up and down the stem of the glass betrayed his tension.

'You're not happy.'

'No.'

'With me?'

'It's not that simple.'

'With me?'

'Some of it, yes.'

He looked away. 'I think we should be frank here. There's nothing to be gained by prevaricating. Yeah?'

As if you could cope with the truth, she thought. 'Yes,' she said.

'Anna—'

It flashed on her, *He knows! He's going to confront me!*

But he only went on, 'Are you jealous of me?'

'Jealous?'

'I've thought for a long time now that you're jealous of me, of the fact that I gave up teaching and you had to carry on. I can understand that. I know we agreed on my taking early retirement, but people change their ideas and I can see it must be hard for you going in day after day while I stay at home. Although obviously I am working.'

Obviously. She said, 'I sometimes wish I didn't have quite the workload. And you could do a bit more round the house.'

'Anna, love,' he broke in, and she knew he hadn't heard what she said, 'I appreciate it can be tough at times, but teaching is your life. It's like a passion for you. You adore the kids, you enjoy your subject, you're at your happiest in a classroom.'

'I wouldn't say that—'

'Be honest, you'd be nothing without your teaching.'

Isn't that the point? she wanted to cry. It felt as though he'd just said something very insulting. She took a swig of wine to stop herself from speaking to hurt.

'I feel as though I have no direction any more,' she said at last. 'Yes, teaching is important to me, but, I don't know, perhaps it's Nathan Woods, I'm not enjoying it as much this year, I feel at times as if I'm not very good—'

'Which is rubbish.'

'Or that something's gone, a spark.'

'You're just tired, it's a long term.'

'And what else is there, what else have I done with my life?'

Jamie was smiling but there was no conviction in it. 'There's us, Anna.'

Quite, she nearly said. But she could see the vulnerability in the set of his face. On the wall next to Jamie's head was a photograph of Jamie and Russ together. She knew, because Jamie had told her, that when it was taken he'd been fifteen and Russ six. The boys were standing in a garden, Jamie directly behind his brother and clasping his arms round him. Anna had admired the protective, fatherly pose. 'It was nothing of the sort. Dad told us to stand like that,' Russ had informed her. It was the one point on which both men agreed. Russ said that Jamie had clamped him so tightly it hurt; Jamie's version was that he had been made to restrain Russ because he was on the verge of a tantrum. 'He was terrifically immature,' Jamie always said. 'Dad indulged him.' 'My brother was a bully,' said Russ.

'What do you want me to do, Anna?' said Jamie now, putting his glass down on a book and turning to face her. 'Tell me what I'm supposed to do here.'

She couldn't bring herself to say, It's too late.

'How about a holiday, long weekend at half-term? That's only a few days away. We could take off into the Lakes, not even book, just see where we landed. I could get some ideas for my writing. What do you reckon?'

'I'll have a lot of marking.'

But it wasn't much fun to crush him.

'OK,' she said. 'Yes, let's do that. Perhaps we can talk some more while we're there.'

He looked pleased. That was that sorted. 'By Windermere, I fancy. Tell you what, I'll get the B&B guide and have a flick through, give us some ideas. Eh?'

She nodded.

'One condition, though.'

Her heart sagged. Was he going to ask for sex again?

Impossible with the bleeding, she'd have to say something. 'Oh?'

'I want you to apologize properly to Ruth and Russ. You never did, I had to. It would go down well if you gave them a ring and cleared the air. Russ was very worried.'

I bet he was, thought Anna.

On the Friday lunchtime before she went away, Anna sat in the school gardens with a book and an apple. She ought to have been teaching a Japanese student but the girl was away on a trip, the same trip that meant Anna was unexpectedly free next lesson. It was warmish, almost no-coat weather. She couldn't stand the noise in the staffroom any longer, and anyway Mrs Hislop was bringing in her new granddaughter to show off some time within the hour. Why did everyone assume you were glad to see their babies?

If she stayed here she might get through the whole period undisturbed. The hedge between her and the main building was ten feet high and the garden laid out in front almost in the form of a maze with walls of cypress and yew, and little paved paths. In this part-enclosed section there were standard rose trees and a sundial. The children weren't allowed here, and the only sounds were birdsong, the far-off cries of pupils from the field over to the right, and the occasional crunch of a car up the gravel drive behind her. So she could be miserable without interruption.

'You should definitely try the flax,' Ruth had said.

'Soya's very good too, I've heard. And Kalms for the anxiety attacks.'

'I will,' Anna had replied, because it was so much easier to pretend she was perimenopausal than battling off the effects of mifepristone. Even Jamie had started to think she was going through the change. Hard to tell what Russ thought.

A movement caught her eye, something flashing past the gap in the hedge. Anna put her book down on the bench and balanced her apple on top. There was a stifled giggle somewhere near. First Years, or smokers. She got up, scanning around her.

Shit, said a male voice on the other side of the yew. Anna stepped close to the hedge where she thought the sound had come from and tried to peer through, but the leaves were too dense to see anything. When she sniffed there was no smell of smoke. She crouched down to see if she could catch a glimpse of shoes through the tiny gap at the bottom of the hedge, then it came to her how stupid she must look so she got up and walked quietly along to the gap and round the corner. Her pumps made hardly any sound on the stone path, but when she got to the next bay, this one a lavender garden, it was empty. She tiptoed on, intending to check the pond area, and saw again a blur of maroon blazer between the black-green bushes. Someone was playing games.

She half ran to the arch ahead of her, sure this time she'd catch whoever it was. But there was only the pink granite obelisk that was a memorial to a previous Head. No fag ends, not even any food wrappers; no trace at all. A flock of sparrows rose on the drive side of the garden.

You could go round in circles here. She came out of the last hedge onto the lawns, her eyes searching between the horse chestnut trees and parked cars. The trouble was, there were so many places to disappear. He could have sprinted onto the playing field in the time it took her to gather her wits, or sneaked back into the building through the main doors. She would not dignify the chase by continuing.

Irritated and tired, Anna made her way back to the bench. Just one lunchtime would be nice, one lunchtime to herself without interruptions from stupid people. This is what Jamie seemed to have forgotten in his retirement, that there was no time in a teacher's day to collect yourself. Way too much to do, and you rushed around under this constant bombardment of trivial annoyances that sometimes made you want to hurl your planner down and walk out of the building.

Then she saw Kali.

'It was you!'

Kali was standing by one of the rose trees, her hands folded. She looked as though she'd been waiting for Anna.

'What do you mean?'

'You were in the garden, on the other side. There was someone with you.'

'No.' Kali frowned. 'Not me. I've only just come here.'

'Well, you shouldn't have. It's out of bounds to students.'

Anna noticed how the girl had pinned her hair up loosely and tried to think what the style reminded her of. Wasn't there a painting of a red-haired girl in a rose garden?

'Mrs Meredith gave me permission. I'm getting ideas for my art project.'

'Did you see anyone running out as you came in?'

'No, no one. I'll go away if you like. If you want to be on your own. I didn't want to disturb you.'

Anna was disarmed by her politeness. 'It's all right. There's only twenty minutes left. And the garden's quite big enough for us both.'

'Yeah, it's nice in here.' Kali began to drift away. 'You can think better, save all your thoughts up and have them here.'

'What's your project about?'

'Blake.'

'William Blake?'

'O Rose, thou art sick. That's the guy. Drew God and the devil and giant fleas.'

'I like Blake very much.'

Kali stopped walking and stared up at the clouds, stretching her white neck taut. 'Oh, me too. Imagine being able to draw and write as well. That is so smart.'

'He wasn't a happy man, though. He suffered from mental illness.'

'Insane genius.'

Anna said, 'You should know I admired your poems very much—'

There was a rustling on the other side of the hedge that could have been the wind, could have been someone brushing past. Kali lowered her gaze to Anna. 'Really?'

'Yes.'

'Cool.'

'I have the book in my car, I keep meaning to give it back. Some of the poems were very mature.' She paused. 'And I don't mean to sound patronizing by that.'

''S OK.'

'You have a gift for tuning into emotions. Some of your lines seemed to express exactly the way I've felt at times.'

Kali raised her eyebrows in surprise. 'You in love too, Mrs Lloyd?'

'Heavens, no. Well, in my youth. I really meant the poems about loss—' For a split second she thought the story of her miscarriages was going to burst out of her, imagined telling this girl her pain and receiving words of consolation from her in the quiet of this garden. To confess, to be comforted. But of course that would have been completely unprofessional, as unprofessional as kissing a pupil. The moment passed. 'Of course,' she managed, 'if you love someone or something, you risk loss as a matter of course.'

'I like writing love poetry,' said Kali. 'It's the easiest sort. You get better language out of love, don't you?'

'I'd never thought of it like that.'

'I mean, love makes me want to write poetry.'

She looked very beautiful standing against the green leaves, a breeze stirring her hair back from her face. An image of perfect girlhood.

'Well,' said Anna warmly, 'whoever he is, the person in the poems, he's a lucky boy.'

'Not a *boy*.'

Anna flushed with embarrassment. 'Oh, I'm sorry, I assumed . . .'

Kali turned away smiling, then looked back. 'He's a man, Mrs Lloyd. A man.'

Chapter Seven

The weekend in the Lakes might have gone all right if it hadn't been for the post that came before and after.

Anna wanted to get off early but Jamie liked to hang around and wait for the mail to be delivered in case it contained an acceptance, although as far as Anna knew he didn't have any scripts out there. Luckily she spotted the letter with Russ's handwriting on it before Jamie did. Capitals or not, he knew his brother's style.

There was no note or signature in the envelope, only a blank postcard of Louise Brooks that she remembered Russ had brought to the caravan for her in the early days. In itself not incriminating, but Jamie would have asked why the mystery and that might have set him wondering. The caravan was cleared and locked now. She hadn't even seen Russ pocket the card.

She'd thought everything was finished, but evidently not. And what else might he send, what other cryptic messages might turn up under Jamie's nose? It was almost as though he wanted to get caught out.

Guilt made her nicer to Jamie than she'd intended, and when, in the bedroom of the farmhouse B&B, he began to caress her legs, she didn't mind. She lay on the old-fashioned bed half reading, half looking out of the window at the view of hills, and let herself be stroked. It was a very brown room, dark-brown furniture, sepia walls with a little diamond pattern on the paper. You had to have the light on all the time.

When she'd first met Jamie he'd been a head of department, she'd been – still was – second i/c. They'd come across each other at a GCSE moderation meeting and he'd challenged the course leader about the mark given to one of the coursework pieces. He had everyone's attention. He argued well, was easy with himself. In the end it was effectively him taking the session, not the examiner. A man like that has to be married already, Anna had thought to herself. But he wasn't.

'You know, I don't think they've decorated this place since the war.'

'I rather like it, it's quaint,' she said, letting her head fall back onto the pillow. 'That landlady was giving you the eye, you know.'

'Hmm. Can't say I was tempted.'

His hands moved further up her leg, pushing at the hem of her skirt. I can't have sex yet, she thought, I'm not ready. She wondered how to stop him.

He must have understood something, because he murmured, 'Relax. This is just for you. You don't have to do anything other than enjoy it. Let me touch you.'

His fingertips at the edge of her knickers, pushing under the elastic.

When you are very sad, she thought, it's like having flu. Everything tires you out and your flesh aches.

Jamie's hands felt good; she closed her eyes, let her mind clear and her body go with the sensations.

Afterwards he lay on his back next to her, an erection obvious under his jeans. She ignored it. If he'd been hoping she wouldn't take him at his word, he was disappointed. 'Just for you,' was what he'd said. 'I don't want you to do anything except lie there.' Physically she felt better than she'd done for a long time, like taking a painkiller for toothache.

'That was good,' she said. 'Thank you.'

'No problem.'

The chintz curtains stirred at the window and the sun coming in showed the dust on the wardrobe mirror. She wouldn't have been surprised to see a Lancaster bomber fly past or hear an air-raid siren. 'It's like dropping back in time half a century, this place.'

'Nice to get away sometimes, isn't it?'

'Yes, it is,' she said. 'Oh, it is.'

Then they came home and this time there was a letter from Adam Gardiner, which Jamie did see.

'What's he doing writing to you?' He threw the envelope down on the kitchen top. 'I thought you'd agreed with his mother that you weren't going to contact him again.'

'He's contacted me.' She hadn't even unpacked yet, there were bits and pieces all over the stairs waiting to go up to the bathroom and no doubt she'd be the one who ended up taking them because, God knows, it never occurred to Jamie to pick anything up as he went past.

'So, what's he say?'

'He wants me to know he's settled in at college and he's doing well. It's a thank you. That's all.'

'He doesn't want to come and stay again?'

'Once he turned up here, once. I didn't invite him and he didn't stay over. Can you at least put the kettle on and make us a drink, Jamie? Instead of standing there going through my private correspondence.'

She pushed past him and opened the door of the washing machine.

'He still can't spell "their", I notice.'

Oh, fuck you, Anna mouthed into the linen basket.

He wouldn't let it drop, either, following her upstairs and sitting on the bed while she laid her make-up back out on the dressing table. 'If his mother finds out she'll be furious. We don't want her shouting the odds on our doorstep again.'

Anna lost her temper. 'You talk as though I had some kind of *injunction* placed on me! For God's sake. The only reason that woman was cross with me was because she realized what a useless mother she'd been all her life. No wonder he listened to me more than he did to her, no wonder he came to me with his problems. If she'd been an adequate role model she'd have had nothing to worry about.'

Jamie waited till she'd finished speaking, then got up and went out of the room. She carried on sorting brushes, lining them up by her make-up bag and not hurling them one after another at the wall as she'd have liked to.

It was all true. The only reason Adam had become so dependent on her was because he was hungry for some kind of proper mother figure. Mrs Gardiner had done nothing but nag and denigrate her son for years – when she paid him any attention – then, when he ran away, it was all hand-wringing and tears. But Anna had never encouraged him to leave home and she certainly hadn't invited him to hers. 'Did you give him your home phone number or address?' Jackson had asked her. He seemed to think this was important.

When her answer was no, he'd sighed with relief.

'That's what the lad said,' Jackson had replied, and she'd realized the question had been a test. 'Did you ever buy him anything?'

'Only a book of poetry. And it wasn't for him specifically, I was going to use it for resources.'

'Did you put in a claim?'

'I never got round to it.'

She could see what he was driving at. If she'd paid for it herself it became a personal gift.

'Anna, did you at any point behave in a way that could be construed as unprofessional towards this boy?'

'Absolutely not.'

That was how the modern world rewarded a dedicated teacher for taking a particular interest in the progress of a struggling pupil. 'You can't be a mother to them,' Jamie had said at the time. 'It's not your job.' That was another moment when she'd been glad she was cheating on him.

So it was a relief to get back to school after all, even though the staffroom noticeboard was full of photos of Mrs Hislop's daughter-plus-baby, and there were pre-inspection visitors in school that day, and it was Year Seven parents' evening that very first night. Jackson was in a fearfully hearty mood, been on some course over the holiday and met an ex-education secretary. 'Charming woman, charming,' he kept saying. 'Told me a few interesting developments in the world of education. Very useful. Very il*lu*minating.' He tapped his nose as if to suggest he'd been invited into the prime minister's private chamber and shown the top ten state secrets. 'Yes, it's good to keep one step ahead of the game in this business.'

After Jackson went out, Andrew said: 'Why's he talk such unremitting bollocks?'

'We are going to have to call him Cliché Man,' said Anna, looking up from her mark book. 'The Idiom King.'

'Idiot King, more like. How do you put up with him, Les? You're in closer proximity than us. Doesn't he drive you mad?'

Les raised his eyebrows. 'I'm known for my saint-like patience. Isn't that right, young Anna?'

Anna thought, I could almost fancy him if he wasn't so ugly. Like her, Les had no children; there was something wrong with his wife, a disability of some sort, though no one was quite sure of the details. It was understood that you didn't ask too much.

He came into the work area and began unrolling charts. 'By the way, you two, I have a bit of gossip you should know.'

'Oh yeah?' Andrew perked up. 'Jackson's hidden vices? Tell all.'

'Nothing to do with our revered HM. No, it's your pal Nathan Woods.'

'Jesus, what's he done now?'

'He's hooked himself up with Kali Norman. True romance, says my informant. They're wearing matching necklaces this morning.'

'God.'

'Yes, touching, isn't it? I mention the alliance, Andy, because they're both in your form.'

'Kali? With Nathan?' said Anna.

'Yep.' Les rolled a rubber band down the charts he didn't need and pushed them end-on across the top of the lockers. 'I haven't seen them, but Mrs Hislop, who spies all from her eyrie, witnessed them embracing on the front drive.'

Not Kali.

Andrew pulled a face. 'Imagine embracing that git, the girl needs her head seeing to. I hope she washed her hands afterwards.'

'I can't understand what she sees in him,' said Les. 'But he must have something, because he was going out with Zoe Parker last half-term and she's very hot property, two years above him as well. Anyway. I believe they got it together at someone's party over the break.'

'Bloody hell, who'd have thought it,' said Andrew. 'And I wouldn't go near him with a ten-foot pole.'

'They like bad boys, these modern women,' said Les, rather sadly, Anna thought.

A girl Anna no longer taught stopped her in the corridor to tell her about winning a poetry competition, and that meant she was slightly late for her Year Ten lesson. As soon as she walked into the classroom she saw that Kali and Nathan were next to each other on the back row. This was in contravention of her seating plan, which now had him sitting at the front on his own. Anna knew she had a split second in which to say something, tell him to get up and move to his usual place, or the moment was lost. His eyes met hers and she failed.

She took herself to the front of the class and stood waiting for silence. Then she sat down at the desk.

'Take out your anthologies,' she told them, and her voice sounded odd. Lin Keane, directly in front of her, glanced up. Two rows back, Kali and Nathan were drawing on the same piece of paper. 'Come on, now.' One inch out of line and she would move him. 'We'll look at another Ted Hughes poem today. "Tractor". Page thirty.'

With infinite slowness, Nathan flicked through the pages of his book. Every time a page flopped over, the hair lying across Kali's right shoulder stirred. She was trying not to laugh.

'I'll read it through first. Listen carefully and note any vocabulary you're not sure of.'

She hardly heard the words as she spoke them; she was watching the back row. After she finished there was a pause, then Martin Fallow said, 'How can a corpse make a noise?'

Anna frowned. 'Put your hand up in future, Martin. Where do you mean?'

'Line thirteen.'

'Oh. Copse. The *copse* hisses. A small group of trees are hissing in the gale.'

Nathan sniggered and she thought he said, 'Wanker'.

'I'm sorry,' Anna snapped. 'Did you have something you want to share?'

'No.' His head went down. Kali was studying her nails.

'And "capitulates" means – anyone? No? "Gives in". Any other vocab questions? OK. So, what I want you to do first is go through and underline any words to do with temperature. Heat or cold.' She turned to the board and wrote the instruction up. 'Two minutes.'

The students hunched over their books, marking the pages. Anna fixed her gaze on Nathan, but he seemed to be working.

It was good news, she thought, about Nicola Fish winning that poetry prize. And nice that she thought to let Anna know. I knew you'd be pleased, she'd said shyly. Anna had given her extra lessons two years ago, out of her own lunchtimes, because the girl had a block with spelling. Not dyslexia, just bad early teaching. Nicola had made her a cross-stitch bookmark at the end of the year which Anna still used.

'OK, then, what do we have?'

Most hands went up.

'Frozen – good – snow – ice -- molten – yes, smoking – white heat – fieriness—' Anna wrote the words up on the board as they were called. When she'd finished, she said, 'Can anyone see a pattern in these words? Or a contrast, a contradiction?'

It was Lin who answered. 'Half of them are to do with heat and half to do with cold.'

'That's right. So why, if Hughes wants to convey extreme cold, does he use vocabulary like "burning" and "molten"?'

Kali was trying to tear a strip of paper from a page of her notepad without making any noise. Anna shot her a look and she stopped.

'Kali, do you know?'

There was only blankness on the girl's face. She hadn't been listening at all.

'Can anyone tell me why Hughes would do this, describe the idea of cold through heat?'

'Because,' said Kali after a few seconds, 'poets never say what they mean.'

Nathan laughed. Anna did too, which confused him. 'Can you explain what you mean by that?' she said pleasantly.

But Kali was too full of being near Nathan to think in a coherent manner. She shook her head and pressed her lips together.

'Is it because,' Sally Marsden coming in now, and it was a crying shame her mother didn't take her to a decent hairdresser, because she really needed a good cut: 'when you get really cold, like when you've been out throwing snowballs, you know, and you come in and your fingers are like, burning, it's like they're on fire, literally, and it's almost like you can't tell whether you're really hot or really cold because it feels the same?'

'What,' said Nathan, full of scorn. 'You can't tell the difference between hot and cold?'

Some of them had got it, others were looking doubtful. Sally appealed to Anna: 'Is that right, Mrs Lloyd?'

'It is. Well done. In some ways it's a difficult concept to grasp. I expect your biology teacher will tell you how it happens, nerve endings and confused messages to the brain, something to do with that. But when you touch a radiator there's a split second where you're not sure whether it's scorching or icy, isn't there? Just a split second. And there's a party trick, a sort of joke you can do with an ice cube—'

'I know a good party trick,' said Nathan.

Kali put her head down on the desk and hid her face with her hair.

'One more remark that isn't directly related to the lesson, Nathan, and I send you out,' said Anna. Her Adam's apple felt too large for her throat and she turned away instead of staring him down as she should have done. Was Les in his office this period?

'You can,' she went on after a moment, 'make someone think they've been burned with a cigarette by just touching them lightly with the corner of an ice cube.' She mimed the action.

'Cool,' said Martin Fallow.

'Although it's not a very nice thing to do. Now, I want you next to look at stanzas four to six and the way in which the tractor is conveyed. Then I want you to answer this question, write it down: How does Hughes . . . feel . . . towards . . . the tractor?'

'Hates its guts,' said Nathan.

'Good,' said Anna, and he looked at her in dismay. 'Try to put it in more formal language, though. Off you go. Something between half and a full page, and you have fifteen minutes.'

She wrote 'personification' on the board then sat down to look at her lesson notes. Almost immediately Kali's hand was up.

'Yes?'

'This is what I meant when I said before about poetry not saying things straight. I mean, how is a tractor like a demon?'

Really she wanted the girl to shut up and get on with her work, but the question was a fair one.

'Can we talk about this after you've done your answer? Anyway,' she added in a lower voice, 'you should know the way poetry works, you write it yourself.'

Nathan's head snapped up. 'Oh yeah?'

'It's nothing.' Kali gave him a shove.

'Poetree, ooh. I'll have to see some of these *poems*. They about me?'

'Get off, it's only old schoolwork.'

'My love is like a red, red nose—'

Anna took a step towards Nathan which made him clap his hand over his mouth and begin writing. Kali looked cross.

For ten minutes there was quiet. Then Sally raised her hand and Anna went round and stood behind her so she could answer without disturbing the others. Sally was pointing at one particular line with the end of her pen. 'I know he hates the tractor, Mrs Lloyd,' she whispered, 'but does he feel a bit sorry for it as well?' As Anna bent over the desk to see, she became aware of movement at the back of the room.

She straightened up and turned to see Nathan waving his ruler in the air like a conductor's baton.

'Oops,' he said, grinning.

'What is it?'

'Is Ted Hughes still alive?'

'No.'

'When was he alive?'

'He died in 1998.'

'What of? Did he commit suicide? Did he get run over by a tractor?'

'He died of cancer.'

'What sort of cancer?'

'I don't know. Get on with your writing, please.'

She went back to Sally's anthology. Then, unbelievably, she heard Nathan say, 'Breast cancer,' and snigger.

That's it, she thought.

Between them there was a row of desks, but all Anna saw was his smirking face. 'Get out,' she said. 'Go and stand outside the room and wait for me.'

Nathan was pretending extreme astonishment, looking round and gaping. 'What? What? What did I do?'

'Get out,' she said again. The class was transfixed.

Suddenly he got up, pushing his chair so it fell with a clang against the pipes on the wall behind, and glared at her. On the display board by his head Anna saw some words that shouldn't be there. *Parts of Speech*, said the title. *Verbs Nouns Adverbs Adjectives*, then lists of examples done by Year Seven. But someone had added in pencil capitals FUCK and SHIT under Verbs and WANK under Adjectives.

'Get out!'

For a second she thought he might strike her, but instead he leant over and grabbed Kali's face between his hands. Then he fastened his mouth on hers – Anna saw the skin of their lips squash and fuse, the muscles in his jaw flickering under his skin – and kissed her. In the endless shameful seconds that passed, Anna was aware that Kali put up only a moment's struggle, then her head was moving between his palms, her eyes closed, just as if they'd been on their own. Part of Anna's mind was shouting, What do I do here? What if he won't leave?

He broke away, trailing strands of Kali's hair between his fingers. 'See you,' he said to her alone, and walked out of the room. Kali swayed in her chair. She was pink around her mouth where he'd pressed against her.

'Are you all right?' Anna asked, which she knew was a stupid thing to say as soon as it was out. Kali looked away and didn't answer.

It seemed to Anna that there was so much hatred still in the room that she would suffocate if she stayed where she was. 'Carry on with your writing,' she said hopelessly, and moved towards the door. If she could find Les, she'd be all right.

Chapter Eight

Jamie was kissing her, kissing and kissing her because she'd asked him to and the surprise on his face had almost made her laugh, would have made her laugh if she had not so badly needed to be kissed. His hands were in her hair pushing back her straight smooth tresses and the pressure at her scalp made her think of Kali's hair wound around Nathan's fingers, and her throat was stretched the way Kali's had been, to meet Jamie's mouth, her lips working wetly against his and her palm flat on the line of his jaw. Russ's cheeks were smoother, a different material almost; he used to groan when she touched his ears and the back of his neck and she thought of Russ swearing as she undressed for him and the way his cock was pinker than Jamie's with less hair and fatter and shorter and his astonished gratitude that she went down on him, not that she ever did for long because it would have been a waste. 'Sometimes I think about you at work,' he'd said, 'and I get hard, I can't stop thinking about you,' and there'd been a rush into her head of power. And now Jamie was unbuttoning her blouse and pushing it off her shoulders, and she wondered whether Kali had had sex and what her body was like, very white she imagined, and had Nathan seen it, and Jamie licked along her collarbone and she shuddered. She remembered her mother kissing a man with sideburns in some bedroom with a skylight, Anna hadn't even known his name, couldn't recall where the room had been. Had she really witnessed that or just pictured it when she'd seen the man come out of her mother's room? He'd used their toilet and he'd come out with his hands on his fly.

Jamie was easing her bra strap over her arm, pushing his pelvis against her; she wanted to desire him but the knot of concentration was unravelling. She heard his voice again as though on tape:

'Wank's a verb anyway, not an adjective.'

'No, they say stuff's wank if it's not very good.'

'They're not going to give him another chance?'

'I don't know.'

Keep kissing.

Mel's answerphone: *I can't pick up right now because I'm bizzeebizzeeeee.* Her own halting message: I just wanted to offload. Again. I know I always seem to be— Ringing for a moan. Give us a bell when you . . .

'I know a good party trick,' echoed Nathan's voice, then Les, 'Can you write up for me exactly what happened, Anna?'

'I can taste your body lotion, it's bitter,' said Jamie as he came at her again, drawing her mouth to his, but it was no good, no good now, and she broke away and had to watch his confused frown as she backed off and pulled her shirt together, shaking her head.

*

'You should see someone,' he said later, angrily. 'A doctor or a shrink. I'm starting to think you have a problem.' She had a moment inside his mind so that she saw events from exactly his point of view: *I've given the whole evening to your school worries, the least you could do is give me sex.* Clearly she'd reneged on the deal.

Later she lay in the dark, fighting off her mother. That man in the skylight room had just appeared without warning, that was the upsetting part. Then he'd used their toilet and left drops on the seat. She'd tried to explain how horrible that was but Miriam had laughed. 'Whose house is it?' she said. 'Who pays the rent here, Madam? I say who comes through that front door. And who stays outside it.' Moaning Minny, she'd called Anna, as if she were the fount of all joy herself.

Mel had been distant on the phone that night and said she hadn't any plans to come to Chester for a while; she was snowed under with work. 'It's hard when you start somewhere new,' she'd said. Which was true.

Finally Anna got up to make herself a drink and sit by the dolls' house.

All quiet in there. The light threw diamond patterns on the Deco fireplace. A packet of Craven A, smaller than a five pence, lay on the mantelpiece. Last time Ruth had been round she'd come barging in here, poked the tiny curtain under the sink, picked up a jar of marmalade between her massive fingers. 'See, I'd have made that back bedroom into a nursery and put the kitchen where the bathroom is. Do you ever swap tips on the Internet with other people who play at dolls' houses?'

'The term they use is miniaturists.'

Russ, who'd only been half listening, said, 'It's bloody political correctness again. For years we called them midgets and no one batted an eyelid. Who looks after the rights of the bog-ordinary bloke?'

In the background Jamie sniggered.

'Beth would so love to have a play with it,' said Ruth, picking at the toilet paper to see whether it would unroll. 'She'd be ever so careful. She's got her craft badge at Guides.'

'It's not for playing with.'

Ruth exchanged glances with Russ. Mean cow, they telegraphed.

'Anna's right,' said Jamie. 'It's definitely not a toy. It's more like, what, a sculpture, a social history sculpture. Anyway, some of the pieces are very expensive.'

'How much?' Russ heard that, no problem.

'Well, that display cabinet was—'

Don't say it, please, thought Anna. Please don't say.

'How much was that cabinet again? Oh, I remember; forty pounds.'

Russ's face twisted. 'For a *doll's cupboard*?'

'Craftsman-made,' said Jamie.

'More like an heirloom, really,' said Ruth, removing her paw hastily from the front bedroom. 'Isn't it a pity you don't have anyone to pass it on to.'

Now, outside the spare-room window, across the street and watching the house, stood a figure that could have been Russ.

Anna pulled the blind down.

*

Parents' evenings were always held in the main hall; that way parents could see when teachers were free, and an open, public environment also minimized the chances of a serious fracas. Even so, most staff had had their sticky moments. Andrew Maye had once had coffee thrown over him, and an NQT burst into tears when one of the mothers had called her incompetent. Les and Jackson patrolled like bouncers, though Jackson's obsequious smile tended to ruin the effect.

In a gap between appointments, Anna looked for Les.

'Are the Woodses here tonight?' she asked as he strolled by, hands behind his back.

He diverted his course and came to stand by her. 'Boycotting the event. As a protest against his suspension.'

'You'd have thought they'd see the opportunity for feedback as even more important.'

'You're assuming,' he said, bending so he could lower his voice, 'that they're reasonable people. Which they're not. Did you really want to see them, you crazy girl?'

Anna smiled slightly.

'Thought not. Have a nice evening, now.'

He drifted off again and she scanned the room to see whether she could recognize anyone. It was strange how some children turned out to be the image of their parents while others had the look of freaky changelings. And the variety of costumes was interesting, too. Some of the mothers had dressed for a cocktail party, others had come in farm gear. A lot of business suits among the men. And here was Lin Keane's mother approaching the table, Fair Isle sweater and check skirt, flat shoes: could the woman be any plainer? She'd made an attempt at make-up, but her lipstick was already coming away. 'Mrs Lloyd, she loves your subject and she loves you. Thank you so much for the special reading list you did her. I think she's about a third of the way through already.'

'One of my stars,' said Anna. 'A super student.'

Interviews like that were easy.

Sally Marsden's father looked apologetic when he came. 'I should tell you, her mum's not around at the moment.'

'Not around?'

'She's taking a break.'

Anna looked the question.

'From marriage.'

'Ah.'

'We're not sure what's happening. I've spoken to Mr Weston about it, he'll fill you in. Rather than go round to all the teachers telling the same . . .'

'Of course. And how's Sally with it?'

Mr Marsden ran his hand over his brow. 'I'm not sure. We're going from day to day. Has she said anything to you?'

'No. She might have spoken to Mr Maye about it, he's her form tutor.'

He shook his head and frowned. 'She doesn't . . .'

'OK. Let her know she can come to me if she needs to. And obviously if she needs a deadline extension, pop a note in her homework planner.'

There was a pause in which his face flushed and his eyes grew bright. Oh, God, was he going to cry? But no, he cleared his throat, clasped his hands on the desk. Well done, Mr M.

'I appreciate that, Mrs Lloyd. Anyway, she likes you. Likes your lessons.' He leaned forward. 'How's she getting on?'

There was another gap after Marsden, then it was the Fallows. Mrs first, clouded in perfume.

'Well: Martin,' Anna began. What to say about the little twit? 'A mixed sort of term so far, some pieces fine and others poor, if you see his grades going right from C- down to E, and no discernible pattern.'

Mrs Fallow turned her elegant neck to peer at Anna's mark book. 'He responds best to praise. He doesn't like criticism.'

'No, none of us does. But he has to behave well in order to elicit praise, I can't praise what isn't there. It would help if he came on time to the lessons. He's almost always a couple of minutes behind the others and punctuality is becoming a concern—'

'Sorry I'm late!' Mr Fallows swung himself into the chair next to his wife. 'Just chatting to Jackson about the new build. Quite an outlay for the school, I should think. Ah, what have I missed?'

'Tell you later,' said Mrs.

'So, yes, and then I often have to tell him off for not having the right equipment, the correct books—'

'Is that a pen?' Mr F. put out his hand and snatched up Anna's Parker. 'May I? Have you a scrap of paper too? Oh, it's all right, I can use the back of this flyer.'

Anna paused.

'It's OK, I'm sorted. Go on, tell us the bad news.' Mr F. settled back and struck an attentive pose. His wife's expression never changed.

'—and he is easily distracted.'

'By other pupils,' said Mrs.

'Often not, no. He'll be in the middle of a task or discussion and he'll suddenly go off on a tangent, start talking about a topic that has nothing to do with the lesson. It's not helpful.'

Mr nodded. 'When's the new block going to be finished, then? I bet it's been fun having all these builders round the place. Jackson was saying he's got plans for a swimming pool, long term.'

After they'd gone, a Year Eight girl brought coffee and a digestive. Four more appointments on her sheet. Les grinned at her from across the room. 'We ought to have a record of scary parents up in the staffroom,' he'd said earlier. 'We could put it next to the student SEN list and the Medical Requirements one, with codes for different quirks. Be ever so handy.'

'Oh, it would. Till the national press got to hear about it.'

They exchanged grins.

Kali's mother next, she thought.

'So we've seen how some published authors set about describing a character,' said Anna to her Year Sevens, 'and now I'd like you to have a go. I want you to write about a person who's made a big impression on you. It can be someone you like or dislike, but it must be someone you've met face to face and can describe in detail. Put your hand down, I know what you're going to say and no, it can't be anyone off the television unless you've actually spoken to that person in real life. No singers or footballers. Doesn't matter how many times you've dreamed about them. That doesn't count.'

Some of the children were exchanging secret smiles and others were looking blank.

'Can it be a grown-up?'

'It can be anyone as long as you know them well enough to describe.'

'Can it be a teacher?' Little smirk there.

Anna folded her hands.

'I'm not going to say that anyone you know is out of bounds. But this writing will be displayed on the main board for everyone to read, so if you were thinking of putting something that might hurt another person's feelings or embarrass them, don't. How would you feel if I let someone do that to you? This is an exercise in English; if I think you've hijacked the lesson to poke fun at someone, I shall be very cross. Are we clear on that?'

She ran her gaze right across the class, taking in every pupil.

'Are we clear?'

General nodding.

'And I don't particularly want any big effusions of love, either.'

Some giggling from the girls by the door.

'Well, then. Half an hour, uninterrupted, sustained creativity, aiming for about a page. Off you go.'

She sat down at her own desk and began to write.

*

She was a woman on the wrong side of everything. Velvet jacket and frilly shirt much too young, jeans zip that didn't quite do up over her belly. This silly comb in the side of her hair like they used to wear in the Eighties. And when she crossed her legs, I saw she had on black pointy ankle boots with a spiky heel. I don't know why those annoyed me, but they did.

'Mrs Norman?'

'That's right.'

My, what an enormous engagement ring you have there. 'Nice to meet you.'

'So, how's Kali settled in?'

Her lips were those of a smoker, puckered into permanent wrinkles: cat's bum mouth, they call it. I couldn't place the accent at first; the intonation was Liverpudlian but some of the vowel sounds were Cheshire and some of them Irish. It was an ugly, mongrel style of speaking that grated on your ears.

'Good, on the whole. Her work so far's been acute and sensitive, if on the brief side. Is she much of a reader?'

Mrs Norman gave a short laugh. 'I couldn't tell you. I've no idea what she gets up to these days. She disappears into her room and the music goes on and that's it. A moody madam. Like me. We're too much alike, me and Kali.'

I doubt that, thought Anna.

Long polished nails, mascara too thick. She had a hard look about her altogether.

'I'd say she's a perceptive student, not without ability. Her comprehension of the texts we've covered has been very mature, but she'll need to work on developing the length of her written responses—'

'So she is behaving herself?'

'Yes; I—'

'Is she going to pass her exams? That's what Owen wants to know.'

'Owen?'

'My Owen. He's the one who's paying the fees.' She rubbed her finger and thumb together.

'Ah. Well, there's every indication that she'll achieve a grade between A and C, though there are never any guarantees and it's hard to be more precise at this stage, right at the start of—'

'That'll do me.'

'I can show you her progress in more detail if we look at my mark book.'

'See, she's never really got settled at school before. We've moved around.'

'So I understand.'

I had a terrible urge to shout out, 'Get your hair sorted! Dress your age!' I don't know whether other people get this impulse, where a single awful sentence lodges in your mind and repeats itself more and more loudly until you can't believe no one else can hear it.

'It would be useful if you could help her keep on top of coursework deadlines.'

'Yeah, I will, yeah.' This said with no conviction whatsoever. 'She's doing OK, though? Is there anything else?'

I'm worried she's still angry with me for mentioning her poetry in front of everyone, Anna thought. But she couldn't say something so personal to this woman.

'Right, then.' Mrs Norman stood. 'As long as we're getting our money's worth.'

I admit I set out not to like her. But even so, she was so much less of a mother than a girl like Kali deserved.

As soon as she heard Jamie say, 'Isn't that Russ's car pulling up outside?' Anna knew something was wrong. If she could have made a run for it through the back door, she would have done. 'I wonder who they've foisted the brats on? Who'd be fool enough to take on that trio? And Christ, look at the expression on Russ's face. Mr Grump, they called him at school and I swear he's getting worse.'

But when Jamie greeted them in the hall it was with smiles and arm-patting and offers of lunch.

'We're not staying,' said Russ. 'Not for long, anyway.'

Ruth shrugged. 'We don't have to rush back. Drama-Shed doesn't finish till four, and Alison said she was OK till—'

'Yes, but I have things I need to *do*, Ruth. When do I ever get any free time? Huh?'

Anna said, 'I'll make a drink, anyway.' She went into the kitchen and stood for a moment with her hands to her temples because she was sure, sure that Russ had come to do some damage. She didn't know what it was but he had this look on him, he wouldn't meet her eye. Guilt and belligerence radiated off him.

She ran the cold tap for too long till her fingers turned numb underneath it.

If he snapped, suddenly, and damn the conse-quences? Jamie always said that if Russ bashed his elbow on a concrete pillar, he'd go back and kick it till he broke his foot.

'OK in here?'

The shock of Ruth's voice almost made her drop the kettle.

'Fine. How are you?'

'Great!'

You look appalling, thought Anna. How can you believe for one minute that fawn slacks and clingy peach sweater is the way to go? The last thing your body needs is more pink.

Perhaps Ruth read her expression. 'Need to get a few pounds off.' She tapped her belly. 'But I think you've lost weight, Anna, have you?'

'Not that I was aware of.'

'You do look quite drawn, still. Sorry. Are you taking the iron supplements?'

'Yes.'

'Now, which brand are you taking? Because some of them don't contain sufficient levels, and some of them contain vitamin C which helps you absorb the iron.'

'I don't know, offhand. The bottle's upstairs.'

'Do you want me to run up and check for you? It's worth it, it really is.'

For fuck's sake, thought Anna, can't you see I'm lying to get you off my back?

'I'll get them later. Would you like a biscuit with your coffee?'

'Ooh, lovely.' Ruth's eyes gleamed, all vitamins forgotten. 'I shouldn't.'

'One more won't hurt,' said Anna truthfully.

When they walked back into the lounge Russ was pacing around, talking politics.

'You should stand for election,' said Jamie. Anna knew he was being facetious, but Russ didn't pick it up.

'I've thought about it. I reckon I could do a better job than Graham Pearce; mind you, a trained monkey could do a better job than Pearce. But you have to have money and you have to know the right people.'

'It's an unfair world, little bro.'

Russ narrowed his eyes but Jamie's expression remained open.

'I think he'd make a good politician,' said Ruth.

Suddenly Russ said to Jamie, 'I need you to look something up on the Internet for me.' His voice seemed loud.

'Yours out of action?'

'We picked up a virus. Something called a Trojan.' Now he caught Anna's gaze. 'So called, apparently, because it *pretends to be something good* and then it installs itself in your system and does *all kinds of damage*. You *can't get rid of it*. It messes *everything up*.'

Was no one else hearing this?

'It's been quite a weekend,' Ruth said. 'Both the older ones were up last night being sick, I was running between them with buckets and we didn't think they'd be able to go to drama class this afternoon, but they seemed fine by ten. Only they've made such a mess of our landing carpet. I was still picking bits of rice out of it just before we came.'

'Thank you for sharing that with us,' said Jamie.

'And then yesterday teatime Russ pulled open the

freezer door and there was red water all down him, all down his trousers, and when I shouted for Tom, because I knew it would be him, it turns out he's been trying to make bath bombs out of soap-and-paint ice cubes. Can you imagine? I thought it was quite funny. You didn't though, did you, Russ?'

'No.'

'Freezing painty water all down his trousers!'

Jamie stepped past them all and went to the bottom of the stairs. 'Shall we Google, then?'

Russ went after him and Anna made to follow, but Ruth blocked her way by stopping where she was and bending over the coffee table.

'Oh, wow, is this Jamie's story?' She picked up a magazine with a black-and-white photograph of a nautilus shell on the front. 'Didn't he have a short story in here?'

'He did, yes.'

'Gosh. I remember him telling us when it was accepted but I hadn't seen it actually in print. What does he think?'

'He's very pleased.' Anna strained her ears for any scraps of conversation on the stairs.

'Did they pay him much?'

'No.' She gave up and turned to Ruth. 'Nothing, actually. A year's subscription to the magazine.'

Ruth nodded. 'Still. It's very smart. Oh look, there's his name. What was the story about?'

'A man who loves his wife so much he shoots her.'

Through the patio window Anna could see a black cat stalking something along the bottom of the fence. She would have run across and banged on the window if she'd been on her own, save the bird or mouse or whatever it was, but she couldn't take the drivelly pet stories that would follow.

'Heavens, Anna, I hope he's not getting any ideas about his own marriage! Better not let Russ read it, I think there are some days he'd like to shoot me.'

'Surely not.'

Ruth folded the magazine and straightened up but stayed where she was, still in the way. 'How's Jamie's script going? I don't like to ask him outright in case he bites my head off.'

'I don't know exactly. He might have moved on to something else. We could go up and see, he loves showing people his notes.'

Without warning Ruth turned and grabbed hold of Anna's small wrist. 'Listen,' she said in confidential tones, 'I don't want to intrude but you're clearly not well. You look dreadful, completely drained. Now, I've been having a little think about the situation—'

What *situation*? thought Anna. What would you know about my life?

'—and I've been chatting to Mum about it, she had a rough time with the Change, and with your mum not being around, I thought you might need a bit of advice.'

Anna felt heat rising to her cheeks, though it was probably from anger rather than anything else. *Discussed it with her mother?*

'So,' Ruth went on, opening her shoulder bag, 'I've brought you round some stuff that might be useful. There's some flax seed.'

'I'm not a bloody budgie, Ruth. I'm not even menopausal, you've got it—'

'No, but you might be on the way, that's before it all happens. That part can go on for years.'

'I'm not even forty-three.'

'And there's a cologne wand to cool you down when you get the flushes, Mum was crippled with them, you just roll cologne on your pulse points and it really helps. And it's so small you can stick it anywhere.'

Don't tempt me, thought Anna.

'And last but not least, some relaxation CDs. You can put them in a Discman and block out stressful environments. I used them a lot after Tom was born. Here.'

Ruth laid the CDs on the table next to the magazine. *Forest Passage*, Anna read. *In the Soul of the Night*, *Spirit of the Plains*, *Mountain Magic*.

'*Mountain Magic*? It sounds like an air freshener.'

'I'm trying to help,' said Ruth.

Anna dropped her head in shame. Who was she to sneer at this woman, after what she'd done to her? It could be that, two floors above them, Russ was dismantling all their lives.

'Sorry. Yes, thanks. I'll try it. Shall we go see how the boys are getting on?'

Ruth shifted resentfully. 'OK.'

Halfway up the stairs she turned and said, 'Oh, I didn't tell you about Tom's incredible shrinking shoes, did I? We had such a laugh about them.' Ruth's sulks never lasted for long.

Up on the top storey they found Jamie supervising the printer and Russ staring out of the window with his arms folded, looking like thunder. Jamie had his mouth all tight the way he did after a row.

'I was telling Anna about Tom's shoe saga,' said Ruth. 'How some nights he was coming home from Reception, oh, it's so funny, and complaining that his shoes were too tight, and then other nights they were fine.'

Russ didn't even move his head, she might as well not have spoken. Jamie caught the sheet of paper as it was ejected.

'We just couldn't work out what was going on, could we? Were his feet shrinking and growing?'

'Here,' said Jamie, poking Russ's back with the printed page.

'And we took him to be measured and his feet were still a size eight.'

Russ snatched the page off him and folded it into tiny squares.

'And the lady in the shoe shop, she didn't know what was going on, it was so funny, they had him in one of those measuring machines and everything. So then I went into Reception – no, wait, it was Russ who took him in one morning, would that have been last Tuesday? No, because you supervise the deliveries on a Tuesday, don't you? Well, it must have been Wednesday. No, it was Tuesday but it was the end of the day, it was when you picked him up, and you said to the teacher, I don't know what's going on with Tom's feet because one day his shoes fit and the next day they don't. Have you ever heard anything like it? And she looked at you as if you were mad, didn't she, Russ?'

He made a 'huh' noise in his throat and stuffed the paper in his jeans pocket.

'But when Tom came out he said his feet were hurting again so you sat him down there and then on the school step and when Russ finally checked, do you know what he found?'

'They were someone else's shoes,' said Jamie.

'That's right! How did you guess? We laughed and laughed, didn't we? You see, the place where the size had been printed was all worn away so we hadn't been able to check, we were just looking at the caterpillar logo on the side. And we said to this other mum, that's the trouble with there only being one shoe shop in town, all the children have the same style.'

I'm going to have to kill you, thought Anna. Right now, where you stand.

After they'd gone, Jamie slammed the front door and took himself straight back to his office. Anna hesitated, then followed.

'What's up?'

Jamie only shook his head.

'What?' She felt squeezed out with fear.

'He wanted money.'

'Money? Oh, my God. How much?'

'Four thousand.'

She sat down because she thought he might see her legs were shaking. 'What does he need that kind of money for?'

'A blip, he calls it. Someone who owes him money going bust and someone else he owes money to putting the squeeze on him. He can't go to the bank because he's reached his limit. He says in a month's time everything'll be back on track.' He sighed and tapped the keyboard. 'What a way to run a business. Bloody hopeless.'

So that was Russ's tack. Proxy blackmail. 'You should have given it to him, Jamie. We've got it, just about.'

'I did.'

She tried not to let her face convulse with relief.

'Then why was he so angry?'

'Because he'd had to come to me and because I'd been able to bail him out. Easier for him in some ways if I'd told him to bugger off. Sheesh, I looked after him for years when he was a kid. Years. You'd think by now he'd be able to stand on his own two feet.'

'Was Ruth in on it?'

'Don't know. I expect.'

They sat in silence for a while, Jamie scrolling through pages on the screen. Then Anna said, 'Was that all?'

'What do you mean?'

'Was that all he said? About the money? Was that what he took you in here to say?'

'Yes. Yes, that was it.' Jamie turned and looked at her. 'What else did you think he was going to tell me, Anna?'

Chapter Nine

Jamie had gone to chair his writing group and Anna for once had charge of the computer. He was in better spirits this evening because he'd managed to produce a short story he wanted to read out (nothing more done on the script, though, Anna noted) and because they had a new member coming. She'd watched him get ready.

'This blue shirt OK with the black jeans?'

'Yes, it's nice.'

No wonder some of them had crushes on him. The glasses he donned sometimes for fine print only made him look more distinguished. Once the writing circle was set up, chairs dragged across the pub floor, he would lean back in his seat and cross his right ankle over his left knee, a man at ease. If she met him now, not knowing him, not viewing him through a pane of resentment, she'd probably fancy him.

She should have been using this hour to check out GCSE revision sites so that she could give them the rating she'd promised her students, but she'd got side-tracked into playing with a search engine. She put in her own name, for fun, and found she was on a basketball team, ran a quilting forum, had written a book on woodland management. Her secret life. And there she was really, on the school's website: Anna Lloyd, English teacher, BA (Hons), PGCE. Strange how coming across yourself like that felt somehow clever and validating.

She typed in Mel's name and turned up a genealogy website and a parish council report. Jamie's was legitimately on three sites, all writing ones. Les appeared only on the Montcliff homepage and she didn't bother with Russ. Then, on an impulse, she typed in Philip Holz.

Review of Modern Watercolour

. . . was impressive. **Philip Holz** says that few people use the technique with understanding . . . as **Holz** asserts. The Twenty First century will see an explosion . . .

He was there. It was him. She clicked on the site.

'Philip Holz, painter and assistant editor of the magazine *Paynes* which showcases work from emerging UK artists,' it said, under a photograph of a man sitting at the base of a huge bronze. His hair was short now but she recognized with a pang his fine features and wide smile. The collar of his jacket was turned up and there was something written on his T-shirt that she couldn't make out. 'You knew you'd be an artist,' she said aloud. 'My God, look at you.' Then she felt foolish, as though he could hear her, and clicked the Back button to get rid of his grin.

There were four other sites listed for his name; she checked them all. No other photographs but some more quotations of his, a review of an exhibition in London and an article on Billy Childish. She scanned them eagerly, looking for – what? Her name? A paragraph slipped in somewhere: *But aside from my interest in paint-ing, I must admit that my existence has been an empty sham ever since I parted from Anna, who I can now see was the love of my life. I was so wrong to finish it and I feel Fate has been punishing me ever since. Now I live alone and pine for what might have been.*

She felt compelled to go and check her lipstick in the landing mirror. 'Idiot,' she told her reflection. But after she'd smoothed her hair, instead of going back to the screen she went into the spare bedroom and began shift-ing boxes around. At last she found her university files and underneath them, a little vanity case. She flipped up the catch and took out the papers in there, a letter and some drawings. She didn't open the letter because she knew what was in it, but she did unroll Phil's sketches. He'd done them early on: two of her face, one in profile (and both drawn from memory during a summer vaca-tion), then a nude study of her lying on a sofa, her flesh coloured in with pastels but the sofa only lightly marked in charcoal. There were two cartoons as well, one of her drowning in an enormous sweater – this after an occa-sion where she'd been forced to borrow his clothes – and one of her holding a placard that said *BAN BAD THINGS*. She studied the drawings at length because she had no photographs from that time, having burnt them in a fit of anger six months after they finished.

It had been a jolt to see his smile again.

She took herself back to the computer and ran another search using a different engine and putting Phil instead of Philip. This brought her up the *Paynes* homepage and a short biography:

Phil Holz, 43, lives in East Anglia and runs his own gallery. His work has been regularly exhibited over the whole of the south-east and he has undertaken commissions from overseas. In 2000 his studies of buildings in Norwich were featured on BBC2's History Makers and in the same year he was asked to be on the panel of judges for the Anglian Watercolour Prize. Recent exhibitions have included the John Russell Gallery of Fine Art and the Norwich Gallery. If you are interested in seeing more of Phil's work you can contact him here: <u>holz@tiscali.co.uk</u>.

That scared her. She could click on that address bar and she'd be in touch with him straight away. There was no mention of a partner, nothing personal at all.

The night they'd got together they'd been sitting in the union bar and he was showing her, on the back of a flyer with a biro, how to draw faces. 'Most people put the eyes too high up,' he said. 'They're actually halfway down the skull. See.' He'd opened his thumb and finger like dividers and touched them to her face. She put her own hand to her cheek and without warning he took hold of her wrist and kissed her palm.

Her mother had hated him. In the summer holidays of '83 he'd come up to stay for a week, and Miriam behaved appallingly. If Philip had proposed, Anna would have packed her bags there and then. He hadn't proposed, though. She thought he might when they got back to uni. He'd taken her up the cliffs one day and they'd sat swigging wine and looking out over the Avon Gorge. She'd been so sure he was going to ask that she'd had the wording of her answer all ready.

She brought his photo back up on the screen, looking

for clues. His smile could have been wistful, rueful. There'd be no harm in exchanging a friendly email or two with him, just to find out what stage he was at. Not to start a romance, she wasn't that deluded.

And yet when she looked down at her hand now, it was shaking with nerves. For God's sake, she thought, you already have a husband and a stalker. This, now, this fantasy of another life was almost more of a betrayal than what had happened with Russ. Madness. Another line from Kali's CD slid into her head,

This is the lie, the lie that bites

It was the stress. Maybe she should give *Forest Passage* a spin.

When Jamie got back she was still feeling guilty, but he was in such a mood he didn't notice.

'Les*lie*,' he said, throwing his cardboard file onto the sofa. 'A man.'

'Were you expecting a woman?'

'Whatever. I don't care what damn sex he is as long as he fits in. But all we had all night from him was smut.'

Anna turned away to hide the beginning of a laugh.

'And I don't see how I can get rid of him because he's a friend of Clodagh's. She thinks he's marvellous, of course.'

'How old is he?'

'Young. Forties, thirties perhaps.'

'Clodagh's toy boy.'

'Looks that way. God, where's the whisky? And of

course what he wants to do is read his porn out, he's not interested in anyone else's writing.'

Not interested in yours, thought Anna. 'Was it actual porn, then? I bet that went down well with the likes of Joyce and Margery.'

'You can imagine. It's not as if there's any embargo on swearing, we're all adults. But it's when it comes at you in a stream of filth. It's bloody boring, apart from anything else.'

'Oh dear.'

'He completely upset the dynamics of the group tonight, just monopolized every discussion, brought everything back round to himself. If he's going to be like that every week—'

Jamie dropped back into the chair and rubbed his brow.

'It's better for you when it's all women, isn't it?' Anna observed. 'That last bloke was a problem as well.'

'It's got nothing to do with whether he's male, female or somewhere in the middle. What I do ask for is a bit of respect, to be able to make a point without someone talking over the top of me. I wouldn't mind, but the only thing he's ever had published is a letter in *Your PC*.'

'Presumably that was porn-free.'

He looked at her. 'You're not taking this seriously, are you? Christ, Anna, I have to listen to you dissecting every single bad lesson with bloody Nathan Woods – which is all of them – but you treat my problem like it was a big joke. Double bloody standards or what?'

'Sorry,' she said. 'Go on.'

'I've finished.'

She left him to make a hot drink, let him have his little sulk. Then she came back in and said; 'I do think you should charge for your time, like a proper tutor. That way you'd discourage the disruptive ones and the others might see you as more, well, prestigious.'

'I have no trouble commanding respect from the serious writers,' he said haughtily.

'That's not what I meant.'

'In any case, I get so much out of it myself, it wouldn't seem fair. It's a democratic experience.'

Like hell it is, she thought. Democratic as long as you're the leader. But she only nodded.

'It's such a pleasure to communicate and draw out of people their best work, because they're always surprising themselves. And the way they listen, with their pens poised, and then they do this smile when they've got something and start to scribble it down. It's . . .'

'I know,' she said.

Between them the gas fire popped and flickered. Jamie fingered the edge of his glass and she clasped her mug in both hands, watching the patterns of interference across the coffee's surface.

She thought of Phil: imagine if it were Phil sitting in that chair across from her. All the little events and decisions in life that got you to where you were. If, if, if.

'Get much done, yourself?' he asked after a while.

'The trouble with the Internet,' she said, 'is that there's too much of it. Whole worlds you never knew existed. Some you'd rather not know about. You chase up and down virtual tree branches like some demented e-squirrel, and in the end get nowhere.'

That made him smile. She felt encouraged.

'Does it frighten you,' she said, 'going into middle age?'

'Not especially.'

'It frightens me. Because, because I wonder what I've achieved in my life.'

What if I'd left you, she imagined herself saying. When you made it clear about not wanting babies, refused to take it further, I could have cut my losses and gone. I stayed because I'd made such an investment in our marriage, and because I loved you, even though I hated you too. Make it up to me, Jamie. Do something tonight to show me I made the right decision.

'Jamie?'

'Yeah?'

'What was it about me that made you want to get married, finally?'

'I liked you more than anyone else I'd met, I suppose. Why did you marry me, for that matter? It's probably as much about being in the right place at the right time, deciding to get hitched.'

'Don't you think it's more than that, though?'

'Well, obviously.'

'And what goes before's important too.' Help me, she thought.

'Hmm?'

He was gazing at her forehead as though he could see right into her, see the image of Phil's smile printed on her mind. Now he moved forward in his seat and clenched his fists on his thighs.

'What I meant—' she began. He held his hand up to silence her.

'Wait,' he said. 'I've had this idea. I need . . . to write . . . a poem.'

'Jamie—'

But he was gone.

Anna was trying to keep herself amused in the staff briefing by imagining sex with different colleagues. Say someone walked in now and held a gun to her head and said, Unless you have sex with one person here I'll shoot you, what would she do? It wasn't a great selection. Andrew was the nicest-looking, but he was cynical and over-smart and she'd heard a rumour recently that he was playing around with Liz Yates, which put her off somewhat. Les would be – no, she couldn't go there, it would be too much like having sex with an uncle. Ian Poole was over-toothy and Tom Maxfield had that awful hair. If it had to be Jackson she'd ask to be shot instead.

She glanced over at Chrissy, who was sitting on the edge of her chair taking notes. Did she have affairs? Probably not. Anna couldn't imagine her doing any activity that would jeopardize the crispiness of the fringe.

'So you need to make a note of that because it will affect some classes,' Jackson was saying. Anna came to with a start. What? What would affect her classes? She tried to peer over Andrew's arm to see what he'd written.

'It's going to be quite a prestigious gathering,' Jackson went on. 'It's the first year London has hosted the

Young People's Environmental Delegation and it's an honour for the school to have been asked to sing in the opening ceremony.'

'Will it be the whole choir out?' asked Chrissy.

'Years Seven to Nine. Out all day. It's a long way down to London.'

'Can you give us the date again?'

'December sixth.'

'That's the last day of the lower-school examinations period. What will we be doing about the children who miss those papers?'

Jackson shrugged. 'There'll be a lot out, won't there? We'll reschedule those exams to the following day.'

Anna had found the right page of her diary. 'Which will be a Saturday.'

'The Monday, then.'

'But we're supposed to be starting reports on the Monday. And I'll have two Years' worth of papers coming in late.'

'There's a chance the ceremony will be on TV,' said Jackson, as though that clinched the matter. 'I'm going to send out a special bulletin to the parents about it.'

I'll never manage, thought Anna in despair. I'll never get them all done for the end of term.

'Fuckwit,' said Andrew under his breath. 'Get your priorities right, Jackson, why don't you?'

The Head beamed on his podium.

After the meeting had broken up, she went straight to Chrissy. 'You've *got* to tell him. I can't get the reports written if I'm still marking papers and I can't write the reports in advance because I need the grades to put on them.'

Chrissy made a sympathetic face that told Anna she had no chance. 'I'll try, but he's so keen on marketing the school there's not a lot I can do. He likes his TV cameras, doesn't he?'

You don't want to bother, more like, thought Anna. Heads of department only taught half a timetable.

'Does nothing in this fucking institution work?' said Andrew somewhere behind her. She turned round and saw him slap the top of the water heater.

'It's not turned on,' said Les.

'Yes, it is. See.' Andrew flicked the switch a couple of times. 'Some of us haven't had a drink yet.'

'Maybe it's fused. I'll give Stu a ring and ask him to bring the kettle up from the workshop while he has a look.'

The bell for the end of break went and Andrew rolled his eyes. 'Brilliant. Mug of cold water it is, then. And when will the photocopier be fixed, Les?'

'Is the copier broken as well?' Anna could have cried.

'Out of toner. It'll be after lunch, I'd have thought.'

So her Year Eight worksheets that she'd been going to duplicate now in her free period wouldn't be ready for lesson four. She'd have to come up with something else quickly. A griping pain in the bottom of her stomach reminded her that she'd started bleeding again that morning. I could walk out of this building this minute and never come back, she thought.

She sat for twenty minutes working out a new activity for the next class, though nothing was really satisfactory, and then she went to the toilet to change her pad. After that she tried to mark some poems but it was hard to keep her mind on the task. Outside the work-room Stu was drilling the wall and someone was playing a tape called *Choisissez Bien!* in ten-second bursts. Then Mrs Hislop called her name.

'In here.'

'A letter for you. I was going to pop it in your pigeon-hole but it says urgent.' Mrs Hislop held out the envelope and Anna took it, her heart sinking. Russ *again*. She wanted to rip the thing into tiny pieces and then drive home and kill herself.

'Thanks.'

'You're still not looking very well. Did you manage to get away over the break?'

'Yes. That was part of the problem.' The words slipped out before she'd thought them through.

Mrs Hislop's mouth made an O shape, and she looked round to check whether anyone else was listening. 'I see.' She moved nearer. 'Trouble at home?'

'Mmm.'

'Anna?'

'I don't want to, here . . .'

'Of course.' *Numéro dix-sept*, went the tape outside. 'If there's anything, if you want to talk to someone about it.'

Anna nodded. It would have been so comforting to let go at last, spill everything out and have Mrs Hislop listen and nod and make soothing noises. Except Mrs Hislop was a nice woman and what Anna had done wasn't, and she could never confess it to anyone. She was beyond the pale.

'I'm sorry. I didn't realize you were having problems. You always seem so' – Mrs Hislop gave a little laugh – 'self-contained.'

'Well, yes.'

There was an awkward pause. *Maintenant, à vous de choisir.*

'Can I help at all?'

'Don't think so.'

'Let me get you something. Cup of tea? We've got some mint Options in the office.'

'No, really.'

À quoi sert un aspirateur?

'If you're sure. A HobNob?'

Anna made herself smile. 'Take more than a HobNob to sort my life out.'

The staff phone began to ring.

'You want to watch your blood sugar,' said Mrs Hislop as she left the workroom. 'I don't believe you eat enough.'

Il sert à nettoyer les tapis; il sert à chauffer les croissants; il sert à laver les fenêtres. Vous êtes prêts? Un, deux, trois, top . . .

Anna picked up the letter and went out.

The garden was empty and very still. There wasn't even anyone down on the games field beyond the far hedge.

I'm writing this, Russ began, *at a children's birthday party and I'm desperate.* In spite of everything, Anna's mouth twitched. What did he sound like? The wind flapped the Timbershop invoice back over itself and she pulled her jacket more tightly around her body.

I'm pleading with you, let me see you again. I think I'll go mad if you don't. Everything's going wrong, my life's all over the place. Sometimes I wonder if it's worth carrying on with it all.

Oh, God, was that meant to be a threat?

I look round me and I think what did I work all these years for because it hasn't made me happy. If you said the word I'd walk out tomorrow. That's the truth.

It might well be. And what would life be like with Russ? It hadn't ever been a consideration. Even in the early days she'd blocked out ideas of anything beyond the caravan bed. They'd never had sex anywhere else, never met up outside of the van without partners in tow. No secret lunches or trips to the art gallery. There wouldn't have been any point – extra risk she could do without – and it would have given him the wrong idea. But you can make any rules you want when you start an affair; in the end they're meaningless.

Let me at least meet you to tell you about the way I feel. You owe me that.

'I don't owe you anything, I've told you,' she said out loud.

Please Anna, please please please.

She had a second's image of Russ on his knees, naked. It was appalling. The trouble was, he was a weak man. We could all give up, she thought. We could all of us throw our hands in the air and walk out of our identities the way you'd shrug off an old coat onto the floor. He should try losing the hope of a baby month after month.

A car went past on the gravel behind the yew screen.

PS, Russ had scrawled under the Timbershop logo at the bottom of the page, *If you don't come to me, I'll come to you*.

Suddenly she couldn't stand the cold any longer. She folded the letter up and put it into her pocket, then hurried across the drive and up the steps to the main doors. Still twenty minutes before she had to teach; a coffee would help steady her nerves.

The first person she saw was Kali, dawdling by the back stairs.

'What are you doing out of lessons?' Anna said automatically.

Kali's face lit up. 'Mrs Lloyd! Got something for you.' She let her shoulder bag slide down her arm onto the floor and bent to reach inside it. 'Here.'

'What is it?'

'My essay on Ted Hughes.'

'But that's not due in till Wednesday.'

'I know, I thought I'd get it in early.'

Through her unhappiness, Anna was touched. 'Thank you. It does make my life easier if I'm not having to chase work. I don't think you students understand that teachers have an existence outside school as well.'

'*I* understand,' said Kali. There were glass beads in her hair; that was against the rules.

'While we have a moment,' Anna said, 'I wanted to apologize.'

'What for?'

'Mentioning your poetry in class like that. I realize now you probably wanted it kept secret.'

'Huh?'

'When Nathan, when Nathan kissed you—'

Kali pressed her lips together to make an unhappy mouth. 'Oh, yeah. Doesn't matter.' She pulled her bag back onto her shoulder and put one foot on the bottom step. 'Nathan's a prick.'

'Sorry?'

'Nathan's a not-very-nice person, Mrs Lloyd.'

'Oh; I thought you and he . . .'

'Not any more.'

'You don't seem especially upset.'

'I'm not.' She tossed her head. 'I'm worth more than that.'

Good for you! thought Anna. She felt warmed. She wanted to say, 'I'm proud of you,' or something inappropriately emotional. Even if her own life was a mess, here was this young girl getting it right. 'Thank you for the essay, anyway.'

'No probs.'

Kali was turning away.

'Bye,' Anna heard herself say. (How stupid, she'd be seeing her that afternoon.) The back page of the essay detached itself and floated down to the lino tiles and as she bent to pick it up, she could see plainly that the assignment wasn't finished. She brought the page closer to her face. Not even half done. What about the other sheets? She turned them over to check in case they were in the wrong order, but there was nothing. A fancy title page, a side and a half of writing, stop.

A little cry of indignation escaped her. 'Kali? Kali!'

'What?'

It was just the last straw. That the girl should wind her up like this.

'Tell me the point of handing in work that's incomplete. What are you trying to achieve?'

'I don't know what you mean.'

Anna's eyes pricked. God, how ridiculous, she was filling up, she was going to cry here in the corridor. It was disastrous. At her feet the chequered tiles fused into a general grey. If she blinked now, the tears would spill.

Then she was being guided to the locker room under the stairs, out of the way. Kali's voice: 'Mrs Lloyd? What's the matter? Mrs Lloyd?'

Anna wiped her face on her sleeve. They were standing in dim light among sports bags and dented metal cabinets.

Humiliation rendered her dumb. To set the context of her distress was impossible; to admit instead that the reason for her tears was this poor ruse—

'Shall I get someone?'

'No!'

'What is it, Mrs Lloyd? Are you ill?'

With a sob, Anna threw the essay down among the bags and put her fingers over her eyes.

She was aware of Kali picking the essay up. 'Oh my God,' she heard her say in tones of amazement, 'there's a section missing. Is that what you're upset about?'

Anna made no reply.

'It's nothing to be upset about. I've got the rest at home, I'll bring it in tomorrow.'

The lie shouldn't have mattered so much, but she couldn't seem to stop the tears. Her chin was wet with them.

'Shit,' said Kali under her breath. 'I'll go and get someone, yeah?'

'No, please.'

'I'll get you some paper towel, then.'

As soon as she was alone, Anna felt calmer. *Stop it, stop it*, she told herself. Year Eight next, and she needed to clear her head, to think over her revised lesson plan. Deep breaths. She could set them a word game from the textbook while she wrote the instructions up on the board. Books: she still had their books, so those had to go back, with debriefing notes. (She blotted her nose with her cuff.) And they could do spelling corrections to start with.

'Here you are,' said Kali, blocking the light momentarily as she came in. 'Okay?'

'I'm fine.' Anna patted at her cheeks with the green towel. She was going to have to use some powder and even then her eyes would still be red. 'You need to get to your lesson. You could be there for the last five minutes.'

'It's only French. Crap language, I'm crap at it. Trust me, five minutes'll make no difference either way.'

'Why were you out of the classroom?'

Kali put her hand to her belly. 'Period pain. Crippling. I had to go get paracetamol from the sick bay.' She paused. 'Are you ill, Mrs Lloyd?'

'Only the monthly blues, like you. It's no fun being female at times, is it?'

And the moment flicked from pupil-and-teacher to two women talking, then back again.

'Go on, Kali. The bell'll be going in a minute. You can be early for your next lesson.'

'Yeah . . .' A split second of gloom and light and she was out of the room, and Anna began straightening her cuffs and smoothing her hair off her face where tears had made it stick.

'Mrs Lloyd?'

Anna jumped. 'Oh! Kali, what is it?'

'Do you wanna go for a walk?'

'What?'

'We could go in the gardens again where nobody could see us. You could tell me why you're so upset.'

Anna didn't know whether to laugh or scold. 'I have a lesson to go to. So do you. What have you got next?'

'Art.'

'You like art, you told me.'

'I know. I just thought you might want to talk.'

'My Year Eights are waiting.'

'OK.' Kali smiled and shrugged her bag back into place. 'But, you know, if you ever do—'

The bell on the wall opposite went off suddenly like a pneumatic drill. 'I'll bear it in mind,' said Anna, through the noise.

Chapter Ten

There was nothing for it but to go to Russ. The idea of his turning up anywhere, at any time, was too much to be endured. Perhaps if she let him have one final say.

So she was driving to the caravan in the early evening dark and thinking not about Russ but about her wedding day, and the person she'd been then and the kind of future she thought she had ahead of her. All Jamie's colleagues had been convinced he was a bachelor for life. She'd worked hard to get him and been jubilant when he suggested they get married. At the time she'd assumed the reason for his proposal was that he felt he'd finally met his soulmate; they were so alike, both quietly independent. Now, though, she thought it was more a calculation that she was someone who'd make the least impact on his life, the fewest demands. They'd been together for almost eight years at that point.

For the day itself she'd worn a black-and-white suit with a broad-brimmed hat. The skirt had to be taken in at the last minute. 'My goodness,' Jamie's father said. 'Look at you. Audrey Hepburn.'

'Welcome to the family, sis,' Russ said over and over

again, touching her arm, her shoulder, until Ruth looked at him sharply.

'There aren't many from your side, are there, Anna?' she observed. 'A shame, no one to give you away, that's really sad.'

Jamie laughed. 'She doesn't come free with a gallon of petrol. That crowd—' He'd pointed to the low wall at the entrance where a group of teenage girls were enjoying a confetti fight. 'They're here for Anna. They're in her tutor group. They sewed her a tablecloth.'

Later, as they drove away to their honeymoon, Jamie said: 'I don't know why people spend a fortune on weddings. That kind of show isn't needed. We didn't need it, did we?'

Two people running cool: it ought to have worked well. And the marriage would have been fine, if she hadn't decided to rock the boat with her unreasonable demands.

Russ was waiting in the caravan, peering out of the window for her. He let her in and she stood sniffing at the damp smell. She had cleaned round before she'd left it, but you can't stop dust from settling in your absence. No bedding, so he couldn't expect any sex. Had they really lain on that nasty mattress?

'Anna.' He held out his arms but she went and sat on the other side of the van, six feet away from him. He shrugged, then folded out the little table and produced a hip flask from his jacket pocket. She watched with irritation as he searched fruitlessly for two cups. *I cleared them all out, bozo*, she thought.

'So what do you want, Russ?'

'You know what I want.' He took a swig from the flask and flopped down on the banquette. 'I thought I'd made myself pretty plain.'

'Me too. Listen, you've got to stop sending me letters and hanging round the house. It's asking for trouble. Ruth's going to work out what's going on eventually, or Jamie.'

'I'm leaving her.'

'No, you're not, Russ.'

'I fucking am.'

Instant, total panic. 'No—'

'Yes, I am. Don't try to persuade me not to.'

She could have flung herself on the floor like the Victorian painting. The blood pounded in her ears. 'Please, Russ, no, you mustn't, I can't leave Jamie, I *can't*.'

'That's answered that question, anyway,' he said, and put the flask to his lips for a long time. At last he finished drinking and wiped his face with the heel of his hand. 'Just wanted to be sure.'

'Why now? What good will it do?' She imagined Ruth's fat face shiny and distorted with grief, with anger. 'You can't walk out on your family.'

'Don't you tell me what I can and can't do,' he cried and hurled the flask at her feet. She jumped out of the way as it bounced into the wood panel skirting of the sofa and skidded across the carpet.

'Jesus, Russ!'

And that was it, he was crying: no surprises there. On the one hand you had Jamie, always so collected and controlled, but it was drama all the way with the brother.

She watched in dismay as Russ pressed his fist against his forehead and hunched his shoulders.

What to do.

Against her better judgement she got up and went to him. 'Come on, now,' she said, putting her arm across his back. 'Come on.'

At once he turned and tried an embrace, as she'd been afraid he would. 'No, Russ. That won't help.'

'It's all going wrong,' he said. 'There's no point.'

'In what?'

'In anything.'

And when he lifted his face, there was such hopelessness in it she felt really frightened.

'Sit down,' she told him, because she couldn't think what else to say. She wished now she hadn't taken away the kettle; at least it would have been something to do, make him a hot drink.

He did as he was told and she knelt near him – not close enough for him to grab, but close enough to indicate support.

'I can't think,' he said flatly.

'You ought to see your GP. You might need something to get you over this; I know my mother used to take Valium sometimes. Not that you'd want to be like her. But they've got new drugs, non-addictive ones.'

'Yeah. I don't – I just—'

She waited.

'You know,' he said at last, 'I've got to my forties and I look round and it's like, where's my life going? Do you know that feeling? Because I've worked so fucking hard for years and years but I'm not actually happy, at all. At all. I have nothing that's my own.' (*Your children!* thought Anna, but she didn't dare interrupt.) 'The fucking bank owns my house, the fucking bank owns my business. What there is of it, 'cause that's nearly down the pan. Ruth contributes sod-all to the household except for moaning and nagging and spending money on tat we don't need. The kids constantly want attention or cash but they won't bloody do as they're told, it's all one-way. Tasha had a bloody awful report last term, seems to think school's a huge joke. Beth's going the same way, and Tom . . . Jesus. I look at him and I think . . . And it feels like it's one huge conspiracy, like I'm working my bollocks off and getting absolutely no reward. I'll tell you—'

His tears had dried now and he was looking a bit wild.

'You need a break,' said Anna. 'The routine's getting you down.'

'It's more than that!' he flashed. 'I'm trying to explain. It's like a con trick. You think your marriage'll be different so you get drawn in and then you find you're on exactly the same treadmill as everyone else. Parents' sodding evenings, and visiting the in-laws – every other Saturday round to lunch because it's written in bloody stone, her mother going on and on about stuff that doesn't matter like who's in hospital this week and which neighbour they've fallen out with – and taxiing the kids about and changing the sheets when one of them has a mate to sleep over and they wet the sodding bed. In the mornings, right, I'm trying to get out the house and Ruth is sloping around in her dressing gown because of course she's got another hour before she has to leave but I still have to help make the breakfast, and trying to make them say what they want is like pulling teeth because they're all gawping at the TV. I've told Ruth to switch it off but she says if she does then they fight. So nearly every damn morning I'm late getting in and then there's a load of hassle from the delivery men.

'I'm so *bored*, Anna. There's never any time for *me*; I have to ask permission before I can go have an hour in the shed. We go shopping and they fill the trolley up with shit and then when I come to get a beer in the evening, the fridge is empty. It's like I come last on the list. And I keep thinking, if I was on my own—'

He paused and looked sideways at her.

'I get it,' she said.

'Do you? I don't think you do. You pick up your pay cheque every month and that's all you have to worry about. But it's a whole different ball game being self-employed. I took a wage cut in July and no one else did. There. Didn't know that, did you? Being the boss is the worst job. Have you any idea how much we paid in tax last year? Fucking ridiculous. I wouldn't mind if you saw anything for it, but when the warehouse was broken into, I had to call the police twice before they'd come out.'

Anna began to relax slightly. She'd heard this part before. The brown curtain above her head stirred in a draught; there must still be a loose fitting round the window. The place needed work, more than a good clean. That or torching. What would the new renters of the caravan make of it? Probably use it for wholesome family holidays, for walking or birdwatching. Normal things.

'I just feel cheated,' Russ was saying. 'Ruth's too busy being a mother and the kids have no respect for me and I get no return on work. You were the only thing that kept me going.'

She saw his hand come out for her.

'Anna, please.'

Please what? She stretched out her arm wearily and he grasped her fingers in his.

'It wasn't all one-sided, was it? Tell me it wasn't. I think I could leave it if you told me that.'

'Could you?' (Oh, thank God.) 'No, it wasn't one-sided. I enjoyed it too.' (At first, a little bit, before you got too needy.)

'At least I know where I stand.'

You always did, she thought.

They sat in silence for a while, then he said: 'You look so unhappy.'

Is it any wonder? she almost blurted. 'I'm fine. I wish I could make us a drink. Are you feeling a bit better now?'

She was so sure he was going to say yes, give her a hug. Hadn't she talked him round, made him see sense? They'd part on good terms finally and she'd go back free of his angry shadow to the disorder that was the rest of her life.

'I'm still leaving Ruth, though.'

She stared at him in confusion. 'For God's sake, why?'

'Because she's pregnant again, and it's the last straw.'

*

It's like suddenly living under ultra-violet light, Anna had written the first time she'd miscarried. While the pupils sat and listed their secrets, she'd poured her grief out on an A4 lined Oxford pad. *I'm amazed at how the landscape's changed. Most of what's around me has receded into a kind of dim grey monotony, but some objects – prams, babies, a shelf of pregnancy magazines – jump out and ambush me. Whack! Whack! when you're least expecting it. It's so bloody horribly disorientating. A month ago I was lying on the sofa feeling dog-tired and queasy, watching a woman on TV cook spiced beef, and I was thinking, 'This time next year there'll be a baby here with me.' And now there won't be. I don't think I can bear it.*

'How long before everything feels normal again?' she'd asked the doctor. He'd talked for three minutes about hormone levels and by the time he'd finished she didn't have the strength to rephrase the question.

Jamie's attempt at consolation was to remind her that she'd not been completely sure herself about what it would mean to have a baby. 'Be honest,' he said, 'you were worried about the impact it might have on us. It's a major life change, you admitted that.' It was true. She had been anxious, on and off, up to the moment where the pregnancy failed, at which point she became surer than anything else in the world that what she wanted was a child. And now none of her colleagues or neighbours understood or gave her any sympathy, and the fact she'd not told them she'd had a miscarriage was no excuse for their callous indifference. She hated them all.

On the day a second card came from the hospital

inviting her to a scan she no longer needed, Anna confided in Mel.

Mel was anti-babies. She'd always said so. 'Women have children because they can't think what else to do with themselves. It's a way of opting out,' was her line. 'It's the only way a lot of them have of achieving anything. The only identity they have comes through their kids. But you only have to look round: a kid on the scene wrecks your adult relationships, ruins your looks and cripples you financially. You're never ever free of the responsibility. Children hang round your neck till the day you die. Show me a mother and I'll show you a sad frustrated cow.'

Though she didn't say any of this when Anna told her about miscarrying. She offered to go with her to the doctor's for some zopiclone and to book them both a break at a spa; a week later she presented Anna with a twenty-pound voucher for Jo Malone. It was the best she could do. Miscarriage for Mel would have meant cracking open the champagne. And she was doing well, she was saying all the right things, but then she went, 'Perhaps it was for the best. These things happen for a reason,' and Anna could have clawed her eyes out.

Which was better, this lack of comprehension or the sneering of the fertile? *Baby on Board. I ♥ MY BUMP.* Might as well have a sign in the window saying, Look at me, you barren old stick. Special rage was reserved for Ruth, with her wide hips and her food-stained lapels; Ruth, who said things like, 'I don't think you really grow up till you give birth', and 'What are we put on this earth for if it's not to have children?' Admittedly, she didn't know about the miscarriages. She thought Anna was being awkward. There's a special place in hell reserved for those who make assumptions about a woman's reproductive plans.

At least time spent with Mel had been safe. A rational adult in a staffroom full of broody hens. God, she missed her. She really missed her.

'How do you know Ruth's pregnant?' Anna managed at last.

Russ closed his eyes for a moment.

'I'm not a hundred per cent certain, but I'm pretty sure. She won't let me touch her boobs, she keeps saying she's tired and she's fatter than she was.'

'That might be too much cake,' said Anna meanly. Her hate glowed like a light sabre in her fists; she wanted to cut through Russ and Ruth and Jamie and leave them bleeding on the ground.

'She's drinking pints of orange juice. And she's been sorting out old drawers, making these little heaps of clothes. I tell you, she's expecting. I know the signs. We've been here before.'

'So you're leaving.'

His face contorted with fury. 'Didn't I always say no more kids? Didn't I? Three's too many, never mind, I wasn't even sure about two – God, *you* knew how I felt so she must have.'

Anna knew exactly how he felt about babies. He and Jamie were not so far apart, on this matter, after all.

'I said it enough times. Shit, I all but hired a bill-board. I've said again and again, I've done the baby thing and I want to move on. It's like being trapped in a bloody time warp, bloody Groundhog Day. Have you *any* idea what having a small baby around involves?'

'No,' said Anna.

'You see, *you* wouldn't know. You get no sleep for years. Imagine that. *Years*. Tash was *five* before she started sleeping through properly, Beth was bad till she was three. Tom still gets up sometimes if he has a lot to drink and needs a pee, and then he won't settle. I *can't* go through it all again, go back to the beginning and start all over— It's like she's tricked me. We'd agreed, Ruth said she'd get something sorted—' He made an unconscious strangling movement with his hands. '—But she obviously didn't. It's *her* fault.'

Anna was imagining Ruth in a hospital bed handing a baby into her arms. 'Here you are, Anna,' she'd say. 'You adopt her' (because it was a girl). But the baby would have that pig-nose, they all did, and she didn't want Ruth's ugly baby, she wanted one of her own. Even if that scene ever happened, which it wouldn't.

'Apart from anything else,' Russ went on, and Anna could hear moments of Jamie's intonation, Jamie's phrasing; 'we can't afford it. I mean, we threw everything out after Tom and there's so much *junk* goes with having a baby, sterilizing units and fucking collapsible prams, and the thought of having stinking nappy sacks sitting round the house again. And then you have to rearrange everything so there's a fucking playpen stuck in the middle of the room, and there's stairgates to put up so you're constantly climbing over them or trapping your fingers in the catches, and every socket in the entire place has to have a guard, even the toilet lid has to have a special catch on it in case the baby falls in and drowns. It gets like a fucking obstacle course. Ruth goes all stupid after she's given birth and like she's only interested in the baby, so that means I'll have to do all the housework because *she's busy*. And it's just as the kids were beginning to get independent, so when we go out they can now all climb in the car themselves and put their own seat belts on, the first time in thirteen years. When you go anywhere with a baby it takes a bloody hour to get ready, and half that's fiddling with the bloody car seat straps. I *cannot* go back to that, Anna. And if walking out makes me a shit, then so be it. I told her, I laid it on the line, you've got three already, no more. No more.'

It should have been me, she wanted to scream. She had to put her hand over her mouth to stop herself; Russ took the gesture to be one of disapproval.

'I knew you wouldn't come with me but I'm going anyway.'

She said nothing.

'I fucking will, you see.' His mouth turned downwards and his eyes started to fill again.

She squeezed the air out of her lungs with an effort.

'I can't help you,' she said.

It was a relief to be back in school with a timetabled day ahead. Jackson was out all morning but he'd pinned a notice up before he left; Anna noticed the cluster of heads around the pastoral board as soon as she walked into the staffroom.

She put her book bag down under the pigeonholes and went over. 'What's going on?'

'Big news,' said Liz Yates, flicking her long hair over her shoulder. 'Our Nathan's going to be a star.'

'Sorry?'

'Oh, but he's a star already,' said Andrew.

Liz smirked and ran a finger round the top of her knee boots. Anna pushed forward to read the message.

NATHAN WOODS Y10 ANDREW MAYE

The school has received a letter from Mr and Mrs Woods informing us that Nathan has been chosen to appear in a television commercial which will be filmed in the New Year. They are not able at present to give us specific dates but believe it will be around February/March and will involve about three days' absence from school. I shall post a reminder nearer the time, but I have assured Mr and Mrs Woods that his teachers will be understanding about homework during this period.

Nathan feels very positive about being given this opportunity and I hope staff will be supportive.

C. Jackson

She snorted. 'Understanding about homework? In what sense? Given that he never does any normally. He's three pieces behind already this term. What's this advert for, anyway?'

'Mazdas,' said Liz. 'I asked him just now. He plays the teenage son in a Family Who Knows How to Have Fun. His job is to slide a surfboard into the back of an MPV and then slap the top of the car. He's got to wear shorts, apparently.'

'God, what a thought.' Andrew rolled his eyes. 'How on earth did he get the gig?'

'He says he auditioned that week he was suspended. His mum and dad were staying near where they were casting and he walked in off the street. He wasn't first choice but the boy they chose got ill or something. Luck of the devil, that one. Mind you, I bet he'll be good at it, I can see him on TV. He's got that confidence.'

The phone rang and Liz went to answer it. Andrew rubbed his chin gloomily.

'I wonder how much he's being paid?'

'Somewhat more than we get for a day's work,' said Anna.

'Ah, but none of us has Nathan's natural charisma.'

'He's going to be awful this week, isn't he?'

'Yup.'

Andrew pursed his lips and she thought what a good jawline he had, almost like a male model. There was a girlfriend, a high-flying business type who earned more than he did and owned property in Chester. And then there was this supposed thing going on with Liz, which she preferred not to think about.

'Well, thank God I don't teach Year Ten on a Wednesday.' She opened her planner on the coffee table: Year Nine, Seven, Eight, Lower Sixth. Not a bad morning's line-up.

Out of the corner of her eye she saw Les come in and make some alterations to the day's notices with a red pen.

'By the way,' he said over his shoulder. 'Your hippy friend's had a bit of bother recently.'

'Who?'

'The ethereal Ms Norman. Not the most popular girl in town at the moment.'

Anna was alert at once. 'What's happened?'

'Some girls in the year below have taken against her. Apparently Nathan had promised to go out with a Year Nine, I forget who, but then he got off with Kali at that party and she got the blame. Then, when she kicked him into touch, that made them even madder. Perverse creatures. Liz intercepted some poisonous notes being passed round during a lesson.'

'To Kali?'

'No, just between the group. It's the usual Year Nine instability. Liz's had a talk to them.' Les sighed and ran his finger along the master timetable. 'I don't know, you females.'

'But she's all right?'

'Far as I can tell. She's the cat that likes to walk by itself. I can't see her being too concerned, can you?' He paused and scribbled something out, drew an arrow down the side of the notice and then an asterisk. 'Ah, damn, sorry, Andrew,' he said. 'There's no one else free then.'

'What have you put me down for?'

'Period four, Tom's class. He's got a hospital appointment this morning and everyone else is out on this history trip.'

Andrew walked over and peered at the board. 'Aw, shit, you are kidding me, Les.'

'Sorry.'

'But it's Year Ten again and I have most of that group period three for Social Studies.'

Les spread his hands.

'So,' Andrew went on, 'that's two solid hours of Nathan Woods, plus I see him for morning and afternoon registration. Can't do it. No way, Les, no way. I'll end up killing him.'

'There really isn't anyone else available. Look, I'd supervise it myself but I'm invigilating. I appreciate it's not ideal.'

'Not ideal? Not fucking ideal?'

Anna made a generally sympathetic face, but the men were watching each other.

'What can I say, Andrew? Send him out if he's any trouble.'

'Yeah, yeah. Spends half his life in that fucking corridor. All I can say is, he'd better not give me any shit because I'm not in the mood.' Andrew stalked across to the exit, scowling. 'And I tell you what, if he wants a fight, he can have one.'

'PMT,' mouthed Les when the door had banged shut. Anna laughed.

As it turned out, Nathan didn't even last through period three; Anna came across him just after 11.30 when she nipped back to the staffroom for a textbook she'd forgotten. He was lounging in a plastic chair with his feet up on the desk that had been set outside for him. His worksheet was on the floor.

'Feet off the table,' she barked as she ran past. He slid his legs down without looking at her. She knew that as soon as she was round the corner he'd put them straight back up again. She must tell Andrew to check that desk for graffiti.

She heard nothing more till the dinner bell went. She was gathering up her Sixth Form essays and chatting to a new girl who'd transferred at the start of term, when Andrew appeared in the doorway.

'Where can I find Les?'

'Isn't he in the staffroom?'

Andrew shook his head.

'Hang on.' Anna checked a sheet in the back of her planner. 'According to this, he's in the hall finishing off a public exam. He should be up by five past, ten past at the latest. Why, what's the matter?'

Andrew paused and looked at the student, but the girl had already taken her cue. 'See you tomorrow, Mrs Lloyd. And thanks for the extra notes.'

'Yes, see you tomorrow. Would you mind closing the door on the way out?'

As soon as they were alone, he said, 'I've got Nathan in detention.'

'Why am I not surprised. What's he done?'

'Nothing spectacular, just the usual insolence. Only I'm not in the mood for it today.'

'You said.'

She watched Andrew's throat jerk with anger, noted the way his gaze darted around. By the time the male students get to GCSEs they're men squaring up to men, she thought. But emasculated by the system. She could tell Andrew longed to roll up his sleeves and take it outside.

'I asked him,' he said, 'for his homework, which of

course he hadn't done. So then I asked for his planner so I could put a note in it to his parents, and he reckoned he hadn't got it. I said, "I can see it, there, in your blazer pocket." So I'm writing an essay in his book – like his parents will care – and I hear him go, "Ooh, I'm scared now." And the lads around are, you know, sniggering. Normally I'd have ignored it but sometimes you get this thing where you think, what the hell, so I said, "You should be, mate." He goes, "Yeah?" And then I lost it. I shouted that I'd had enough of his smart remarks and it was about time he understood that he's not nearly as clever as he thinks— Some other stuff, too.' Andrew put his fingers to his temples for a second. 'I was really shouting, Anna.'

'What was his reaction?'

'His face went white and I thought he might swear at me, but he didn't. I moved Martin and Umair from either side of him because they were pulling stupid faces and he's worse with an audience. So, when he was sitting on his own and I was sure he wasn't going to respond, I turned back to the board, and straight away I heard this chair scrape. He'd got up and gone to sit next to Martin. That was it – and we were only twenty minutes into the lesson. I booted him outside but I kept the classroom door open so I could see he was still at his desk. I didn't want him just taking off.'

Anna nodded, imagining the possibilities for a boy like Nathan left to roam the building in the uninterrupted quiet of lesson-time.

'He was in the corridor for an hour and a half, then?'

'No, because towards the end I realized he'd gone,

must have sneaked away while I was helping someone. I was about to send to the staffroom for help when he reappeared. "Been to the bogs," was his excuse. But he'd got a packet of crisps in his pocket and a can of Lilt, so I assume he had a little trip to the vending machines. That's when I told him he was in detention.'

'What did he do?'

'Shrugged. Came with me, started his worksheet. But he's legged it again. I had him in room 16 but when I went to check two minutes later, no Nathan.' Andrew sat down on the student desk in front of her and gripped the edges on either side. 'He could be anywhere and I know I should be looking for him but I need reinforcements, Anna. I am so bloody furious, I don't trust myself—'

I don't trust you either, she thought. She picked up her books and thrust them into her bag. 'You need Les.'

'Yeah.'

'Right. Well, you try the office, I'll see if he's in the staffroom. Try not to punch anyone's lights out on the way.'

He gave her a weary look. 'You know how it is, though, don't you?'

She decided not to reply to this.

Outside in the corridor she passed Kali, who gave her a thumbs up for no apparent reason. Anna hesitated, but the girl had passed in a waft of perfume. Her hair was down today and spread out over the shoulders of her non-regulation coat.

'I got your essay,' called Anna. Kali turned and smiled, walked on.

In the staffroom Anna learned that Les had come out of the exam and was now tied up interviewing a sixth-former, but Jackson was back in the office. He can sort Nathan out, then, she thought. It's what he's paid for.

She made herself a drink and went to unpack her lunch, except that when she pulled open the fridge, her sandwich box wasn't there. Had someone taken it? Surely not. She had a quick glance round the staff all the same. Had she even brought it in? Or was it even now sitting on the drainer at home waiting for her to add a yoghurt? That seemed likely, given the state her mind was in these days. Fuck. That would mean trailing down to the canteen.

The phone rang and she remembered Andrew again.

She could look for Nathan on the way, that would be a help.

Chapter Eleven

She saw him almost straight away. You couldn't have said he was hiding, but he wasn't drawing attention to himself as usual, and he'd chosen a seat facing the corner farthest away from the door. No one was sitting with him. The shape of his back was warning enough.

Anna stepped between tables. Before she bought her lunch, she would tell Nathan to get up to the Head's room. She was not going to get involved in any confrontation, simply tell him to move.

No reaction when she spoke his name. He carried on eating as though she wasn't there.

She tried again. 'You're in detention. Leave that and go to see Mr Jackson.' She might have been invisible. 'Now, please.'

Nothing.

She squatted down so that her face was level with his shoulder. It gave him a height advantage but it meant he couldn't ignore her so easily. 'Nathan. Come on.'

'I'm not leaving my burger.'

'I beg your pardon?'

'I said—' He turned his head towards her and enunciated the words as though she were stupid: 'I'm not – leaving – my – burger. I've paid for it.'

'That's beside the point. You shouldn't have come down here when you'd been told to stay in room 16.' She tried to speak crisply and without aggression. 'Go on, Mr Jackson's waiting.'

'You pay for it, then. There's no way I'm leaving food I've bought unless you give me my money back. You owe me two quid.'

'Don't be ridiculous.'

'I'm not going, then.'

'Oh, come on, Nathan.' Irritated, she put her hand on his shoulder and in that split second she knew her mistake.

Nathan leapt to his feet, screaming, *'Get off me get off me get OFF ME.'* The sudden volume stunned her. Simultaneously he made a sweeping movement with his arm and something cold struck her very hard on the cheekbone. She cried out and covered her eyes on a reflex. China smashed on tiles behind her. She was aware of him pushing past her.

The dining room went quiet.

'Mrs Lloyd?' That was one of the dinner ladies. 'Is she all right? Hey, young man!' Arms guided her to a bench. A voice nearby said, *Oh, my God, did you see?* 'Has he hurt your eye, Mrs Lloyd?'

Anna took her hand away, feeling giddy. 'It hasn't broken the skin,' someone said. 'He went berserk, didn't he?' The dining room murmur was rising again, or perhaps that was her ears whooshing. Below her eye a band of skin throbbed and she moved her fingers back to her temple, shielding herself from the light.

'Oh, God.' That was Liz Yates. 'What happened? You all right, Anna?'

'Where is he?'

'Nathan? Stormed out. I'll ring the staffroom in a minute.'

Then she heard Kali's voice. 'Get some ice. When my mum's boyfriend hit her she always put ice on it.'

'No, I'm fine. I need to go and wash my face, that's all.' If she could get to the toilets she'd be all right. A girl close by hissed, 'Is she crying?'

'Let me take you, Mrs Lloyd.' Kali put an arm round her waist.

'Thank you, Kali,' said Liz. 'But I'll see to her.'

Anna let herself be led across the quad to the staff cloakroom and waited till Liz had dragged in a plastic chair from the room next door.

'Sit down. You look like you're about to puke.'

In some very rough schools the children carried knives, she'd read; swore at the staff daily. Last week she'd read in the *TES* about a teacher being raped by a pupil. The Head at Jamie's school had been threatened with a baseball bat. This was nothing, really.

'I'm OK, it was just a surprise. Let me look in the mirror.' There was a red mark under Anna's eye, as though someone had dabbed their finger on a lipstick and then wiped it across her cheekbone. The rest of her face was gaunt and poorly-looking but she wasn't damaged. Reflected over her shoulder she could see

Liz's bright complexion, her enquiring eyes. 'Did you see what happened?'

'No. I only looked when I heard you shout.' Liz soaked a hand towel in cold water and passed it over to where Anna leaned against the sink. 'You'll have a bruise.'

'Do you reckon?'

'Well, a small one. He was livid, though. What on earth did you say to him?'

'I only asked him to go back to his detention.'

'Is that all?'

'What do you mean?'

'Nothing. It just seemed like a huge reaction if all you did was that. What you say.'

'He's not a *normal* boy, is he?'

Someone had left their hairbrush poking out from under the net curtain. There were hairs in the sink, and spots of black mould on the windowsill. Everything seemed grubby.

Liz said, 'You do have to go carefully with him.'

'Why the hell should I? Just because he doesn't like to have to do what everyone else has to. Why should he be a special case?'

'I haven't taught him since last July.' Liz swung her hair, glanced at her reflection. 'To be honest, though, he's never given me any bother. Don't know why. I know he drives Andy up the wall, but that's more of a personality clash.'

'I do hope you're not implying it's somehow my fault this has happened?' snapped Anna, throwing the towel into the sink so she splashed her own skirt.

'No, I didn't mean that.'

'What *did* you mean then?'

Anna Lloyd, always so cool and collected. She watched Liz falter.

'Jeez. You're shaken up, you might need to go home this afternoon. I only meant Nathan can be hard work, that's all. That was all. I'm going to – go and find someone.' She moved swiftly towards the door. 'Stay sitting down in case you faint.' Then she was gone. Anna could hear the heels of her boots tap-tapping across the parquet.

She had a sudden memory of her mother in knee boots and a skirt like Liz's; Miriam flirting with Phil the night he arrived, leaning against him at the table, laughing loudly at his jokes, playing with her hair. That night Anna couldn't bring herself to have sex with him because it felt as though her mother were sitting on the end of the bed (whereas in reality she was holed up next door stewing in dope and sourness). 'Did you ever know your father?' Phil had asked her sometime in the small hours. 'Never.' 'Perhaps you're like him, then.' Because you're nothing like Miriam, he meant.

There was a clunk as the fire door outside shut and Chrissy came in.

'Goodness,' she said. 'Been doing six rounds with Mike Tyson?'

Anna shot her a look. 'Where's Nathan?'

'Walked out. The Head's on the phone about him now. Are you OK?'

'Not really.'

Chrissy folded her arms. 'Go home, Anna. I've

checked your timetable and I can absorb your Year Sevens.'

'I can't. I promised them I'd hear their plays today.'

'Hear them next time. Come on, pop up and see the Head, then get your bags.'

'But I'll be fine in a minute. Let me have something to eat and a cup of coffee.'

'Anna.' Chrissy moved closer. 'The Headmaster wants you to make a brief statement, then go.'

Something in the intonation.

'I'm not suspended, am I?'

'Good Lord, no. But we felt it would be better. You can run yourself a nice bath, have a glass of wine. Think of me stuck teaching Upper Sixth, eh?'

They faced each other. If I argue, Anna thought, I'll make it worse.

'The Head only wants to get the facts, that's all.'

'Yes.'

'And if you go via Matron's room, she'll put a bit of arnica on your cheek.' Chrissy touched her lightly on the back. 'You were in the wrong place at the wrong time, I think.'

Events replayed themselves in Anna's mind: Nathan screaming, the plate, Kali asking for ice, Liz's boots. 'What did Liz say about it?'

'Liz Yates? Haven't seen her this morning. Was she there?'

'She went to get you.'

Chrissy frowned. 'No, it was Kali Norman who told me you were here, came thumping on my office door, very upset. I thought at first it was her that Nathan had hurt.'

'Was she all right?'

'Oh, fine. Enjoying herself, probably. They do like their drama, these teen girls.'

So she had been an exciting episode.

'Too many soaps,' said Chrissy. 'Every schoolday's another thrilling instalment.'

Anna dropped her paper towel in the bin and went out.

Contact your union, was Mel's advice.

Anna heard her own breathing in the receiver. 'Really? You think it's that serious?'

She'd been expecting kind words and general sympathy, not a confirmation that the trauma of the day was only the prelude to a whole raft of trouble. It almost felt as though Mel had gone against her, though she knew that was an unreasonable reaction.

'If it's what you said, then I'm sure everything'll blow over. But it's as well to know your options, that's all.'

'Don't you think the Head should've had him in? Torn a strip off him?'

'Without a doubt. You know Jackson, though. Anything to avoid confrontation. I'm amazed it's not the school motto.'

This is not what I needed, thought Anna. You should have told me Nathan was a bastard but that I'd be OK.

'—I wish you hadn't left,' she blurted. A stupid thing

to say, because how could Mel respond? *Don't worry, I'll hand my notice in and come back next term.*

'Poor Anna,' Mel began. In the background a mobile phone was going off. There was a pause and a brief exchange with the caller before she came back to Anna. 'Sorry about that. So, yeah. What can I say? You're not having a good run, are you?'

Jamie was more sympathetic, but the fee for counselling turned out again to be sex. How does it happen that you go from desiring someone to not, she thought, as he mauled at her nipples.

When they'd first got together she'd been impressed by his skill and control and by the way he understood her body. She knew there'd been a lot of girlfriends before her but she'd never seen any evidence of them, no tokens or mementoes, until she'd helped clear out her father-in-law's house and found an old photo album. Long-haired Jamie in V-neck sweater with a succession of pretty women. Some of them leaned against him, some held his hand. One was sitting in his lap. The plainest had her arms tight round his waist in a desperate gesture. He wore the same detached half-smile in every picture.

In a little panic of jealousy she'd brought the albums home and asked to be taken through them, but he'd only been interested in the very early photographs: him and Russ as children.

'See that,' he'd said. 'We used to climb that tree and drop twigs on people walking underneath. Russ got caught once. I never did. Look at this one: Russ is pretending to be a dog, I remember it.' And there was Russ on all fours and Jamie holding up something like a lead. But when Russ had seen the picture he said, 'My brother tried to strangle me with that belt.'

Jamie laughed. 'Don't be so melodramatic. You asked me to put it round your neck. It was your idea.'

'I was choking!'

'No, you weren't. You made out you were to try and get me into trouble. Which was your forte.'

That part of his life was clearly far more vivid for Jamie than the years with the girls, so she'd left it.

And he'd really seemed to love her. They'd spent whole days in bed, till they felt weak and druggy and the room smelt of sex. Now, of course, she resented his stamina and the fact that he always waited for her to come, which meant he pumped on and on like a machine while she strained underneath, struggling to ignite the spark of her own orgasm. He held back as he did in everything; holding back his sperm to keep her barren, willing them not to swim. So sex had become a battle, with her trying to draw him out. Because there was always the idea, even when the dates were against her, that this time might be the one where she got pregnant and she hung onto that thought, it kept her going as the bed rocked and the headboard shifted against the wall.

'Do you think they'll expel Nathan?' she asked when they'd finished and Jamie was lying on his back, his hands behind his head.

'Don't tell me you were thinking about that little scrote while we were . . .?'

'No, of course I wasn't.' Mostly she'd been thinking about Kali, and Liz.

'Damn good job. I'd say, if he was in the state system, he'd be out like a shot. Bearing in mind his record. But with an independent, I'm not so sure. Depends whether his dad plays golf with one of the governors, doesn't it?'

Fuck you, she thought, for being right.

She'd half expected to be barred from work the next morning, met by the bursar at the gate with her P45. But she walked straight into Jackson's office. He shut the door at once and began to talk, giving her no chance to interrupt.

Anna learned that, on arriving home, Nathan had told his mother he'd been assaulted by a teacher. She'd phoned his father, who'd come out of his Chester office and driven straight to the school, where he'd demanded to see Jackson. Possibly to buy himself some time, the Head had asked Mr Woods to wait till Nathan could be brought in. But Woods claimed he had the full story, which was this: that Nathan had misunderstood about the detention; he thought Mr Maye had said he could get his lunch first, then come up and do the work. That he was surprised and distressed by Mrs Lloyd's abrasive manner. She seemed to be intent on humiliating him in front of his peers. That when she grabbed him by the shoulder he became frightened and jerked away, accidentally knocking the plate off the table. That he was so confused and upset by the incident, all he could think of was to get himself home.

Anna didn't dare speak in case she howled or a stream of abuse came out.

Jackson said, 'They're looking for an apology.'

What would he do now, she wondered, if she picked up his glass paperweight and smashed it into his face? Heat travelled through her as she imagined the splintering of nasal bone under the weight of her hand, the slippery resilience of splitting flesh.

'Anna?'

Through the window she could see a roofing lorry reversing in, long rafters strapped in cuboid bundles laid in the back. She'd ridden in a flatbed once; she and Miriam stranded somewhere when the car had broken down, thumbing a lift on a country road. There hadn't been any room left in the cab for Anna so she'd sat in the gritty trailer part, bouncing around insecurely. Every time she'd turned round her mother had been laughing with the men. You wouldn't be allowed to do that these days.

'I'm the one with the bruise.'

Jackson looked unhappy. 'He says it was an accident.'

'It wasn't.'

'Do you have any witnesses?'

'I don't know. Do I?'

'I'll have a word with the dinner ladies this morning.'

Jamie could knock your teeth out, she thought. With one blow.

She'd had enough; she turned to go.

'Are you prepared to take it to court, Anna?'

'Yes,' she said without hesitation, but she knew it

was a lie. Jackson came forward and opened the door for her.

'Well, think about it,' he said. As if she wouldn't be going over it endlessly for the rest of her life.

They greeted her in the staffroom like a hero.

'Let me make you a coffee,' said Andrew as soon as he saw her. 'You deserve it. Badge of honour.' He touched his own cheekbone and that made her hand go to her bruise.

'All right?' said Les.

'Not really.'

Liz was in the corner watching Anna with curiosity. She nodded but stayed where she was.

'Well, I'm going to do your break duties for a fucking month,' Andrew was saying as he handed her a mug. 'I'm sorry you got clobbered, but I'll definitely make it up to you. 'Cause anyone who gets Woods expelled deserves a medal. Services to education. You should get an extra spine point for it.'

'Don't get ahead of yourself,' she said quietly.

'What do you mean?'

She couldn't look at his sharp, eager face. To begin explaining, to take the weight of his indignation on top of her own.

'Andrew,' said Les, 'shut up. Anna, my office. Bring your drink.'

She avoided assembly. Just let Jackson ask where she'd been, just let him. Listen to an invertebrate like you preach? she'd say. You wouldn't know a moral code from a sausage roll.

A slow walk down to the bottom of the playing field and back again would dispatch the trite story and prayer, she'd heard them all before. No prayer existed that would encompass the wishes swirling round her head just now.

She passed the smokers' copse where the ground level dipped, and turned so she could skirt the football pitch. The sky was bitterly cold but bright, the mud rutted hard under her shoes. When she looked back at the school it was like a painting, with the grey central tower and the formal garden in front of it, then the field. There was a light haze over the grass.

A figure was coming out between the tall yew hedges and moving along the fence to the top gate; Anna squinted to make out the detail. When she knew who it was, she folded her arms and waited.

'Are you all right, Mrs Lloyd?'

Kali's voice sounded thin across the winter air. She was still a few yards away but Anna could see the glint of metal below her ear lobes. Her hair looked redder than usual. Celtic Goddess in school uniform.

'You must be freezing without your coat. What are you doing out here, Kali?'

'He's a bastard, Mrs Lloyd. I told him so as well.' The girl came up close and stood with her hands in her pockets. A purple chiffon scarf, thin as a rope, was twisted twice round her neck. 'Before he went yesterday I told him straight. I saw him getting his bag and I knew he was off, so I had a go at him for you. Ask Mrs Meredith, she heard me.'

'I'm not doubting you.'

Their breath steamed out in front of them and rose up as one cloud.

'He was well worked up, I thought he'd throw a plate at me. He would have if there'd been one handy, I tell you.'

'Kali—' Anna felt suddenly hopeful, '—did you see what happened in the dining room?'

'Yeah.'

'Did you?'

'Yeah. Most of it.'

'Where were you standing?'

'By the door.'

'Did you see me put my hand on Nathan's shoulder?'

Kali looked as though she were considering. 'Mmm, I didn't exactly see all of it. I came in when you were holding your eye. I saw that bit.'

The lowest clouds above them were rolling fast, like speeded-up film. Giant shadows crossed the grass like curses.

'But I can pretend I did,' Kali went on. 'I'll go to the headmaster and tell him Nathan threw that plate at you deliberately. Whatever you want me to say. He did, didn't he?'

Anna sighed. 'Why aren't you in assembly?'

'I was running an errand for Mrs Hislop, I had to give a message to the exam invigilator. I saw you on my way back so I thought I'd come over and ask if you were OK.'

'You're never where you should be, Kali Norman.'

'Oh, I wouldn't say that, Mrs Lloyd.'

Now, at the top end of the car park, children were filing across to the music department. Anna checked her watch. 'We have to go in. Lessons are starting.'

'S'pose.'

'Get back to the warm. Your hands must be like ice.'

Kali examined her own fingers, then touched them to her cheek, and to Anna's. The sensation was an electric shock that shot through her scalp and neck.

'Oh!'

'Sorry. Proved you right, though.'

They walked back up the field together. When they reached the gate and were about to part, Kali said, 'Don't be so sad. You always look sad.'

'Do I?'

'Yeah. Underneath. Really miz.'

'Is that what the pupils say about me?'

Kali shook her head. 'Only me. I don't think anyone else has noticed.'

('Why are you always so bloody miserable?' Miriam had shouted, banging the bedroom door back against the wardrobe. Anna had been sitting under the duvet doing her homework. 'Serious isn't the same as miserable,' Anna remembered saying. 'Someone in this house has to be serious.' Miriam – drunk – had laughed so hard she'd doubled up.

Miriam howling with laughter on a boat, on a river cruise somewhere, a place with red clay banks; taking off a ring, holding it between finger and thumb for a second then throwing it into the brown water; some lads on the bank whistling; Anna feeling ashamed.)

'I just lost someone,' Anna heard herself say.

'Oh, Mrs Lloyd, I'm sorry.'

'A baby.'

Kali's eyes went wide. 'God.'

That called Anna back to herself. 'I shouldn't have told you that, forget it.'

'No, I'm glad you did.'

'Don't tell anyone. I shouldn't have said.'

'I won't.'

'You need to go.'

'Yeah.' Kali shook her fringe out of her eyes. 'Mrs Lloyd?'

'Yes?'

'You can trust me, you know.'

Chapter Twelve

As ever, being in school helped calm her. Paul Abel from Year Ten stopped her in the corridor and gave her a copy of his GCSE piano composition, a piece she'd heard him playing in the hall the week before and complimented him on. Her Year Sevens were working well and sparking off each other; her Lower Sixth were lively and cooperative. On a good day, there was no job like teaching.

Mel used to nag her to apply for promotions but Anna always said, 'Why would I want to take on more admin? It's being in the classroom I like.' Although in her more honest moments she would have admitted she was not head of department material. Jackson regarded her as a loose cannon, and no matter how impressive her exam results were, he didn't want anyone on his senior management team speaking frankly about their mother's cannabis use. Well, that was OK. She was better off out of it. One thing she didn't need was more of Jackson in her life.

Break she spent at the photocopier, so it was dinner-time before she went back to the staffroom. She'd been in there thirty seconds before she heard Tom Maxfield say to Andrew, 'Lay one finger on me and I'll chuck this plate at you.'

She meant to go for a long walk around the grounds but when she got to the back entrance she saw it had started to rain. Part of her would have liked to stand in a downpour till she took a chill and died, but a more rational voice told her that, since she was close, she might as well visit the Sixth Form Centre and chase up a late essay.

She could hear the boom of a bass beat from several yards away. As she got to the door, one of the Lower Sixth stumbled out wearing tinsel round her wrists. 'Christmas party,' she said when she saw Anna.

'Christmas is weeks off yet.'

'We're getting in the mood. You have to work up to these things.'

Inside the common room it was darker than usual because the curtains at the far end were closed. The comfy seats had all been shifted round so that they were in a semicircle, and someone had carried up a half a dozen staging blocks from the drama department. A boy who Anna had taught when he was in the first year was singing into a microphone, leaning into the stand with his eyes closed. His hair was short and spiked, and under the reddish lights he looked as though he'd walked off an album cover. I remember you crying because you'd left your coat on the bus, she thought.

'Hi, Mrs Lloyd!' Daisy from her Lower Sixth group was sitting on the row closest to the door. 'Did you want something? Or have you just come for a good time?'

'Oh, you know, I was sitting in the staffroom doing

my marking and I thought to myself, what I really want to do is listen to some extremely loud karaoke.'

'That's the spirit. He's good, isn't he?'

'He is. Are you all having a go?'

'God, no. I sing like a cat with tonsillitis. Do you want some Pepsi?' Daisy picked up a litre bottle and a plastic cup. 'We've got stacks.'

'You're fine. What I was really after was You-Na's essay.'

'Not in today.'

The song finished to whoops and cheers, and another boy climbed up. As soon as Anna heard the first bars she recognized the track from Kali's CD.

> *They come along, these precious moments*
> *Out of nowhere*
> *They fill your head, lift you up inside*
> *Out of nowhere*
> *You keep your cool, you stay alert*
> *I'm gonna give you strength to push away the hurt*
> *Out of nowhere*

'Do you know this one?' asked Daisy. 'You were mouthing the words.'

'I do, actually.'

'Well, get up there. Show them how it's done.'

For a mad second she imagined doing that, stepping up to the mike and singing in front of them, and their stunned admiration; something by Bowie or Free, or one of the Pretenders' songs, because people used to say she had a look of Chrissie Hynde. And that made her think of when she was seventeen and a man called Gary who'd only been around for half a year before Miriam had two-timed him, but who'd helped Anna one night when she'd got back from a party having drunk too much. Miriam had been asleep, but Gary had heard her struggling with the front door and come downstairs to find her being sick. Without fuss he'd cleaned the sofa and got her out of her dirty jeans. 'You need to watch yourself,' he'd told her matter-of-factly. What she understood now but didn't then was that he could so easily have taken advantage, she wouldn't have been able to stop him. There was no need for him to be so nice.

'Go on, Mrs Lloyd, you'd be great.'

What I could do is go up there and make a speech, Anna thought. I could say, *I'm beginning to see now I might have made my life harder than it needed to be. Relax, cheer up, enjoy yourselves, use your time wisely. Don't worry too much. You have all those years ahead.*

'Lost my voice,' she whispered and put her hands round her own throat.

Daisy grinned.

> *Where do I start? How does it end*
> *Breaking the surface as my heart begins to mend*
> *Out of nowhere*

'Yeah, yeah. I believe you.'

Near the stage two girls were holding hands and dancing. A knot of boys by the curtains were throwing Smarties into the air and trying to catch them in their mouths; she would have to tell them to clear up afterwards. A new song started, one she didn't know, then halted. Some problem with the machine, or it was the wrong CD. The mobile in Anna's jacket beeped and she took it out to peer at the screen.

You have one new text message.

If it was Russ she was going to throw the phone out of the window. But it was from Mel: *End of term hell! Sorry haven't been around much. Speak soon promise. Hang in there girl! X X*

An image came to her of the three of them sitting by a canal at a pub table, Mel taking herself off to the Ladies and Jamie saying, 'Nice girl, Mel, but a bit horsey. I keep wanting to offer her an apple.'

She would go home and make a wax model of Nathan, or stick his picture to a dartboard, or write a letter telling him what a shit he was and then burn it. *Get out of my face*, yelled the new vocalist. *I don't want you in my space.*

She would get through this crap time.

Almost as soon as Jamie had left for another session at the Lion, his writing folder under his arm, Russ's car swung into the drive. Anna was marking poems at the kitchen table and saw the red Mondeo at once. 'Fuck,' she said out loud, then swore again as the driver's side opened and only Ruth got out. Anna's mind flicked through the various reasons her sister-in-law might pay a lone visit, and produced no positive options.

Despite wanting to drop down flat on the carpet, she made herself go to the front door and open it.

'This is a surprise.'

'I told Russ I was going round to Mum's.'

Anna's heart sank. 'Why?'

'I don't know.'

'You'd better come in,' said Anna.

Ruth followed her through into the lounge and drooped onto the sofa, still clutching her saggy handbag. She was wearing old-lady sheepskin boots and a belted mac that did nothing for her. Anna couldn't see any obvious signs of pregnancy, though.

'Aren't you going to take your coat off?'

Ruth shook her head. 'I'm not staying long.'

'Drink?'

'No.'

Get on with it, thought Anna. If you're going to announce our doom, let's have it over with. 'So why the subterfuge?'

Ruth frowned, her face worked.

'There's something wrong with Russ and I thought you might know what it is.'

'Me? Why should I?'

'Because he might have told Jamie and Jamie might have told you. They're so close.'

In spite of her fear, Anna almost laughed. God, Ruth, you're such a good judge of character.

'Russ looks up to his big brother. Always has done. He asks him for advice.'

'If you think that, why not speak to Jamie about it?'

'Because he wouldn't tell me. He doesn't take me seriously.' Ruth lowered her face. 'I'm a bit frightened of him, to tell you the truth.'

There was a pause for reassuring noises to be made, but Anna remained silent, considering, as another hot wave of guilt washed over her. It hadn't occurred to her that Ruth might sometimes pick up on Jamie's irony. Perhaps she was smarter than they'd given her credit for.

'He hasn't said anything to me. What do you think's the matter?'

Ruth's mouth went down at the corners. 'Me,' she said.

I'm going to have to stop you there, thought Anna. Let me freeze this frame while I go upstairs, pack my suitcase and leave this island forever.

'You wouldn't understand,' Ruth went on. 'You and Jamie have such a strong marriage. He adores you. Look at you, your lovely figure. You have time together, and you're comfortably off, not always worrying about money, it makes a difference.'

'We have our moments.'

'How could he not be happy with you, Anna? You're clever and pretty . . . I irritate Russ, that's the truth.'

'No.'

'I do. I annoy him.' Her coat gaped at the bust. Nothing of Ruth's ever fitted properly. 'But it's hard, you know, when you have no privacy and you're at the beck and call of everyone. You and Jamie can just hop in the car and drive off for a weekend; we haven't had a night on our own since before Tom was born, that's five years. Even if we had the time, it's finding the cash.'

'Everyone has their rough patches.'

Ruth carried on as though Anna hadn't spoken. 'And I know I'm a mess, I'm well aware of it, but you tell me how to do glam when you're fretting over every penny and you spend your life running round like a servant after your family. Even the bloody dog thinks I'm at his beck and call.'

'I'm sure Russ doesn't feel that way.'

'He does, he does, I can tell.'

'But what about your kids? You gave him children—'

Ruth started to cry and Anna cursed herself. If only Jamie would come back or the phone would ring.

'I'm not the person to advise you here, Ruth. I'm, I'm too close to it. Have you tried talking to your mum?'

For a second Anna was back in Miriam's hallway, holding the phone and crying. Two weeks after the split with Phil and she'd thought he was ringing to get back with her. Halfway through pouring her heart out, she'd realized that the TV next door had gone quiet and that her mother was listening in. 'I only eavesdrop because you never tell me anything,' Miriam had snapped afterwards. 'You force me into it.'

'I can't tell Mum, it'd break her heart.' Ruth took a shuddering breath, buried her face in her hands and mumbled something into her cuffs. It took a moment before Anna worked it out. *I'm worried he might leave me.*

Russ in the caravan, reaching out.

'Honestly,' she said quickly, 'he's not said anything to Jamie. I'd know if he had.'

'Would he tell you?'

'Oh, yes.'

'You see, your marriage is a good one. You don't have secrets from each other.' Ruth sniffed and wiped her top lip with her index finger. She looked for a moment as though she was going to pull herself together, but then her features twisted and the tears broke out again. 'Do you ever,' she said, 'feel like you've done nothing with your life?'

'God, yes.'

'*Do* you?'

'Of course.'

'Oh.' Ruth looked confused. She leaned over and began rummaging in her handbag. 'But you do loads with your days. Sometimes all I do is pick up dirty clothes and move piles of rubbish around. I try to sort the house out, get rid of some of the clutter, but no one ever helps.' Liquid dripped from the end of her nose.

'Do you want a tissue?'

'No, I'm – I need to use your toilet.'

She went out and Anna got up and paced around. Could she phone Russ, warn him, or would that make it worse? Her mobile was upstairs. Then the cloakroom door clicked open and Ruth was standing in the hall with her face wet and hopeless.

'What? What's happened?'

'Can I borrow, have you a tampon or something I could use?'

Anna stared.

'Tasha must have taken my spare one out of my bag. I wouldn't mind if she'd replace it. She's so selfish.'

'They're in the first-floor bathroom cupboard. Help yourself. No, I'll get you one, stay there.'

Anna ran up the steps, her heart thudding. She tipped up the box of Lillets so they scattered across the floor, grabbed one, left the rest and ran back down to Ruth. 'Are you all right?'

Ruth was still sniffing pathetically. 'Just cross with

Tasha. She's always taking my stuff, as if she doesn't have everything she wants on a plate. We're too soft with the kids. We've made a rod for our own backs. Well, she can bloody well start buying her own out of her pocket money, I shall tell her.'

She took the tampon and disappeared back into the cloakroom.

Not pregnant, then! Not pregnant, Russ was wrong and it would all be OK. There would be no crisis after all. And no visiting Ruth in hospital again to watch her coo and primp like some latter-day Virgin Mary.

Anna went over to the drinks cabinet and located a whisky miniature. With shaking hands she unscrewed the top, then held it to her lips and swigged the lot. A column of warmth spread down her, and her breathing slowed. She dropped the bottle in the bin and sat down to wait. Then she changed her mind and took out some Shiraz. When Ruth emerged, there was a glass set on the coffee table for her.

'Heavens. I can't,' she said. 'I'm driving.'

'One drink. You're fine with one.'

Ruth managed a weak smile. She'd re-powdered her face but she still looked a sight. 'Go on, then.'

'Well, for God's sake, get that coat off,' Anna said.

Even just an hour after Ruth had left, Anna had trouble remembering what was said and what she'd only imagined saying. There'd been an awkward embrace at one point, three seconds of physical pressure; that was after Ruth said, 'I know you don't think very much of me.' Which Anna had denied, but maybe not convincingly enough because Ruth had replied, 'It's all right, it doesn't matter.'

She recalled Ruth praising her job and her home, and saying again that Jamie made her nervous because he was so clever. So Anna had pointed out some of his annoying habits, knowing that they'd probably be reported back to Russ but deciding that might not be a bad thing. And every so often in the conversation she'd had this hot, crazy impulse to tell Ruth about the first miscarriage and how she'd given the baby books and the cot mobile away because she thought they'd tempt fate, although now she realized she didn't have that degree of control over her life. As though anything she did had an effect either way. Ruth would have expressed such astonishment and sympathy. Why didn't you tell us? she'd say.

Because it's so much easier to pretend that babies aren't your thing than to have anyone guess what you're really thinking when you're forced to admire someone else's child. They go, Do you want to hold him? And you think, If I touch your baby I'll be so consumed with jealousy I'll make a dash for it or I'll strike you or I'll scream till they have to sedate me. Better to spare everyone's feelings and feign indifference.

Ruth had gone to her car happier and reassured, full of shame-inducing thanks. As a parting gesture she'd admired Anna's new earrings. 'You don't usually wear those dangly ones, do you? What are they, little moons?'

Pearl studs were Anna's favourite. 'I don't know if they're me, really.'

'No, they look nice. They don't go with your clothes,

though. You'll have to get one of these Indian tops they're all wearing, and jeans with velvet on. You could get away with it. Not like me, my backside.'

'Me in an Indian top. I don't think so. I'm a little older than you, remember.'

Ruth glowed at this moment of self-deprecation. She'd been smiling when she'd driven off.

Anna had gone back and poured out the rest of the wine. What a sister-in-law she'd been. And nothing now that could be done about it. Ruth's anxious, trusting expressions, her simple words of kindness, were like skewer after skewer through the heart. It wasn't her fault she was fertile.

To blot out the guilt, Anna was going to have to go upstairs and Google Phil's name again. There was still half an hour till Jamie came back.

Anna had been to five different schools as a child. She'd had two years in a Guildford first school, transferred to the middle school, then they'd moved to Exmouth. At ten or eleven she'd done a short, terrible stint in a village primary outside Nantwich. Then a complete run at her secondary education, all eight years in the same place, but always with the threat that Miriam might take it into her head to up sticks again with no warning, which made it impossible to settle. At eighteen Anna had gone off to university without a backward glance, everyone else crying on the phone that weekend after term started and Anna raising a toast to herself in the student bar.

Jamie, who was interested in childhood generally, liked to ask about her early life. Having lost his own mother at the age of thirteen he wanted to know about hers: why didn't they get on? Was she really as bad as Anna remembered? 'You do tend to retain the worst of a situation,' he'd said.

So she'd told him how Miriam never wanted children, would often say so. She freely admitted pregnancy had been a tactic that went wrong. If it was meant as revenge on her over-strict parents, it had backfired; she had not felt more in charge of her life with a baby of her own, on her own. 'It sounds ridiculous,' said Anna, 'but I don't think she'd understood there would be a child at the end of it. And eighteen years of it. More.'

'Was she threatened by you?' Jamie was clearly thinking of the dynamic between him and Russ. 'You must have been a bright girl to make up for all that disrupted education. Perhaps she felt inadequate.'

'I did read a lot. Miriam didn't like that, she thought it was weird. But there wasn't anything else to do most of the time.'

And then there was Miriam's background: an inflexible religious upbringing that had her leaving home for good at seventeen and throwing herself at the first man who showed an interest. Anna, who'd created for herself a vision of a cheery old couple standing in front of a white cottage with lupins in the garden, nagged to meet her grandparents. But her mother would not budge. 'I'd have enjoyed growing up in a traditional kind of household,' Anna had said once, during a row. 'No, you wouldn't,' Miriam had snapped. 'Believe me!' Sometimes she hinted there'd been violence. The grandparents died and Anna learned anyway they'd lived on an estate in the middle of Stoke.

'Wasn't Miriam *ever* nice to you?' Jamie had asked.

Common sense said she must have been. Anna was fed and clothed, received birthday and Christmas presents. 'She wasn't the right sort of mother for me, though.'

'You probably weren't the right sort of daughter.'

Anna had shown him her school photographs and even she'd had to admit she didn't look like a very approachable child. Some kids were naturally carefree and sunny; Anna's eyes were piercing and dark and her brow was set on the verge of a scowl. Perhaps she had just been unlovable. 'You look as though you're busy framing the rights of man,' Jamie had said. But that picture was taken on a bad day when she'd found out her favourite teacher was going on maternity leave and it had felt like her heart was going to break.

Had she been a difficult child? She'd have liked to ask her mother now, adult to adult. But it's hard to forgive people when they're not around any more.

Nathan was still away. 'They're getting his arm checked out by a physiotherapist,' said Les. 'Poor lamb.'

'Les, I only went like this—' Anna reached out and put her palm to his shoulder. His face stiffened for a second as she touched him, then relaxed as she drew away.

'I know, I know. It's ridiculous. They're probably trying their luck with Claims Direct.' He put on an advert voice. 'Have you been lightly brushed by a petite lady? Suffering severe muscle damage and mental trauma as a result? Call us and we'll rake you in a pile!'

Anna tried to laugh for politeness.

'Bad joke, sorry.'

'No, it's me. I'm coming in every day geared up for this ghastly apology I'm supposed to make and then he isn't here.'

'I don't believe he'll be back before Christmas now. Try and put him out of your mind.' Les turned to the noticeboard and began to remove drawing pins from the out-of-date slips.

'How come?'

'More auditions, I heard. Unofficially.'

That cheered her. A Nathan-free run-up to the end of term.

She took her books through to the work annexe and spread them out, meaning to go over the remaining lesson plans for Year Ten. But then she thought of Les and how kind he'd been about everything. Had she said a proper thank you to him?

She pushed her chair back under the table and went out of the staffroom and across to his office. The door was open so she called his name. No reply, but she stepped in anyway. He might be back any minute.

It wasn't an especially tidy office, but then it was a busy one. On the desk was his album of cuttings; anything the kids did that made the newspapers, Les carefully clipped out and stuck in a scrapbook. The book then sat in reception for visitors to peruse. He was obviously about to add another article because there was the glue stick and scissors next to it. On one of the shelves there was a photo of his wife sitting on a white rock in front of a very blue sea; that must have been before she got ill. It made Anna sad to look at it.

A scratchy sound like a mouse made her jump, but it was only a sheet of fax paper flipping over in the breeze. She watched as it crept along the surface of the desk. One page of the album turned itself over. She moved round to close the top window for him.

In the yard below was a group of girls playing some sort of game. They'd taken their blazers off and they were covering someone. No, hugging them. No. That wasn't right. What were they up to? From this angle she could see only the tops of their heads, and the ripple-pattern glass blurred the detail. Then she recognized Kali in the centre of the circle and it dawned on her something unpleasant was going on. This was not a game at all.

Anna banged on the window and heard only the thin rap of her own knuckles in the room. The sound did not penetrate. She watched in dismay as the girls on the outside raised their arms in unison, then she was running out of the office towards the back stairs.

Chapter Thirteen

It was hard not to look for your younger self among the pupils. The quiet, the shy, the intense, the dark, all aroused Anna's special interest. Sometimes – as with Adam Gardiner – she felt she should be compensating for the deficiencies in their lives. Which was ridiculous.

'It's not your job,' Jamie had said. 'You go in, you teach, you come home. That's the way I always worked.' (Easy for you, Anna thought. I'm not made like that.) 'Because otherwise you burn yourself out. Just as well you aren't in one of these inner-city comps where there's a crisis every five minutes. You'd be on the carpet inside a week.'

As she raced down the stairs to where Kali was, she was also running out of that playground in Nantwich, with the other girls screaming at her to come back and her heart churning with the stress of breaking the rules over the need to escape. 'Bloody palaver,' her mother had complained. 'Called out of work and only been in the job a fortnight.'

So Anna would not stand by now and let a pupil of hers be bullied. She rushed out of the side entrance and swept her gaze round, but the quad was empty apart from some Year Seven boys stamping in puddles. 'Stop that!' she called, and they did. She hurried across the car park then down to the field. Not there, unless the group was hidden behind the dip. Was it worth going all the way down to check? No, because they couldn't have got that far in such a short time.

That left only the garden.

By the time she reached the clipped hedges she was panting and had a stitch under her ribs. The pain made her stop and stretch her back; she was standing in the quiet centre of the garden where the paths all crossed, the granite obelisk behind her and a dark arch of leaves on four sides. She turned slowly. The air was so cold it hurt her lungs.

In the far distance the choir were practising for the carol service, the swoop of *tra-a-vli-ing* over and over again; *tra-a-vli-ing*. As she listened it became more distinct. Perhaps someone had opened a window. Two sparrows skittered out in front of her, jerking across the stone like dead leaves blowing. As soon as they registered her presence they ducked and took off, and she could hear the fluttering of their wings. Under her soles was the unevenness of a frozen moss ridge.

She took a step forward, even though she didn't want to leave, and into her head came Jamie, hunched over his computer. Jamie standing in the kitchen, frowning: 'Why do you want a baby? If you could explain it to me.' 'I can't,' she'd said. 'I don't know.' There was no explanation, no way of putting her feelings into words. 'I've told you, it's a drive.' He'd looked at her uncomprehendingly: 'I didn't think you were the mumsy type.' Cue an image of Ruth spooning food into Tash's mouth; trying to unwedge a plastic starfish from the bath plughole; Ruth saying she sometimes wanted to walk out and leave them to it. Russ and Ruth, so much in common after all.

The star of mercy, the star of grace, sang the choir. By now she was at the entrance, stepping out onto the drive, and back inside her right mind. Kali. She was going to do one more circuit and then go back up to the staffroom and write a report. *Shall lead thi-iy heart to its resting place.* The voices tailed off again. She crossed to the window so she could watch.

Students stood in rows with sheet music held out in front of them. Their faces were set identically, jaws open, heads up . . . *thy ha-art to the infant king—* The sound was so sweet it was impossible to imagine those mouths framing swear words or taunts. Light and dark scalps shone under the lights. These were healthy, confident children who expected to do well in the world.

What exactly had been going on in the yard?

She went the long way back, taking in the top of the field again and the car park, the dining room, the science labs. Just as she was about to give up she walked past the art room and was astonished to see Kali in there, overalls on, hair tied back. Anna went in at once.

'Hi, Mrs Lloyd.'

Anna paused. At the far end of the studio the student teacher was pegging up wet paintings, but otherwise the room was empty. A radio played faint rap music in the corner.

'What are you doing?'

'I'm washing palettes,' said Kali cheerfully. 'Helping.'

'Oh.' Anna couldn't think what to say for a moment. 'Have you been here long?'

'Don't know. Have I, Sue?'

Sue? Anna felt a twinge of something. The student teacher was dumpy and plain but she was young. '"Miss Williams" to you, Kali.'

'Oh, yeah.'

'I'm not sure,' said the student.

The place smelt of powder paint and varnish. Along the whole of one wall were studies of barbed wire and knives. Kali was drying brushes on a rag and saying something about earrings, but Anna stopped her.

'What was happening in the yard?'

Kali shrugged. 'I don't know. I was in here.'

'I saw you from Mr Weston's office, about ten minutes ago. You and a group of girls.'

'Not me.'

'It was you. I recognized your hair. Who were the girls? I couldn't make them out from the tops of their heads.'

Kali put the brushes down and looked puzzled.

'They were all round you, jabbing you with their fingers. You had your hands over your ears. *You seemed in distress.*' Anna leant forward as she lowered her voice.

'Honestly, I've been here for ages, haven't I, Miss Williams?' The student gave an embarrassed smirk but said nothing. 'Hey, how's your eye now, Mrs Lloyd?'

In cases like this you told the pupil that there was nothing to be gained by keeping quiet; that silence perpetuated abuse; that the school had a clear policy on bullying. Words meant to inspire confidence. But none of it seemed right for Kali, and anyway you couldn't talk about this stuff with someone listening in. The student teacher was bumbling round by the kiln now, unrolling chicken wire.

Kali sighed and tilted her head. 'Stop worrying all the time. Stress is bad for you.'

Then she smiled so brilliantly that Anna could believe this girl had spent a happy lunchtime washing art equipment to the sound of Radio One. Nevertheless:

'It wasn't anyone in your year, I don't think. They were – sort of – poking you.'

Kali turned away and picked up a jam jar of glue spreaders, leaving Anna stranded.

'Well, if you think of something you want to tell me.'

'Yeah.'

'We have systems in place.'

'Great.'

'You promise you'll come and find me if you need help?'

'Sure.'

A catch clicked; the student slid out a wide flat drawer and began to lift up the sheets of paper inside. When she bent over, you could see a bulge of fat at the waistband of her denim skirt. The DJ on the radio was laughing and playing a noise like a bouncing spring.

'I mean it, Kali.'

'I know you do. Thanks.'

When I was at Nantwich, Anna thought, I used to help tidy the stock cupboard to keep out of the playground.

And at morning and afternoon breaks I hung round the staffroom window. But I was unhappy, you don't look unhappy. You look in control. Perhaps I was mistaken after all.

'We could make a start on this mod roc, if you've got time,' said the student. She ignored Anna completely. A more experienced teacher would have appreciated the situation and withdrawn at the start.

'OK.' Kali began to roll up her sleeves.

Anna stood for a few seconds, then left.

Jamie was not in when she got back that evening. He'd left no note, and there was nothing on the answerphone. She dithered about starting the tea, then turned the oven on while she thought what to do. Why would he be late? He never went anywhere. She thought of the excuses she'd made over the last two years. Except that if you're being unfaithful, you plan it better; the last thing you should do is take off mysteriously if you've something to hide. Maybe he'd been having a breakdown and she'd not noticed.

But no, here he came now, striding up the path with his hair flopping in his eyes. Man on a mission.

The front door banged open. 'Hi!' he shouted down the hallway.

'Where've you been?'

'Sorting something out. For you.' He came through and laid a briefcase on the coffee table, then stood back. 'There you go.'

Was he trying to tell her he'd got a job?

She watched as Jamie bent down and unzipped the side, peeled away the vinyl lid.

'Ta-daaa.'

'A laptop.'

'It's yours.'

'Oh—'

'Because it's crazy you not having your own computer. I know you said you didn't need one, but you can use this anywhere. Sitting on the sofa, anywhere. You can research your English sites and your dolls' house stuff on it, install your own icons and favourites. Go on it whenever you like.'

He prised open the hinge so she could admire the keyboard and screen.

'Very swish.'

'You deserve it.'

Why? she thought.

'Is it new?'

'Newish.' Jamie settled himself on the centre cushion of the sofa and switched the machine on. 'Clodagh bought it four months ago and couldn't get on with it, says the screen's too small for her eyes. She was going to put it in the free paper and I said, How much do you want for it? And she said about six hundred, which is brilliant because they're well over a thousand in the shops and it's got all its paperwork.' The screen loaded with a picture of Marge Simpson.

'You can take that off for a start.'

'Yeah, yeah, customize it however you like. Nice Inshaw print or something . . . But it's good, isn't it?'

'What's it in aid of?' she said at last, trying to keep her tone light.

'That's the best bit.' He looked up, face triumphant. 'I've sold a story.'

'Really?'

'Yep. *Broken Sky*'s taken that one about the refugee, do you remember? Where she's lost in London and she meets a pimp. It's a really hard mag to get into, as well.'

'And they pay! That's fantastic.'

'Well, fifty quid. But it's the prestige.'

Prestige won't pay the council tax, sang a voice in her head, a line that had come to her weeks ago and that she'd rolled around, though she knew she would never say it out loud. She must not frown. So he had spent five hundred and fifty pounds of money she'd earned without consulting her. Miriam's cross face popped into her head. *Where did you get the cash for it?* Holding up the china horse Anna had wrapped as an apology for breaking the front-door glass. She'd helped herself out of her mother's purse and never thought it might be a crime. *I'm already out of pocket because of you, why would I want to waste more cash on tat like this?*

'Congratulations,' she said. You weren't supposed to think, That's my money; that's yours. More evidence this marriage wasn't working.

'I thought you'd be pleased. And now you won't have to wait for me to finish in the evening before you go online or do your worksheets. I can transfer all your files off my machine. Do it tonight, if you want.'

'Great.'

'It'll be better us each having our own computer space,' he said. He was already tapping away, absorbed.

She went to choose a ready meal out of the freezer.

Later they had sex in the lounge. When they'd finished, Anna lay on the rug in the firelight and thought about Kali. 'What were you like when you were at school?' she asked him.

Jamie raised himself up on one elbow. 'You know all this, I've told you.'

'Tell me again. Were you bullied at all?'

He wasn't. The usual fights, he said, that boys got into, but he always gave as good as he got. 'Russ used to say I bullied him.'

Anna knew her cue. 'You were only being firm with him. It was a difficult position for you.'

'Exactly. And he was a daft bugger. You never knew what he was going to get up to next. He'd just get an idea and be off, damn the consequences.'

She knew he was thinking of the time Russ was late home from primary school – Anna had heard this anecdote so many times she could picture it like one of her own memories – and Jamie had had to go look for him. He'd found his brother balanced halfway along the iron wall of the railway bridge, a thirty-foot drop to his left onto tarmac. A knot of lads cheered from the bank. Jamie screamed at the boys, then climbed across and dragged him off. When they got to the safety of the grass, he'd given Russ a wallop for being stupid. Russ had never forgiven the humiliation.

Which made Anna think of her own railway game: how, in Exmouth, she and another girl had taken it in turns to lie with their ear pressed against the rails on a quiet stretch of track and wait for the other to shout that she could see a train. You hadn't to take your head away till then, even though by that point the noise was rumbling through your skull like actual wheels. They played the game most of one summer until a woman dog-walking said she'd tell the police. 'Not like you to do something that stupid,' Jamie had remarked when she'd told him. She didn't know why she'd even risked it once, let alone repeatedly. Except there was such a feeling of being brave and clever, this surge of defiance as you lay there, your muscles all tensed to humming-point for the leap away. She'd never had a buzz like it since.

She rolled across to where he was stretched out and put her head against his bare shoulder. 'Haven't you ever done anything reckless?'

'Not when the danger had no point. I'm not a coward, but there's a time for risk.' His confidence both annoyed and impressed her. 'And I certainly would never do something I didn't want to just to wow the crowd. That was half Russ's trouble.'

Anna had first touched the cold metal track to prove her friendship. She hadn't told him that part, though. 'I'm not a victim, you know,' she said sharply.

He looked down at her, surprised. 'What? Where did that come from?'

Then she was back in the past again: Miriam at the dressing table winding up her heated rollers and telling her that bullying was part of school and it prepared you for life. She'd spoken out of the mirror. *It helps you grow up.*

Even now there was a lot Anna still wanted to say to her mother. But Miriam had cleverly put herself out of reach by dying; no more answers required.

When the doorbell rings late, you assume it's bad news. It was; it was Russ. Anna was in her bathrobe rinsing down the shower. She came onto the landing to hear him say, 'Can I have a word with you in private?' and Jamie go, 'Sure.' That had her running down the stairs.

Jamie was in the kitchen when she reached the hall so it was just her and Russ. He scowled when he saw her. 'OK?' she said, pulling a *WHAT!* face at him. They heard the freezer door clunk shut.

'It's all right, you're safe,' he muttered nastily.

Jamie emerged with a glass of ice cubes. 'I've bent my bloody nail back on that plastic tray again.'

'I've told you to run it under the hot tap for thirty seconds first,' said Anna. She wanted to sink onto the bottom step, and leant against the newel for support.

'So, come on through.'

Russ moved forward towards the lounge and Jamie glanced up at her. 'Sorry. He says—'

'I know, I heard him. I'll see you upstairs.'

He went through and pushed the door to behind him. 'God,' she heard Russ say before it closed, 'Anna's still looking a bit rough.'

Safe? she thought. When will I ever be safe again?

But it turned out to be only money. Jamie explained it after Russ had gone.

'He's had a cheque come through from a company that went under, something to do with the way creditors get paid.' Jamie took his shirt off and she watched him from the bed. 'What it was, he hadn't expected to see any of it but he got a fair chunk when they divvied up, plus there's a big order come in as well from a new customer. So, wonder of wonders, he's paid me back.'

'Was that it?'

'Yep. Puts him back on the moral high ground, we're quids in, everyone's happy.'

Anna lay back against the pillow. She felt very tired.

'He's got a downer on you at the moment, though,' went on Jamie, unclipping his watch and laying it on the dressing table.

'What do you mean?'

'Little barbed comments.'

'Such as?'

'Oh, you know. I shouldn't have said anything. It's only Russ grumbling on, he's always got someone in his sights. Usually me.'

'But what did he say?'

Jamie lifted the covers back and climbed in next to her. 'It wasn't anything. How he thought you didn't look on top form, that was all. But I told him, it's the end of term and she's knackered. I wouldn't mind if he was married to a raving beauty. God, now if I started on Ruth—' He reached up and switched off the light. After a silence he said. 'Have you had a fall-out with her?'

Her own breathing loud in the darkness. 'No. Why?'

'I was trying to work out why he might be so pissed off with you.' She was wondering how to reply when he said; 'I suppose you're too different, that's the trouble.

That's why you annoy him, you're another species. He can't fathom you.'

That was true enough. 'Let's not go to Ruth and Russ this Christmas,' Anna said quickly. 'Let's go off on our own somewhere.'

She was expecting a battle: We've said we'd go, Everywhere'll be booked up, How about we make it next year. But Jamie just said, 'OK.'

Still, it was a long time before she got to sleep.

Anna now went to the school garden whenever she could. Some lunchtimes – the ones she wasn't marking or report-writing or giving extra tuition – she took a book but other times she sat and thought. But there was always a sense of waiting, like an angler on a bank.

Ade, who had been Miriam's first Nantwich boyfriend, had taken Anna fishing once. She'd been invited because she was good at keeping quiet and also because Ade was under the impression that the way to curry favour with the mother was through the daughter. Anna had accepted because she was fed up of sitting in her bedroom. Also, she was curious about seeing a fish die. She asked about that on the way to the river: do you hit them on the head or let them suffocate? How long does it take? Could a dead fish come back to life if you threw it back? Ade was very patient with her and she could see even then that Miriam would get bored with him soon. He promised her she could help him reel the first fish in. But she missed the action because he only had one bite the whole two hours and that was when Anna had wandered off round the river bend and was watching water voles. 'Trouble is, you can't *make* a fish take bait,' he said as they trudged home. You'd do well to remember that, thought Anna, looking at his receding hairline.

Kali came to Anna on the last Monday of term. She appeared under a cypress arch as though she'd been conjured up. If I were an artist, thought Anna, I'd paint her like that, standing with her hands in her pockets, looking at the sky.

'So.' Anna laid her book on the bench.

'What do you mean?'

'How's it going?'

'I handed my essay in. Didn't you get it?'

'Yes; that's not what I was referring to.'

Kali twisted on the spot. 'Oh. Yeah, it's cool. Definitely.'

'Not spending too much time washing palettes?'

Jamie had said to her, 'Don't go barging in. You can end up doing more harm than good. Most of these spats resolve themselves, anyway. It's teen-female dynamics, best not tampered with.' Great form tutor he'd been.

'I like helping out,' said Kali.

'OK.'

There was a pause; Anna wondered whether Kali would go away, but she didn't. The silence stretched out companionably. After a minute, Anna closed her eyes, and when she opened them again it was because the slats of the bench had shifted under her and she knew the girl had sat down.

'I didn't want to come to this school,' she said, looking down through the archway to the far gate. 'I didn't want to move.'

Carefully, so as not to startle her, Anna turned her body so that she could see Kali's expression.

'Aren't you happy here?'

'Are you, Mrs Lloyd?'

The question took her aback. 'No, I'm not. But that's because, I've told you why I'm not happy at the moment.' Meet honesty with honesty.

'I've been thinking about that. Your baby.'

'You mustn't. I shouldn't have told you.'

'Why not?'

'Because it isn't professional of me to burden you with my personal life.'

'But you expect me to tell you mine.'

'Come on now, you're intelligent enough to understand the distinction. I'm in the role of carer here, whereas you're—'

'Except you did tell me.'

It's like being behind glass in this place, Anna thought. It's got a different feel from the rest of the school. As though the rules here could be different. She let herself examine Kali's face while she thought what to say. No make-up today, which made her more vulnerable, especially her eyes with their fair lashes; the skin was absolutely unlined. In her blue irises there were flecks of brown. She could have been any age, from twelve to twenty.

'Kali, who would you say were your friends here?'

'Depends what you mean by friend.'

'All right; who do you go round with?'

A flick of the lashes. 'Loads of people. Or no one. Depends on my mood.'

'Mr Weston said there'd been some bother when you split up with Nathan. Some girls were cross about it? Jealous?'

A tremor ran over the flanks of the hedge next to them.

'They say I've been stealing.'

'No! That's terrible.'

'I've had worse, Mrs Lloyd.'

The phrase and its intonation played through Anna's head for a while. She recalled the day Nathan's plate had hit her, and Kali's comment afterwards. *When Mum's boyfriend beat her up*, she'd said, *she used an ice pack*. At least my mother never subjected me to anything like that, thought Anna.

But before the Miriam thoughts could start up, Kali broke in. 'Can I say something?' She shook some strands of hair away from her mouth where they had blown across, and leant forwards earnestly, not waiting for a reply. 'That baby, yeah? It *was* real.'

'No,' Anna said gently. 'There was nothing there. We saw it on the scan.'

'It was a baby to you, though. Doesn't matter what the doctors said, it was a baby in your mind.'

A baby of the mind, thought Anna.

'And another thing,' Kali continued, 'when you lose someone I reckon they don't go away, not really. What I think is, yeah, they change into light, so if there's light around you, that's the person you've lost. Like, ripples

on water and sunsets and even candle flames. That's
what I reckon. So they're all around you all the time.'

'There's a poem like that.'

'Yeah? Well, it's what I think.'

Today the sun was only a pale shine behind grey
cloud. If anyone else had told her that her babies had
turned into light, she'd have been furious with them
for the sentimentality. But it would be nice to believe
something like that. Jamie had told her that there being
no foetus made it much easier. A blip, he'd said, not even
a proper miscarriage.

'They said I was stealing from their lockers,' said Kali
quickly, 'but I was looking for something of mine that
they'd taken.'

Anna was still imagining light on water. 'What?'

'Nathan had given them a letter of mine, one that I'd
written to him – told you he was a git – and they were
passing it round and taking the piss. It was awful. They
were reading it out. They wouldn't give it back. They
said it wasn't mine.'

'You're saying they had a love-letter that you'd
written?'

Kali snorted. 'Not *love*. Personal—'

'I'm with you. That's very mean.'

'I thought so. I only wanted it back. Anyone
would've done the same.'

'Look,' Anna took a deep breath, 'which girls were
involved? I'll have a word. We'll get this sorted, I
promise you.'

But Kali had stood up and begun to wander away
from the bench.

'He won't be back, you know.'

'Who? Nathan?'

'Yeah. Gone for good.'

The way Kali spoke made Anna's scalp prickle. 'You say that almost as if you'd put some kind of spell on him.'

'I wish.'

'Why did you go out with him? I never understood it.'

Kali shrugged. 'He's confident, he thinks everything's a laugh. It was sort of easy being with him, if you know what I mean.'

'Not really.'

'No, well. I soon realized he was a bastard. So anyway, he's gone to join a drama school where his Talents can be Properly Recognized.'

Nathan gone! It was all Anna could do not to whoop aloud. 'Does Mr Jackson know?'

Kali shook her head. 'It's supposed to be a secret till he's got in, or had his interview, whatever, only he can't keep his mouth shut. The sixth form know because he told Zoe Parker. Don't say anything yet, though. For God's sake don't mention my name.'

'I wouldn't. I wouldn't pass on anything you'd told me in confidence.'

'That's OK, then.'

'Just as I know you won't talk about my own situation.'

The sentences balanced in the cold air.

'Never, Mrs Lloyd.' Kali's face was an oval of sincerity. 'I would never do that.'

Chapter Fourteen

'I've got a theory about Russ,' said Jamie. 'That the reason he doesn't like you is because he sees you as a symbol of something unattainable.'

Anna, sitting at her desk painting a miniature meat safe, didn't trust herself to speak.

'See, you're sorted. You don't live in a mess. That's why he hates me too. We represent a lifestyle he can never access because of the choices he's made.' He leaned against the door jamb looking pleased with himself, waiting for her to agree.

Anna carried on painting and eventually he went away.

Kali didn't come the next day, although Anna had cleared her lunchtime deliberately, coming in early to get photocopying done and rearranging a meeting with a Sixth-Former.

She waited in the same spot as before for an hour, a book on her lap and her eyes watering with the cold. They'd made no firm arrangement. Why should the girl be anywhere in particular? No one had been let down.

Little birds moved among the leaves. One of them,

some nervous grey thing, was calling over and over again *not-fair, not-fair, not-fair, not-fair*. If you could time-travel, she thought, this might be one of the places you'd go from. If you could go back and warn yourself against events.

Most days she tried very hard not to let her mind slide onto the miscarriages; there was no point, she was used to thinking by instinct around them. No amount of self-analysis could conjure up a baby.

But sitting here now she found that she wanted to be sad. She wanted to remind herself what she'd lost: not simply a baby, but the approval of society which smiled at pregnant women in the street and stopped to admire the contents of a pram, as though the mother had done something astonishingly clever. Parent-and-child parking spaces mocked her when she went shopping, TV advertisement breaks in the middle of late-night films showed happy parents eating butter-substitute, sniffing washing powder, driving family cars. If you were infertile there was always this sense of letting the side down. Childless women were selfish, and parents jealous of your long nights in bed and uncluttered homes marginalized you as a punishment for bucking the trend.

In her head she'd often practised being a mother. She saw herself (and it was like a real memory) walking around a science museum with a little boy, explaining the exhibits to him and answering his questions. After the visit, she'd have taken him home and done experiments in the kitchen like growing crystals and freezing soap bubbles. Or sometimes it was a girl whose hair she brushed and plaited; sometimes a baby she held up to a full moon, its round eyes glittering.

Now, when she tried to imagine Jamie as a father, she got a block. All she could picture instead was Russ's cross face as he stood in the middle of his lounge shouting about Lego. All that joy wasted on him. And Ruth, buying sweets over comics in the supermarket, sticking the TV on for sixteen hours at a stretch, throwing out books because they took up ornament space. She recalled Natasha asking for advice on how to do French nail polish 'because Mum bites hers to stumps' and Tom bringing her his dolls to dress, knowing even at three he'd get no sympathy in any other quarter. 'You're very patient with them,' Ruth had once said, grudgingly. To which Anna had not replied, And you're such an ungrateful bitch.

Then there were those mothers who went on holiday and left their children in the house alone, who smoked over the heads of their asthmatic babies, who never made physical contact except in anger; news stories that made her jab the radio mute button or turn the page quickly. Because what kind of mad world was it, where beautiful babies were every day placed into the arms of monsters?

The final vision Anna allowed herself before she went back inside school to thaw was the one of the white cottage, her dolls' house realized. The garden was full of lupins and hollyhocks and she was there, behind the green gate. If Jamie ever discovered her affair she'd take off and find that place. She'd walk out and leave everything behind like her mother had always done.

*

It was on the penultimate day of term that Kali delivered her news.

Morning break, and Anna was in the corridor with Lin Keane discussing *Talking Heads*.

'They're so funny and so sad at the same time.' Lin shook her lank hair in admiration. 'And they're so real, aren't they? That one with the old lady, I was nearly crying at the end, and the bit about wrapping the baby in newspaper, God.'

'It's a very moving line. Interesting that you picked it out.'

'Thanks for lending it me, anyway.'

'I had a feeling you'd like the style. And if you're thinking about A-level, that's one of the texts we look at.'

'Is it? Wow.' The girl glowed. 'I thought the books would be harder than that.'

'We get through a variety of texts, some of them more accessible than others. But you wouldn't have any trouble, Lin. I take it you are considering English Lit?'

'Will you be taking it, Mrs Lloyd?'

Anna was about to say she didn't know, when someone coming up behind her seized her arm and fumbled down it to her hand. 'What—?'

Kali was unfolding Anna's fingers and pressing something into her palm. There was a smell of cigarette smoke overlaid with patchouli for a second, then Kali had detached herself and was walking quickly away. The same tingling shock she'd felt after the plate hit her was beginning in Anna's chest.

'Wait!'

Lin's mouth had gone tight and annoyed. She said loudly: 'What's the A-level Language course like?'

'Give me a minute,' said Anna.

She unpleated the note as fast as she could and read; *I need to see you.* Nothing else. 'When?' Anna called, but Kali had rounded the corner and was out of sight. In the background, Lin sighed and turned away.

The door to Les's office opened and Jackson came out, almost knocking Anna over because he was too busy looking back and blethering. 'Watch yourself, there,' he said when he noticed her staggering to one side. He was in an enormously good mood, clasping his hands and beaming. 'Aha! Mrs Lloyd, would you like to walk with me to my room?'

She hated it when he attempted roguish. 'I was actually—'

'It won't take a moment. Will it, Mr Weston?'

Les raised his eyebrows at Anna and she knew she should do as she was told.

'After you, Mrs Lloyd.' Jackson flourished his arm in mock gallantry.

They had not gone more than ten paces when he said, 'Do you know what I'm about to do now?'

Could be any brand of bollocks, she thought. 'I have no idea.'

'When I get to my room I shall call in Mrs Hislop and dictate to her a notice to go up on the staff board.' Here he left a dramatic pause.

'Oh?'

'About a friend of yours.'

'Nathan Woods?'

He stopped in surprise. 'How did you guess?'

'A hunch.'

'Well, it'll be public knowledge by lunchtime but I thought you'd appreciate hearing ahead of everyone else: he's leaving. Left. Going to a performing arts college in Manchester and hoping to make a career in television.'

They were by the doors to the hall now and Anna could see the back of Kali's head through the glass panel. Jackson noticed her gaze slipping past him and shifted so his bulk was blocking the view.

'Good news, eh? For you.'

'So I shan't have to make a formal apology?'

'Not unless you want to.' He meant this as a joke, she assumed. 'No, I think the Woods have other things on their plate now. Forget the lad. Put him behind you.'

'Right.'

'So, there you are.'

It dawned on her that he was waiting for a thank you. Jackson was evidently under the impression he had sorted the situation for her. But why should she be charitable to this man who always got himself in the way, uselessly?

'We've been lucky,' she said as the bell began to ring for the end of break. When it stopped he was still looking hopeful. 'Thanks,' she said. Now she would hate herself all morning.

She waded through lessons five and six, then hurried straight to Kali's form-room. There was no one there, which was what she'd expected, so she went to the staffroom to grab her sandwiches. It was imperative she get down to the garden as soon as possible.

As she was extricating her lunch box from behind the ranks of selfish stupid yoghurts in the fridge, Andrew Maye clapped her on the shoulder.

'Result!'

'What?'

'Nathan's out.'

'Yes, I know.' One of the front pots leaned, fell and rolled towards the edge of the shelf. She jammed the heel of her palm against the wire just in time.

'Isn't it brilliant?'

If he would just leave her alone. 'Yes.'

'What's up?'

'Nothing. I've got a meeting.' She knew she'd snapped and wasn't surprised when he backed off and pulled a face at Liz. Finally Anna managed to slide the plastic box out, grabbed her coat and umbrella, and made for the door.

Chrissy was expecting her down in room 16 to help tidy the book cupboard, she knew, but too bad. The excuse had been framed: *I had a pastoral emergency, Chris. These things won't wait.* It was true. Pupils like Kali didn't open up too often. For all Anna knew, it might be desperate.

She must look mad, she thought, sitting on this freezing bench under an indifferent sky. But Kali appeared within minutes, wearing a man's black overcoat and black fingerless gloves. She came forward till she was standing opposite the bench, and looked down at Anna.

'I'm leaving,' she announced. 'I'm leaving the school.'

Anna was immediately thrown into confusion. 'When? Why, for God's sake?'

'Soon. Mum says it's not a good thing for her to depend on Owen's money because it ties us down.'

'But she's engaged to him.'

'I know. They don't always get on, though.'

For God's sake, thought Anna. 'Well, you don't! It's not all roses round the door, you know. Marriage, being with someone, is about having bad times and good. To expect anything else is . . .' She was about to say, childish.

Kali stuck her hands in her deep pockets. 'Yeah, anyway, she was saying it's at least two more years' worth of fees and she wasn't sure about that kind of commitment if it didn't work out with Owen.'

Bit late to think of that now, wasn't it? Anna searched the girl's face, trying to gauge how upset she was.

'Do you think she means it?'

'Not sure. Mum makes these snap decisions. Could be on one day and off the next.'

I know all about that kind of behaviour, Anna thought. 'She could just have been having a moan. People say things when they're fed up that aren't necessarily true.'

'Maybe.'

'How would you feel if she did take you away?'

'Crap,' said Kali. Tiny drops of moisture clung to her hair like silver beads.

'Look, it's starting to rain, do you want to go inside?'

'No.'

'Then sit down.'

She patted the bench and Kali drew in beside her. 'Let's get this umbrella up,' said Anna, shaking out the spokes and pushing at the handle till it clicked. She rested her fist halfway along the back of the bench so they were both sheltered, the canvas casting a greenish light as though they were under water. 'That's better. So: I thought you weren't especially settled here?'

'I am.' The response was emphatic. 'I was just starting to feel I belonged.'

Anna wondered about this, but said nothing.

'It's like, I know I don't go round with a big group, but I don't think you need to be with people all the time to feel good. Do you?'

'No. But that's something I've worked out over years. I wouldn't have had the confidence to think that way when I was a teenager.'

Kali gave a sad laugh. 'I am exceptionally mature for my age.'

'You are, aren't you?'

'It's a curse, Mrs Lloyd.'

'I imagine it can be.'

Anna had an image, out of nowhere, of the two of them walking along a sea front on a winter day; this would be years in the future when Kali was grown up but Anna was still the same age. They might sit in a cafe together and watch the water and talk about life. The soundtrack would be *Brood: Four Oceans*. Jamie was not in the picture.

She was brought back to the present by Kali shifting

about awkwardly and pulling at the sides of the huge coat.

'Oops, sorry, Mrs Lloyd. Hang on.' Her hand moved around under the thick material. 'Look, I wanted to show you something. If I can get the—' At last she managed to draw a square white envelope out of her skirt pocket. 'Here.'

Anna frowned. 'You want me to open this?'

'Yeah.'

'Are you sure?'

It was Kali's turn to look puzzled. 'It's only a Christmas card. What did you think it was?'

God, what a fool. 'Your secret letter.'

'Huh?'

'You said some girls had taken a letter you sent Nathan—'

'Oh, no.' Kali's focus shifted to somewhere beyond them both. 'I did get that back, though.'

'So it's sorted?'

'Yeah.'

'If you're sure.'

'Definitely. And there's a present in it, to say thanks.'

Over the years Anna had received many gifts. Some came from the parents – good wine, Crabtree & Evelyn, Thornton's – and some directly from the pupils themselves. In the cupboard by the dolls' house she kept a nodding boxer dog, a hand-painted mug, a pebble with eyes, a friendship bracelet, a plaster badge of a horse's head. There were cards and letters and drawings and photos. It restored her to go through these things from time to time; proof that she had made some difference with her life. Her favourite present ever had been a clumsy portrait of Emily Brontë by a girl who'd begun the year hating Anna, hating English. When Anna had taken the drawing up to the staffroom on the last day of term, Andrew had been showing off a bottle of cuvée. 'That all you got, Mrs Lloyd? Bad luck.' 'Ah,' Les had observed, 'but to earn your prize, Andrew, you had to put up with the loathsome Mrs Goodridge phoning you weekly about darling Ivan's progress. She's sold you short. You deserve an entire case.' The drawing was better than any vintage champagne, but there was nothing she could have said without sounding pious. 'You'll just have to try harder next year,' Andrew had told her.

Kali reached across and tapped the paper edge. 'There's a poem in it, Mrs Lloyd.'

Inside the silver and white snowflake card was another sealed envelope.

'Shall I read it now?'

'Up to you. It's about, you know, light.'

Anna scanned the message Kali had written under Season's Greetings. *Thanks for helping*, she'd put. *Keep in touch.*

'I don't think I've done anything.'

'Yeah, you have. It's enough that you listened. Mum never listens.'

Mrs Norman in her velvet jacket and straining jeans. I don't imagine she does, thought Anna. No time for anything as dull as a daughter. She said in a rush: 'You know when you said your mother's boyfriend hit her? Does that ever still happen?'

'Oh, no. That was ages ago. It was only a couple of times.'

Anna experienced a tiny dip of disappointment. A second later, she was horrified at herself. 'That's great, glad to hear it. You understand why I had to ask?'

'Sure.'

'Will you be all right over Christmas?'

'Yeah, course.'

'I'll give you my address and mobile number.' Though what could she do from Devon?

'Great, thanks.'

'And I'll read your poem when I'm on my own.'

'Whatever.'

She felt the bench move as Kali stood up.

'It's a real shame about your baby, 'cause you'd have made a brilliant mum, you know. You would. Life's just shit sometimes, bad things happening to good people.' She shook her hair over her shoulder and sighed. 'Just shit. Shitty and unfair.'

Anna moved her lips to say yes but no sound came out.

'Anyway.' The rain was drawing Kali's hair into dark tendrils round her cheeks. 'See you, then, Mrs Lloyd.'

But Anna could only nod and raise her hand.

Chapter Fifteen

They made themselves go for a walk before they exchanged their gifts; this was a Christmas Day ritual that had started the year they got married, though Anna couldn't remember who'd first suggested it or why. Other fixed points had been lunch round at Russ's, and doing the *Daily Mail* bumper festive quiz all afternoon while Ruth said things like, I am definitely getting a stone off in the New Year.

But this time Ruth and Russ were miles away, might have ceased to exist for all Anna knew. She was walking down a high-hedged Devon lane with Jamie. The only sounds were cawing rooks and, faintly, a church bell.

'If there was snow it would be a perfect Christmas scene,' she said.

He was hanging back, fingering a bramble leaf. Then the notebook came out and he made some jottings. 'Funny how so many things have veins,' he said. 'Leaves, marble, us.'

'I suppose.'

'When you look at the world with a writer's eye you see all these connections.'

Anna would have liked to ask him about progress with the script but she didn't want to spoil the day.

After a while they strayed away from the right-hand bank and walked confidently down the centre of the road.

'Some of these stiles are really old,' she said. 'I wonder how many people have climbed them over the years?'

Out with the notebook again. When he'd finished, he came alongside her and took her hand.

'What?' she said.

'Nothing.'

Back in the thatched hotel they sat by a log fire and unwrapped their gifts. 'This is so much nicer than going to your brother's,' she ventured, as he picked at the Sellotape on her parcel. 'Perhaps we could do it every year?'

'Tricky. They expect us, we're part of the day.'

'Do they really want us there, though, or are they just being polite?'

Jamie shook his head. 'I tell you, Ruth was gutted when I told her we weren't coming this year. But she did agree a break would do you good – oh, Anna.' He pulled the paper aside and drew out a slim book with a green cover. 'Allison McVety!'

'It's signed.'

'Wow. Where did you get it?'

'eBay. They do quite a few poetry books on there.'

'And, hey, a dictaphone.'

'For when inspiration strikes.' She knew by his face she'd hit the target.

'Thank you.' He leaned across and gave her a swift kiss. 'Yours now.'

He watched while she undid a miniature Clarice Cliff tea set. There were tiny cups with triangular handles, a matching milk jug and pot. Each plate showed an orange tree and a hill. 'Oh, my God. They're amazing. Where did you get them?'

'An artist called Sally Meekins makes them. I could show you her website but then you'd know how much I paid.'

'I promise not to look at the prices.' Anna was still taking out each little object and turning it between thumb and forefinger. 'They're perfect, aren't they?'

'If you say so. Not my line. I thought you'd appreciate them.'

Russ and Ruth – Ruth, in fact, since Russ had probably never chosen a Christmas present in his life – had got for them a foot-long wheelbarrow filled with dried lavender. 'Nice,' said Jamie. There was also a parcel from the children, which turned out to be half a dozen packets of dolls' house food plus a box of real-size Milk Tray.

Jamie inspected a tiny plate of fondant fancies. 'It's all cakes and sweets. See, Kit Kats and Liquorice Allsorts and, what are those, Viennese whirls. Jesus. But you won't be able to use those in a wartime house, will you? Never mind the anachronistic wrappers, what you've got there is about a year's worth of sugar rations for an entire village. How wonderfully typical of my sister-in-law.'

'There's a little telephone as well.'

'Not a mobile, is it?' He was laughing now.

'No. Victorian. Stop it, Jamie. It's the thought that counts.'

She couldn't let herself mock for the same reason that, this year, she'd bought Ruth a Dior bath set instead of some pig-related pot. Russ would even now be unwrapping a giant DIY manual, which was the most unromantic present she could find.

'What did we get them, anyway?' he said, gathering up the torn paper. 'In case it's me who picks up when Ruth phones to say thanks.'

'One of these days I'll make you do the gift-shopping,' she said.

She had a sudden memory of a Christmas years ago: Jamie attempting to show Tash how to use K'nex to make a model car; Tash only wanting to turn out rows of identically spiky bracelets. 'So much for trying to break the gender stereotype,' he'd said, throwing his model back into the box. Another year he'd complained Beth's snotty nose was putting him off his turkey. The look of horror when Ruth asked him to lean across and wipe the baby's top lip for her. 'You'll feel differently when it's your own,' Ruth had said, to Jamie's grimace.

But Anna shook the pictures out of her head. She was not going to drop back into that groove today.

They spent the afternoon in their room, Jamie watching TV and Anna on the laptop. Several times he looked longingly over but she couldn't tell whether it was at her or the machine.

'Shall we give them a ring?' he asked at one point.

The phone had been switched on all day because Anna had wondered whether Kali might call.

'OK,' said Anna, but neither of them did and the phone stayed silent. Still, it was the best Christmas she could have hoped for, under the circumstances.

Mel came down to Chester for the sales.

'Fantastic to see you!' Anna, meeting her at the station, was struck shy and awkward. 'It seems like a lot longer than four months.'

'I'll say it does. This place doesn't change, though, does it?'

They fought their way from shop to shop.

'You could have stayed over with us, made a day of it,' Anna said, standing back as Mel pushed through racks of sweaters in Next.

'No, I have to get back to Greg.'

'Who?'

'I told you about him.' Mel unhooked a hanger and held it up, then against herself. 'What do you think of this?'

'You didn't.'

'What's the label? It's wool, so—'

'You never mentioned him.'

'I *did*, Anna. Teaches PE. Bald but sexy. I definitely, oh, God, it's chaos in here. Look, let's go get something to drink.'

I knew it, thought Anna as they fought their way across the packed street to the Rows; there's something different about her.

They queued without talking. When they finally got

a seat Mel said, 'I have mentioned Greg, told you about him weeks ago, because you said divorcees often came with baggage.'

Shoppers streamed past the window, vacant-eyed and loaded with carriers.

'I didn't realize you were seeing him. I thought you were just sizing up the available talent.'

'I was, at the time. There've been developments.'

'Evidently.'

In all the time Mel had taught at Montcliff she'd had only had one boyfriend, and that had been an on-off affair because he lived in Cornwall. She claimed it was an arrangement that suited her. 'It's perfect. I can do what I want most of the time, please myself, and then he's there when I fancy some horizontal aerobics. I'm too busy to be married, any of that shit.' But Anna could tell things had changed.

'It's been a hell of a term,' Mel was saying now. 'I told you the department's pretty crap because the guy I took over from couldn't be bothered and the staff were more or less used to doing what they liked. Plus now the second i/c's suddenly announced she's retiring at the end of this year, and she's not for taking on a load of new ideas, she just wants to coast her way out. Mrs Popular I'm not. It's one bloody big headache.'

'Why did you go, then? You were happy here.'

'Because you have to move on, don't you? You do, Anna. I don't necessarily mean careers and stuff. You have to, kind of, refresh yourself every so often. Try something new. Otherwise . . .'

'Otherwise what?'

'Oh, I don't know. It was time to flex myself; bigger department, bigger school. Marginally more dosh. But I do miss you lot. God, I even miss Jackson. Our Head's never there and when he is he's miserable as sin. At least Jackson smiles.'

'Smiles and smiles and is a villain,' said Anna. It was a joke they'd shared before. 'You've finished with Launce, then? Our man in Cornwall?'

'That was only ever recreational.'

'You like your independence.'

Mel pursed her lips and blew on her latte. 'Well . . .'

You do, you do! thought Anna.

'I'm forty-one,' Mel said, as though this explained everything. 'So anyway, tell me about my replacement.'

'There's nothing to tell. She keeps herself to herself.'

'But she's supportive?'

'Yeah, pretty much. So far.'

'Is she one of the Broody Hens?'

'No.'

'Sounds like your type, then.'

'I suppose she could be worse,' said Anna, without enthusiasm.

After coffee they went to more shops. Anna had never seen Mel so interested in clothes; she was picking up girly tops and chiffon skirts, nothing like her usual style. And had she put on weight?

'How'll you go hiking in that?' asked Anna, as Mel held an ankle-length gypsy number to her waist. Mel just laughed. There was something almost flirtatious in her manner which had Anna all at sea.

They picked their way through the people and racks

until Mel announced she wanted to try an outfit on. 'Come in the changing rooms with me,' she said. 'Grab anything.'

'It's too stuffy, there's no air in here. I'll wait by the door and watch for you coming out.'

Mel shrugged. 'Suit yourself. Semaphore your opinion to me.'

Anna pushed through to the exit and stood by a rail of fuchsia and petrol blue blouses. Imagine wearing colours like that. She unbelted her grey coat and let it fall open.

It was disorientating and provoking. Mel's life had clearly moved on, but why the secrecy? Why hadn't she told Anna about it? This relationship with Greg must have been brewing for months.

But then Kali's words came back to her: *You expect me to tell you my secrets but you don't tell me yours.* Anna hadn't confided anything of importance to Mel for a long time. To begin explaining what had happened recently, she'd have to reveal earlier concealments. It would become complicated and shameful. And there wasn't time now, this wasn't the right place, and perhaps Mel wasn't even interested any more.

Mel appeared now at the far end of the store, waving. When Anna looked up, she held her arms away from her sides like a paper doll. She'd chosen a paisley tunic in dull greens; dreadful. Anna nodded non-committally and Mel beamed. There was such a plump smugness about her today. Dear God, might she be pregnant? Mel did a little curtsey and disappeared back into the cubicles.

Anna snatched up the blouse nearest to her and, as she did so, caught a glimpse of herself in a long mirror angled to the door. A pale face under dark hair and this vivid pink silk below; it didn't look like her. She could really have been someone else. There was a moment where she wanted to hug the material to her and just run through the alarm, which was ridiculous because she could certainly have afforded to pay, and in any case, where would she run to? But she held onto the blouse and carried on gazing at herself. You couldn't see the mac and black sweater underneath at all. Movement at the edge of her vision: Mel had come out again, this time in a crop top.

Anna mouthed *No* and was turning away with the intention of hanging the blouse up again when she caught sight of Russ coming across the precinct out of Watergate Street. She didn't recognize him at first; her attention was drawn initially by the way he moved, walking so purposefully through the slow-milling crowd, barging people aside so that they frowned and exchanged glances. His coat flapped about him and he was scowling, and as he drew near, she saw he was staring straight into her eyes.

She stepped back in alarm. For God's sake, he looked as though he was about to knife her.

Never breaking his stride, he came through the entrance of the shop, right up to her, and grabbed her upper arms. His fingers dug in hard, and even through the cloud of shock she wondered whether he'd leave bruises and what Jamie would say.

Before she could speak Russ pressed his mouth

down against hers and she tasted mints and whisky as his wet stiff tongue slithered against her skin. She clamped her lips together, and that made him hold her arms even more tightly. He was probing her face and working his jaw against her and she wanted to shout out, but her mouth was full of him and she could only moan. The sensation of being stifled added to the panic and she made to wrench away; he just moved with her, like something welded onto her flesh. She began to wonder whether she might suffocate as the kiss went on and on in a series of images, real and remembered: a tiny round window in the church apex opposite, a pigeon in silhouette, the caravan curtains, someone's Doc Martens, Kali's hair, an aeroplane trail, and Russ's angry eyes fused into one unfocused blur.

At last, when she was thinking she might faint, he let her go and she staggered back against the wall. You total *bastard*, she was going to yell at him, and damn that couple in the corner looking at her, for Christ's sake hadn't they got anything better to do than stand around gawping? She wiped her face on the back of her hand and then, more aggressively, on her cuff. The skin all round her mouth felt scraped raw.

But Russ had gone. In the seconds while she collected herself he had turned and walked off into the mass of shoppers round the Cross. In fact, where was he now? She'd lost sight of him almost immediately. Her biceps throbbed where his fingers had been and her legs were shaking. She realized she was still clutching the blouse on its hanger.

The couple who'd been watching had lost interest

and were counting coins out of the man's wallet. No one else seemed to have noticed. She swung her head round, taking in the whole store, but she didn't see anyone she recognized, thank God. Half the bloody school went shopping in Chester. She'd once been half naked in a changing room and come face to face with Jackson's wife.

And here came Mel again.

'You were right, I looked a dog,' she said, swinging her bags. 'V-necks make your face appear longer, I read that in a magazine.'

'Ah.'

'Which is something I do not need. That's nice, though. You'd look nice in that.' She lifted the sleeve of the fuchsia blouse. 'Are you going to try it on?'

Anna's mind was racing. She stared at Mel. *Do you know what's just happened to me? I've had an affair! I lost a baby! That special pupil's left! Why didn't you tell me about Greg?*

She could have opened her mouth and come out with anything.

'Mel?'

'Yeah?'

'—Are you expecting?'

'Expecting?'

'Are you pregnant?'

'No! Hell, no.' Mel laughed in a hurt way and looked down at herself. 'Wherever did you get that idea? Shit, have I put on so much weight?'

Anna shook her head and half turned away while she collected herself. She wanted badly to be home.

'Is the baby thing still bothering you? I thought you'd finished with all that.'

'I have.'

'Oh. Good.' Mel sounded relieved. ''Cause, I can tell you now, you went a bit mad for a while. Like you couldn't see anything else.'

You try going through it, thought Anna. 'No, it's in the past.'

'Right. Only, this afternoon you've been . . . Like you were cross about something. What's on your mind? Have I done something wrong?'

'School stuff, Jamie. Hormones,' said Anna. 'Nothing to do with you at all.'

'What are you up to?'

In a strange role-reversal, Jamie was waiting for Anna to finish on the laptop, hanging around in the doorway of the spare room. The main computer was out of action, away at the menders, leaving a dark rectangle in the dust on his desk. Jamie was bereft.

She closed the screen quickly. 'Researching a GCSE site,' she said.

'Again? There can't be any more sites left to check.'

'They're always updating.'

He came forward to see but she'd brought a page of eBay up instead.

'I could install that anti-spyware for you, if you like.'

'Tomorrow.' She tapped words into the search engine. *Deco, Thirties.*

'You're finding it useful?'

'Huh?'

'The laptop.'

'Oh, yeah.'

He stood next to her, flexing his fingers. 'I like your blouse,' he said after a while.

'Mm.'

'You're like an Eastern princess. Turkish Delight. Is it silk?'

1930, she typed. 'Don't know.'

'It's nice to see you in a bit of colour, anyway.'

'Yeah.'

'Takes years off you.'

Wartime, Forties. 'Good.'

At last he slouched off to watch TV.

As soon as he'd gone, she opened up the site again.

It was duplicity by omission; well, she'd had to tick one box that said she was under eighteen, but that was the only time she'd lied. In any case, what mattered was intent, and she was on the site to help.

She'd checked out InkJet at Lin's request, initially. Did Mrs Lloyd know there was an Internet writing site where young authors could post their work for peer review? Anna had not known, but thought it sounded interesting. However, to access the review forums you had to register, and this was where things had become awkward.

She'd had to construct a profile for herself – age, location, username, interests – and since the truth would not do she'd had to spin herself a false identity. So she was Cayenne, sixteen, from Shrewsbury, into Brood and Françoise Sagan and how embarrassing would it be if

Jamie were to glance over and see her details? She could imagine only too well the kind of comments he'd make. Birthday cards with '16' badges on the front, remarks dropped in front of Ruth and Russ about how young she was looking, was she using a new face cream, etc. The joke would run and run. That's if he saw it as a joke. He might equally well decide her behaviour was perverted or borderline schizophrenic. And yet all she was doing was reading students' stories and giving them feedback and encouragement. An extension of marking, that was all, but much more fun because of the banter and because these were people who were writing for the love of it, not as a homework exercise. *Be Part of the Jet Set!* said the banner across the top of the screen. It was a buzzy environment, one to lose yourself in. Addictive.

Here came Jamie again, now with coffee. She half lowered the laptop lid as he came near, as though she were a child in the middle of a spelling test.

'Give me a shout when you've finished so I can do your spyware, won't you?'

'Uh-huh.'

He paused, then turned and peered in through the front of the dolls' house. 'Found anything interesting lately?'

'Still browsing.'

'The hallway's better now you've redone the carpet. I didn't even know you could get miniature stair rods.'

'There you go.'

'Hey, you might even find some dolls that are right, one day. I know you're not keen, but Ruth was saying she'd seen some Victorian villa on TV where the lady-doll of the house is sitting in her boudoir talking to her husband, then, if you go round the back, the lover's climbing out the window on a ladder. Sort of visual gag.'

'Hilarious.' Anna was thinking how nice it would have been to show Kali the site, get her to post some of her poems. She wondered how the girl was and what she was doing at this moment. Sitting in a lonely bedroom, crying?

'You could have your family crouched under the table as if it was an air raid.'

'Mmm.'

He lurked behind her, opening the little windows and fingering the edge of the roof tiles.

It crossed her mind fleetingly that if she did show him the InkJet site he might understand. He was a writer, after all. But the moment passed. Too risky, too inviting of ridicule or worse.

'So, I'll be downstairs. Give me a shout.'

'I will.'

He didn't move.

'Don't forget your coffee.'

'No.'

The staffroom had been painted in their absence and the chemical smell was still sharp and offensive. Anna was starting term in a mean mood.

'Can you *believe* where the holiday went?' said Tom Maxfield, as he always did. He was bent over the coffee table sorting papers energetically. 'It is amazing, isn't it? I mean, where does the time go? Eh? Where does it go to?'

'Sorry, can't cope with philosophical questions this early in the morning,' said Les.

'Mind you, we had a brilliant Christmas,' Tom went on. 'Marshall had this mad idea to go carol singing. Just go, you know, round the houses!'

'That is what carol singers do,' said Anna.

Les grinned at her. 'Did you take your guitar, Tom?'

'I did. It was great. Everyone appreciated it. *Silent Night*, you know . . . *O Little Town.* Brilliant.'

'Well, I went out and bought myself a huge telly,' said Ian Poole. 'Sixty-one-inch screen. Absolutely massive, it is. The effect's fantastic as well, it feels like you're actually in the film.'

Anna watched his lips struggling to shape the words over his irregular teeth. You'd have been better spending the money on good dental work, she thought. A set like yours, you'd want to whip them all out and start from scratch.

Andrew entered, shaking rain off his umbrella. 'Anyone seen Jackson?'

Les nodded.

'So you all know about the inspection?'

'That was supposed to be announced at the staff meeting this afternoon,' said Les.

Andrew shrugged. 'He's told me. Told me in the corridor just now.'

'We've finally got a date?' asked Tom.

'This time next year.'

'Oh, that's ages off,' spat Ian. 'We can all relax again.'

'Not quite.' Les pushed a pin viciously into the noticeboard. 'We need to be getting all our documentation into place for the autumn term and focusing on record-keeping and pupil assessment. That's got to start as soon as possible. Your heads of department'll be talking to you about it. I know, it's a sod. This is why the news was being saved till the end of the day, to let you get your breath back.'

Anna wanted to go up and pat his shoulder. He looked so tired. What kind of Christmas had he had, she wondered? Next to him, Andrew, sleek and well-sexed, stretched his arms above his head as though preparing for gymnastics. She caught the flash of a new, expensive watch on his wrist.

'Fuck 'em. If the inspectors are going to come, let's get it over with. But I'm not putting on a three-ring circus for them. They can see me teach as normal.'

'I think that's the idea,' said Les.

'There was a note from Chrissy in my pigeonhole,' Anna broke in, to distract. 'She's putting on a mini drama festival at Easter, wants something from every Year. Any ideas?'

'Oh, fucking marvellous,' said Andrew. 'Just what I needed on top of mocks and modules and pre-bloody inspection meetings. I think I'll turn round and go home again.'

'Maybe we can work something out together . . .'

'The trouble with Chrissy is, she's no conception of what it's like to teach a full timetable. Yeah, I could put on a drama festival if I had four non-contact periods a day. Sorry, Anna, I'm not doing it and I'm going to tell her so.'

Ian wandered over to the sink and flicked the water

heater on. 'How big's your TV, Andrew?' he asked. In the far corner, Tom was patting out some tune on his thighs like a drummer in an asylum.

Anna took herself into the workroom and stood for a minute deep-breathing and watching the rain pour down the glass. The sky was dark grey, and the elder by the windowsill glowed ultra-green under the approaching storm. All the strip lights were switched on in school, some of them still with the torn ends of Christmas decorations attached. It gave the place an eerie, flickering air. She thought of Jamie at home, brewing his coffee and sawing open a new packet of bourbons. How much time did he really spend writing? On the other side of the workroom wall, Chrissy's voice asked Andrew whether he had any thoughts about an Easter drama festival. 'Anna and I are getting together,' she heard him reply, and Chrissy's bright, approving intonation filtered through the clatter of milk bottles being unloaded. Time to get going.

She was on her way to assembly, moving with the crush down the main corridor, when she spotted Kali slipping through the double doors into the hall.

'Andrew?' Anna pushed and dodged to catch up with him as the line of students shuffled forward.

'What's the matter?'

'I've just seen Kali Norman.'

'And?'

'I thought she'd left. I thought her mother took her away—'

She stopped herself; it wasn't appropriate to talk about a pupil's financial situation here in public.

'Calm down, dear, it's only a pupil.' Andrew was smiling down at her in a way she didn't like. 'She turned up this morning with a letter to say she's staying. But since we hadn't got round to removing her from any lists yet, it hasn't made any difference. I'd crossed her name out in the register but I can Tipp-Ex it back in again.'

'What was the reaction of the other kids?'

'Nothing, far as I can tell. I don't think she'd spread it round that she was leaving.'

They had reached the doorway and he went ahead of her. Mozart filled the hall; no further conversation was possible. Anna walked past the chair she usually took, so she was further away from the stage and close to the line of Year Ten. Then she let her gaze rove naturally around until it came to light on Kali, as if by accident. There she was! Anna tried to catch her eye but the girl was looking at the floor, her hair hanging down so it obscured her features. Was she happy or sad to be back here today?

Jackson began to speak, the usual spiel about new opportunities and respect for oneself that he always gave at New Year. Time for a hymn, and she could smell Liz's perfume, over-sweet and synthetic, coming from the row behind her.

Think how all-seeing God thy ways
And all thy secret thought surveys

Anna thought of Russ kissing her in town and felt a rush of nerves. Then, out of nowhere, came a Miriam memory: the last time she'd seen her mother. Miriam had been subdued. She'd followed Anna round the flat, watching her pack.

'It's not been all bad, has it?'

Anna had given no answer, which perhaps in retrospect was cruel.

'Are you taking your old books? I can't store them, I haven't the room.'

Her own grand reply; 'I'll send for them.' Send who? What had she been talking about? The books would be out with the rubbish first thing, they both knew.

They could have ended with a row. Anna could have said, *Isn't this what you've wanted for years? You can do what you like at last. Why so glum? You should be cheering.* But that would have been dangerously close to real communication and the last thing Anna needed, just as she was bowing out.

'Well, I don't know. It's going to be funny without you round the place.' Miriam's parting shot.

And Anna had said: 'I expect you'll survive.' But in what tone? Sometimes she recalled the words as lightly reassuring, sometimes they came across as a sneer. They could have been either. Miriam could have heard it either way.

Everyone was clapping: Anna jerked out of her dream and back into the hall where two children were receiving prizes they'd missed at the end of last term. Jackson smiled benevolently On the back row one of the sixth-formers was sticking a pencil point into her thigh, and a Year Eleven boy by the window yawned openly. Kali turned her head to look at Anna.

'God, that man loves himself,' someone muttered as

Jackson drew himself up, nodded at them all, then stalked out. The boy playing the piano struck up his allegro and the front class began to peel off and file through the main door. Anna stayed where she was, waiting for Kali to come past, then she could fall in with her. But people jostled around and the boys trailed off, and the girls, and where was she? Anna spotted her hanging back at the end of the Year Elevens and wondered whether Kali meant her to go across; and then Chrissy was at Anna's shoulder asking about a theme for the drama festival because it would be nice to have all the performances linked in some way, and if they were going to do that then they ought to establish it soon before people started to get their ideas down.

'I haven't had a chance to think about it,' said Anna. 'We've only been back in school an hour.'

'I appreciate that. Just dropping the seed into your mind. Can you spare me ten minutes before the staff meeting and we'll brainstorm it, attack it and get it out of the way?'

The woman was impervious to a bad mood. Perhaps it was all those layers of hairspray. Where had Kali gone now?

Outside the hall doors it was a mass of bodies. But she was there, in with the Year Elevens, laughing with them, a little group around her. She looked radiant, a different girl from the one who'd drooped so mournfully in the garden only three short weeks ago. Anna walked up to them, uncertain.

'Kali!'

Now she was standing here she didn't know what to

say. How stupid of her. They were waiting for her to speak. 'It's lovely to see you.'

She saw two of the other girls exchange glances. The boy nearest, Neil Patrick, lifted his chin in the air as though to dissociate himself from the conversation.

'Yeah?' said Kali.

'I've found a website you might like—' Silly, she didn't want to share the details here, in front of them all. But even as she faltered, Anna glanced down and saw that Kali was holding Neil's hand. If it had been anyone else she would have told them instantly and without fuss to stop it.

The rest of the group were drifting away. Neil loosened his grip on Kali's fingers and she looked up at him, alarmed.

'I'm not sure that's—' Anna began.

'Catch you later, Mrs Lloyd.'

Kali put her arm through Neil's and let him steer her back into the flow of students. They moved down the corridor together, a closed unit, a couple.

Chapter Sixteen

She was completely unprepared for Jamie's attack. Despite the draggy staff meeting, the whingeing and point-scoring, Anna had driven home in a good mood. More than good. Chrissy had told them the drama festival was off; it clashed with some big athletics meeting that no one had put in the diary but that still took precedence because it involved other schools and couldn't be shifted. 'No other slot's available, sadly,' she'd said, while behind her Andrew punched the air. And Kali had waved at Anna across the dining room, but she'd been wise enough not to go over. Leave the girl to chat with her new friends. Neil Patrick was no Einstein but he seemed all right. Better than Nathan, at any rate.

So when she climbed out of the car she was thinking of how to convey to Jamie her happiness without him going silly on her. 'Praise the Lord, Wonder-Girl's not left after all,' she could imagine him saying. 'Hallelujah.' That was OK, though, she could take a bit of ribbing today.

She let herself in and went through to the lounge, meaning to get straight on the InkJet site and catch up with the chat. It was gloomy at the back of the house and she switched the light on as she passed through the doorway.

Jamie was sitting on the sofa absolutely still and quiet, no TV on, no music. He had her laptop next to him.

'Hell, you gave me a fright.' Anna dropped her schoolbag and grimaced.

He frowned and folded his hands together, as though he was about to pray.

'Is there anything you want to tell me, Anna?' he said.

It was a line she'd used herself with students, often: this football that smashed the window; this packet of cigarettes we found behind your locker. It sounded bizarre in the context of her home and she might have laughed had it not been for Jamie's expression.

'What?'

'I said,' and his tone was icy, 'is there anything you want to tell me, Anna.' This time the *tell* was punctuated with a nod at the laptop.

Her heart began to thud. It was important not to get tricked into anything.

'With regard to what?'

'With regard to certain websites you've been visiting.'

'How do you know which websites I've been visiting?'

He sighed as though she was being very stupid. 'You click on "History". It gives you the details.' He turned to the laptop and dabbed at the touch pad. A bar appeared at the side of the screen with a great list of pages; Anna saw InkJet over and over again, her log-in name, her user profile, and all the threads where she'd contributed. Jamie must have seen her Brood avatar and her sign-in page, and had he read her latest postings in the chat threads? In recent evenings she'd begun to create a personality to match the ID. One comment in a discussion about TV adaptations had provoked general chat and some enquiries about her personal life. She'd been forced into invention, and once you let slip one lie it stopped seeming such a big deal. To the people in the forums she was a Year Ten student, arguing with her mother and bored with her boyfriend.

A forty-two-year-old impersonating a teenager. It would look very bad to Jamie, to anyone.

'Have you been seeing him, Anna?'

'What?'

'Have you been seeing him?'

'Seeing who?'

'Philip Holz.'

The name, coming out of the blue like that, hit her like a thump in the chest. Years ago Anna had told Jamie about Philip in the hope that he'd reveal some of his own romantic past. Jamie had listened for a while, impassive. 'And why would I want to know this?' he'd said when she finished.

'Because you're interested in me?' she ventured.

'Interested in you, yes, but as you are now, not as you were.'

'But the way I am now is because of experiences I've had. I'm a product of my past.'

'We all are. It doesn't mean I want your entire love-life

laid out like the Bayeux tapestry. You began when I met you. If we ever split up, that's where you'll end.'

That was not the way Anna had been expecting the conversation to go. She'd never mentioned Phil again.

Now Jamie swivelled the laptop right round to face her. 'Look. You've been on his site every day for the past fortnight. That's as far back as the history goes. But I know you looked at it months ago, on my machine. I didn't say anything then.'

She thought of all the lines she would have used if she'd been guiltless.

'Sorry, what are you accusing me of here?'

'You heard me.'

Anna attempted a dismissive laugh. 'I've not been having an affair with Philip Holz.'

'You've been emailing him?'

'No! Look in my Sent folder.'

'You could have deleted the messages.'

'I haven't. I haven't been in contact with him at all.'

'But you've been calling up his page every day?'

That had become a routine, saying hello to Phil's picture before she moved on to other sites. All she could do was hang her head.

'Anna, do you promise me you haven't been speaking to this man?'

It was as though she'd split into two, one half of her wanting to throw herself down in supplication, the other wanting to rear up in terrible fury that Jamie should have dared to spy on her like this. Check her history? Whatever happened to trust? But then she remembered that she didn't deserve to be trusted, and the recognition of that fell on her like a weight.

'People go on friendsreunited,' she said lamely. 'It was only that. Checking out the past.'

'A bit more than that. Every day, Anna. Some might say obsessively. I mean, why?'

The question hung in the air while she battled with herself. The first chance she got she was going to look at Jamie's history, and ask Andrew how you deleted your own. Had the laptop been intended as some kind of trap?

In the end she said, 'It was a silly sort of fantasy, that's all. Harmless. Wondering where my life might have gone; don't you ever do that?' She thought of Jamie's face when he'd slid his hand up her skirt the night before and she'd stopped him because she felt too weary. 'Neither of us is happy, let's face it.'

'*I* am, Anna. Well, I was.'

She'd tried honesty and it was the wrong thing.

'Although lately it feels as though you've been a long way away,' he continued, and she thought of Cyril Raymond and Celia Johnson at the end of *Brief Encounter*, the music swelling and the credits rolling. *Whatever your dream was, it wasn't a very happy one, was it?*

'I haven't been in touch with Philip. I promise. Do you believe me?'

Jamie stood up. 'I want to, Anna. I want to.'

He stepped past her, out of the room. She thought he'd only gone to the kitchen but, seconds later, the front door banged.

*

Kali, a lunchtime football widow, was sketching in the garden while Anna marked Year Seven books. *Church – churches, ox – oxen, woman – women, appendix – appendices*. Kali bent over a leaf, lifted its edge slightly with her forefinger and then selected a different pencil from her box. Although the air was crisp, the sun on their faces was pleasant. Far away someone was practising Erik Satie.

When she was at primary school, one of Anna's favourite books had been a story called *When Marnie Was There*. Not just because the heroine had her name, and not because she was another lonely little girl. It was the plot that had drawn her; the Anna of the novel sent away to strangers and befriended by a ghost-girl who eventually turns out to have been her own grandmother. Imagine that. How time could make or miss a friendship.

Kali had been in the garden already when Anna arrived. They hadn't spoken yet, only smiled at each other.

Today Kali wore her hair in a lopsided twist with wisps escaping around her neck. There was a silver cross at her throat which swung forward when she leaned over, then fell back against the triangle of flesh revealed by her open collar. Her tie had been pulled well down, out of the way. Anna observed the way the girl's lashes lowered in study, the way she tilted her head to catch the different angles of her subject. Kali was frowning now, putting the end of the pencil to her lower lip. Against the dark green of the hedge her face looked nearly white; she would have to take care in the sun as she grew older, skin as pale as that. Dress her in a long gown and she'd have made a Victorian heroine, or even medieval. Keats's Belle Dame, Tennyson's Lady of Shalott. What kind of a woman would she grow into? Was she waiting to be rescued, or to ensnare?

Anna caught the exercise book as it slid onto the bench. The slap of palm against cover made Kali look up.

'You made me jump.'

'Don't let me break your concentration.'

''Sall right.' She held the drawing away from herself critically, then took another pencil. 'I was thinking,' Kali continued as though they'd been in the middle of a conversation, 'about that Anne Hathaway poem we did last term.'

'What about it?' A series of unhappy Nathan images flashed on Anna's memory.

'I was thinking what it's like to lose yourself in someone like that. So your identity kind of blurs into theirs. D'you get me?'

'It's been a long time since I felt that way.'

Anna thought of Jamie stalking about the place, casting her sideways looks to check whether she was noticing his aggrieved silence. Perhaps a good screaming match would have sorted it, but Jamie never screamed. In fact, the angrier he got, the less he said. She could have apologized, but she was damned if she was going to apologize for something she hadn't done, even if the point was a technical one. And so it went on.

She realized Kali was staring at her.

'It's not just the baby you're sad about, is it, Mrs Lloyd? Is there something else wrong as well?'

Jamie retrieving the laptop from the bin and wiping it down with a damp cloth, plugging it in wordlessly and firing it up on the table next to her. 'Like I'm going to be using that again,' she'd snapped at him. 'And have you sifting through my stuff.' But she had done, because the habit had become a compulsion, and also out of spite. Pressing 'clear history' wiped her tracks now. Sod him.

'Draw your leaves,' Anna said.

If she'd been an irresponsible kind of woman, she could have said to Kali, I think my marriage might be coming to an end.

She'd always thought of Jamie's coolness, his unflappability, as a sign of stability and inner strength. Now she saw it as a weakness. He didn't have the resilience to tackle or explore his feelings; much easier to freeze up.

When Anna walked in and found Jamie holding one of her letters up to the light, she realized they'd reached a whole new stage. He'd had the grace to drop the envelope and busy himself with emptying the coffee filter. Anna hadn't said a word. She'd ignored the letter on the table, made herself take a yoghurt from the fridge and leave the room. Later, when he was upstairs, she came back. The envelope was handwritten, with a local postmark, so she could see why it had attracted his attention, but all it turned out to be was a reminder note from the dentist. Anna made sure she left it out on the side table near his glasses.

It made no difference, because a week later she was unsealing an envelope when she realized there was something wrong with the glue under the flap. It was the wrong consistency, too tacky, and the paper had tiny creases where it had been previously curled back.

Dear Mrs Lloyd said the note inside, *Surprise! Max B. here, bet you weren't expecting that??? Never said thanks for the reference you gave me and also for talking to Mum like that, she's done a complete turnaround and now thinks it's cool to have a son in the music biz. I'll never be rich but I'm going to try dam hard to be happy. You only get one shot at life!* There was a URL at the bottom of the page. Anna knew before she checked it that Jamie would have been there first.

'So what did you think of Max's band?' she asked over supper, her tone light as though it were an ordinary conversational opener.

Jamie stopped cutting his meat but made no reply.

'Why bother gluing the letters closed? You could save yourself the trouble. Just go ahead, feel free, open all my mail.'

'You get way too close to your pupils,' he said finally, and went out, leaving his meal on the table.

'—And it helps if you read your poems out loud.' Anna took the book from Kali's hands and examined the page again. The day was breezy and the paper bent at the edges under her fingers.

'But isn't there a rule about when you start a new line? That's what I want you to teach me.'

'There is no rule in free verse. It's instinct and ear; you have both, I don't know why you're asking me. Look at this section you've written here:

> As each word drops
> it lands like ink
> and spreads in spirals
> lovingly

'See, you understood that "drops" had to be at the end of the line for impact, and that "lovingly" had to be separated from the line above so that it would slow the pace of the poem down to the speed of ink diffusing in water.'

Kali let out a short laugh. Down on the field, someone was blowing a whistle. 'Did I?'

'Yes. Perhaps not in your conscious mind. You have a feel for where the words need to go, that's all.' Bestowing the compliment bathed Anna in warmth like a shaft of sunlight. It was such a pleasure to share ideas like this, to connect.

'I just do it, you know. Stick the words down.'

'Yes, but not everyone has that language sense. It's like an ear for music. Very difficult to teach. Your talent comes from inside.'

'Yeah?'

The girl had taken a strand of reddy-gold hair and was winding it round and round an index finger.

'You'll give yourself split ends,' said Anna.

A heavy sigh. 'It's my hair.'

'Well, yes, but it'd be a shame to spoil it. It's so lovely.' Without thinking, Anna reached out to touch a curl. It was the kind of unthinking gesture she would have made with Tasha, or Tom: fond, maternal.

But Kali flinched away.

'Oh,' said Anna lamely. 'Sorry.' Heat rushed to her cheeks. The question formed on her lips: what did you think I was going to do?

Kali twisted away on the bench and got to her feet. 'I should go.'

'Didn't you have another poem to show me?' Anna held onto the book, patted it reassuringly.

'Doesn't matter.'

'Come on, now. You said you wanted to ask me about rhyme.'

Shrug.

'This one.' Anna ploughed on.

> I'm an outline, a sketch
> He shades me, he adds depth
> With him I become 3D
> He draws me.

'You see, I like the way you've caught just the suggestion of rhyme and metre here. Simple but so effective. And I love the central idea of someone activating you, bringing you to life, and with that clever use of word-play on the last line.' She was gushing now. Still Kali hadn't sat down. 'Because I think it's coming from the heart, your poetry, yes? And that will communicate itself to the reader. I had a boyfriend once – this is years ago – who drew me; he's a professional artist now. And I always felt, well, like you obviously do with Neil, that he could see right into me—'

Kali's face only darkened. 'This poem's not about Neil.'

'Oh, OK. Whoever—'

'It's not about anyone *you* know.'

'All right.'

''Cause it isn't.'

'Right.'

'Anyway, I've got to go.'

A car pulled into the visitors' area on the other side of the hedge and David Gray blasted through. Kali stood up and held out her hand for her book, her mouth tight.

What happened there? thought Anna. Did I move too fast?

She stayed alone in the garden for the remaining twenty minutes of lunchtime, then on into the next period, which was a free. A thousand different skies raced over her head. Ivy grew round her feet and her hands fossilized against the bench arms. An image came of her mother stalking ahead on a beach somewhere, moving at such a rate that Anna couldn't keep up. One of her flip-flops had come off and then, when she bent to retrieve it, her bucket of special shells that she'd been collecting had tipped over, and she'd shouted at Miriam to stop. But Miriam had carried on. Anna stood and cried in the sand till a sunburnt man took her arm and asked whether she was lost. Had he run after Miriam for her, or called out? 'My mum always walks too fast,' she remembered saying to him. When Miriam came stropping back he laughed and said to her,

'O-ho, didn't quite manage to escape that time, did you, Mummy?'

And the scene had appeared in dreams. Newly married Anna had gone to the doctor for sleeping pills and he'd insisted on her seeing a professional about relaxation techniques. She'd been furious about it. But no counsellor, no tablets.

The counsellor asked if anything was especially on her mind and Anna had, for something to say, recounted the last dream she had: that she was building a sand-castle at speed because Miriam was on her way and it had to be completed before she arrived, and the sand-castle was supposed to be the Taj Mahal although it had coloured minarets like the Kremlin so she knew it was all wrong. Then, just as it was nearly finished, a man whose face she couldn't see began pushing pebbles into the sides of the towers and breaking them and she'd woken up shouting. The counsellor asked who the man might have been but Anna didn't know. 'Do you think there's any significance to this dream?' he'd said. After the session had ended, she'd been allowed to make an appointment to get her prescription. 'All round the damn houses for fourteen pills,' she'd complained to Jamie.

She was thinking about going back inside the school – there were a million and one things she needed to do before the next lesson – when she once more caught a flash of movement in the gap between the hedge and the wall at the far end of the garden. No pupil should be in here without permission; she would have to go and see who it was.

She walked quietly down the path till she got to the obelisk, then looked around. Further down were two figures on the stone ledge, half hidden by a lilac tree. Anna saw slim brown knee boots, kicking playfully. Then Liz laughed and stood up, came out of the leaves pulling at her companion's hand, and it was Andrew who emerged from the screen of leaves, and who came forward easily into an embrace. She took in their furtive caressing, the smug exchange of smiles; then the way their backs went rigid the second they realized they had an audience.

'It's—' began Liz.

'Oh, go do it somewhere else!' Anna heard herself cry, and then turned and ran, the image of their shocked faces printed across her vision like a camera flash.

'I'm not like that.' She spoke aloud to herself in the car on the way home. *But you were*, said a voice in her head. *Just as bad. Worse, because you cheated in cold blood.*

She saw again Liz's hand come up round the back of Andrew's scalp and pull him closer, the intimacy of the gesture putting Anna immediately in the wrong for watching. And that made her angry. What would Liz say to her husband tonight when he asked how her day had been? Or Andrew to his girlfriend? It felt to Anna as though she'd stumbled across herself and Russ, and been confronted with all the shabbiness of the affair.

But I wasn't myself, she said. It was a way of coping.

Doesn't matter what Jamie denied you, you know what you did was a terrible thing.

Well, it's over.

You hope.

Was it too late to go home and redeem things with Jamie? If she rushed in and kissed him and told him she loved him, and that she was sorry, sorry, sorry— But what exactly are you apologizing for, he'd say. And there she'd be, stuck. Because it couldn't be a genuine apology without a full confession, could it? White lines flicked under the car and Anna felt sick suddenly. She pressed the brake and pulled over in front of a farm gate.

After she had wound the window down and sat for a minute, she took out her mobile and dialled Mel's number. Anna could offload about Andrew and Liz, get that out of her head, then make arrangements to meet up. And if the opportunity arose, she might confide in Mel about the affair. No, that was too risky. But she could have a moan about Jamie, at least—

'Hi, Melanie speaking.'

Thank God, Anna almost said. 'Mel, it's me.'

'Oh, give me a sec.' There was a pause and Anna could hear a man's voice in the background, and Mel giggling. At last she came back on. 'Hiya, Me. How you doing?'

'Are you busy?'

'Not especially.' Her voice became muffled. *'Greg, stop it!* Sorry, I'm fine. *Don't you dare. Look, I'm trying to talk to Anna.'*

'Shall I call back another time?'

Another pause, then Mel returned, contrite. 'Sorry about that. Somebody's full of the joys of spring this afternoon.'

'I can ring you tomorrow.'

'Don't, he's behaving himself now. *I should think so. On your knees. Bad boy.*'

Anna let her gaze wander to the hills in the distance, and then across the field beyond the gate. Smoke rose from the chimney of a brick cottage to her left, washing hung on the line outside.

'Anna? Are you still there?'

'Just about.' She laughed to show it wasn't a jibe.

'Because it's so weird you phoning right now, it really is. I was going to get in touch this evening, yeah. We've got some news for you.'

And here it comes, thought Anna. She clenched her jaw, steeling herself for baby congratulations.

'Go on.'

'We're going to hand our notice in at half-term.'

'And?'

'And leave teaching. I know, it's mad, isn't it? We'll see the Easter term out, then we're off.'

'Where?' Anna was astonished.

'Dunno. Travelling. We're going round the world. Greg's been to Singapore, Thailand, that sort of area, and I've been round Europe, but we want to cover as many countries as we can. Not plan or anything, just go, see where we end up.'

'How long for?'

'A year, maybe. As long as the money lasts.'

'My God. You've only just been promoted.'

'I know! But guess what? I don't care. It's Greg, he's crazy. You're going to have to meet him before we set off, he's so . . .'

Anna said, 'He certainly seems to be having a big

influence on you,' but she was wasting her breath. Mel's voice had gone tinny again as she held the phone away.

'*Stop showing off, you nutter. Yes, you are. Mad as a Jack Russell. Come here and say hello to Anna. Come on.*'

Some scuffling.

'Helloooooo.' Greg's voice sounded high for a man, but he was putting on a silly accent so it was hard to tell. 'Helloo helloo.'

'Hello,' said Anna.

'So you're a teacher, too? Ever fancied chucking in your job and going on a voyage of adventure?' He must have realized this sounded like an invitation because a second later he added, 'There are lots of places you could go with your husband.'

If I went, Anna thought, I'd go alone.

Mel was back on. 'God, he's a handful. Worse than any of the kids. *Ow. Well, you are. Go away now.* Hey, I forgot to say, did you phone for anything special?'

'Only to chat.'

'This evening of all evenings. You must have felt the vibes.'

'I must.'

Chapter Seventeen

When Jamie went out to his writing class it was like the air pressure lifting; Anna was able to expand her lungs fully again. Her muscles relaxed. She ate a biscuit and took off her shoes. Then she went upstairs to his office, because if he could search through her stuff, she could search through his.

'I can't believe you're being so weird over a website,' Anna had snapped after he'd gloomed his way through another evening meal. It was like sitting opposite a gargoyle, she thought; the chin in the hand, that grim mouth.

'It's what the website represents,' he'd said darkly, and she hadn't dared to ask any more. Later, as he was gathering his notes together, he said, 'It's like when you notice a stain on the wallpaper. You've never seen it before but once you know it's there, you can't stop looking, it's so obvious.'

She affected a laugh. 'Sounds like a line from one of your stories.'

He'd packed his papers and left the house.

Anna switched the computer on and, as she waited for it to load, sifted through some of the clutter on his desk. More poems, odd lines scribbled on Post-its, a letter he'd never mentioned congratulating him on a £25 writing prize. And some of the latest script.

KNOCK ON GINGER
A drama by
James Lloyd

<u>EXT. ARMLEY PRISON. NIGHT (DAY 1)</u>

<u>INT. ARMLEY PRISON. NIGHT (DAY 1)</u>
An inmate's cell. The room is depressingly bare but for one corner where dozens of sheets of paper covered in handwriting have been stuck to the wall. Two men lie in bunk beds. The lower man is sound asleep but the upper one - KEITH MASON - mumbles and flings his hands out. As his palm opens it shows the clear imprint of a key in the flesh, even though his hand is empty.

MASON (V/O)
Prisons, keys, locks. They're all just words to me. Meaningless. When the night comes, I can go wherever I want.

<u>INT. ARMLEY PRISON. CORRIDOR. DAY (DAY 1)</u>
A warden walks along the row of doors, unlocking as he goes. As he gets to MASON'S door, something makes him hesitate. He listens, then opens the peephole. What he sees makes his eyes go wide with horror. Alarm bells begin to ring and other wardens come running.

So this was his latest, and he hadn't said a word about it. When a project was fresh he liked to talk through his ideas daily, asking her opinion and reading extracts out. She put the script down, feeling suddenly flattened by loneliness.

The screen had loaded. She sat herself down at the desk, pulled the chair up, and clicked on History – because she knew how to do that now – all the while justifying herself in her head. If Jamie walked in here, she'd say, You started it, you were the one who made these new horrible rules. She was expecting him to have cleared his internet tracks, but there was almost a week's worth of listings in there. Perhaps he was making a point.

Anna scrolled down. Babel Fish, BBC, classic cars on ebay, Flash Earth, various writers' sites, some Victorian erotica (how typical was that; tasteful even in his pursuit of porn) and a bunch of trivia: cyber fireworks, solitaire, Fruit Shoot, virtual bubblewrap. Nothing more incriminating than procrastination, though it was galling to think of him sitting at home popping bloody virtual bubbles when she was out at work. Still, no girlfriends here, ex or otherwise. If that was what she was looking for. She didn't know.

Next she went through My Documents; not much new there. After that she moved on to emails. Here were exchanges with editors of small writing magazines, lots of topic reply notices from the BBC drama message boards, updates and newsletters from his story groups. She moved the bar down and down. How many messages a day did he send, for God's sake? Then the line jumped out, <u>holz@tiscali.co.uk</u>, and Anna went dizzy with horror.

'Fuck,' she said out loud. Her hand was dithering so much she could barely open the message.

Dear Anna (Dear Anna!),

Great to hear from you, and sorry I haven't got back sooner. Life here is mad, and moments where I can catch up with myself are rare. I guess it's pretty much the same with you. Everyone I know moans that there aren't enough hours in the day.

The gallery is really busy, not that I'm complaining. We're hosting a series of new watercolour artists this summer and the extension isn't ready, so I'm trying to supervise that and keep my own painting going – tricky. Things will get easier when Romy starts at nursery. Then Astrid can go back full-time and finances will be less erratic. My gallery's being featured on TV soon, a prog called Flatland Art, but I don't know whether that's regional or national. Watch out for it in July. We're hoping it'll bring a lot more visitors in, anyway.

Let me know how things are with you if you get a moment. Still standing up for Freedom and Justice all over the place?

The original email Jamie must have sent wasn't attached so she immediately checked the Sent folder and then Deleted. There was no trace of it. But she could only too well imagine the kind of thing he must have written. The shock, outrage, the humiliation was almost unbearable and she moaned and put her hands over her face.

Phil at a summer ball in his DJ, all the girls looking at him as he carried drinks back from the bar; walking with her up to the Suspension Bridge and her shoes hurting so much she had to take them off and go barefoot in her taffeta frock. Phil riding his bike round the lawn outside her hall of residence. That was the first time she'd ever seen him. 'Who's that fool?' she'd said to the people she was with, trying to sound dismissive because even then she felt an irrational jump at her heart. Later that week she'd spotted him in town with a blonde and had been surprised by how upset she'd felt. Another image came of them sitting in adjacent carrels at the university library, supposedly studying for exams but instead sending paper dart messages over the divide to each other. She so wished she'd kept his letters.

How could she contact him now?

Dear Phil,

   That last message wasn't from me at all, it was from my bastard of a husband checking up on me. Yes, that's the kind of man I ended up with.

   Not that I'm in a position to challenge him. Hoist with my own petard.

   It's a long story.

The clock in the doll's house room told Anna it was after three. Impossible to lie quietly in the dark feeling the things she was feeling. *Dear Phil, More and more I want to run away from the mess I've made. I think maybe I've never loved anyone except you. Please abandon your wife and chil-*

dren and come and save me from my life. Jamie hadn't even stirred when she'd got out of bed.

She moved the house round on its turntable and squinted through the side windows. All well in the kitchen, with its hanging resin pheasant and new Acme mangle; and in the master bedroom above. The Lloyd Loom chair she'd repainted looked good, though the curtains weren't hanging properly yet. She'd have to take them out and redo them, maybe put a stitch in the top to keep the folds right. Slippers by the fender, false teeth on the cabinet, and for a moment she forgot scale and was peering into a real house.

But now, what was that in the middle of the bathroom floor? Anna swung the structure gently towards her. Had something fallen off the wall? She pushed her chair away, went across to the main light switch, stood blinking for a moment, then came back to examine the bathroom again.

'Oh!' She couldn't stop herself from crying out. A dead bluebottle lay on its back, casting a giant dirty shadow behind it. It looked monstrous in that setting, beyond what she could deal with. She opened the house right up and put her hand inside, then withdrew with a shudder. Ridiculous, but she couldn't touch that crispy black body. There was nothing handy to poke it out with, either. Finally she blew hard at the fly and it slid across the lino, hit the bath and came shooting back into her face. She let out a yelp of disgust and flapped at her hair.

Jamie was standing in the doorway.

'What the hell are you doing?' he said.

The bluebottle was at her feet, and it was tiny. Anna pointed pathetically at the carpet.

'There was a fly in my dolls' house.'

If he'd at least walked over and put his arms round her. But he only cast his eyes round the room, half-nodded, and left.

'I tried ringing you,' said Les.

Anna had been off school for three days with a throat infection. She'd come back before she was ready, partly because she couldn't afford for her GCSE set to lose the time, but mainly because hanging around with Jamie had been a drag.

'Why, what's up?'

Before Les could reply, Tom Maxfield thrust himself between them. 'Sorry, but I had to show you this.' He waved a paper in front of their faces. 'It's wee Jayne Roper from Year Seven. You know, talks like that—' He stuck his tongue between his teeth in imitation of a lisp. '*I don't get it, Mr Maxfield.* So I gave them all a little test on angles, the one we always give at this stage of the course. And one of the questions was, Find the angle BAC. See, see what she's put.'

Les took the sheet between his thumb and forefinger to steady it. Anna leaned over and saw, in child's handwriting, an elaborate arrow and the explanatory note, *There it is*.

'Priceless, isn't she?'

Anna smiled briefly. 'I'd say you had more work to do there.'

Les made no comment at all, and Tom withdrew to share the joke with someone else.

'This nuthouse,' said Les. 'Come into my office where we can have a bit of privacy.'

'Am I in trouble?'

'Not you.' They went into his room and he shut the door. 'Your friend Kali.'

'What about her?'

'She's been suspended. With a view to expulsion, but that last's confidential so don't go spreading it around.'

Anna sat down.

'I knew you'd be concerned,' he went on. 'I'm aware you've been taking a special interest in her pastoral care. I'm sorry she's repaid you like this.'

'What's she done?'

'She's been stealing and it's been going on since last term.'

Relief flooded through Anna. 'No, you're wrong,' she blurted. 'I know all about that. It's a mistake. Some Year Nines had taken a love-letter of hers and she was trying to get it back, that's all. In fact, I almost came to you with it but she said she had it sorted. I can vouch for her.'

Les was shaking his head. 'I think there's more to it than that. Other girls' possessions were actually found in her locker.'

'They could have been planted.'

'They could.' His face showed that he didn't think so. 'You need to see Jackson, have a chat with him. Be aware, though, that there's also another element to this.'

Anna felt herself flame with indignation.

'You mean there's a question mark over the fees so the Head's booting her out, that's what's at the bottom of this, isn't it?'

There was a knock at the door but Les ignored it. He waited for a few seconds, then lowered his voice. 'Jackson's been speaking to the headmistress at one of the previous schools. He suspects there are drugs involved.'

'No way, she's too mature.'

Les shrugged. 'You know how touchy he is on that particular topic. With good reason, too, the way the papers are over independent schools and bad behaviour. Look, I can't say any more, I shouldn't have told you as much as I have. You must promise you won't say a word to anyone else till it's cleared up, yes? Otherwise we'll all be in trouble.'

He drew his hand across his brow as though he might have a headache.

'So Kali's not in school at the moment?'

'No. You can set work to send home, if you like.'

He opened the door for her. From the end of the corridor she could hear Tom yelping hilariously. 'Priceless, I call it. Priceless.'

Jackson told her not to get involved.

'Categorically. I'm dealing with it. It's being dealt with.'

'Are you going to interview those girls?'

'I'll make a note of what you've told me.' Which meant he wasn't. 'I appreciate your concern but you are not Kali's tutor and you don't have the full picture.'

So give it to me, she almost shouted, but it would have been pointless.

'And please don't speak to any of the students about this, either.' Jackson must have known she might tackle the Year Nines herself. 'I need your full cooperation here, Anna.'

You need me to stop bothering you and go away, she thought. That's your definition of a core teaching skill, passivity. God forbid anyone should take an initiative.

'I'll keep my mouth shut, then.'

'Good girl,' he said.

By four o'clock she wanted nothing more than to get home.

She found Jamie in the bedroom, having a clear-out. Anna went straight over and put her arms round him; he didn't respond but she wasn't going to give up. 'Have I had a day,' she said.

'I don't know. Have you.' His tone was flat.

'It's awful, you won't believe what they've done.'

He held a T-shirt up to the light, then crumpled it into a ball and dropped it at the foot of the bed. Not in the mood for guessing, then.

'They've suspended Kali. Can you believe it? They might expel her, too. Because some girls say she's been stealing. It's outrageous. There are all sorts of accusations whizzing about. Jackson's in a big panic anyway because of a pre-inspection visit, and there's no getting through to him. Les wants to help but his hands are tied. The trouble is, no one knows her like I do . . .' She tailed off. 'I didn't even get a chance to say goodbye.'

Jamie twisted the neck of a bin bag closed. 'I'm not interested.'

'Don't say that. I know you think I'm silly for getting involved, but someone has to. It's not a crime to care about your pupils.'

'Stop it, Anna.'

'Stop what?'

'Talking. I don't want to hear.'

This was too provoking. 'Excuse me. I listen to you banging on about your writing group and your scripts.'

He raised his hand to silence her. Then he reached across to the chest of drawers and took a piece of paper from the top.

'Tell me what this is.'

Even from where she stood she could see the Halifax logo. He had opened her bank statement, the one that showed payments for the caravan.

'I can see it's something you've had set up for a while.' Jamie flicked the page angrily with the back of his fingertips. 'So what was this money going out that stopped in February? Why did you keep a whole separate account that was secret from me?'

'You had no right to open that letter,' she said, panic flooding through her.

'Don't talk to me about rights. Don't you dare talk to me about rights.'

From downstairs the front doorbell rang like a mad alarm.

'Who the hell's that?'

'I don't bloody know, do I?'

They glowered at each other. The bell rang again, this

time in a jaunty pattern as though someone was spelling out Morse code.

Anna moved first.

'You're not going to answer it, are you?'

She paused.

'Do not go downstairs. Anna!'

It was enough. She left the bedroom, and Jamie fuming in it. This would give her time to think.

She opened the door to find Ruth beaming on the step. Russ was lurking behind.

'Surprise!'

'It certainly is,' said Anna.

'Goodness, you're pink. Are you having a hot flush?'

Anna thought that perhaps she was.

'Or did we interrupt something interesting?'

Jamie had come down to the landing and was staring insanely.

'We thought,' said Ruth, her bulk filling the narrow hall, 'we'd pop in on our way back from Chester. We've been up to the Sealand estate to look at bathroom suites.'

Obviously they were supposed to ask about this.

'I didn't know you were having work done.'

'No, well, we only had the idea last night.'

'You did,' said Russ over her shoulder.

'You agreed. You said the bathroom was the most depressing room in the house and when you sat in the bath you sometimes felt like weeping.'

'I've always had a soft spot for your palm-tree tiles,' said Anna, then cursed herself because it was the kind of snidey remark that Jamie would have made.

Russ sighed. 'Thing is, as soon as I make money, you

spend it for me.' But he spoke without malice. Ruth nudged him.

'What's it for, then, if you can't spend it? He's had a big order,' she said proudly. 'We heard yesterday. The county council.'

'We've been lucky, put in the right quote. It's so hit-and-miss, competitive tendering. But it's a good job to pull in because you get on the books, and because they're not going to go bust on you.'

Jamie, who was still on the stairs, sparked into life. 'Excellent news. Come through, what are we all standing out here for?' Only Anna recognized the tautness in his delivery, the set jaw and stiff movements that betrayed his real feelings. He stepped down to usher them into the lounge, and a casual observer would have seen nothing but a cheery family gathering.

When she had made them drinks, Anna sat by Ruth and let her go through washbasin designs and tap options. Russ talked to Jamie about cash flow. It was crazy; did Jamie find it crazy to be chatting down here about nothing while the row squatted upstairs, waiting for them? She tried hard to pay attention to the tile catalogue.

'Chinese blue, or camel?' Ruth was asking. 'And which border?'

Christ, as if she cared. They could decorate it with pressed tea bags as far as Anna was concerned. 'Blue.'

'I thought so. But Russ is more of a browns man.'

Across the room Jamie lounged, apparently calm. The longer this normal conversation went on, the more she began to wonder whether she'd dreamed the episode before, or if Jamie had decided that it was not, in the end, worth bothering about. Perhaps his immediate anger had drained away and he was feeling more rational. There: he was smiling. That was not the face of a man who was about to blow his marriage apart. She tried to catch his eye but he was examining some figures Russ had scribbled on the telephone pad.

By the time Ruth levered herself out of the sofa to go, Anna had convinced herself that simply maintaining a bright tone might bring Jamie round.

'Well,' she said as the front door closed, 'that makes a nice change. Not the usual tale of woe we get from that quarter. What was it that Russ was showing you?'

But when she turned, she was talking to herself. Jamie had gone straight back upstairs and now she understood what was happening. She ran up after him.

'You're packing, aren't you?'

'I don't know.'

'How can you not know?'

'It depends on what explanation you can give for hiding this money. You see, the very best construction I can put on it, Anna, is that you want to live a kind of "life apart" from me. That you're not really in this marriage the way I am.'

'That's not—'

'And that's the best construction. The best.'

'I always thought that's what you liked, independence. An independent wife. That's why you married me.'

'There's independence, and there's being in a completely different groove.' He stopped folding T-shirts for a moment and looked at her. 'I don't know what you used this cash for, but I do know you kept it a secret from me. Were you planning to run away? Are you paying someone off? Explain it to me.'

'It's only a bank account, for God's sake.'

'It's tangible evidence of the way you hold back all the time. You've been distant for months; more than distant, furious. I know something's been going on with you, Anna, I'm just not sure what. I'll ask you again, is it to do with Philip Holz?'

'You'd know,' she spat. 'Sending him emails. *In my name*.'

Jamie blinked with surprise, but then recovered himself. 'It was quite reasonable of me to investigate, given your obsession.'

She wanted to hit him for his smugness.

'All right, here it is: I hired a static caravan. I used to go there after work sometimes when I felt too depressed to come home. That's what the account was for.'

'On your own?'

'Yes!'

'I don't believe you.'

'You have to.'

'No, I don't, Anna.' His face was rigid. 'I don't have to at all.'

He carried on taking clothes out of a drawer while she stood digging her nails into her wrist.

'It's my money, I'm the one earning it,' she blurted finally.

It was the only time he raised his voice. '*Our* money! Ours! That's what marriage *is*. You share. I'm aware you think my writing's a waste of time and that I contribute nothing to the household – though I note you were fine about coming in on my dad's inheritance—'

She struggled for a reply. There were so many awful unformed sentences whizzing around their heads that could have been plucked out and spoken.

'I've not been happy,' she began, 'for a long time.'

'That's *you*, though, isn't it? Your natural disposition to overanalyse and brood. You make a hell in heaven's despite, it's what you've always done.' He swallowed and in the beat of silence afterwards she saw pictures of her mother, Phil, the hospital scan room with its empty screen.

Did she dare raise the baby thing again, try to spell out once more the impact of his selfishness? But she was too frightened he'd see into her head, and somehow make connections. *Let's see: she wanted a baby so she—*

Then Jamie spoke again, slowly and deliberately: 'You never see what you have, only what you haven't. It's like you're looking through a distorting glass. Everything's ugly, including yourself. Jesus. Doesn't it ever strike you, Anna, that unhappiness seems to follow you about?'

The injustice if it took her breath away. She felt herself expanding, becoming light-headed with the effort of getting the words out.

'How can you speak like that when you never feel anything at all? There's nothing to connect to, with you. How dare you accuse *me* of being detached? You're the one who holds back all the time, you're always holding back.'

'Oh, God, here we go.'

'Jamie, listen.'

'No, you don't.' He was shaking his head angrily. 'Don't make this into the having kids thing again. Because we've done that one to death and I'm not going to feel guilty because of holding a rational preference. It's just not fair, Anna, trying to make me something I never was. Stop punishing me. Stop trying to shift blame onto me. I'm not the one keeping secrets.'

'I didn't *mean* that.' She could have hit him in her fury. 'I meant the way you were downstairs with Russ, switching off to be all pleasant and then switching back on to argue. Like that!' She clicked her fingers. 'That level of detachment. It's not normal.'

'You were the one who let them in,' he said coolly, and zipped up his suitcase. 'What did you expect me to do?'

She followed him down the stairs. 'You're leaving?'

'Looks that way.'

'Aren't we going to talk some more?'

'I think we've said all there is to be said.'

'No, we haven't.'

But he had opened the front door and gone through it while she was speaking.

Chapter Eighteen

She was supposed to be on outside duty with Liz, but Liz had gone on a field trip and hadn't bothered to find herself a stand-in. A misdemeanour that was no big deal until a child injured himself or there was a serious bullying incident, and then the whole school could be up in court, all over the press, for negligence. Not that that kind of thing ever happened to Liz.

Anna walked down the side of the art block, then across the courtyard to investigate a knot of Year Sevens by the car-park wall. A Sixth Form boy belted past her with a football under his arm and yelled to his mates on the field; she saw the powerful shoulder muscles moving under his shirt, the huge soles of his boots. To her left, two bored Year Eight girls were tugging at the wire fence round the tennis court. 'Stop that, please,' Anna called and they let go at once. The Year Seven group dispersed. A boy all on his own shuffled his feet in the gravel, raising clouds of white dust. 'Look, I'm on fire, Mrs Lloyd,' he said as she went past. Colin Rafferty. He always played alone.

So Jamie's absence was serious: he had taken the computer. Every other day he came round to pick up post and leave lists of instructions. Sometimes she replied to them. *When are you coming back?* she'd written on one. There hadn't been any response yet.

She was waiting for the impact. At the moment she felt as she had when Miriam died; in limbo. School helped. The routine was a comfort, and the timetable so busy there was no time to think much about Jamie until she got home. There'd be a dip then, a half-hour where the house felt horrible and she longed for someone to tell about her day. Something to eat and drink bucked her up, though, and then there was marking and planning to tackle, and an hour's TV or a session on the Internet took her through till bedtime. And it was a relief to lie down and just sleep, not have to go through the pre-sex ritual. His hopeful, generalized stroking, her rolling this way (yes) or that way (no), and if no, sometimes a more assertive movement such as pressing himself against her back, and then her turning towards him (yes) or curling up further and doing tired breathing (no), and if no again, his shifting away and sighing and the darkness prickling with accusation. Now the bed was her own and she roved across the mattress at will and kept the reading light on with impunity.

She passed through the gate at the bottom of the car park and surveyed the field. Boys threw themselves around, collided and swore in the centre of the football pitch. Round the edges other students strolled, or sat on blazers to talk or share a Game Boy. Daisy Bishop, in breach of school rules, stood with her arms round Christof Bannerman's neck, kissing.

It had been tempting to confess the Jamie situation to

Les that morning when he'd been waiting for her to finish on the photocopier.

'Everything all right, Anna?' he'd asked.

'Yes. Why shouldn't it be?'

'You look tired, that's all. You were yawning all the way through assembly.'

'Yes, well, it's hard to be riveted when you hear a story for the twentieth time. If we have that one about the poor stowaway once more I shall have to run on stage and wrest the book from Jackson's hands.'

'*My home is far across the sea where the birds are like flying jewels.*'

'Stop it.'

Les pursed his lips. 'However would Jackson manage if *Inspiring Tales* were to go walkabout?'

'And perhaps mysteriously find its way onto a bonfire? There's a thought.'

Les's eyes drooped at the corners, meaning he looked sad even when he smiled. She had, out of nowhere, a vision of him clearing away an invalid tray, loading a washing machine with bedding. Perhaps he too sat watching TV alone in the evenings. If she could tell anyone about Jamie leaving, it would be Les.

I don't know what to feel, she could have said. I miss my husband but I'm relieved he's gone. I'm angry with him but I'm also angry with myself. Sometimes I feel sorry, or guilty, or let down, or miserable.

She said, 'Actually, I'm having some trouble sleeping.'

He leant in, concerned.

'I go off OK, but then I wake up convinced there's an

intruder downstairs. I can hear creaks, like someone's coming up the stairs. It's happening nearly every night. And I know it's just my imagination, I know there isn't someone in the house really, but by then I'm all wound up.'

'What does Jamie say?'

That would have been her opportunity.

'I don't bother him,' she'd said.

Daisy and Christof were now walking back towards the school building, holding hands. Anna watched them for a while, then turned and scanned the far side of the grounds. By the school pavilion three Year Nines were play-fighting with litter-pickers. She would have gone across, but they spotted her and lowered their weapons. She stood and glared, arms folded, till they retrieved a wrapper and dropped it in a bin bag.

'You know,' Les had said, 'you shouldn't get too strung up over Kali Norman, if that's what's getting to you. You did your best by her. I'm sure your attentions'll have a lasting impact, wherever she goes. Never be ashamed to have thought the best of someone, Anna.'

She bit her lip; it was not the time to begin an argument. Mrs Norman had been persuaded to take her daughter away. This was different from an expulsion and saved everyone's face. But Anna still seethed at the injustice. Nothing had been investigated properly. Decisions had been rushed through because of Jackson's paranoia. Now she would not see Kali again. It felt as though a light had been switched off. The school seemed so much dimmer for the girl's absence.

'Let's not go there.' She lifted the lid of the copier and

slid out the master sheet. 'Anyway, it's more than that. Everything's out of joint, Les. The kids are like zombies this week, all my Sixth Form lessons are disrupted with this bloody field trip. Not a single one of my Year Tens has handed their coursework in; even Lin Keane and Sally Marsden had excuses. And I can't chase them tomorrow because I'm out all day at a moderation meeting. I tell you, it feels like one long slog at the moment. I need,' she finished, 'something, something *good* to happen.'

The bell rang and, in the silence after, they heard the far-off thunder of children's feet. Another day starting.

'You and me both,' Les had said.

Something was going on at the bottom of the field, by the hawthorn hedge; a group of older boys clustered suspiciously. It was too open a spot for smokers, but the body language of the students nearest was self-conscious and heads were turning, checking around. Anna quickened her pace.

By the time she got halfway down the football pitch she could pick out individual faces. Martin Fallow was there, and Vaseem Malik, both with their blazers thrown on the ground and their collars open, tieless. She frowned, trying to make out the figure in the middle, the boy wearing a long black coat and sunglasses like some refugee from *The Matrix*. Then she heard him laugh and knew it was Nathan.

The moment she recognized him, she was almost floored by the weight of her loathing. Her legs went heavy and would hardly carry her forward. *Ignore him. Go and get Les.* But then, for God's sake, he was a fifteen-year-old boy. That was all. If she walked away now, and they saw her, she would never keep order again.

At the centre of the group Nathan nodded his head to an inaudible beat and his mirror shades glinted; impossible to tell whether he had noticed her or not. What was he passing round now that had the others so fascinated?

'Oh yeaaaaah,' he said loudly, like the man in the Gillette advert.

She cleared her throat.

'Nathan?'

He looked round, presenting blank lenses at her, then turned back again. Dismissed.

'Nathan, what are you doing here?'

Some of the others shuffled and studied the ground. Martin was pushing his hand down into his trouser pocket and sniggering.

'If you're on school property without staff permission, you're trespassing. Do you have permission?'

'Not exactly.' He said this to the boys, to make them laugh.

'Then you need to leave.'

'Or?'

'I'm not getting into an argument. That's the situation. If you've cleared it with Mr Jackson, a one-off visit is fine, but you can't just drop in when you feel like it; no one can. It's the rule. Have you even reported in at the office?'

For an answer he bent down, picked up a stone and threw it far into the trees on the other side of the hedge.

'Come up now and sign in. Perhaps we'll see Mr Jackson on the way and you can . . .' She left the sentence hanging, then set off briskly across the grass towards the top gate as if she expected him to be following her, though she was certain he would not. As she walked, she was aware of eyes on her. Every one of her muscles felt awkward, nothing in her body would move by reflex. Her arms seemed to be hanging oddly so she clamped them to her sides; no, that was no good. In the end she clasped her hands behind her back like an actor in a period play, knowing she looked ridiculous but unable to manage any other arrangement.

Something made her turn and she found, to her surprise, that Nathan was behind her.

'Good. If you come up—'

His voice was low but distinct. 'Bitch.'

She almost stumbled, struggled to regain her stride. If she could get to the staffroom, Les would sort things out.

'I said, bitch.'

They were almost at the gate; only the car park to cross and up through the courtyard.

'You can't touch me now, Mrs Lloyd.'

She didn't feel like a forty-two-year-old woman. Context fell away and she could have been fifteen, like him.

'You are one sad lezzy bitch. You've got no life outside of school, have you? You've got no friends, you've nothing.'

Anna shrank further; she was ten, backed into a corner of the playground while a boy with grey skin and a suede-head cut called her spicky.

'You can't tell me what to do any more.'

Find Les.

'Look at you, running away. *Tea*cher.'

She stopped, fatally. 'For God's sake, Nathan,' she exploded. 'I asked you to go and sign in, that's all, because we have a legal requirement to know who's on the premises. Look, if you have personal problems, don't take them out on me.'

'*I* don't have personal problems—'

'Drama college not worked out, has it, or are you—'

'—you think you can boss people around because—'

'—this school's been so much better for you not being here—'

'—such a *fucking* lezzy bitch—'

Suddenly he flung his arm out towards her face so that she flinched and gasped.

'Ha! Had you there,' he cried, triumphant. 'What's the matter, Mrs Lloyd? Something up?'

Around the car park children were staring. She must not run. She must not run.

The staffroom reeked of solvent; Stu, in his overalls, was cleaning graffiti off a desk, erasing a marker-pen cartoon of Jackson. 'You'd think he'd be flattered,' said Stu. The artist had given the Headmaster an enormous penis sticking out of his trousers, but they knew it was meant to be Jackson because of the grin.

In the corner by the dais, Ian Poole stuffed his mouth with trail mix. Anna watched as he dropped a peanut, hunted around, located it deep in his crotch. He hooked the peanut out, popped it back between his lips and scooped into the bag again. 'Oops,' he said as another shower rolled off his palm.

'Open a window, Stu,' said Andrew. 'Otherwise we'll all be high as kites this afternoon.'

Anna was feeling light-headed anyway, and still shaky. Les had commended her for keeping her cool. She had gone straight to his office and reported the incident, then sat and written a brief report while he went off to deal with Nathan. 'And you won't say anything to the others about this yet?' he'd warned her before he left. As if she wanted that lot dissecting events. She wondered how Les was getting on. He had not come back.

'Did you hear about that school,' said Ian, 'where the Headmistress made the staff take probiotic yoghurt at break-time? To boost their immune sytems. I'd hate that. Yoghurt turns my stomach. I'd be puking all morning.'

They had no real jurisdiction over Nathan any more, apart from removing him from the school grounds, and he could walk back up the drive any time he wanted. Unless they posted some kind of sentry, which even she could see was overkill. All he had really done – again – was use aggressive language. She could hear Jackson now telling her it was Essentially a Low-level Incident. 'My first school in Manchester,' he'd go, 'one of the pupils went for the deputy with a chisel. You've no idea what some teachers have to put up with.' That's what he'd say. Jamie would be more sympathetic. But then she remembered he was not around to tell; her world had shifted and nothing was in its proper place any more.

'Now if Jackson made us start each day with a stiff

whisky, that'd be nearer the mark,' said Andrew. 'That'd set us up for the rigours ahead. You reckon?'

Ian screwed up his empty paper bag and cast about for the bin. 'Hey, Stu,' he called. 'Did you know there's something written underneath that desk as well? When you tip it back.'

They all turned to look as the desk was laid on its side. Same artist, different target.

'Who's that, then?'

Stu came round the other side and squatted down, evaluating. The next second he was attacking the picture with his cloth.

'Who was it?' persisted Ian. 'Was it one of us?'

'Well, it wasn't you, Ian,' said Andrew. 'Given that it was wearing a bra.'

Stu scrubbed harder.

'Was it Liz?'

'Shut up, Ian.'

'Eh?'

'Bloody kids,' said Stu. 'It's not like they come from bad homes. They've no excuse.'

Anna, who had been closest to the drawing, had seen it all: her haircut, her prim stance, bizarre black underwear. Stu's attempting to shield her from the insult somehow made it worse. She wanted to fold herself up in the chair and turn out the lights.

'Someone's done this survey,' said Ian, 'and the average teacher laughs or smiles every three minutes. Did you hear that on the news? Every three minutes. We must be in the wrong school. I say, we must be in the wrong school.'

The door banged open and Tom Maxfield came in, swinging a pair of nunchakus. 'What do you think of these?' He held the top baton in his fist and began whirling the lower one about near Stu's head.

'I should stay under that desk if I were you,' said Andrew. 'Where did you get them, Tom?'

'Confiscated them from Philip Mathieson. He says he needs them in school to do an English talk, or something. That right?'

'I don't know,' said Anna. 'I don't teach him.' With luck, the nunchakus would flip back and crack him in the face.

'Hey, Andrew.' Tom caught the loose stick, held both out in front of him like motorbike handlebars. 'I've just seen your mate.'

'Who's that?'

'Nathan Woods.'

'He's not here, is he? Fuck. What's he want?'

Tom looked smug. 'Says he's coming back.'

'What? No way.'

'Yeah, I've been having a little chat with him. He says he's not ready for drama college yet, he wants to do his GCSEs first and then apply. His tutors feel he's talented, but maturity will add depth to his performances.'

'In other words, they find him an irritating little twit and they want rid.'

Anna watched the two men squaring up, and felt hopeless.

'He's still waiting to hear when his advert's being screened,' Tom continued, rattling his chain cheerfully.

'What I don't understand,' said Ian, 'is why leave and then come back?'

'Loads of kids do it. Lucy Elford went to Spain for two terms and then turned up in Year Nine, do you remember? And Daniel Leroy went to Cassels because he reckoned he was bullied, but he got bullied at Cassels as well so he came back here and re-did Year Seven. The grass is always greener.'

'He's winding you up,' said Andrew. 'Winding us up. At least, I hope to God he is.'

The telephone rang and Anna escaped to the annexe to answer it. An outside call.

'It's Mrs Taylor here. Zachary's mother.'

'Oh, yes, Zach.'

'I needed to speak to—'

Outside, Andrew was close to shouting. 'Hang on.' She pulled the door closed in an attempt to shut out the conversation outside.

'Go ahead.'

'Well, mm. It's about Zach.'

'Yes?'

The mobile in her pocket bleeped. Jamie? She slid it out with her free hand.

'OK, well, what it is, he's not happy about doing PE. In fact, he's getting himself in a state.'

More muffled bickering. *Just because he says it, it doesn't mean it's going to happen. He's not the Almighty.* Anna struggled to bring up Messages on her phone.

'Is he? Poor Zach, I'm sorry to hear that. Some students find it difficult to—'

Mel. *Rdy 4 off. Nxt tm u hr frm me i'll be in thailand!*

'The problem is, if I can speak confidentially, Mrs Yates—'

Bugger, the woman thought she was Liz. Never mind, she could relay the information.

'—he's a sensitive boy.'

'Of course he is.'

'And he's got these—'

'Yes?'

'He's got breasts.'

'Sorry?'

'I've told him he'll grow out of it, if he loses a bit of weight, but at the moment they're quite prominent under his T-shirt and the other boys are calling him Playtex, and it's very hard for him in the changing rooms because he has these, well, they are boobs—'

'Boobs?'

'Yes. It's very awkward for him.'

Andrew again: *You needn't sound so fucking pleased about it.* Ian's nervous laugh in the background. Then Les: *Now, what's the problem, chaps?*

'I understand,' said Anna. 'I've got them myself.' She put the phone down. Let Liz sort it out.

'Anyone seen Anna?'

'Here I am.' She dropped her mobile back in her pocket and came out of the annexe.

Les was looking anxious. 'You OK?' he asked.

'I don't know.'

'Master Woods is off the premises, anyway.'

Andrew stood up. 'For how long, though? Come on, Les, give.'

'I can't tell you.'

'If he comes back—'

'It's no good meeting trouble halfway. The truth is, I don't know what's happening.'

Anna watched Les's eyes flick down to the left. That was a sign someone was lying, wasn't it? She settled herself at the coffee table and began to read the *TES. GCSE pass rates a joke, says minister.* Twenty seconds later Tom leaned across and swept the newspaper away, towards him. She gaped in indignation but he failed to notice.

'The point I'm making,' he said, laying the nunchakus on the floor to make room for the paper, 'is, I've never had a minute's trouble from the lad. I subscribe to Abraham Lincoln's theory: if you look for crap behaviour, you'll find it.'

'And what's that supposed to mean?' Andrew turned his scowl in Tom's direction.

It was enough.

Anna picked up her bag, wrote a note to Les, and put her planner, with its lesson outlines, in Chrissy's pigeonhole. Then she left the school.

Chapter Nineteen

Anna drove first to the supermarket; she was laying in stocks for a siege. Once home, she made an appointment to see the doctor and extract a sick note. She had toyed with the idea of going away – the image of sitting in that sea-front cafe still hung around at the back of her mind – but she didn't have the energy. Then she flicked the answerphone on, went to bed and slept round the clock.

She dreamed: Adam Gardiner had come to her house again. You have to stay away, she told him, or I'll be in trouble. No, he said, we're married. You married me so I could get away from home. She started to argue but the scene changed to something else that she didn't remember.

When she woke up she was very hot and thought she must genuinely be ill. She showered, drank a glass of milk, wrote some notes on lesson cover to post. But she could not shake off the awful feeling of the dream.

The phone rang and she hung over the banister to listen to the message. *Oh, it's Les. Look. Anna.* There was a silence after that where she could hear him breathing, hoping she was there and would speak to him. *Can you call me back when you've a minute?* At last the dial tone. Chrissy would be next, of course.

Anna went back to bed. This time the dream was about Miriam: they were on the beach and her mother was digging a hole. What are you doing that for? Anna asked. Because the foundations here are so poor, Miriam told her, you have to go a long way down. But the tide, said Anna. If you build here it'll get washed away. Can't you see what's going to happen? No, said Miriam, because I'll make a wall. And all the time the water was rushing in.

The phone was ringing again. Anna lay in bed and thought about watching television with her mother, *The Fall and Rise of Reginald Perrin*. The opening sequence had shown a man shedding his clothes and swimming out into the sea, faking suicide so he could start a new and secret life. 'I'd love to do that,' Miriam had said, with real longing.

Later Anna got dressed and went to her appointment. She cried a little, and the doctor signed her off for two weeks. 'You're not the sort of person to swing the lead,' he said. By the time she got back she was exhausted, but she made herself put the slip and lesson notes in an envelope and address it to Jackson. If she'd broken her arm or been in a car accident he'd have to shape himself; there were mechanisms in place for staff absence. Not her problem. 'Are you really not well?' she imagined him asking, his voice full of suppressed irritation despite the smile. 'I'm not myself,' she said aloud. That was the best answer for now.

She knew she ought to eat something so she made

herself arrange some chicken pieces on a plate with a slice of bread, and took it upstairs, even though she had no appetite. While she was sitting on the bed looking at the food, the front door Yale clicked and she heard someone step into the hall. Jamie said, 'Anna?' He spoke low, as though he was hoping he wouldn't get a reply. She kept quiet. He closed the door behind him.

A minute passed. Now he'd be going through the post she'd left on the table. The pipes hissed as he ran a tap. Then the happy-robot voice of the answerphone: *You have. Two. New messages. Message. One: Oh, it's Les. Look. Anna.*

Bloody infuriating of Jamie to waltz in and start listening to her calls like this. There might be anything on there.

Message. Two: Hi, Anna, Chrissy speaking, from school. Sorry to hear you aren't feeling too good. Is it, what is it? Can you let me know? Anyway, I've got your planner with some lesson notes, but I do need to clarify one or two points with you. It's quite important. If I could maybe have a chat with you when you're— Anna could detect panic in the intonation. Normally she was so utterly conscientious; they wouldn't believe she'd just dropped everything like that.

The front door banged and Jamie was gone again. Anna went down to see. The house was so quiet she could hear the rustle of carpet fibres under her feet.

He had left his cup on the mantelpiece, and the throw over the chair had been disturbed. Slender evidences. She could put the cup away on the shelf and straighten the throw, and it would be as though he was never there.

There was still most of a bottle of whisky left in the cabinet. If she made a huge effort, she might just get back up to bed again.

Anna was dreaming again. Not about Phil, but about little Colin Rafferty. She was in the playground and someone was saying, 'Colin's set himself on fire, Mrs Lloyd.' It was her fault because she hadn't taken enough notice of him. She became angry and shouted, 'I'm fed up of dealing with attention-seeking kids! That's all I do, all day!' The alarm began to go off, and Les was there looking shocked and sorrowful. Then he had covered Colin with a coat and was beating and beating him, thumping away as if he was trying to break bones, and Anna was awake and someone was leaning on the bell and banging hard at the front door.

Her first reaction was panic. It was almost midnight, so there must be some dreadful emergency. The noise stopped and that was even worse, because what if the house next door was ablaze or there was a police raid or something, and they needed to evacuate the area? She jerked and struggled with the covers. Jamie had had an accident; no, he'd hanged himself. They were coming round to show her the suicide note.

At the top of the first landing she paused to listen, then crept down the next flight till she could see the door. As she watched, the letter box opened and slim fingers poked through, then withdrew. A female scared voice came from the slot: 'Mrs Lloyd? Please open the door, Mrs Lloyd. Please.'

'Kali?'

Anna almost fell in her haste to get down and undo the lock. She didn't know what she was going to find on the other side, but in the event it was just Kali, on her own and unharmed, with a carrier bag at her feet and a halo of light across her crown from the street lamp.

'I need to come in,' she said. Exactly as Adam Gardiner had a year ago, when she should have told him, No, you can't stay here, it's not appropriate, go home to your mother.

'Of course,' said Anna. 'Come out of the cold. I'll put the gas fire on.'

'Someone was following me.'

'What?'

'I thought there was someone behind me.'

Anna peered past Kali's shoulder, but the square was empty. 'I can't see anyone.'

'No. I was probably just spooking myself. There was this weird bloke on the bus doing strange noises, snorting and stuff. Looking at me.'

'And he got off at the same stop?'

Kali shook her head. 'Ages before.'

'Well, then.' *What are you doing here?* Anna tested the sentence out in her head but it sounded ungracious. 'Come through, I'll make coffee.'

They sat opposite each other, close to the fire. Kali hunched over her mug and jiggled her knees up and down nervously. Anna had put more whisky in her own drink.

'Are you in trouble?'

'No. What makes you think that?'

Anna laughed. 'It's a bit late to be out alone.'

'I'm sixteen,' said Kali in her young, high voice.

God, I've missed you, Anna thought. She said, 'I'm forty-two and I'd think twice about walking round on my own after dark. Does your mother know where you are?'

'She's in Ireland. Hey, I smell brandy. Can I have some? To warm me up?'

'Are you telling me your mother's abroad and you're on your own?'

'It's OK, Trent's looking after me, I'm staying at his.' Kali smiled faintly. 'He's a family friend.'

'But your mother's left you?'

'She had to go and sort out some business with a will and I didn't want to trail over there. She'll be back at the end of the month. God, didn't your mum ever leave you at sixteen?'

'They were different times,' said Anna. The flames wavered between them, Miriam stuffed clothes into a canvas bag, dropped a shoe and cursed. 'What about Owen? Has he gone to Ireland too?'

'Yeah. But it's OK. Trent's OK.'

'So where is he?'

Kali stood up and began to walk round the room. 'I really like your pictures, Mrs Lloyd. Is this one old?'

'It's a modern print by an artist called David Inshaw. What about Trent?'

The girl turned away from the wall with a patient

expression. 'He can't be expected to play babysitter twenty-four seven, he has work to do.'

You're reciting what you've been told, thought Anna. 'And he's at work now?'

'He had to go to Manchester for a couple of days to meet some people. He's going to give me a ring when he's finished.'

The situation was wholly unsatisfactory. She wondered whether she should phone Mrs Norman; then again, what would she say? Kali was safe, no one had broken any laws. Kali wouldn't thank her.

'Why did you come here tonight?'

'I just wanted to see you.'

Anna recognized that would have to do for now.

'OK. I'm going to make us some supper,' she said. 'And you're going to tell me all your news.'

Anna, sitting in the school examination hall, newly married, optimistic. Thinking of children; thinking of a daughter. Imagining what they will do together, what she can give. What kind of mother will she be?

She will give her daughter a love of books and reading and study. She will encourage her to make the best of her looks, but not to set too much store by beauty. She will guard and protect her from all harm.

So here they were, cooking together. Anna moved round the kitchen collecting ingredients. She felt capable and busy.

'Take this plate and grate some cheese, will you? Bottom shelf of the fridge. The grater's hanging up.'

'The trouble is,' Kali was explaining, 'Trent can drive, it's all right for him. If he wants anything he can hop in the Saxo. He doesn't look at Broxton from my point of view which is, like, I don't know anyone and it's miles away from Chester.'

'But why did you come to me?'

'You were near.' Kali stared into the fridge, illuminated. 'And 'cause I started to see how some of the stuff you told us was relevant.'

Anna laughed. 'Thanks very much.'

'I mean, to do with Trent.'

'How?'

'Because – you *know*.'

'I don't.'

'Well—' Kali seemed stricken by shyness all of a sudden. 'We got it together, at last. After messing about for a long, stupid time—'

'You and Trent?'

'Yeah.'

'Oh! What happened to Neil Patrick?'

'That wasn't ever anything. I've known Trent for ages. He's really important.' A vague look came into her eyes for a moment. 'Do you remember that poem we did about the frozen tractor? When you said there was no difference between extremes of temperature?'

'That's not quite right.'

'Yeah, you said when you touch an object that's really hot or really cold it confused your nerves, the sensation was the same.'

'Only for a second. You can soon tell whether you're

being burnt or not. Look, do you want me to grate that cheese?'

'Sorry, no. I was thinking, though, love's like that. There are times you feel so strongly that you can't decide what it is you're feeling. You get *consumed*. Do you know what I mean? You can love someone for a long time and not be sure it is love. You might even think it's hate. And then something happens and you understand.'

'How do you mean, something happens?'

'The person goes away for a while, or you see them with a girl.'

Anna had been stirring a pan, watching butter melt into milk, but she stopped and looked up. 'How old is Trent?'

'Twenty,' said Kali promptly, but there was a sliding note to the word which didn't sound right.

There's a game going on here, thought Anna.

She will teach her daughter to respect herself. She will give her the confidence to feel the world is hers for the taking. She will always listen.

'I'm happy for you, if you've found someone,' said Anna. You need some stability, she could have added. 'And I should mention, I was very sorry about the business at school; I thought it was disgraceful the way Mr Jackson handled things. I did go to see him, but . . .'

'How do you mean?'

'Well, I know you were effectively pushed out without a proper enquiry. I was very angry about it.' Jackson's pious jowly face, his outraged brows.

'No, Mrs Lloyd. You're wrong. I left Montcliff of my own accord. It wasn't the right school for me.'

Anna didn't know how to greet this statement so she said nothing at all. She bit into her toast and watched Kali bending over her plate, her hair draped over her shoulders in a shining curve, her bracelets glinting as she wiped up a blob of egg with her finger and licked it off.

'So, anyway, I'm making a new start at Hazelwood after half-term. Hey, Trent makes a brilliant Welsh rarebit. He's a better cook than Mum.'

'Is he, now,' said Anna.

She will try not to be too judgemental.

'Aren't you tired, Kali?'

'No. Are you?'

Anna was surprised to find she wasn't. 'But it's past midnight and we need to think about getting you back. I can't drive you—'

'Why not?'

'I had a drink before you came.' How long ago was that? She wasn't sure. 'But I'll pay for a cab.'

Kali shot her a simple look of fear. Don't make me go back to an empty house on my own, her face said.

'I know a reliable firm. I can ask for a woman driver.'

'Can't I stay here?'

'That's not really a good idea.'

'Why not? Wouldn't your husband like it?'

'Oh no, it's certainly not that.' (But then, imagine if she sent Kali back and something happened to her?) 'It's because . . .' The girl's expression was pleading. You came to see me because you were lonely, thought Anna. Then Jackson's figure loomed into her consciousness.

Professional parameters, he was saying. Except Kali wasn't her pupil any more; it was a different relationship now.

'We have a spare bed in my study,' she said. 'Come and help me put some sheets on.'

Anna woke at two with the sense that someone was in her room, but when she switched the bedside light on, there was nothing. Then she remembered Kali and got up.

Blue glow from the living room TV flickered across the door frame.

'Couldn't you sleep?'

The girl, half dressed, was hunched up in Jamie's armchair. She had the sound down but the picture showed a woman dancing, naked except for a metal collar.

'It's a documentary,' said Kali. She reached for the remote and flicked through three or four channels rapidly – male newsreader, a Mediterranean street, US football – and settled on a car chase along a red-orange mountainside.

'There's no need to turn it off,' said Anna.

''S OK.'

The leading vehicle went into a spin and ricocheted off a boulder.

'Your husband,' said Kali, 'he's not here, is he?'

'We'll talk some more in the morning.'

Cars rolled and exploded in front of their eyes.

But in spite of the late night, Anna woke the next morning feeling refreshed and positive.

This was a good thing she was doing, generous and grown-up. She would keep an eye on Kali till her mother came home, and hope the woman was shamed by Anna's example. Even afterwards, Anna could be Kali's mentor. She could offer more poetry sessions, or help her catch up with the GCSE course. She saw herself slotting into Kali's life, advising her on colleges, providing her with references, giving counsel. Everyone needed a figure like that, a person outside the family, to whom they could speak freely. She would be there for Kali. Jackson had got the girl so wrong; he didn't know her at all.

It was well past ten when Kali came down.

'We'll have brunch,' said Anna, and began to assemble ingredients. Meanwhile Kali wandered in and out in varying degrees of toilet. Anna, laying rashers on the grill and slicing tomatoes, trying not to look up, nevertheless caught glimpses: white thighs, black knickers, the brown tattoo, a grey shirt with a toothbrush in the pocket.

'Do you need to borrow anything?' Anna asked. It was dawning on her that Kali had come prepared. *Expecting* to stay the night. She wasn't sure what she felt about that.

At this moment the girl was standing by the window brushing her hair, like a figure in a modern painting.

'Hey, by the way, I like your dolls' house,' she said. 'It's cool.'

Anna decided the carrier bag of clothes demonstrated Kali's trust in her, and went back to turning the bacon.

She was in the process of transferring sausages from the grill to the oven when she saw Russ's car pull up. She dropped the pan onto the hob as though it had burnt her.

'Come with me,' she said to Kali, who'd been sitting at the table reading a magazine.

'Where?'

Just out of sight, Anna almost said. No way could she cope with Russ just now. 'Quickly. Upstairs.'

Kali was laughing as she went up the first flight.

'What's going on?'

'It's someone I don't want to see.'

They sat together on Kali's bed and listened to the doorbell ringing over and over. After a while it stopped. Anna knew that meant nothing, though. Next came a hollow knocking from the back of the house; Russ was at the French windows, trying to get in via the lounge. They could hear his muffled calling.

'Who is it, Mrs Lloyd?'

'*Hush*,' said Anna urgently. She could guess only too well why he was here and she couldn't face him.

Minutes passed. The dolls' house door hung open and the tiny hall mirror trembled slightly on its chain. 'I think they've gone,' whispered Kali.

Anna shook her head, and at the same time there was a rattle at the front of the house and Russ's voice came through quite clearly.

'I know you're in because you've left the grill on.'

'Fuck,' said Anna. Kali giggled.

'Open the door or I shall stand here all day.'

He would do that.

'Wait here,' she told Kali. 'Do not come down.' That was one complication she could do without. Russ raising his eyebrows and making inappropriate comments. In any case, she did not intend letting him past the hall.

She went down to the kitchen and switched off the gas. Russ appeared at the kitchen window. 'I have to speak to you,' he mouthed. There was moisture on the glass where his breath had been.

As soon as she opened the door he was inside.

'I ran across Jamie in Prees this morning,' he said excitedly.

When Anna said nothing, he pushed past her into the lounge.

'I'm busy, Russ,' she called after him. 'You can't stay.'

'I saw him as I was driving past. Walking up the high street. So I asked him what he was doing there. And do you know what he told me?'

'I've got a doctor's appointment in a minute.'

'Do you know what he said? He said he wasn't living here any more. He said he was having some time out. Time Out.' He nodded significantly. 'What does that mean, Anna?'

It was stupid to stand in the hall. She followed him through.

There was more light in the lounge and she could see he was wearing a new jacket and possibly new shoes. Had he lost some weight as well? He was looking better groomed than usual.

'He's finishing an important script,' she said. It sounded unconvincing even to her ears. 'A prison drama he thinks the BBC might take. He wanted to concentrate extra hard so he gets it right, no interruptions. You know what he's like.'

'He's left you.'

'No, he hasn't.'

Russ smiled and sat down, leaning back and crossing his legs in the way Jamie always did, with his right ankle over his left knee. Make yourself at home.

'It is true,' Anna went on, 'that he's having a break. But it's not permanent. He's left all his CDs and DVDs, see for yourself. His writing magazines are all in the stool.' She lifted the lid to show him.

'Hmm. Turn-up for the books, though.'

That was it, she had to make him leave. 'I'm going out,' she announced. 'Now.'

Russ stood up and came forward. 'I wondered at first if he'd found out about us. But no, he'd have floored me, wouldn't he? Broken my jaw, or something manly.' He gave a foolish grin. 'So it's obviously something just between the two of you. Whatever are you going to do, all on your own?'

My God, thought Anna, he thinks we're on again.

'I'll manage.' She took her coat from the peg and picked up her bag. 'Right, well, you really must—'

But she never finished the sentence because he had grasped her hands in his so tightly her wedding ring hurt. 'Come back to me,' he rasped. His lips were moving towards hers.

She shook herself free.

'You don't mean that.'

Russ had stepped back and was staring at her, his whole face on the edge of a sneer.

'No, I don't. You're right. As ever. My mistake.'

He really hates me, thought Anna. She held the front door open and he walked obediently through. As she shut it behind him he turned and said, without any apparent trace of irony, 'You know, Ruth's *twice* the woman you are.' He would have added more, but she swung the door closed and the clunk of the lock drowned him out.

'Jesus,' she said, and leant against the wall. All the tiredness had come back; she wanted to slide down onto the carpet and close her eyes.

A movement on the stairs. Anna turned her head.

'Kali?'

The girl was standing on the third step up, her arms folded.

She said, 'You're in a bit of a mess, aren't you, Mrs Lloyd?'

Chapter Twenty

Most of the light in this room was coming from a fibre-optic lamp in the corner, but there was an illuminated bar round the door edge as well; Kali liked to leave the landing bulb on, she said. Anna preferred gloom. It was less abrasive on the eyes.

Earlier the room had looked shabby, with mismatched curtains, and a patch of terracotta over half the wall where someone had begun painting and then given up. The place needed a clean, the lines of joss-stick ash wiping away and the carpet hoovering.

'Your mother left you here?' Anna had exclaimed when she first walked into the flat. There was black mould on the windowpanes, cobwebs hanging off the picture rails.

'They left me at Owen's,' Kali said. 'I came out here because the house felt too big. Why, is there something wrong?'

Anna bit her lip. She didn't want to spoil things. That was Miriam's line, the ever-critical. Anyway, in the dimmer light the place looked folksy and chic, colours like she remembered in Phil's room at uni. There was a faded Persian-type rug in the centre of the floor and scarves hanging off the wardrobe door, a poster of Magritte's dove over the fireplace. Kali's boots lay on their side under the window.

She had driven Kali back to Trent's in the early afternoon, but when they got there the place was still empty and Anna hadn't wanted to leave the girl on her own. It seemed like a careless thing to do.

Nevertheless she'd made herself go home. For six hours she stayed there, wandering from room to room, opening the dolls' house and adjusting furniture, nibbling plain biscuits and checking out of the window repeatedly for Jamie or Russ. The walls might have been made of glass for all the protection she felt they offered.

Finally she rang Kali. She had a duty to check everything was all right.

'Have you heard from Trent yet?'

'Back tomorrow afternoon, for definite.' Kali sounded small over the phone.

'And have you got everything you need? I forgot to ask before I left.'

'There's no bread or milk, but I'm eating crackers. Oh, and I've found some very old fruit tea at the back of the—'

'Let me drop some supplies off. I can be round there in twenty minutes.'

The girl put up a feeble resistance. 'It's OK, I've got a bit of cash, I could probably . . .'

'No arguments. I'll see you.'

Anna had gone joyfully to her own cupboards and filled a cardboard box with groceries she thought Kali might like. As a mad afterthought, she took her sponge bag; it could be left in the car. Fuck Jamie, fuck Russ, fuck Jackson and Liz and everyone.

Kali was playing Brood when she got there and they unpacked to 'Prisoner You':

> *Gonna make you a prison of love*
> *Bars of guilt, locks of need*
> *A moat of loneliness all around*
> *You will follow where I lead*

Anna made supper and then read a Stephen King novel she found in the bathroom. Meanwhile Kali sent some texts, painted her fingernails, wrote in her poetry book. Girls together.

'I must go,' Anna said twice.

'Yeah,' said Kali.

Neither of them moved. It got dark outside.

At half past ten Kali stopped writing and said matter-of-factly, 'I can lend you clothes and stuff. You can sleep in my bed and I'll have Trent's.'

There was no point in protesting.

Kali's velvet tunic was on the radiator, her empty WKD bottles on the bedside table. Anna lay on top of the duvet and stared at the triangle of starry sky where the curtains did not meet. This is where I need to be just now, she thought. I'm doing no harm.

Mid morning she took a cup of tea through, but Kali was still sound asleep. Anna perched on the end of the bed and watched her. Do you usually spend the night in here? she wanted to ask. Are you taking care of yourself? Does your mother know you're in love with the person she left in charge? What kind of family friend is he, anyway? Perhaps she could ask these things. Anna leaned closer; Kali breathed with her mouth open. There was a wet patch on the pillow, a tiny cut on her top lip.

After a minute, Anna got up and opened the tatty curtains. As she walked back round she paused by the wardrobe mirror to consider herself in purple velvet. My God, she thought, look at you. Who was that woman? Not Anna, for sure; somebody far more interesting. It wasn't right, though, until she changed her way of standing, relaxed her shoulders, moved her feet apart. She lowered her face and peered again at herself from under her fringe. Was that better? In the background Kali sat up and said, 'Oh, cheers.'

Anna turned round at once.

'Sorry to wake you. I'll go.'

''Sall right.' She picked up the mug of tea and took a long swig. 'Shit, though – I was having this dream. Ugh. Thank Christ it's the morning.'

'Nightmare?'

'Just a bit. Bizarre.' Kali stretched one pale arm above her head, splaying her fingers. 'Do you ever dream you're getting off with someone you don't fancy? I mean – ' disgusted noise – 'what's going on there? Hey?' The arm dropped to the duvet, defeated.

'Anyone I know?'

'Not really. And then you wake up and it's like, thank *God* for that.' Even without make-up, in a creased T-shirt and with her hair mussed up, she was lovely.

'I've had those dreams too. They're very common. They don't mean anything, just your day unravelling.'

'Yeah? Sheesh. You're great, you know everything.'

'I'll make some breakfast. Let you get dressed.'

But Kali had already thrown the cover back and was stretching her long bare legs out across the mattress. Anna slipped out quickly and closed the door behind her.

The toast she had made was cold by the time Kali came out of the bathroom. Anna heard her humming, then there was a faint burst of guitar as a text came through on her phone. At last she walked into the kitchen. Today she wore a black lace blouse with a high-neck collar, and jeans. Her eyes were outlined in kohl.

'That was Mum saying hello.'

'Everything all right?'

'Uh huh. Just checking in.'

Anna thought, *That woman.*

'Kali, can I ask you something?'

The girl raised her head. 'Sure.'

'I was wondering whether your mum knew you and Trent were – together. An item.'

Kali shrugged. 'Not sure. It happened after she left. I don't think she'd mind, though. She's always teasing me about him.'

'Have you known him a long time, then? How did he become a friend of the family?'

'What are you getting at, Mrs Lloyd? Are you worried he's not *safe*?'

'Yes, if you want the truth.'

''Kay.'

'You're very young, still—'

'Old enough to be married.'

'Technically.'

They eyed each other across the table. Anna had never felt less the grown-up. Kali said, 'He's fine, stop worrying. You'll meet him soon. Come and help me with my hair.'

She brought her chair round and handed a brush to Anna.

'I want it in two small plaits taken from the sides, here, and then clipped together halfway down. Do you get me? I can do it myself but it's hard to make it equal.'

Anna began to comb through the back strands, remembering the time in the garden when Kali had flinched away. They'd come so far since then, it was astonishing.

She worked gently so as not to tug and the hair slipped through her fingers like silk.

'Trent's mum,' said Kali, 'was a friend of my mum, back when we lived in Manchester. He used to babysit me, sort of.'

'Which must make him a lot older.'

'No. He was really young himself. And then his mum got killed and we saw a lot of him, but then we went to Ireland and he moved in with his uncle in Blackburn for a bit. Now we live near each other again, it's really good.'

And he's responsible, mature? Is he decent? Anna wanted to ask.

Kali tipped her head back confidentially. 'Trent's taught me all sorts.'

'I can imagine.'

'Honestly, not like that. You'll like him when you meet him, Mrs Lloyd.'

'For heaven's sake, call me Anna. It's not as if I'm your teacher any more.'

Even when you looked close, you couldn't tell what shade this hair was. The roots were dark, but lower down some strands were orange and some of them almost blonde, and they changed in the light as you handled them. She pulled the plait taut and studied the colours as if she was about to draw them.

'No, you're not, are you?' said Kali.

When Anna was sixteen, she thought boyfriends were nothing but a whole lot of trouble.

Before she brought the first one home she'd suffered agonies. 'You won't be funny with him?' she'd felt compelled to ask Miriam.

Her mother had laughed. 'What do you think I'm going to do to him?'

Walk round in just your dressing gown, start sobbing, offer him a joint. The possibilities were endless. But in the end her mother had plumped for being simply rude.

'My old teacher had a pair of glasses like yours,' she'd said, pointing at the boy's face till he blushed. 'They didn't do a lot for him either. What's your dad do? Ae-ro-nautical en-gin-eer? Fancy.' Miriam had smirked and pulled faces. 'How the other half live. What must you think of us?'

So Anna hadn't had many relationships at school because it hadn't seemed worth the bother. If she'd lost her virginity at that time she was sure her mother would have somehow known about it, which was a thought not to be borne. Miriam was a woman who feigned indifference, then went through your diary while you were out.

But since she'd been here she'd hardly thought about Miriam. Anna's neat fingers passed strands of Kali's hair over and under; the second plait was nearly done. The elastic to secure them was round her wrist and there was a black ribbon draped over the back of the chair for finishing off. On the radio someone sang:

> *Happiness is just a trick*
> *It's all in the mind*
> *A mental aberration*
> *Madness of a kind*

Anna had lifted the two plaits together and was comparing tensions when Kali said, 'You been having an affair, then?'

Come back to me, Russ growled again in Anna's ear; she could still feel his clutch on her arm.

There didn't seem any point in denying it. 'I was. Not any more.'

'Oh.'

Kali groped behind her for the ribbon and passed it up.

'It was over a long while ago.'

'Yeah, I heard you. It didn't sound as though you liked each other very much.'

'No, I don't think we ever did.'

'Why d'you have an affair, then?'

'Well—' The ribbon slipped from Anna's fingers and fluttered to the floor. She bent to pick it up again, hiding her face while she framed an appropriate lie. 'There are lots of reasons people have affairs.' She noticed, as she concentrated on tying the knot, that her hands were trembling. 'Sex is a complicated business.'

This was no good.

'I was angry with my husband, Kali. That's why.'

'What had he done?'

'It was because we couldn't have a baby.'

'Was it his fault?'

'It felt like it. He wasn't that bothered and it felt like I was on my own, I don't know how else to describe it. Having an affair was a kind of revenge, I suppose. Punishment.' At last Anna managed to pull the loops of the bow through and knot the ribbon tight. 'It's hard to explain; it made sense at the time. But please, for God's sake, never let on to anyone about it.'

'I never would.'

'I know, I know you wouldn't. There. You're finished.'

Kali put her fingers up and patted the back of her head.

'I'd like to pay for you to get your hair shaped sometime, at a really good salon,' said Anna. 'If you wanted, obviously.'

The girl rose slowly, as though she were at a deportment lesson, and made her way to the bathroom. 'Imagine if you'd got pregnant by the other bloke,' she called. After a minute she came back in. 'Smart, thanks.'

'Talking of which, are *you* looking after yourself, Kali?'

'Whatever do you mean, Mrs Lloyd?'

'Come on.' It was hard for Anna not to sound irritated. 'If your mum's not here to give you personal advice, then I—'

''S OK, I know what you mean. And yeah, I'm sorted. Thank you.'

Anna began to gather up the brushes and clips. 'Right. Good.'

'I've got my lucky stone.' Kali hooked a finger inside her collar and drew out a silver chain with a ring of haematite fastened to the end. 'Here. This'll stop me falling.'

Anna's eyes widened.

'It really does work,' Kali went on, pulling the chain taut and running the ring up and down its length. 'Something to do with your body's natural magnetic fields. They used it in the olden days. It's never failed me yet.'

Then she began to laugh. 'Your face, Anna.'

'What?'

'It was a joke.'

'A joke?'

'Yeah, of course. I wouldn't be so stupid. Did you really think I'd be so stupid? I mean, a lucky stone? Yeah, right.'

'I suppose not.'

'Oh, God, now you're cross.'

It was true, she was. No, not cross, embarrassed. She

felt a fool. 'It's not something to make fun of; I was trying to help.'

Kali came over and put her arms round Anna's neck. She smelt clean: mint and bodyspray. 'I know, you've been a good friend to me. Sorry for winding you up.'

The stray copper hairs at the edge of Anna's vision grew thick and vanished as she let her focus relax. Her gaze travelled to the window nearest, then to the tree outside. She pulled away. Kali was still smiling.

'I really had you going, though, didn't I?'

'You certainly did,' said Anna.

She needed to get out for a while, so she took herself down the lane in the direction of the garage. She could pick up some kitchen spray and give all the cups a good swill, wipe down the cupboards. No need to go mad, though. She didn't want to look as if she were taking over.

As Anna walked, she wondered about Jamie. What would he be doing now? Perhaps he *was* writing; he might have been telling Russ the truth. It was possible. A sudden awful vision interrupted her, of Russ marching round to his brother's new place and confessing everything out of mad spite. Jesus.

But no, that wasn't going to happen. She understood finally that Russ was too weak to field that kind of upheaval. Even if – and here was a crazy thought – even if she'd turned round and said to him at any point, OK, then, let's you and me take off, he wouldn't have had the nerve. For all he complained about his dull life, it was what he could cope with. The rest was fantasy.

But Jamie. She screwed up her eyes like a seer and concentrated; she used to be good at getting into his head. He'd been an easy man to read, till lately. Lately she'd felt out of her depth.

I haven't gone for good, she imagined him thinking. *Too much effort involved in that course. I'll just stay away a while longer, to teach her a lesson. Teach her to appreciate me. It would be different if I had positive proof of an affair, but it probably is what she said, that she needed some time alone. I have all day to myself but she never gets that because of work. And she does like her space. If only she'd been up front about it. But then I suppose it wouldn't have been completely private. I can kind of see that. Anna wouldn't have an affair, she's too sensible.*

I'll go back when she realizes she needs me. I'll try again, if she does.

The garage had come into view. She halted, considering. It would be a good move to text Jamie and let him know she was all right. She didn't want him contacting the police when it dawned on him there was no one home.

She called up her address book and scrolled down for his number, but as she did so another idea popped into her head. She imagined Jamie in a bar talking to a woman. And a new voice-over to go with it: *I'd say a little fling, given the circumstances, was justified. After all, we're adults. If Anna feels the need to hide part of her life from me, then I have the right to do the same. We'll be quits, and I can go back with my self-respect intact.*

It was all too plausible. Jamie rolling around on a

strange bed with someone else. How did she feel about that?

I might even get a few good stories out of it. It's all life experience.

Actually, that hurt. She shook her head to disperse the picture from her mind and fished in her jeans pocket for her money. Bleach. And more washing-up liquid and a new dishcloth, if they sold them. She crossed the forecourt, stepping over petrol-sodden sand. It occurred to her that she hadn't been able to make her mental-Jamie say he loved her and he missed her, but she was here at the garage shop now and the moment had gone. Maybe later.

'Your head's wrong.' Kali studied Anna from the far end of the sofa.

'Thanks very much.'

'I mean, we ought to do something with your hair and make-up so it matches the clothes. Hippify them. 'Cause that top looks quite good with your colouring.'

'This is me, it's how I am.'

'It's how you've chosen to be; I could make you look completely different. Listen, we could crimp your hair underneath so it fluffs it up . . . You definitely need some stronger lipstick and some mascara.' Kali leant across and made quick gestures round Anna's face. She lifted a wing of hair critically. 'Yeah. Go on, let me. You'll be amazed at what I can do to you.'

And that was how Trent came across them, sitting in candlelight and painting each other's faces.

Kali heard the key in the lock first. 'He's here!' she

said. Anna expected her to leap up, but she stayed where she was.

So this was Trent. Tall and olive-skinned, in a black overcoat; serious-faced. He dropped his holdall on the floor.

'Hello. Who's this?'

You're older than twenty, thought Anna. She pushed her hair out of her eyes and stood up, offering her hand. He looked down at it and laughed.

'Who is it, Kali?'

'I'm Anna Lloyd. Nice to meet you.'

'She's my friend,' said Kali.

'Right.' He did take Anna's hand at last. 'OK. Make yourself at home; oh, I see you already have. What are all the candles in aid of? It's still light outside.'

Kali pouted. 'We wanted atmosphere. Don't open the curtains, you'll spoil it.'

'I wondered what the fuck was going on.'

He sat down heavily.

'What've you got for me, Trent? Anything?'

'Depends on whether you've been a good girl or not.' He glanced across at Anna. 'Has she been a good girl?'

'Exemplary.'

She could tell by Trent's expression it was a stupid thing to say.

'Ooh. Exemplary.' His lips twisted upwards. 'Who are you again?'

Anna started to explain but Kali cut in. 'I told you, she's a friend from school. She's been keeping me company. And cooking. She's an ace cook. She'll cook you a meal if you want.'

Trent closed his eyes and put his head back against the chair. 'That'd be good.'

Kali nodded at Anna meaningfully.

'Right, then. I'll do an omelette for everyone, shall I?'

'Whatever,' said Trent.

She took herself into the kitchen end of the room and filled the kettle. Her new reflection, with its carmine lips and blue-lidded eyes, wavered up and down the steel flank; she held the kettle steady and frowned. Kali had made her look like something between a vampire and a prostitute. Heavy beaded earrings swayed against her cheek. If Jackson could see her now he'd have a fit.

The kettle overflowed into the sink and she turned the tap off hastily. Yesterday she and Kali had made the meal together. Anna had shown her how to do a proper shepherd's pie with fresh ingredients.

'Like *fuck* you will,' hissed Kali from the living room, and giggled. She must have moved onto Trent's lap; the chair back hid them both but her bare feet were sticking over the side. 'You're mental,' she said. There was some muttering and a squeal.

I'll cook this damn omelette and go, thought Anna.

The food stuck in her throat. She had put the meal on the table but Trent had taken his to the sofa, so Kali had too. Anna sat on her own. The omelette sat cold and foul on the plate in front of her. She pushed her chair back and stood up.

'I think I'll be on my way. You two don't need an audience.' That sounded rather bitter, but it was too late, the words were out.

'Yes, we do,' said Kali at once. 'Stay.'

Anna didn't reply. She went through to the bathroom and gathered her things. When she came out, Trent was pretending to bite Kali's ear.

'I'll see you.'

'No, wait—' But Kali made no attempt to break free or get off the sofa.

Anna slipped through the door and down the stairs. It was better to go now, under her own volition. The evening was dropping cool and the inside of the car was damp and chilly. The curves of the bonnet were outlined in yellow light from the warm bright window of Trent's kitchen above, but she didn't look up.

When she got home, Miriam was waiting for her. It's your fault, she told her mother. Your fault I can't form proper relationships. Dragging me round, being such a cow I couldn't bring people home.

Get over yourself, said Miriam. *You were born solitary. Don't go blaming everything you are now on me.*

The post was piled on the bottom stair, so Jamie must have been round earlier. That felt slightly reassuring. She looked for a note but he'd not left one. There was, however, a card from Ruth: Thinking of You, a cartoon teddy holding a daisy. *Hope things are back on track soon. Give me a ring if you want to talk*, she'd written.

Just when Anna was thinking she couldn't feel any worse.

She unpacked and made a drink and went up to the dolls' house to see if that made her feel better. Out of nowhere came a terrible pang to see Ruth's kids, for everything to be back to normal again. She would like to be sitting at their dining table back before the affair was even thought of, with Russ whingeing about taxation and Ruth scolding someone, Jamie wearing that superior half-smile his face tended to slip into when he was with his brother. At this minute, with nothing but silence waiting downstairs for her and the sense of a howling storm gathering on the horizon, she would swap places with Ruth. Truly, bodies and all. The lot. The dolls' house was dusty and the beading was coming off, she noticed, under the front eaves. She revolved the structure slowly. It remained a model that she could not enter.

She thought of Jamie teaching her the names of fossils when they were on honeymoon and making fun of her when she got belemnite wrong and congratulating her when she found a crinoid. That day she'd thought about stopping the Pill and how it would all happen after, how her life was all about to change.

There's irony, said Miriam.

The trouble was, not having children put you out of the loop. You didn't meet women through your antenatal class or at children's parties or in the playground at 3.15. You couldn't join in the chat about schools in the area or how to get your kids to eat vegetables or how you were nothing more than a glorified taxi service or where the best child-friendly hotels were. You had no eighteenths or weddings to plan. Other women went, Have you got kids? And you said no and they shut right down on you. As if you had nothing else to talk about. As if you were the one who was being aloof. You were on this island of selfishness.

If she could at least have discussed the way she felt

with Jamie, properly, without it turning into an attack. 'Some days I feel really desperate,' she'd confessed to him once. And he'd gone, 'But why, Anna? You've got everything.' Another time he'd said, 'Not wanting a baby doesn't mean I don't love you.'

Miriam rolled her eyes. *Why do you always fix on the one thing you haven't got? You were always that way.*

—But I'm not just being awkward! You've got no idea. Nobody has. It's like a bereavement. It goes on and on.

Ah, stop feeling so damn sorry for yourself.

Oh, well, you'd know all about that, said Anna.

She went into the bathroom and began to wipe off the make-up that Kali had so carefully applied. The blue shadow left great smears under her eyes that she had to scrub with the corner of a towel, dragging at the fragile skin. There were lines of lipstick all over the towel, like blood.

To finish off, she filled the sink with cold water and plunged her face into it, held the pose, thought of Jamie. Jamie standing in the kitchen after they got back from his dad's funeral, unknotting his black tie wearily. I only cried once when my mother died and I've never cried since, he'd said. Maybe you should, she'd told him. Why, he'd said, what good would it do? And she'd thought, how do you explain the benefit of tears? You either get it or you don't. Whatever kind of man had she married?

A noise like a drill through the muffle of water: the front doorbell was ringing as though someone was leaning against it. Sodding Russ again, that would be.

In a rush she pulled her face out, water running horribly down her neck and back and between her breasts, and her hair hanging wet at the front in chilly ribbons. She groped for a fresh towel.

You're like me. Miriam again. *I could never keep a man.*

'Oh, no, I'm not,' she muttered. 'I'm not like you at all. At least I try to take charge of my own destiny.'

But when she peered out of the bathroom window it was not Russ; that was the Head's car she could see parked opposite. Jackson come to see her. Jackson. She dropped down on her haunches by the sink. It was so wrong, Jackson being here in her world when he really only existed at school.

After thirty seconds he tried the bell again, but with less vigour. She longed to kneel up and see whether he was walking away from the house, oh, please let him be walking away, but how awful if she was seen. Part of her wanted, even through the horror, to burst out laughing like a child in a game.

After a while everything was quiet. She got to her feet. The car had gone.

Jackson would never be the type to hang round corners sneakily, but he was persistent. When Anna got to the bottom flight of stairs she was not surprised to see a cream envelope on the mat. *Mrs A. Lloyd* was typed on the front, starkly, next to the school crest. The letter inside was two lines long and asked her to contact him re arrangements for cover. There were no clues as to how cross he was.

She would have to consider sending in some more lesson plans, but the very idea made her want to groan with weariness. Her brain was a fog. She took the letter and placed it face down in the kitchen drawer while she struggled to gather her thoughts. As she pushed the handle closed, her mobile went off. Jesus. What now? Where was the bloody thing? The ringtone was coming from the jacket hanging in the hall. Flustered, and thinking of Kali, she pulled the jacket round, dragged the phone out of an inside pocket and pressed Accept.

'Am I speaking to Anna Lloyd?' said a man's voice which too late she recognized as Jackson. The oldest trick in the book. How could she have fallen for it?

'Yes,' she said.

'I called round.'

'I was lying down.'

'Of course, of course.' He sounded even more on edge than usual. 'So, how are you?'

'Sick.'

He waited for her to elaborate but she didn't.

'Yes, I received your doctor's note. Very bad, very sorry to hear you're under the weather. And obviously we're keen to give you the support you need.'

But, thought Anna.

'Thanks.'

'Have you had a chance to speak to Chrissy Eames yet? I know she's quite concerned.'

'I will do.'

'Good. Good. Because it's important for the students, of course, continuity, we need to minimize disruption. Have you any idea how long you're going to need to—'

'Not yet.'

'No. I see. I should imagine it's tricky, something like this. Stress, it's very tricky.'

'Mmm.' Tears were close.

'Can I ask, is it a domestic or . . . a professional problem?'

She found she could not answer, sensed Jackson's sudden appalled realization that he was on the phone to a crying woman.

'I. We. I'll call again in a few days,' he said hurriedly. 'Look after yourself.'

The second the phone was switched off she felt better. In the staff handbook it said you could have up to six months off for illness, and she might be ill. The doctor said she was. Her contract was still valid. All this she could say to Jackson if she needed to, next time.

It was cold standing in the hall. She pulled the sodden velvet neckline of Kali's top away from her breastbone and peeled the garment over her head.

This was the plan: she would launder the top and take it back, with some more groceries, tomorrow. Maybe she'd slip Kali a little cash, too. She could have a couple of hours there at least while she checked on Trent.

That meant there was only the night to get through on her own.

Chapter Twenty-One

'It is weird, though.' Kali sat back and waved her bottle to demonstrate the full scope of the weirdness. 'When you think about it, you being here.'

'You came for me,' said Anna.

The bell had rung shortly after twelve. Anna had gone to answer and found Kali under the porch light hugging herself with glee. 'I've told Trent I need you. You have to go back with us, now.'

There wasn't anything to think about. Anna had picked up her overnight bag, checked the back door, and gone.

'Yeah, I know. That's weird as well. I am a bit mad, though. If you hadn't noticed.'

Trent took the phone away from his ear. 'You're a bit pissed. Go easy on those things, we're nearly out.'

'I can get your groceries,' said Anna. 'It's no bother.'

'What I mean is,' Kali went on, 'she was my teacher and now we're hanging out. Don't you think that's bizarre?'

'I don't care. You can do what you like.'

And that was from the man who had been left in charge of the girl, thought Anna. She said, 'I don't believe age matters all that much. It's people that matter, personalities. We're just three individuals.'

'Three individuals,' said Kali. 'I like that.'

'In any case, you've taught me probably as much as I've taught you.'

'Yeah? How come?'

'Well. You've helped me get a better perspective on life, in some ways. And you've introduced me to me some words I didn't know.'

Kali laughed. 'Oh, yeah. She didn't know what a weston was, Trent, or a shedhead.'

'I love the way young people are creative with language,' said Anna.

'There's loads you don't know about, actually. What we are going to have to do is sort your clothes, because you're just too f'king . . .' the bottle waved again '. . . neat. You really need to scruff up. We could go shopping.'

As Kali was speaking, Anna found herself slipping into a memory: she was in a supermarket and she'd stopped to admire a little boy's flashing trainers. She bent down and spoke to him and he showed her how they worked, stamping for her to bring up the sequence of lights. He was a sweet little boy with dark brows and blond hair you wanted to touch. Suddenly he'd looked up and said, 'Where's Mummy?' The aisle was empty. His mother had not noticed when he stopped and had gone on without him. He'd become upset. Anna took his hand and dragged him guiltily up and down the aisles; at last, in despair, she'd taken him to the help desk and they gave a message out on the tannoy. When the mother came she was angry, even though it had been her own fault for not keeping a proper eye on her son. Cow, she'd called Anna. Interfering cow.

She came out of it.

'You're too much – yourself,' Kali was saying. 'I could *transform* you. I could make you as *cool as me.*' She giggled and leant forward as if she meant to get up, then stopped with her eyes closed. 'Whoa. Shit.'

'See,' said Trent. 'I told you to go easy.'

'Think it's flu.' Kali flopped against the chair arm. 'I think it's Archers.'

'When I move—'

Anna sprang up. 'You should drink some water. I'll get you a glass.'

'I wanna go to bed.'

Trent sighed and slipped his phone into his pocket. 'Give me a hand.'

They took an elbow each and walked Kali to the bedroom. Anna helped her lie down and tucked her in. 'You need to pace yourself,' she said. 'You've only got a light frame. Women have to be careful with alcohol.' She stroked the girl's hair but there was no response; Kali seemed to have fallen instantly asleep.

Anna stayed for a few minutes, then went back through to the lounge. Trent had moved to the floor and was reading a music paper.

'Did you know she was drunk?'

He looked up. 'I was the one who told her to stop, if you remember.'

On the sill outside sparrows squabbled and fluttered. She watched them for a minute, moving her head to align the nearest tree trunk with the window frame. That was better; it left a pane clear, and boxed in the smaller branches tidily. Because there was no order in this place, no authority.

She turned and looked round the flat in dismay. At least if the kitchen was cleaner.

Anna wiped round the drainer, stacked some bowls, wrung the dishcloth out and draped it over the tap. Then she poured herself some orange juice and drank it leaning against the sink. Someone needed to unload the washing; her, she supposed. She squatted down to open the machine and clawed the sodden clothes into an empty vegetable tray because there was no basket. They would have to be hung over the radiators. Afterwards she would take the Stephen King through and sit with Kali till she woke.

Or she could use the space to find out more about Trent. She filled a second glass with juice and carried it over.

'Here you are,' she said as though he'd asked for it.

He raised his eyebrows in surprise, but took the juice from her. Anna began to lay out the wet clothes, waited till he'd turned two pages before she spoke again.

'She's a lovely girl.'

'Yeah.'

'Have you known her long?'

'Since we were kids. I used to baby-sit her.'

'I thought you'd have been too young.' Anna tilted her head ingenuously.

Trent snorted. 'I'm ten years older than her. How old d'you think I was?'

So he was twenty-six. If he was telling the truth. Anna wasn't sure if that made the situation any better or not. She shook out a pair of blue knickers with a butterfly on the front.

'What do you do, Trent?'

'Little as possible.' He leant over the page, frowned, and then started to tear at the bottom corner.

'You don't have a job?'

'I do courier work, but's casual. Sometimes I'm needed, sometimes I'm not. That's how it is.'

Anna watched him detach the last bit of paper, fold the strip into a square and fit it into his jeans pocket. He needed a shave, but his mouth was nicely shaped and his teeth good. She could understand how Kali might be attracted to this man.

'Kali seems fond of you.'

'She's a great kid.'

Yes, but what are your intentions? Anna longed to ask. She wanted to say, Don't hurt her, don't take advantage, keep her safe. 'Oh, she is, a great girl. Very mature in many ways. But I think she's quite vulnerable underneath.' She waited a moment before adding, 'I'm sure you know that.'

Trent turned the newspaper over and studied the front. It was a black-and-white picture of a man screaming.

'So what's your interest?' He spoke without looking up.

Anna's heart skipped a beat. Before she could stop herself, she'd said it: 'She reminds me of my daughter.'

It could all have come out, then. If Trent had shown

a spark of sympathy in the beat that followed, she might have told him everything she'd ever felt for the girl. Listen, she'd have said. I get this sense that there are children of mine out there that I've never met. Because where do these lost children, the children that we never have, go to? They're somewhere. And now I think I've met one of them. You think it's mad, but you don't feel the connection. For years it seems like I've glimpsed her on the edge of my vision and now here she is in full view and I want to do nothing else but look. She feels like mine. It's gone beyond a game.

'Your daughter?' said Trent.

Anna waited for him to ask some more. Her pulse was thudding and she gripped the sofa arm as if it might tip her off.

But he wasn't interested in family chat. 'She rates you,' he said. 'Although she thinks you need sorting out.'

'Take a hell of a lot to sort my life out.'

He shrugged. 'Yeah, well. Don't take it so seriously. It's all just stuff, people messing with your head, power trips. None of it lasts.'

'Thought for the Day.'

'If you like. And if it all gets too much, just leg it. 'Swhat I do.'

Trent sat back on his heels, appraising her. He stared until she blushed.

'What?'

'Funny, though.'

'What is?'

'Kali's teacher.'

'Not now she's left.'

'But you are a teacher. Which is fucking weird. How come you're not in school?'

'I've got a doctor's note.'

'Oh, yeah? Handy.' He got stiffly to his feet, yawned, and stretched his arms up and then wide. His T-shirt lifted and showed a silver belt buckle and a line of brown flesh.

'Shouldn't we go check on Kali?'

Trent dropped his arms against his sides. 'That's what I was going to do.'

She repositioned the seat cushions on the sofa more neatly. Within seconds he was back.

'Sparko. She'll be out for hours.'

'Do you think she's all right?'

'She's drunk, Anna. That's all.'

But you can be sick in your sleep and choke, she thought. 'I'll go through later and make sure she's in the recovery position.'

'Whatever.' He hitched his trousers up, flashed his belt again. 'Do you want a coffee? I need some caffeine.'

She followed him to the sink. When he reached up to get the jar from the shelf he had to shake the hair out of his eyes. That was a bit Phil-ish, the way he'd brush his fringe back to study more carefully some precise texture or shade. He wasn't really like Phil, of course. His expression was tighter and hungrier, a different personality altogether.

'So what did you teach?'

'English.'

'Yeah?' He shoved the cutlery round in the drawer.

'I quite liked English. Much as I liked anything. I did a poem about a comet once, the teacher read it out.'

For a moment Anna saw the small boy, interested in pleasing, happy to have been noticed. She said, 'Did you study it at A-level?'

He snorted unpleasantly. 'Not exactly. Special Needs.'

'Dyslexic?'

'How did you know?'

'A guess. It's not an automatic bar to achievement, though. Did the school give you extra support?'

'Did they fuck.' He dropped the teaspoon in the sink with a clatter. 'They weren't interested. It doesn't matter now. I'm not illiterate or anything.'

'You're obviously OK with street names.'

Trent looked blank.

'When you're being a courier.'

'Oh,' he said. 'Yeah.'

She took the coffee from his hands. 'Funny what you were saying before about legging it,' she went on. 'I was on teaching practice years ago and I was in this really rough school, but it was OK because I had a mentor. He was called Mr Goodwin, John Goodwin, and although the students were lively in his class they more or less behaved. Everyone told me I was lucky to have him as a supervisor because I'd learn a lot. He seemed to have everything sussed.'

Trent settled back against the units and she did the same.

'But I went in one morning, and he'd told me the night before he'd have these worksheets copied for me and they weren't, and that was unusual, and no one could find him. He hadn't come in and he hadn't called. So they began to get worried because he was normally so conscientious. I think the deputy head went round to his house, but there was no one in. A rumour went round that he'd hanged himself, which was completely wrong because in the end it turned out he'd just run away. He'd driven to the station, picked a train at random and was staying in a B&B two hundred miles away.'

She recalled even now her outrage and sense of personal abandonment, even though she understood that the effect of his absence on a student teacher would have been the last of John Goodwin's considerations. The state of his mind, she wouldn't have featured in his consciousness at all.

'Bet he got the sack.'

'I think the head gave him compassionate leave and he went back a term later. It was weird, because everyone assumed he was coping.'

'He had an extra holiday out of it.'

'He needed it for his breakdown.'

Trent drank his coffee and made no comment.

'The thing is,' she said, 'you can't always tell what's going on with someone, they might look fine, and then have this awful tragedy going on behind the scenes. There's this man I work with who's got a disabled wife and I think things are pretty grim at home, but he's always so brave about it.' A memory of Les flashed into her mind: being in his office the day before term started, a CD playing of Ray Charles's 'I Can't Stop Loving You'; Tom Maxfield barging in and saying, Strewth, this is miserable music and Les going, It's the blues, Tom. It's meant to be miserable.

'People are complicated.'

'Damn right.' She smiled and he smiled back, a brief flash. 'Everyone has these layers to them.'

'I reckon the only time you get the truth out, you get to see what someone's really like, is when they're drunk.'

'I'm not so sure about that,' said Anna.

Trent rubbed his chin.

'I think,' she went on, 'the tricky one is knowing yourself, and there's no amount of alcohol will reveal that. All over the world you've got these people going to doctors and shrinks so they can have someone else explain their personalities away, and—'

She broke off because Trent had put his drink down and was moving towards her: a prickle of acknowledgement passed between them, like a spark, and she knew he was going to try and touch her.

'No!' she cried, and ducked out of his way.

'No?'

'*No.* What the hell do you think you're playing at?'

'Just wanted to see what you'd do.' He was laughing at her.

'Your *girlfriend*'s in the other room, for God's sake.'

'Yeah?'

She could have hurled her cup in his face. 'Look, who the bloody hell do you think you are? You're supposed to be in loco parentis here. Do you honestly consider it appropriate to go round—'

'Jesus, keep your hair on.' He grinned nastily. 'She said you weren't that way.'

Anna wasn't sure what he meant; was too angry to care. 'Haven't you any scruples?'

But Trent had turned away and was tipping his coffee down the sink.

The skin over her cheekbones felt tight and hot. She left him where he stood and went into Kali's room.

The girl was still asleep, mascara print round her eyes. Anna sat close to her on the bed and touched her sleeve. She could still smell Trent's tobacco.

If she'd had a daughter, she'd have read to her every night. She'd have told her stories about misunderstood witches, and princesses who rescued princes. She'd have stayed with her through nightmares and stroked her to sleep. It's a mother's job to watch in the darkness.

Something made her look round and there was Trent in the doorway. She scowled and he disappeared.

When she turned back, Kali had opened her eyes.

'Now, how are you?' said Anna gently.

'Can you get me a bowl?'

There was a waste-paper bin under the desk; Anna brought it at once. 'I'll put it here, next to the bed.'

Kali nodded. She looked awful.

'Could you try and drink some water?'

'Umm.'

When Anna went through to fill a glass, Trent was nowhere to be seen. She checked the bathroom but it was empty. Where had he gone? Was his car still there? She drew back the curtain and looked down at the street. The Saxo was just pulling away.

'Anna!'

She ran back into Kali's room and held her while she moaned into the bin.

At last Kali stopped retching. Anna wiped her face with one of Jamie's handkerchiefs, then supported her while she took a sip of water. Afterwards, Kali leant against her and she took the warm weight of the girl's body.

'You silly puss.'

'I know.'

'I blame myself, I should have stopped you. Never mind. Soon be better.'

She found she was rocking Kali slightly, as if she were a child.

'Anna?'

'Yes?'

Kali's head moved against Anna's collarbone. 'You won't leave me, will you? Promise?'

'You have my word,' said Anna.

She was back in school and there was a fire drill. Les had told her to call all the parents individually and inform them. That'll take forever, she'd thought, and we need to get the children out of the building. But he'd made her take all the registers to the office and go through the contact details. She'd started with Kali but could get no further because there was nothing in the pupil notes. 'No,' said Les when she asked him, 'there's no need because she knows the number off by heart.' 'We don't, though,' said Anna. 'What use is that in an emergency?' Then Trent had burst in, although it wasn't Trent, it was

Nathan because that's the way of dreams, and said they had to get Kali out of the school first because she was pregnant and mustn't inhale smoke.

Kali had made it clear to Anna she was not going to give up her mother's number.

'It's OK,' she'd said. 'Trent's got it.'

Trent. 'But what if there's an accident and he's not around?'

'Trent's the one in charge,' Kali said, as if that settled the matter. Then Anna's own phone had rung and it was Jamie wanting to know where she was.

'You still in Abersoch?' Because this was what she'd told him.

'No. Moving round the coast. I'm in Barmouth today, might go down to Aberystwyth tomorrow. Or I might go inland.'

'You haven't got your car.'

'I'm using public transport, it's more interesting. Look, I'll keep my mobile on. And I'll text you.'

'What about work?'

'I've got leave.'

'*Are* you sick, Anna? Tell me, what's going on?'

She'd switched the phone off. See how he liked being left.

Now she got out of bed and pulled on a Chinese robe Kali had lent her. She drew the belt tight and tucked the neckline across securely in case Trent was around. Then she crossed the corridor to the bathroom. Locked. She listened for a few seconds and heard Kali singing on the other side of the door. *If you're so deep/ If you're so deep/ How come you can't see/ The way I feel.*

Quickly, she went through to the lounge. No sign of Trent. She put her head round the door of his room, but there was only the thrown-back duvet, a single imprint in twisted sheets where Kali had been lying. Her mobile was on top of her jeans by the radiator.

Anna snatched the phone up and ran with it back to her room, closing the door behind her. She brought up the address book and scrolled her way down it, but her hands were trembly and the blipping of the keys was too loud and she didn't seem to be able to take the titles in. And all the while she was thinking, How can you do this when she trusts you? But sometimes you had to act in a way you didn't like, for the greater good.

There. She highlighted the number. Was there time to scribble it down? But where? She had nothing to write with in this room and she didn't want to venture out into the lounge and waste valuable seconds hunting for a pen and paper. What to do? The next moment she'd jabbed Call.

'Hullo?' A man's voice, Irish.

'Is that—' She shut the door again hastily. '—I need to speak to Mrs Norman. Is she there?'

'You mean Caroline? I don't know where she is.' He went fainter but she heard him say: 'Does anyone know where Caroline is?' Then he was back. 'No, I'm sorry, she's around somewhere. She might have gone up the parade. I'll get her to call you back.'

'She can't call me back. Just tell her that her daughter's not very well and she might need to come home.'

'Oh, OK. And you are?'

'Just tell her Kali needs her.'

The voice sounded hesitant. 'I'll pass that on. She'll be back in England in a week or so anyway, but I'll make sure she gets the message. So what's the problem, exactly? Who are you, again?'

'A friend,' said Anna weakly. Prickly with horror at what she'd done, she switched off the phone and ran to replace it on top of Kali's clothes.

By the time Kali came out of the bathroom, Anna was sitting at the kitchen table, failing to read a magazine and feeling like death. Why was trying to do the right thing always so fraught with complications? She began to rehearse excuses to herself.

'Don't look so miz,' said Kali, coming up behind her and giving Anna's hair a little tug. 'We've got a busy day ahead.'

'We have?'

'Oh, yeah.'

She draped her clothes over the chair back and began to unbutton her nightshirt.

'Packed.'

The shirt dropped to the floor. Kali stood, unembarrassed, in her knickers, and put her hands on her hips. 'God, look at that belly.' Anna let her gaze slide across. The girl was patting her stomach and grimacing. 'Look at the state of it. I'm going to have to do some sit-ups or something.'

'Don't be ridiculous. You're like a wand.'

She was, too. Smooth and white and lean, with small uptilted breasts. An artist's model, new and vulnerable.

Kali sucked in a lungful of air, then let it out again explosively. 'Be OK if I go round holding my breath.'

'For goodness' sake. You are *not* to worry about your weight. You're on the slim side, if anything.' (Now your mum, on the other hand.) 'Really. You mustn't get into all that dieting business, not when there's no need. It's hard to hang onto a positive body image these days, but you must try.'

'Mmm.'

'And your skin's very fair. Do you wear a sun-screen?'

'No.'

'We'll get you one. Next time we're near some shops. A really good brand.' There was so much this girl needed doing, so much she needed help with.

The tattoo was like a brand on that clean skin. Kali saw her staring. 'Do you like it?'

She came close and turned her body so her shoulder was in better view: a bird with its wings touching above its head.

'I don't know,' said Anna.

'Touch it. It's henna. I have it freshened every couple of months.'

Anna raised her fingers but was too shy to make the contact. She changed the gesture to one of picking up the shirt. Kali ran her palm over her own bicep.

'Free as a bird, that's me.'

'Watch out for cats, then.'

Kali laughed. 'I spit on cats. I eat cats for breakfast. Anyway, today. Today's about you. I've got plans.' She reached for her jeans.

'Have you?'

'Oh, yeah.'

'Am I allowed to ask what?'

'No,' said Kali. 'I'm the boss now.'

It felt like a dream, but it wasn't one; this was a bright afternoon in Piccadilly Square, Manchester. Shoppers were streaming towards her in a mass, jostling, hard-faced. The pitching sensation of standing still while everything around you shifted reminded Anna of driving into a snowstorm. She was disorientated and her wrist throbbed.

She knew exactly how she must look, standing there. It was as if she could go outside herself and observe, but really it was the extrapolation of a memory from two hours ago, when she'd stood in front of a full-length store mirror with Kali nodding behind her.

Trent had come back to the flat mid-morning. Had he been out all night? Kali threw herself at him and he kissed her for a long time, then took her to the bedroom. Anna cleared some beakers away and washed up. She knew instinctively there was no point telling Kali about the business in the kitchen.

When he emerged later he looked smug; Anna could have hit him. 'Stuff to do, people to see,' he said. 'You girls fancy a trip?'

'More than,' said Kali. 'Anna needs some new clothes. Badly.'

'I do?'

'You do. Doesn't she, T.?'

Trent had faked a yawn. 'Don't look at me, I'm not

trailing round fucking TopShop with you. I've got business to do. I'll drop you in town and leave you to it.'

'Suits us,' said Kali.

Now Anna was tricked out like a gypsy in boots and waistcoat, her hair whipped around by the wind. 'I'd never have gone for an outfit like this on my own,' she'd said as Kali selected an appropriate scarf and earrings to finish off.

'Exactly.'

Kali had chosen everything: the jeans with their velvet hems, the beaded belt, the grandad shirt.

'You're sure it's not too full-on? I don't want the mutton look.' Anna had squinted, trying to imagine she had never seen herself before, that she was someone whom she'd glimpsed in a crowd.

'No, it's good. Ruffle your hair so it's not so neat.'

She did as she was told.

'I might lose the belt.'

'Trust me.'

This dark-eyed woman in the mirror, what kind of life did she lead? Anna tipped her head, tried a smile, ran her fingers through her hair. A rack away, Kali slipped herself into a suede coat.

'Now, that's nice,' said Anna. 'Are you going to get it?'

Kali pulled it off and hung it back up. 'Can't afford it. You should get your stuff, though. Ask to wear them out. You can stick your old clothes in a bag. The new you starts here.'

It does, thought Anna.

'Better than sloping round your old gallery.'

That had been Anna's first suggestion. 'You're right. It has been.'

'I mean, there's Art, and there's clothes. Do you see what I'm saying? What? Why are you laughing?'

Anna said, 'I have this idea. I'll tell you when we get outside.'

All her life she'd been one of those people who observes from the sidelines. Now she was in the middle, involved. Anything might happen.

The shop smelt of surgical spirit and that took her to A & E and then to the miscarriages. But she would not think that way now.

'What I want,' she explained as the pierced man ran a razor lightly along her forearm, 'is a record of today. Whatever happens to me in the next few years, whatever's waiting for me when I get back, I want to be able to look at my skin and remember.'

His gaze flicked to hers, then away, uninterested. He squeezed yellowish cream out of a bottle and spread it on her arm with a spatula.

'So, a line?' he said.

'A plain line, like a bangle, yes.'

She could tell he thought it was a waste. All around were pictures of panthers and butterflies and Red Indian feathers and Chinese letters. You could have had all this, his expression said. 'A line it is, then.'

'Are you sure you want to go through with it?' said Kali, leaning forward. 'Looks fucking painful to me. 'Cause you could have one done like mine where they just paint it on.' The needle started to buzz, drowning her out.

The man took Anna's arm, pressed it flat against the tabletop, and began.

'Did it hurt?' Kali wanted to know as they walked out of the studio. She seemed impressed.

'Yes. But I wanted it to.' She'd watched the whole process, the needle tugging under her flesh. 'That's what made it real. Do you understand?'

'No, I think you're mad. How long will it last?'

'He says five years. It starts to fade after three. Probably.'

'Then will you have it done again?'

'It depends on where I am,' said Anna. She couldn't imagine the future at all.

They passed a beggar on the corner, a young lad. He had no dog or instrument or *Big Issue*s. It was him and a plastic box for coins. What's your story? thought Anna. Where are your parents? She dropped in a pound and hurried away.

Kali waited for her to catch up and they walked on, elbow to elbow.

'Is Trent, you know, a bit older than you originally told me?' asked Anna after a companionable silence.

'Oh.' A blush and a grin. 'A bit. Mmm. But he's cool, he's OK. He is.'

'I see.'

'Sorry.'

'There's no need to lie to me, Kali. I'm your friend.'

'Yeah.' She smiled brightly. 'But telling someone what they want to hear isn't the same as lying.'

'Oh, it is,' laughed Anna.

'What, telling them something that'll make them feel better, stop them worrying? I thought that was a white lie and it was OK.'

'You're a rogue, Kali Norman.' Anna took her arm and squeezed it. 'A rogue of the first order. You want taking in hand.'

Kali halted for a moment, and sighed. 'I do. You're so right.'

'You know, it's strange,' continued Anna as they fell back into step. 'I admit, I kind of—'

'What?'

'—set out to change you, and here you are changing me instead.'

'Yeah? How change me?'

'Show you new things. Paintings, sculpture, music. Have you ever heard the second movement of the Emperor Concerto, or Ravel's *Pavane*? They're so beautiful you want to cry. Or films, Powell and Pressburger's *Red Shoes*, that sort of . . . Has anyone ever taken you to see a ballet? There's all this wonderful art out there that I know you'd love. I want to widen your horizons. Just, make you happier, really.'

'I am happy.'

'So am I.' She caught sight of herself in a mirrored shop window and it was true. She *walked* happier. 'Listen,' she said on an impulse, 'do you want that coat? Because I'll buy it for you.'

She had expected some protest, but Kali only grinned and said, 'Yeah, great.'

Afterwards they stood in Piccadilly Plaza by the

fountains and she tried to recall her Year Seven class. What faces she could conjure were blurry; she couldn't drag up more than half a dozen names. It was as if that part of her brain to do with school had atrophied. Les always said (and she'd never believed him) that if you wanted to measure how much you'd be missed from a place, you should fill a bucket under the tap, then stick your hand in. When you pulled your hand out, what kind of a hole did you leave behind in the water? Institutions moved on quickly. The individual was always dispensable.

Kali appeared across her line of vision, hands in the pockets of the new coat, stalking a pigeon. Anna glanced around the square, then set off across the tram lines to a newsagent's. 'Wait there,' she called over her shoulder.

The disposable camera was in a plastic wrapper inside a cardboard box. Anna had to use her teeth to get into it.

'What's that for?' asked Kali, leaning forward. The breeze blew her hair back from her face so that she reminded Anna of a ship's figurehead. That colouring!

'No reason,' she said. Except it had been the best day for as long as she could remember. 'Smile.'

When they met up with Trent he looked ill. 'I'm wrecked,' he said. 'Come on.'

Anna had assumed they would be walking to his car, but instead they set off down a different street that seemed to be taking them in the wrong direction. She wondered if it was a short cut. Kali held onto his arm and Anna had to walk fast to avoid falling behind. 'Where are we going?'

'Have to see a mate.' He said a name to Kali that Anna didn't catch.

They walked for almost half an hour. As they moved away from the town centre, the streets became increasingly narrow and grubby. This was Manchester away from the consumer front of glass and steel; a whole network of dark brick, and gable ends supporting tatty billboards or showing the ghosts of ancient advertisements painted directly onto the walls. Anna wondered whether the people who lived there minded having their houses used that way, or whether they'd had any choice. There was litter, a lot of graffiti, a door with broken glass panels, the side strut from a folding push chair propped against a wall. She had the sense of being watched, though there was hardly anyone about.

The overflow from a second-hand furniture store blocked the pavement and they had to step round a vinyl office chair, a bedhead, a nest of black ash coffee tables. A display of artificial flowers poked out of the mouth of a china frog. *Cash Generator*, said a sign in the window. 'Is it far?' asked Anna, but Trent answered without turning round and she didn't hear what he said.

Eventually they stopped outside an end-of-terrace with a bay window. The backdrop to the window was white pinboard, against which was propped a faded sign: *The Customer is King*. Anna was about to make some comment to Kali about the dead flies on the windowsill when Trent produced a key and let them in.

They followed him straight up the narrow stairs and

waited on the landing. He unlocked a second door – plain, flat, unpainted – calling as he went through.

'Have you been here before?' Anna mouthed at Kali.

'Not for a bit,' she said.

Trent took them into a lounge which smelt of cigarettes and air freshener. Anna thought she had never seen such ugly cheap furniture in her life. The only obvious nod at decoration was a velvet wall-hanging above the gas fire of Ganesh, the elephant god, picked out in gold and pink. He held a flower in one hand and an axe in the other.

Kali collapsed on the tatty sofa and unzipped her boots. 'God, I'm fucking shagged,' she said.

It wasn't nice to hear words like that coming out of the girl's mouth. But what could you say without sounding an old fool? Anna looked round for Trent, but he'd gone. 'Do you think he'll be long?'

'Not sure.' Kali located the TV remote and switched onto CBBC, some drama about a talent contest. She settled back to watch.

After a few minutes Anna went and stood outside the bedroom, listened, then knocked. 'Is it OK if I make a drink?' she said through the wood panel.

There was a pause. Then the door opened and the face of a young Indian man appeared, inches from her own. He was so close she could see the individual hairs above his top lip, darker acne scars on his cheeks. She stepped back out of his space. 'Yeah, help yourself,' he said.

An image of Miriam came to her: Anna home from secondary school and asking, 'What's for tea?' Her mother saying, 'Anything.' 'You mean nothing, then.' Helping herself to tins of dubious age, pouring their contents onto thin curled bread. 'Girls should be able to cook,' Miriam had snapped when she complained. 'I'm teaching you to be independent.'

'Are you hungry, Kali?'

'Starving.'

'Right,' said Anna. 'Let's see what we can find in this kitchenette.'

There was not much in the fridge. She opened cupboards and drawers, hunting for cans. 'Will tomato soup do you?'

'Whatever. Great.'

So Anna then had to find a tin-opener, a saucepan, bowls and spoons. And they were strange cupboards, full of items you wouldn't expect, like rows of film canisters and tiny brown bottles, and miniature self-seal plastic bags. In the bin where she dropped the soup cans there were strips of empty blister packs. She picked one out to examine, but the foil was too damaged to read the print. She poured the soup out and took it through.

'There doesn't seem to be any bread.'

''Sall right.'

Kali took the bowl and rested it on the sofa arm. She began to eat slowly, her attention still on the screen where a young man was singing into a microphone, a middle-aged woman making notes on a clipboard. *Lovin' you's no kinda life*, the boy crooned.

'How well,' said Anna, 'do you really know Trent?'

'Huh?'

'I mean, do you know what his job involves? What it is he delivers?'

'No idea,' said Kali. 'Not interested.'

When the boy finished his song, a pretty girl in the wings clapped enthusiastically. But the middle-aged woman was frowning.

Anna lowered her voice. 'Could he be involved with drugs, do you think?'

'What?' Kali's head whipped round. 'No way. Absolutely no way. For fuck's sake.'

'It was only—'

'No way. Stop saying that. You don't know what you're talking about.'

'I do know that there are certain—'

'No way, Anna. Read my lips. No drugs.'

'I was just concerned.'

'Yeah, well.'

They sat in silence for a while. Anna's soup went cold; she couldn't eat it. Ganesh looked down on them placidly.

The programme finished with the boy being told he had failed. His girlfriend had got through to the next round. She told him it would be OK, and then the credits rolled. *Newsround* came on.

'I never asked,' said Anna, 'were you named after the Hindu goddess or was it just because your mum liked the word?' It was something to say.

'I am a goddess,' said Kali.

'What of?'

'Destruction, creation, liberation.' She ticked them

off on her slender fingers. 'I'm the beginning and the end.'

'That's what I thought.'

'Because in endings there are beginnings and in destruction is creation. One of Mum's boyfriends told her that and she wrote it down. And then she got pregnant and that was a beginning and an end, because he left us. The bastard.'

(Miriam clearing out drawers, tipping clothes and papers into bin bags. She was always the one to leave. It's the best way, she maintained, but never with any elaboration. She was a woman easily bored.)

'There's a lot of it about,' Anna said, eager because this was something she could share. 'When I was a little girl I had no dad either, and Miriam, my mother, just wasn't interested.'

'I know, you said. She dragged you round the country and you hated her. It stopped you making friends. You wish you could tell her a load of stuff.'

'Because it does damage you if you feel you're not wanted early on. The root of it was, she wasn't cut out for motherhood at all, I see that now, although at the time I assumed it was my fault. There are things we should have talked about and resolved.'

'But you're grown up now. Why does it matter? You should be over it.' Kali's eyes never left the TV.

'I should, shouldn't I? Yes. And yet. No, you're right, it shouldn't matter so much. The trouble is, you think you're going to get to a magic age where everything sorts itself—'

But she got no further because Kali's phone was

going. 'Speak of the devil,' she said, peering at the screen. 'My mum.' She put the phone against her ear.

Floods in India, said the man on TV, depletion of the ozone layer, a miraculous escape from a cable car over Grindelwald. The tattoo burned; Kali's face was changing and clouding, her brow creasing in puzzlement. 'What? No. No. Who said? When?' Her eyes locked on Anna. 'Did she?' A grimmer, more downbeat intonation. 'Did she?' And finally, a rare species of bird had had twitchers from all over the UK racing up to Scotland, and Kali said, 'Well I'm fine, she was just messing about, no, she's no one, there's no need, yes, I will.'

The phone clicked shut.

'OK,' said Kali, her face like stone. 'Do you want to tell me what's going on?'

Chapter Twenty-Two

'We're staying here tonight,' Trent announced when he finally emerged.

'Why?' asked Anna.

'Because I've not finished what I have to do.'

'I need him to look after the place for a couple of days while I'm away,' said the Indian man. ''It's not a good area, you know?'

'Where will we sleep?'

'In the bedroom?' said Trent.

Fuck you, thought Anna. I shall go, I'll walk out of here and get a cab, then a train, then another cab. But she didn't. It was dark outside and she didn't know whereabouts she was in the city. And the idea of struggling all that way, leaving another mess behind her only to get home to an empty house: she couldn't stand it. In any case, there was still Kali to be placated.

'I *trusted* you,' the girl had said, making Anna feel as though she'd been sliced through the chest with a razor. 'How could you do that behind my back?' It had gone on for nearly an hour. 'Oh, yeah, concerned for who?' she'd said. 'Do you *want* my mum to come back and spoil things?'

No, Anna hadn't wanted that. In the sulk that followed, her mind wandered. She struggled to work out what day it was and what she would have been teaching. The sick note would have run out by now, but she felt no panic or guilt. School had nothing to do with her. She could not visualize herself in a classroom any more, which was astonishing.

'Tell you what, I'll take you out tomorrow and treat you to some new shoes to go with that coat.'

Kali nodded faintly. That was promising.

'Or something else, if you'd prefer.' She spread her hands. 'I don't know how else to make amends.'

''Kay.'

She could not, she told herself, in all conscience, leave the girl here. Not in this city, this flat, with these two men. She had to stay.

And tomorrow she'd redeem herself. She was not going to let this relationship fail too.

That night, on the Indian man's couch, Anna dreamed that her head was on a railway track and her wrist was tied down with hot wire. 'You will undo me when the train comes?' she said. 'I have to wait for a flag,' said her companion, whom she couldn't see. But it was Mrs Norman who was supposed to wave this flag and Anna knew she wouldn't do it, on purpose. The train was coming and she was going to die.

The next morning was sunny, which cheered her slightly. But by midday there was still no sign of Kali.

'Hello?' Anna knocked gently on the bedroom door. There was scuffling, but no reply. She didn't dare go in.

'I'm popping into town.'

Still nothing. Well, she wasn't waiting any longer. She needed a toothbrush urgently, and some fruit, and bread, maybe travel wash; and the pains in her belly told her she'd need tampons before the day was out.

'I've been up since seven,' she muttered to herself as she pulled her coat from the back of a chair. Her tattoo was on fire.

Unsure of the general direction back to the city centre, she followed the signs from before: the furniture on the pavement, the broken pushchair, the Poisonhead fly-posters that showed a baby on a pile of nettles. After a long time walking she found herself back in Piccadilly.

She bought the items she wanted without difficulty, then she sat outside a cafe and texted Jamie to say she was on her way down to Fishguard. She could almost imagine herself doing that journey round the Welsh coast, sitting in a country bus with a book in her hand. She would check into little quaint B&Bs. There would be bracing cliff walks. A more wholesome adventure, but a duller one. She would not have been wearing this petrol-blue scarf or these velvet jeans; she would not have been sitting under a brilliant sky, watching crowds of strangers, to the soundtrack of a busker playing a penny whistle. I don't know what comes next, she thought; it's astonishing. Anything could happen today, tomorrow. Her stomach clenched with fear and excitement.

And here came Miriam, forcing herself into the

present, pulling Anna back to the past as though she were on elastic.

'Go away,' she told her mother. 'Kali says I should be over you and she's right.'

What you need to do is get out, said Miriam. *Go home. Before you do some damage.*

Really, it was as though the woman had never died.

'I'm not the one who's damaged Kali. I'm providing some stability.'

You're pushing in where you're not wanted.

'She came for me specially because she wanted me.'

Housekeeper and cash machine, that's what you are.

'I have a duty to take care of her till Mrs Norman comes home.'

Says you.

'She's my friend.'

The sound of Miriam's laughter, echoing.

'And where exactly did cynicism ever get you?' asked Anna, squinting into the warm sunshine.

Kali was up and about when she got back. 'We've got something planned for tonight,' Kali announced when Anna was cooking supper. 'You'll like it.'

'Fucking daft idea, a seance,' said Trent, from the sofa. 'We should go drinking instead.'

'No, 'cause you're not supposed to leave the flat empty, remember?'

'Anna can stay in. She wouldn't mind. She'd rather do that than go round the pubs.'

Excuse me, she thought, I am here.

Kali put her arm round Anna's shoulder. 'Anna'll want to do what I want to do, isn't that right?'

'A seance sounds fun,' she said. 'Do you have to have special equipment?'

'Just a glass and paper, and the candles.'

'Waste of fucking time,' said Trent, but mildly because he was watching TV. Breaking news scrolled across the bottom of the screen: a shooting in Moss Side. 'That's near here,' he said, almost proudly.

'Not that near,' said Anna, glancing at Kali.

A head-and-shoulders shot of a young man came up and some statistics appeared next to it. Then the face of the newsreader looking concerned, bowing his head very slightly the way they do when they're delivering grim tidings.

'Mate of mine once got shot,' Trent continued, leaning closer to the TV. 'I had to go with him to casualty.'

'Oh, my God. Was he all right?'

'Yeah. Shot himself in the leg. Twat.'

The screen changed to an outside broadcast.

'By the way,' said Anna to Kali, 'I brought you back a few bits and pieces. Toiletries, that sort of thing. Some moisturizer with sunscreen, a clean hairbrush . . .' In the background Trent made clucking noises, but Anna ignored him. '. . . some spare knickers, just plain white ones. I thought you might be running low.' She reached for the bag and handed it across.

'You bought me knickers?' Kali pushed her hair back and rummaged in the carrier. 'Eew. That is so weird.'

'Someone has to think about these things.'

Trent got up and stretched. 'You two are so fucking gay,' he said as he passed.

Anna's face flamed, but Kali laughed.

'In your dreams,' she said.

When it was dark outside, Anna helped set out tealights. Kali wrote the letters of the alphabet on Post-its and set them round the coffee table. They had to sit on the floor to be level with the glass.

'Hang on, before we start I need the loo.' Kali got to her feet.

'Again?' Trent rolled his eyes. 'You only bloody went five minutes ago.'

Ann followed her to the toilet.

'You want a tampon? I've got some.'

'No, I want a pee. Fuck's sake.' She gave Anna a look and closed the bathroom door.

Anna went back to the table.

'She was up twice last night as well,' said Trent. 'And she reckoned it was too hot, kept throwing the duvet back and waking me up. It wasn't hot last night, was it? I was fucking frozen when I woke up this morning.'

The candles wavered together, making the shadows duck and sway.

'She might have an infection,' said Anna.

'Too much information.'

'I mean, she might be sickening for something.' The girl re-entered the room, walked round the sofa and sat down cross-legged on the carpet. 'Do you feel sick, Kali?'

'No. Jeez, what is it? I went for a piss, that's all.'

But Anna was remembering her early pregnancies and how she'd first known her body was changing when her sleep was broken by the need to empty her bladder. She thought about the washing she'd done over the past fortnight. There had been no evidence of Kali having a period.

'OK,' said Trent. 'So what do we do?'

'Keen to get started?'

'Keen to get it over with.'

'Shut up and concentrate.' Kali put her finger on the glass and nodded at them to copy her. 'Is there anybody there?'

It was possible to hear the traffic, very faintly. A long way away a car alarm was going off. Trent let out a snort.

'Shut *up*.'

'Are you after anyone in particular?' whispered Anna.

'My nan.' Kali's breath made the flame nearest shiver.

Trent kept his head down.

Into Anna's mind came the white house with the green windows and the hollyhocks in the garden. The foliage was alive with birds. An elderly couple stood on the step, waving.

The glass gave a lurch.

'Fuck,' said Trent.

Simultaneously they leaned forward and the glass moved again.

'Where's it going?' hissed Kali. 'Shall I ask it a question?' Anna looked across at Trent, expecting to see a smirk, but his lips were apart as if in wonder. 'Who are you?'

The glass stopped.

'Shit, though.' Kali leant back on her heels. 'Shall I try again?'

Anna wasn't sure. She didn't like the feeling in the room, Trent's frown, the quivering, distorting light. But she didn't want to break Kali's moment. She put her finger back. The glass remained still.

After a minute, Kali dropped her hand to her side. 'Looks like they've gone.'

'Nipped outside for a ghostly fag,' said Trent. He mimed a smoking action. 'Buggered off to the ghost-pub.'

'Be quiet.'

The wall-hanging above the gas fire stirred. You could imagine there was someone in the room, waiting.

'Come on,' said Kali. 'It feels closer now.'

They reached into the centre of the table. Almost at once the glass started to slide again. *B*, it touched.

'My nan's name was Bridget!' said Kali. 'Oh, God.' *O. L. O. X.*

As Kali tilted her head, trying to make sense of the sequence, Trent exploded into laughter.

'For God's sake,' snapped Anna.

'You *bastard*.' Kali pushed herself away from the table and folded her arms crossly.

'Had you there.'

'It's not funny.'

'Yes, it is. It's hilarious.'

'Only if you're about ten.'

'Yeah, yeah.' There was a brief blast of rap music from the floor below. Trent got to his feet. 'I need a beer. All this excitement.'

He went into the kitchen and Kali followed him. There was a scuffling noise; Trent said, 'Ow, that fucking hurt,' and Kali said, 'Good.' Then there was the sound of the fridge door shutting and a moment later Kali ran out laughing. 'You come back here,' Trent called, but she did a swerve into the bedroom. 'I'm gonna sort you,' he said. Next they had a tussle with the door, Kali squealing from the other side, and after half a minute he forced his way in and everything went quiet.

You're nothing but an audience, said Miriam.

'It's about time you shut it,' Anna hissed, and the tea-lights flickered again under her breath. She inhaled deeply, like a girl at a birthday party, and blew them all out in one go.

Then she got up and made herself a cup of hot milk and watched a man on TV hunt killer sharks. After that she took some washing off the radiators and folded it into a pile ready for putting away.

She was considering going to bed when Kali and Trent reappeared.

'Mum's texted,' said Kali, without looking at Anna. 'She'll be home on Tuesday. And there's been a change of plan. We're going back to Trent's tomorrow, so you can pick up your stuff.'

'Right.' Anna swallowed. 'That's good, then.'

'No more *pants*-shopping.'

'As you say.' She bent to pick up the Ouija glass and unpeel the Post-its from round the edge of the table.

Then, suddenly, she stopped, because she'd had an idea.
'Actually, I'd like another go.'

'What at?'

'This. The Ouija.'

'Yeah? Why?'

'Because I would.'

'You look a bit weird,' said Kali, peering at her. 'You
all right?'

'Absolutely fine. Come on. If you're going to do it,
do it properly. Everything's set up still. We might as
well. You're not too tired, are you?'

'No.'

Trent appeared, swigging lager out of a tin. 'What's
occurring?'

'She wants another try.'

'Eh?'

'I think we should.' Kali snatched a cigarette lighter
from the chair arm. 'Why not? One more go. If it's what
Anna wants.'

'Oh, well, if it's what *Anna* wants.'

'Fuck off, Trent. You owe me, anyway.'

'What for?'

'For pissing about before. Come on, get yourself over
here and stop being such a pain.'

He did as he was told.

It happened that the street lamp, or illuminated
shop sign, that had been shining through the curtains
last time had now gone out; the room was darker than
before. Anna switched the gas fire back on, half for
warmth and half for the extra light.

'OK. Let's really concentrate,' she said, settling

herself in front of the glass, taking charge. 'Clear your minds.'

Trent opened his mouth to make a quip, then shut it. Anna closed her eyes.

For twenty seconds all she could think of was the day she'd just had: the shopping, the TV news, Trent sneering, sharks. Her brain swarmed with images and noise. But she concentrated on her breathing and the darkness, and soon little flashes of the past started to come, like scenes glimpsed from a train window. Memories of the miscarriages, the tests, the scans she consciously pushed away. She would not drag her babies out of the peaceful dark.

Miriam came soon enough: *It'll be fun living on a boat. An adventure. We can go wherever we like.* 'Wherever you like,' Anna had replied. Miriam had turned away and pressed her hand against her brow. *God, you're hard work, you are*, she'd said, and started to cry.

'It's not happening,' said Trent. 'Anyway, I need a slash.'

'Wait,' said Kali crossly.

A man shouted in the street below; a car horn bibbed. Then it went quiet, and time fell away again.

— Christmas over some pub with another of Miriam's boyfriends. Anna tearing off wrapping paper, saying loudly, 'Not this one. It was the blonde one I wanted.' Wordlessly, Miriam picking up the doll by its heel and dropping it across an ashtray, so that forever after its hair would smell of smoke—

The glass under her fingers slid away from her and she came round with a jerk.

'There's someone here!' mouthed Kali.

A., the glass said. *L.*

'Aren't those your initials?' asked Trent.

Kali drew herself up straighter. 'Is there,' she intoned, 'a message for Anna?'

Y., said the glass. Anna's chest went tight.

'Holy fuck,' said Kali, reaching across herself for Anna's free hand.

M.

There was a pause.

'Who is this?'

The glass twitched but stayed where it was.

'Do you know an M.?' Kali asked breathlessly.

'My mother,' croaked Anna. Every hair-root on her scalp was prickling.

B. O. A. T.

'What's the matter? Does that mean anything to you?'

'You know it does.'

Kali gave Anna's wrist a squeeze. 'What about the boat, M.?'

The glass stayed quiet for a while. Anna found she was shivering and she had to clench her jaw to prevent her teeth from chattering. A picture came to her of Miriam's boyfriend picking the doll out of the ashtray and shaking his head in disappointment: *I was brought up in a children's home, me. I never had no toys I got to keep.* So typical of Miriam to send a memory like this, of Anna's own deficiency, now.

Trent said, 'This is fucking creeping me out.'

'Have you anything else to say?' said Kali. 'Anna, have you anything you want to ask your mum?'

Where to start?

'Yes.'

'Go on.'

Anna's mouth was very dry. 'I'd like her to say sorry.'

One of the tea-lights went out. A line of smoke, thin as a thread, rose up, taking their gaze with it.

'You did that,' muttered Trent.

Kali shook her head. 'Is that it? Have they gone?'

But Anna stayed still, watching the glass, willing it; she was not surprised when she heard the tiny scrape of it starting up once more.

S. O. R.

Her whole body tensed.

R. Y.

'My God,' said Anna. 'Oh, my God.'

The glass moved on.

T. E. L. L. T. R. E. N. T.

'Tell me what?' The young man cocked his head earnestly.

H. E. S. F. I. T.

A hiss of breath from Kali. 'You twat.'

'Aw, shit, though,' cried Trent, pulling his arm up and out of the circle, laughing. 'Ain't it the truth? You heard it from the spirits. I'm just the messenger, me.' As he got to his feet, the glass fell on its side and rolled in an arc to the edge of the table.

'What? What?' Anna turned her head between them, confused. 'Why did you do that?'

'Dickhead,' said Kali, smirking.

'Me?' Trent pointed at himself theatrically.

'You were the one pushing.'

'*You* were.'

Kali unpeeled one of the Post-its and threw it at him. 'Dub-brain. "Tell Trent he's fit"? Yeah, right. Stick the lights on while you're over there.'

The room was suddenly very bright. It hurt Anna's eyes so that she covered her face.

'Someone had to do something or we'd have been there all frigging night.'

There was some whispering behind her, then a sharp intake of breath. 'As if,' Kali said. Trent left the room.

'Tosser,' Kali called after him. There was a pause. 'You OK?'

'I have a headache.'

'You're not cross?'

Anna made no reply.

'No way. You didn't believe us, did you? I thought it was obvious we were mucking about. I thought you were shoving it at one point.'

'Why would I do that, Kali?'

The girl shrugged. 'You were the one who wanted to carry on. Can't blame us.'

Trent's voice came from the bathroom. 'Told you she wouldn't think it was funny.'

Kali shrugged and got up.

I'm saying nothing, said Miriam.

Much later – it must have been about four in the morning – she fell into a light doze. She dreamt that Jamie was a little boy and it was wartime and he had lost his mother. 'I'll look after you,' she said to him, and he held her coat sleeve gratefully. Then she was Kali, arguing with Trent. He was cross with her because she was late for her *Pop Idol* audition. 'They're holding them now, in Piccadilly Gardens,' he said. But she couldn't go because she was pregnant. 'It's OK,' said Trent. '*Anna'll take the baby.*'

I knew it, she thought. That's it. I knew there was a reason I was here.

As soon as she woke up she understood what she had to do.

The flat was empty. No answer to her knocks on the bedroom door, and when she peered round there was no one there, just a mess of belongings. She did not know where Kali and Trent had taken themselves off to this morning, but it didn't matter. It was another sign.

If she was going to stake any kind of claim, it had to be today, before she and Kali parted ways and the mother came back.

She went quickly into their room and began to hunt. First she pulled the duvet right back as though she were about to strip the bedding. The bottom sheet was smelly but unmarked. Under the pillow was the T-shirt Kali had been wearing at night; Anna drew it out and shook it straight, turned it round, put it back. Next she sorted through a pile of dirty clothes from the day before.

She had no clear idea of what she was looking for: too much to hope for a positive pregnancy test lying around. But there might be other clues. In the bin she found only sweet wrappers and the gas cartridge from a hot brush. The bedside table held small change, lip gloss, a gold chain, two elastic bands, a lighter and a bottle-top.

Anna turned her attention to Trent's backpack. She lifted it onto the bed and tore at the Velcro flap. Then she plunged her hand inside and felt around. Something soft on top: a screwed-up T-shirt. Underneath that was a pair of trainers, and then a hard, cold, rectangular object that she recognized as a tobacco tin. She pulled it out and prised off the lid. There was a nugget of wrapped dope in there, plus a packet of Rizlas. So, thought Anna. She put her hand once more into the backpack, pushing down deeper to touch the bottom. A penknife, she identified, and some coins, another lighter, a US flag key ring, a small notebook and a pen, some batteries, sunglasses, a steel tape measure. Trent's. There was nothing of Kali's in here.

She rose and went to stand in the middle of the room with her palm against her forehead. It occurred to her she might look in the bathroom.

One sliding door of the cabinet was missing, which meant half the contents were permanently on display: Ralgex, Rennies, paracetamol. With a hooked finger she tugged the door in its groove to the other side, revealing King of Shaves, hair wax, hair gel, Head and Shoulders. Above the scummy sink was toothpaste and soap. This was all the Indian man's. If Kali *had* brought Pills or Durex, where was she keeping them? Anna's guess was that she hadn't, that she was using nothing at all. It was important to be sure, though.

She took herself back to the bedroom and searched

again through Kali's old clothes. Then she had an idea: she laid herself flat on the carpet and peered under the bed. But there was nothing in that space except magazines and shoes, and so much dust it made her chest tighten. She scrambled to her feet and looked at the backpack once more, considering. As well as the main section, she saw now, there were extra compartments she hadn't investigated. She leaned across, grabbed the bag and set to, unzipping and wrenching and probing, turning out pockets to the seam. All she found was a bunch of receipts, a plastic pouch of tobacco, and a beer mat with a phone number written across it. At last, in something like a fit of giddy hope, she upended the backpack, shaking it so that the contents went everywhere, coins bouncing off the mattress, the penknife hitting the headboard and dropping somewhere by the bedside table.

Through the wall came a sound that might have been the door of the flat opening.

She began to scrabble the things together, fingers fumbling. The backpack, lightened, toppled slowly off the bed. There was the clunk of a door closing and, a second or two later, a blast from the TV. Anna grabbed at the vinyl strap, hoiking it up, ripping at the fastening, trying to stuff Trent's huge trainers down far enough to get the T-shirt back in on top.

'What in the name of fuck are you doing?' said Kali from behind her.

Anna dropped the bag at once. This was not the way she had planned events.

'I need to talk to you. Is Trent about?'

Kali came further into the room. 'You're looking for drugs, aren't you?'

'No.'

'You fucking are. When I tell Trent you've been going through his stuff—'

So he wasn't here yet. That was good.

'I was not looking for drugs.'

'What, then?'

Best to come straight out with it. Anna took a breath: 'You're pregnant, aren't you?'

'I'm *what*?'

'Come on, Kali. What have you and Trent been using?'

Blank look.

'I mean for contraception. You didn't really believe in that magic stone-thing?'

'Oh, for fuck's sake, Anna!'

She could see Kali was really angry now, but she had to press on. 'You see, it's very tempting to say to yourself, It won't happen to me. And then deny what you're frightened of. And sometimes your body gives out these signals but they're very subtle, and you don't pick them up at first.' The first time Anna had been pregnant she'd thought there was something wrong with her seat belt because it had started to hurt her breasts.

'Right.' Kali dropped her coat on the bed and folded her arms. 'If you must know, fuck, this is embarrassing, we use condoms. Usually.'

'But not every time?'

'Well, Trent doesn't always, he sometimes— Oh, this

is gross. I'm not telling you what we do in bed. Who do you think you are?'

If this were an afternoon TV film, thought Anna, I could use a line here about being a good friend or just someone who cared, and the soundtrack would be broken piano chords. Kali would sink down and hug me and we'd both cry. 'Look,' she said, 'we have to be practical. I'm speaking as your friend and advisor, here. If there's any chance at all you might be pregnant, you need to have a plan of action.'

'But I'm *not*.'

'How can you be sure?'

'Because. Because I'm not, I'm just not.' Kali's hands made fists in front of her. 'What are you – do you want me to be pregnant?'

There was an awful pause. My God, she can see inside my head, Anna thought. 'Of course not,' she said briskly, but the intonation was wrong, she could hear it herself, clear as day.

'You *do*!'

'No, no, it's just that if you are, I'm in a position to help. I wouldn't let anyone bully you, and if you felt that you needed someone to look after the—'

'You do, you do.'

'I could help you take care—'

'You're fucking *mental*, you are.'

'I'm trying to help because your mum isn't around—'

'You've no need.'

'I've every need. If your mother swans off.'

'Don't you diss my mum,' cried Kali furiously. 'You

don't know anything about her. She trusts me, for a start, which is more than I can say for you. And I've got Trent.'

'And what kind of a man is he?'

Kali sneered. 'Like you're in a position to lecture anyone about relationships. Know what?' She was backing away. To Anna she still looked huge, towering. 'I was thinking this last night. Who are you anyway? You're not really anything. You're too old to be a friend, you're too *weak* to be a teacher. You are *so* not my mum.'

'Well, I've tried—'

'You're not my mum. You are *not* my mum. You're just a fucking emotional vampire leeching off me, yeah? Like you're living off me, living through my life. And it's no fun any more, it's not normal, you're not normal.'

Anna shifted up onto the bed. Her legs were numb and tingly and she did not trust herself to stand.

'That's hardly fair,' she began.

But Kali was shouting, 'Get out! Get out!' Her hands were on her head as though she were protecting herself from a terrific noise, and there was something that was not Kali in her eyes.

'I'm sorry,' said Anna. 'I'm sorry. I got it wrong.'

'Too *fucking* true.'

'We'll make it work. You're not yourself.'

'I'm *exactly* myself. This is *who I am*. You don't know me *at all*, Anna.'

'I know you better than you think.'

'You know fuck all. You don't even know what you're like yourself! Just get fucking *out!*'

She's going to hit me or throw something, Anna thought.

'*Now!*'

That was it. Anna ducked past her and ran into the lounge. She grabbed at the clothes which were draped across the sofa, stuffed them into a carrier, glanced wildly round. If Trent came back and saw Kali in this state, there was no knowing what he'd do. But if she could go for a walk till the storm had blown over.

'You fucking sad bitch. Fucking pregnant!'

Kali had opened the door to the flat and was clutching at the handle.

'I'm looking for that camera—'

'You sad fucking lezzer, just GO. GO.'

For a second Anna thought she couldn't do it, couldn't pass Kali where she stood; better to throw open the sash and hurl herself out of the window onto the concrete below. A swoop and then the end, easy.

'*GO!*'

She clasped her bag to her chest and ran, like someone in a fire, pushing past to burst out onto the landing, down the stairs and out into God knows what, the street, the empty normal street.

People moved across the square at their own tangents, following their own concerns. Hard faces, old faces, young, laughing, bleak. Meanwhile Anna sat at a metal table outside a cafe and cried. The old Anna would never have done anything so public, but she wasn't that person any more and there was no going back, that was for sure.

She cried out of humiliation, and for the girl she thought Kali had been; for the babies; for Miriam, left badly and forever out of reach; for the betrayal of Ruth and Jamie and even Russ.

No one came over, no one took the slightest notice.

After a while the tears subsided and she managed to drink her cold coffee. It was bitter and nasty but she took it anyway. And as she sipped she went outside herself, saw the thin middle-aged woman with the miserable face and the incongruous clothes and it struck her: no one was coming to rescue her, it was a ludicrous idea. She was in a mess and she had no idea where to go. Someone across the street was playing Brood.

> *I'm in a cold cold place*
> *Under a cold cold sky*
> *Now I've fallen from grace*
> *Now salvation's passed me by*

You sad fucking lezzer, said Kali's voice again.

Anna took out her phone and stared at it hopelessly. Did she dare ring Jamie? Who else should she call? Wildly she cast about, ran through a flick-book of unsuitable candidates: Mel, Mrs Hislop, Ruth, even Chrissy. Then her thoughts lighted bizarrely on Les. Or was it so bizarre? Les would know what to do, he'd have the right words. He'd listen patiently and be supportive and make no recriminations. *It's never a mistake to have thought the best of someone, Anna.* Les with his scrapbooks and his blues music and his photo of his healthy wife. Once he'd been talking in his office about holidays, and he was explaining how difficult it was for him to book hotels with all the right gear, ramps and stuff. She'd said, embarrassed, 'It must be really hard. I don't know how you keep going.' 'Because I love her,' he'd said simply.

She hung her head at the memory. Les was not hers to call on. It should be Jamie: obviously, you ring your husband when you're in trouble. Unless your marriage is all but over, and even then, you at least go back and end it properly, like an adult. Running away's childish. It solves nothing.

She waited for Miriam to comment, but nothing came.

'I'm not my mother's daughter,' she said out loud.

And Jamie's response from sometime in the past: *Whoever said you were?*

She dialled her home number, and waited.

He picked up at once. 'Where are you?'

'Manchester. I wasn't in Wales.'

'I know. We got a bank statement today with cash withdrawals. I'd have contacted the police if you hadn't rung me by this evening. Why, Anna? Why've you been lying? Why've you had your phone off? What the hell is going on?'

She took a deep breath, but her voice sounded odd and strangled. 'Jamie, can you come and get me?'

In the pause that followed, and to keep herself from screaming, she counted up the side of the tower block where the height was marked in metres. 100, 200, 300. If you stood on the top you were 335m up. What would it feel like to be so far above everything?

At last she heard him clear his throat. 'What makes you think I'll come, Anna?'

'Please. I'm in a state. I don't know what to do. I've been really stupid.'

'Tell me honestly,' he said, and she stuck her finger in her left ear so she could block everything else out except his words: 'have you been with someone? A man, I mean. I need to know.'

'No.'

'Is that the truth?'

'I swear.'

'Because if you've been, if you say to me now – I don't think I could stand it.'

'Honestly. I'll tell you about it.'

'Oh, Anna.' There was a choking, gulping noise at the other end of the phone. 'I thought you'd gone for good.'

With a shock she realized he was crying. Jamie, crying. She frowned, trying to picture him with tears on his cheeks, his face screwed up and vulnerable, and she couldn't do it. It was such a surreal image. Jamie, who never cried. Yet here he was; she could hear him as clearly as if he were standing next to her. And she understood, if she went back to him it would not be to be saved.

'Just come and get me, Jamie.'

He made her wait a long time before he replied.

'Tell me exactly where you are,' he muttered. 'I'm on my way.'

Afterwards

'It's not the end of the world.' Jamie threw a pebble down the scree slope in front of them and they watched its skittery tumble-skip to the heap of slate at the bottom.

'I wonder how many people have made that joke,' said Anna.

'What?'

'I said—' She cupped her hands round her mouth against the wind. '—I wonder how many people have made that joke. About World's End.'

He shrugged and reached for another stone.

'Here.' Anna passed him a shard in the shape of a triangle. He took it graciously, even though there were slate fragments all around him.

Have you been here before, he'd asked as she'd parked the car.

Now he was shouting something again.

'What? I can't hear you.'

Jamie shook his head in exasperation, and shuffled nearer. They sat elbow to elbow in the buffeting air. 'I said, you can see such a long way. It's amazing.'

'I came here when I was depressed.'

'Yeah?'

'It helped. A bit. This view.'

'I can understand that.' He frowned. 'I didn't realize you were so unhappy. Bit hacked off, but not . . . I mean, that you ended up going to a schoolgirl instead of telling me. It's just . . .'

I did tell you, Anna thought, looking down past the shivering bracken bank to the mottled-green valley, its miniature houses and ponds and trees and drystone walls.

'I feel. I feel as if I should say sorry.' Jamie put his head back and spoke to the clouds, so she only just caught the words. 'Would that help?'

Only if we don't have to specify what we're sorry for, she thought. Otherwise we're on very dodgy ground.

'If this was a lake,' she said, 'we could skim stones. All these flat ones, they'd be brilliant.'

'It might have been a lake once, or a glacier; these would have been layers of mud. Before humans and their petty little problems were ever thought of.'

Of course he'd asked her to be honest with him, but there's honesty and honesty. Sometimes the bald truth wasn't accurate enough. Anna could be honest about what she wished had happened, and what she'd make sure did happen if she had her time over again.

'I'm sorry about not wanting children. It's just the way I am.'

'—Don't.'

She would like to go down and see that little white farmhouse closer up. It looked idyllic from up here, though probably when you got near you'd find it was in need of painting, or had some nasty extension round the back, or was in ruins. All she could make out was a tiny white square. Imagine living here among all the green.

Anna shaded her brow and squinted. 'I think the landscape's too rolling for glaciers. Don't they leave a flat bottom, or something?'

'V shapes and U shapes. V shapes is rivers.'

'It isn't V-shaped, either. Liz Yates would know.'

'Liz Yates can fuck off.'

'Yeah.'

In a different field a horse was moving back and forth along the length of the hedge, galloping for the joy of it.

'What are you going to do about school? Will you go back in September?'

Anna watched the horse. Up to the top corner it went, then back down to the far gate. 'I'm not sure.'

'You'll need to let Jackson know soon.'

'Yes.'

'We'll sort something, whatever. But I think you'll want to, once you've got your head together.' Jamie picked up two rocks and chipped them against each other, hunching over like a caveman. 'No Nathan, for definite. And what about all those cards and messages you got off people? They really miss you. I can't imagine Tom Maxfield getting letters from the kids. Letter bombs, maybe.' Anna smiled in spite of herself. 'And old Chrissy's beside herself, can't wait to have you back. She was telling me, that new supply's useless, he can't keep order.'

'It's nice to be wanted.'

'You *are*, Anna.'

'Goodbye, Mr Chips.'

'Don't make light of it. You're a bloody good teacher; see yourself properly for once. You change lives.'

'Oh, yeah, looks like it.' She laughed bitterly.

'Kali was an aberration. She was beyond fucked-up before you ever got to her.'

'I made a mess.'

'No, Anna, I'm not having that. She was a hopeless case, accept it. And maybe you had to—'

'What?'

'Maybe you had to go away to see. To see us. To see what there is to save.'

She fixed on the mare's-tail clouds far above his head.

'What I mean is,' he said, 'would we be here if it wasn't for Kali?'

I'm not giving her the credit for that, thought Anna bitterly. That's a screenwriter talking. And where *are* we, anyway?

'What's done is done,' he went on. 'Now you just need to get on with it.'

Ah, yes. The easy bit.

She picked up a long sharp piece of slate and jabbed it into the centre of her palm. All those layers of rock, compressed time. A hundred years maybe between each horizontal fracture.

'Then you need to understand.'

'Go on.'

'Too much going on in here.' She put the stone point to the centre of her chest.

'What, Anna, what? Tell me.'

'It's hard. You know already.'

'No, I don't. Explain to me again. I'm listening.' The breeze whipped his hair back from his forehead, exposing pink skin, making him look older. His eyes brimmed with the cold.

'Well, sometimes I don't – There are times when I don't know who I am. Like I'm floating about, untethered. Free-form.'

'Go on.'

'Or it's like the way an engine needs a load to pull for it to run properly.'

'Since when were you an expert on engines?'

'Heard it somewhere, one of those daft things that sticks in your memory . . .' She shook her head. 'I don't know if you're getting what I mean. It might not be the same for men. And anyway, you're happy with who you are. But most women – they have— Maybe it's partly to do with identity. If you're not a strong person. There are so many things I'm not, see; I'm not a mother, I'm not a daughter, just now I'm not even a teacher.' The wind blew spitefully in her face so that she blinked and turned her head away. 'Not much of a wife, either, let's be honest.'

'That's not for you to say, is it?'

The wind blundered about and Anna's fingers slowly froze. Glancing down, she saw that tattoo on her wrist was standing out darker today, because the cold had drained her natural colour. It was still a shock to see it, to raise her hand to turn a tap, or brush her hair, and catch a glimpse of that foreign dark line. There'd been scabbing, and the scabs had fallen away and now the skin was smooth to touch, but marked. It will fade, though, she told herself. The man in the parlour had assured her of that.

Suddenly, out of the silence, Jamie said: 'So this is the deal. Do you see the bottle as half full or half empty? I don't mean to sound trite, Anna, but that's what it boils down to.'

'I can't pretend it doesn't matter. The baby thing.'

'I understand that now.'

'It does. A lot. And I have to find a way of living with it.'

Jamie hung his head. 'I love you. Simply, you're the only woman I've ever met who I wanted to marry. I'm sorry that's not enough for you.'

She said: 'If you were writing a drama about a marriage and the couple were trying to move on, what would you have them doing?'

'What?' He looked up, frowning. 'Seriously?'

Anna let herself lean against him. 'Uh-huh.'

'God, I don't know.'

'Please.'

'Hmm. OK. OK, I'll run with it . . . Right: if this were a drama and you were the troubled wife, I'd have you picking up a rock, a big one. Like that one there, that'll do.' He pointed to a thick lump of slate by Anna's feet. 'Go on.'

The slate was cool and sharp. If she'd clenched her stiff fingers round it hard enough, the edges might have actually cut her skin.

'Then you'd say, "This is the past, it's going." Or "I'm jettisoning my mistakes" – no, that sounds too formal. But, giving this sense that you were moving on.

So something like that. Maybe you wouldn't speak the line out loud, you'd just look like you were getting ready to sling away your baggage. And then you'd throw it, throw it away, up into the air, and that would be the final shot.'

'Except life isn't that simple.'

'No, it's not.'

'You can't cure your problems by flinging stones about.'

Jamie sighed.

'I don't have any answers, Anna. But you can't carry a great lump of rock around with you forever.'

Layers of blue-black mineral caught the light and gleamed. The edges were like teeth, imprinting her palm.

'I thought she'd been sent to me. That's what I thought.' Kali standing by the yew hedge, sketching; Kali yelling, her face distorted with hatred.

'I know. Chuck it anyway,' said Jamie, nodding at the slate.

'Will it help?'

'Try it and see.'

She pulled her arm back like a shot-putter, then flung it out with all her strength. Her muscles sang with tension.

The slate left her hand and arced high up over the valley, hanging for a moment against the blue-and-white sky.

picador.com

blog
videos
interviews
extracts